FIC CAMPBELL, L.
Campbell, Lisbeth, author.
The vanished queen
34520003829592

THE VANISHED QUEEN

Kelley Library
234 Main Street
Salem, NH 0307
603-898-7064

THE VANISHED QUEEN

LISBETH CAMPBELL

SAGA PRESS
LONDON SYDNEY NEW YORK TORONTO NEW DELHI

1230 AVENUE OF THE AMERICAS, NEW YORK, NEW YORK 10020

This book is a work of fiction. Any references to historical events, real people, or real places are used fictitiously. Other names, characters, places, and events are products of the author's imagination, and any resemblance to actual events or places or persons, living or dead, is entirely coincidental.

Copyright © 2020 by Lisbeth Campbell

Sonnet #212 © 2017 by J. M. McDermott. Used with permission.

All rights reserved, including the right to reproduce this book or portions thereof in any form whatsoever. For information, address Saga Press Subsidiary Rights Department, 1230 Avenue of the Americas, New York, NY 10020

First Saga Press hardcover edition August 2020

SAGA PRESS and colophon are trademarks of Simon & Schuster, Inc.

For information about special discounts for bulk purchases, please contact Simon & Schuster Special Sales at 1-866-506-1949 or business@simonandschuster.com.

The Simon & Schuster Speakers Bureau can bring authors to your live event. For more information or to book an event, contact the Simon & Schuster Speakers Bureau at 1-866-248-3049 or visit our website at www.simonspeakers.com.

Interior design by Davina Mock-Maniscalco

Manufactured in the United States of America

1 3 5 7 9 10 8 6 4 2

Library of Congress Cataloging-in-Publication Data is available.

ISBN 978-1-9821-4129-5
ISBN 978-1-9821-4131-8 (ebook)

For survivors

#RESIST

The big, black, ugly bird that clings
to rooftops in the city, long of wing
And long of neck, naked, warty thing
That swoops out of the twilight, singing
Songs of ugly hunger, early death
Where lost breaths are swallowed breath
by breath, we walked in city streets, enwreathed
in sidewalks, green grass and oak leaves wreath
the idylls of we who pretend until the bird
black bird cawing in the break of dawn, a word
of darkness, swoop upon the rooftops, heard
in bedrooms still dark, waking to a dead word
A kitten half-eaten by the dogs of moonlight
The wicked tooth, and harpies own all twilights.

—Mikos Rukovili

PROLOGUE

WHEN KAROLJE BECAME king, he ordered rooms in the library to be mortared shut. Sometimes Anza imagined the insides of the rooms, dark, the books and papers ravaged by mice, the furniture and floors thick with the dust of those twelve years. Karolje had expelled most of the masters and locked nearly all the buildings. In the College now there were three masters and barely sixty students, who studied under the ever-watchful eyes of Karolje's soldiers. The city had once had numerous printers and booksellers, most of whom had abandoned their shops or turned to some other business or been killed.

Moonlight silvery-blue on the square and the library made her hesitate. The white harpy droppings streaking the roof tiles were bright. Rumil bumped into her. Jance looked back and said, "Are you about to quit?"

"We aren't going to be inconspicuous," Anza said. They had all drunk too much raki, but she remembered to keep her voice down. It was after midnight, and the College required them to be in their rooms.

"I have the bloody key," Jance said. "All we have to do is cross the square."

"Shut up, both of you," said Rumil. He was always nervous about breaking rules.

They did. It was fall, a crisp coolness in the air that the raki dispelled nicely internally and left pleasant on the skin. Jance walked forward, confident, arrogant. That was the trick, of course; if you looked like you were skulking, you were much more suspect.

No one stopped them. They walked up the steps to the library portico. It was too dark to see any of the carvings on the door. Jance said, "Don't crowd me," and Anza and Rumil backed up.

The key scraped against metal as Jance tried to fit it into the lock. Then came the snick and the turn. He pushed, and the door opened.

All three of them had been in the building before, usually sent on an errand by a master, but never at night. The moon shone through the high windows and left blocks of silver light on the threadbare carpet. The staircase ascending to the gallery loomed. To the left, the rooms where the permitted books were shelved were full of darkness.

Jance stepped in. Rumil said, "Now what? We know what it looks like. You've won the bet."

"Afraid of ghosts?"

"It's a library, not a mausoleum. You won't be able to see a damn thing in there."

"Leave, then. Are you coming with me, Anza?"

"I'm staying, but I'll explore on my own," she said. She glanced at Rumil. He shook his head and turned around, shutting the door as he left. With the door closed, the building was larger, darker, the moonlight catching on the rail of the stair faint and insufficient.

Jance said, "I knew he wouldn't come in. I stole some other keys too. I'm going to try them in the north wing."

"Give me one." She held out her hand.

He placed a smaller key on her palm. "I don't know what it unlocks," he said. "It might belong with another building. Meet me back here in an hour."

She put her foot on the stairs. Each step was loud, each creak an explosion.

The gallery, which circled the entrance hall, was lined with locked doors, former offices for the masters. She had walked past them in the daytime and seen the scars where the masters' sigils had been forced off the doors. At either end a windowless staircase led up to the third floor, where the forbidden books were walled off. The bricks covered the doorways in tidy rows, solidly mortared, impossible to pass through.

Once she had asked her father why Karolje walled the books away instead of burning them, and he had said, *Those were the early days.* Before the war with Tazekhor ended, before the killings began, before the queen vanished. Mirantha had disappeared three years after her husband was crowned, and no one spoke of her. Her vanishing was one of the stories everyone knew and no one could remember hearing. The thought was disquieting in the darkness, the silence.

She went to the nearest room and tried the key.

It fit in the third door, but stiffly. She twisted harder. There was a horrific screech from the lock. The hinges were not much quieter when the door swung open.

The air flowing out was stale and musty. Dust lay on the floor like velvet. Books were stacked unevenly here and there, some leaning against each other, on mostly empty shelves. Where the moonlight hit them, the gilt on the spine was bright. A table had been shoved out of place, and one of the two chairs was on its side. Soldiers like her father had come, forced the master or student out, and locked the door. Any books that were illegal would have been confiscated. Anza was surprised the College had been allowed to keep the key.

Softly, as though the floor were fragile, she walked in. Clouds of dust raised by her footsteps showed in the moonbeams, wraithlike. The shadows of the lead bars on the window made a lattice in the silver light. When she stepped forward, the lattice fell across her legs, caging them.

Absurdly, she righted the chair. She went to the window to look out at the empty square. No movement, no shadows. Her breath fogged the cold glass. Jance's taunt to Rumil suddenly seemed fitting. The library might have been a tomb, full of the dead and their uneasy shades.

She turned back to the room and saw that on one shelf the books were arranged neatly, carefully. They had not been searched by soldiers. She crossed and pulled the books off one at a time, opened them in the moonlight. Each had an owner's mark on the first page, its details illegible in the faint light. A history she knew to be banned, printed before it had been illegal. Essays. Another history. A volume of poetry, small enough to fit comfortably in one hand. The poet, Mikos Rukovili, had been executed for treason years ago. A thick treatise of political philosophy. *The evil of kings is that they obtain their power through plunder and reiving and maintain it with oppression.* She returned it hastily to the shelf; knowledge of the contents alone could get her killed. A discourse on natural philosophy, illustrated with drawings in bold dark lines. A play.

How had they survived the king's purge? Her tutor had had such books, and though he did not live in daily fear of king's men in the small village, he had kept them hidden. When he taught her from them, he leashed his dog outside and locked the door. *This is what Karegg is like now*, he said, and she had understood that he was an exile. She had accepted the risk of learning with him, but she had never thought to find cracks in Karolje's censorship within the College itself.

The book at the end of the shelf was thin and bound in a dark green leather, still relatively new. It fell open near the middle. She touched the corner of a page and felt the roughness of the pulp. The library scents of paper and leather and glue and dust bowed to a smell of orange blossoms and lavender and mint.

Moonlight revealed line after line of handwritten words marching across crisp pages in dark ink, written in the Eridian alphabet. Anza sounded out the first few words and realized that only the alphabet was Eridian, not the language. A protection against hasty glances or uneducated companions. Someone's journal. There were no dates. She read a little further, then stopped at a word as fear clogged her throat. It was a name, a name she recognized. Her fingers trembled.

Her body screamed at her to run. She told herself she was not such a coward. She took several deep breaths, of the sort she had learned to take before she nocked an arrow to her bow. The journal had been kept, not destroyed. It mattered. If she did not take it now, it might not be seen for years, its voice further silenced. Someone had to read it.

She slipped it under the back of her shirt and beneath the waistband of her trousers. Impulsively, she took the poetry too. She looked at the owner's mark again. This time, knowing who the journal writer was, she could read the mark.

The poetry fit into the loose pocket of her trousers. She did not dare try to take any of the other books. She retreated and brushed the dust off her shoes in the doorway. She wiped her hands on her pants and locked the door. Then she hurried back down to the library entrance.

The waiting until Jance appeared seemed hours. The comforting warmth of the raki had faded, and she expected soldiers to appear at any moment. She gave Jance back the key as soon as he was close enough to touch.

He dropped the library key twice before he got the door locked. Each time Anza started with surprise at the clank of metal against stone. They walked back together, more quickly than they had come, silent. She was glad to separate from him in the dormitory. They did not say good night.

Once inside her room, she changed rapidly into nightclothes by the light of a candle, forbidden this late. She briefly lifted the edge of the curtain to look for anyone passing outside. The flame swayed, shadows ebbing and increasing. Wax trickled over the rim and hardened on the side of the taper in rigid lines that reminded her of bones. She rotated the candle and huddled into her cold bed with the journal.

The first pages were a lesson book of some sort, in a child's hand, but near the middle it had started to be used for its new purpose:

> *I know it is dangerous to write this, even in this foreign script. But I must put it in words somehow, or I will go mad. I would rather be killed for my deeds than because I have lost my mind.*
>
> *It is three months since Karolje was crowned, and he has not relented about the boys. There is always a guard or two with them when they come or if I go to see them. I have stayed away from the schoolroom. If I go to the garden to walk with*

them, I am always joined by some other woman, usually the wife of one of Karolje's favorites. Everything I say to my sons will be reported to their father. I cannot put Esvar on my lap and tell him the things he needs to hear to have a chance at growing into a good man. I cannot tell Tevin when his father lies. I can only let them know they continue to be loved.

Still I have not seen him *alone. Karolje keeps him close, an adviser. This frightens me. The king must know, and he will kill me for it sometime. I am sure my maids have told him everything he asked.*

When she finished reading, Anza blew out the candle, almost a stub now, and held the closed book on her lap. She ran the tip of one finger over the stamped seal on the cover. The queen had been careful in what she wrote—only near the end was the lover named, after he was dead, impaled as a traitor. Being careful had not protected her.

Anza knew she would be haunted by the journal's last line for the rest of her life. *When I am gone, Karolje will pay.* A curse, a wish, a promise.

1

AFTER CAPTAIN HAVIDIAN bungled a raid on the resistance and was beheaded, raids were overseen by one or the other of Karolje's two sons. Usually the task fell to Esvar, the younger, who hated it. Karolje was punishing him too. He wanted to be among the resisters, fighting the king, instead of rounding them up for the dungeons and torture chambers. He found himself afraid to go to bed those nights. Once he was alone in the dark, the thoughts and memories swirled around and around in his head, pulling him into some unimaginable abyss.

Tonight was likely to be no different. Low, heavy clouds had kept the day from ever warming, and now that the sun was down the air was cold, more like spring than early summer. In the gardens of the Citadel, the trees would be bending with the wind blowing strongly out of the northwest. Esvar hoped the rain held off.

The unpaved street was narrow, crowded with rickety houses whose upper stories blocked out most of the sky. Rats, undeterred by the horses, foraged among a nearby stinking pile of garbage, their scaly tails snakelike on the dirt, bright eyes gleaming in the lantern light. In daytime, the poverty would show in missing planks, in stained and ragged curtains, in grubby, too-thin children with infected sores on their arms and legs. The dank smell of the waterfront a few blocks away clung to everything.

The lightless house was three buildings down from the cross street where Esvar waited. Karegg was filled with abandoned houses that had become ratholes for the resistance, and raiding them was routine. The watchers had already confirmed that no one had left by front or back, door or window. The soldiers in the rear should be in position by now. Four soldiers on horseback blocked each end of the street. The ten other soldiers had all dismounted and were ready, stunning whips in one hand and daggers in the other. They had short swords, but they were instructed not to use them unless their lives were at real risk. Karolje wanted the captives able to talk.

Esvar looked the soldiers over one last time. "You and you," he said, pointing, "will wait outside." One looked too nervous, the other too eager. In the few months he had been leading the raids, he had developed an eye for both timidity and viciousness in his men. "And you, Rozik." Rozik was capable of keeping the men under control if any of the resisters fled toward them.

"All right," Esvar said, familiar apprehension tight within him. His horse's ears twitched. "Go."

The soldiers jogged away from him to the house. The three men Esvar had ordered to stay back fanned out, a lantern on the ground between them and the house, while two men broke down the door. Shouting, the soldiers poured in.

Shouts. A scream of pain. Esvar unclenched his fists. This was the worst of it. The watchers had said six resisters were inside, which was no challenge for seven trained soldiers. The greatest threat was the cramped space. In close quarters a knife strike could be deadly. The stunning whips, long enough to lash a raised arm into paralysis before a blade could ever touch, should dispose of the threat. Should. There was always room for something to go wrong.

Shutters banged as neighbors closed them. No one wanted to see what was happening. Ignorance was the only shield these people had against Karolje. Not much longer now. His eyes scanned the house restlessly from top to bottom.

He saw not the object but the motion, the disturbance in the darkness, as something arced from one of the upper windows. "Get down!" he yelled, but before the words left his mouth there was a boom. The world went silent. Flame spouted to the sky from the street, spilled lamp oil burning madly. His horse reared, its mouth open in a scream he could not hear, and he reined it in with effort. In front of the house, a man writhed on the ground, his arm wrapped in fire, while clods of earth rained down. One struck by Esvar and sprayed his face with soil.

He dismounted and ran forward. His ears were ringing. The heat of the fire struck him like a blow, but he continued to the injured soldier. The man's face was distorted and reddened with light and flame, his open mouth shining in the firelight, the sound inaudible over the noise in Esvar's ears. Esvar flung his jacket over him and beat at the flames.

He smelled hair burning, and flesh, and the chemicals of the explosive. The light danced unsteadily as tears from the smoke filled his eyes.

Soldiers were upon him. One lifted the injured man; the other grabbed Esvar by the upper arm and hauled him away. There was a sudden pain in his back as the mail shirt he wore was briefly driven into his flesh. He spun and saw the arrow on the ground. It was steel-tipped, a military arrow. Where the hell had that come from? Beside him a soldier fell, a feathered shaft protruding from his neck.

They ran. An arrow grazed his shoulder. More arrows skipped against the ground. He looked back with swollen, painful eyes. The lurid flames painting the houses against the night transformed the street into the entrance to hell.

Panicked neighbors fled directly into the soldiers cordoning the block. As Esvar watched, appalled, a sword cut down the slender figure of a youth. Other soldiers followed suit. He raised his arms, shouting, but he could not hear his own voice. The soldiers likely couldn't either. Firelight gilded the blades and the trappings of the horses.

Esvar pushed past a terrified woman and reached the soldiers. He waved them aside. For a moment no one moved; then the soldiers stepped out of the way, and the fleeing people scattered into the night. A few lay dead or injured.

The clouds chose that moment to disgorge themselves of torrential rain. Had Esvar still believed in the gods, he would have dropped to his knees in a prayer of gratitude. The water stung on his bare arms, hurting more than rain ever had. His skin was burned and tender. He was soaked through almost at once. He crossed his arms against the cold and turned his face upward, hoping the rain would clean his eyes.

The street darkened abruptly as the fire went out. There was just enough light from the lanterns to see bodies on the street. At least three were soldiers. It had all happened fast.

Someone brought him a cloak. He put it on and watched grimly while men bustled around him. His trousers clung to his legs. Slowly the stinging in his eyes and the noise in his ears abated. Raindrops fell into the water-filled holes in the street.

"My lord? Sir?"

Esvar turned. "What is it, soldier?" He could tell his voice was louder than normal.

"There were three resisters as tried to flee out the back, sir. We caught 'em before the fire. Two men and a girl."

"Are they hurt?"

"No, sir."

Better for them to have perished. Esvar wished he could send the prisoners to their death before the interrogators got to work. Karolje would know, that was the damnable thing about it. Karolje always had a way to know. Men were too frightened of him to do anything other than spy on each other.

"Where are they?" Esvar asked.

"In the cart, sir."

"I'll see them. What about the others?"

"Two died. One got away."

He swore to himself. Karolje would be furious.

In a swirl of cloak and squelch of boot, he walked the dozen yards to the guarded cart. It was a wooden box on wheels, bigger than was needed for only three prisoners; they had expected to bring back half a dozen. An oil lamp hung from a rod over the back of the cart, where a man stood guard. No one was supposed to talk to the prisoners once they were locked in, not even to ask names. Questions were all saved for the Citadel.

Esvar motioned for the door to be unlocked. He wanted to see what he had. He would not defy the rule and speak to them, not when the rest of the raid had gone so wrong. The guard was Karolje's man, and a report of any transgression would make its way to the king. He wished he could select soldiers for the raids from the few dozen men sworn to him and his brother, but Karolje did not trust him that far.

The door swung open. The rain against the top and sides of the cart echoed in the space of it. A wooden bench ran front to back against either wall. The prisoners, separated from each other, were chained by their wrists to the bench. Their ankles were bound with fire-twine. Any movement against the rope would burn and blister their skin.

The men were both in their early twenties. One kept his head bent, but the other glared. The woman, younger than them, had her eyes closed, her mouth set.

She was not the woman he had hoped to find. The leader of the resistance, who called herself Sparrow, was known to be significantly older. The three prisoners were all too young to have any authority and were not likely to yield anything new to the examiners.

The guard locked the prisoners in the darkness again. Free them, said the voice of his conscience. He quashed it as he always did, by telling himself he protected the throne for his brother. After fifteen years of rule, Karolje was ill, fading. His fierce grip on city and country would not last forever. When Tevin was crowned, he could reverse the laws and edicts.

Esvar saw no point in waiting any longer to go back to the Citadel. He walked to his horse and rubbed as much water off the saddle as he could. The cloak was heavy and sodden. He mounted and chose three men to accompany him. Karolje would be no easier to face in a few hours.

✦ ✦ ✦

He had stripped his life down to its essentials, and there were not many ways for the king to punish him. Karolje had ceased physical violence against him some years ago, and the failure of the raid was not significant enough to render Esvar useless. He made his report on bended knee and endured the acid cuts of scorn he was accustomed to.

Dismissed, he rose. Karolje sat straight in his high-backed wooden chair, his clothing loose on him, his hands bony and pale on the chair arms. He had not reached gauntness yet, but it was coming. Though he still met with the chancellor, the spymaster, and a few other men, he no longer appeared before ordinary courtiers. It was years since he had allowed himself to be seen in the city. Around his neck he wore the ancient Vetian pendant of office, a silver wolf's head. Legend said that nine hundred years ago Kazdjan the first king had laid the first stone of the Citadel on the spot where he wrestled a wolf to its death. The jet eyes of the wolf's head were as black and baleful as Karolje's own.

I could kill him, Esvar thought, as he often did. The guards would slay him at once, but it would give the crown to Tevin.

Except it wouldn't. Esvar knew he lied to himself when he justified the raids as for his brother's sake. As soon as Karolje died there would be a power struggle for the throne, and Tevin might well lose. Each prince was the other's only ally. The king had made no secret of his contempt for his heir, and since his illness had become evident a few months ago, many of the lords had ceased pretending loyalty to Karolje's successor. Esvar and Tevin still needed Karolje to live long enough for them to discourage the circling dogs and to bribe, threaten, or cajole as many courtiers as possible to their side. Lord Goran the chancellor, Karolje's cousin and next in the succession after Esvar, had numerous adherents. Lord Doru Kanakili, the spymaster, had fewer adherents but more assassins and the ambition to match.

The corridors were empty of anyone but guards this time of night. Esvar had changed out of his wet clothing before reporting to the king, so he went directly to his brother's workroom. The soldiers at Tevin's door stepped aside for him to knock. The vigor in Tevin's call to enter was forced.

On one side of the room was a large desk, which had on it books and papers and a filament light, turned off now. On the other side were a sofa, a low table, and a few upholstered chairs. The only illumination came from an oil lamp and what remained of a fire. Rain spangled the window glass. Tevin sat on the sofa, a half-empty cup of tea on the table.

"What happened?" Tevin asked. He was a handsome man, capable, five and a half years older than Esvar, who had just turned twenty-one. When he wanted to be, he was intimidating in his own way. Esvar had two inches on him, but Tevin could make him feel much smaller. Right now he looked weary. His gold-brown hair shone in the light.

"We got three, the inexperienced ones. They had explosives. And military arrows." Briefly, he recounted the events.

"You didn't know they had archers," Tevin said.

"It doesn't matter. I should have left that soldier to die instead of trying to save him. If I'd stayed where I belonged, the soldiers would not have killed the neighbors either." He slammed his fist into the palm of his hand. He missed Havidian, who had been a good soldier and still maintained his honor, a difficult task in the Citadel. The captain would not have made so elementary a mistake as Esvar had.

His brother looked steadily at him. "The resistance had to know that setting off an explosive would frighten people out of their homes. They made that choice, not you."

A few years ago, the resistance strikes had not amounted to much: a watchman stoned on patrol, damaged sculptures and defaced paintings of the king, broken glass on storefronts that displayed the royal seal of goods. But since last autumn the attacks on soldiers had been more daring and more deadly. Explosives were another step toward insurrection.

Esvar said, "There are enough people killed every day without having to make chances for soldiers to kill more."

"Which means that if the resistance has gone there, if they are ready to go to full-out war against the king and don't care about incidental deaths, or want to use them to rouse people, we have to hit back hard at them too. I'm not going to let Karegg get any bloodier." Tevin left the sofa and poured wine into a cup. "Here."

It was an attempt to take Esvar's edge off. He did not want to be dulled, but he sipped obediently. If it had not still been raining, he would have returned to the city and found a dark tavern where he could be completely unknown. Obscurity was the privilege of being the younger son.

The wine was better than he would get in a tavern. He sat on the sofa, put his feet on the table, and said, "It's a bloody disaster no matter how we look at it. I want trained men for the raids. A group of them, who know how to do it. Not whoever draws the duty. Get me two decent officers who can choose good men." Men who were able, incorruptible, and unexcited by cruelty.

Tevin sat beside him. "I know one man you can work with. He was just promoted to lieutenant, and he seems to have actually merited it. His name's Jance Mirovian. I suggest you take him unless you think he'd not fall in line enough. He was educated at the College. Finished two years ago and came on as an officer. Havidian trained him. He's a cousin of Lord Darvik, and it would be useful to have Darvik feel flattered by you."

"Who paid his commission? Darvik?"

"Darvik paid a third and Mirovian's father paid the rest."

Esvar hated paying out favors—the recipients usually immediately wanted another one—but Darvik had a following among the minor lords and was popular with the wealthy merchants. Tevin read people well. It was the men like Darvik, who had friends in both Citadel and city, whose support Tevin would need.

"I'll take him out with me," he said. "See what he's made of."

That was something he had far too much experience in. When Esvar was sixteen, Karolje had sent him east to put down a rebellion in the mountains. The fighters were peasants, untrained, crudely armed. It should have been an easy slaughter. But Karolje had salted the company with men who questioned his orders, disobeyed, mocked. He stood by the campfire the second night, recognizing the test, and the next day he ordered three men hanged. He was obeyed. Then they killed the rebels.

Upon returning to Karegg, he sat in his bedroom at the open window and held the edge of a knife to his wrist. He did not want to die, but he did not want to live this way either. His room overlooked the gardens, and outside the grounds the lake, shining in sun, and circling it the tree-covered hills, green and glossy. He remembered the dead men swinging on the rough gallows before they were cut down. He had passed the test, but Karolje had won.

At last he had sheathed the knife. If he killed himself, the game was over. He refused to let the king beat him that way.

Tevin said, "I don't give a damn how many of Karolje's men are killed on these raids, but I can't afford to lose you. If Mirovian's not suitable, we'll find someone else. If I could, I'd send you away altogether."

"An assassin can kill me anywhere. Where would you send me?"

"To the shah of Milaya and his eight daughters. I'll need a queen."

"You're not serious," said Esvar. "If you want to marry one of them, you're going to have to give the country in return." Milaya was everything Vetia was not: large, rich, powerful. Sending a Milayan princess to Vetia would amount to exiling her.

"Nasad will get a grandchild on the throne."

"The lords will never stand for that, Tev. If they even think you're considering it, they'll force someone else on you."

"Will they challenge me with Nasad's army behind me? Killing me would guarantee war."

"They'll challenge you before a betrothal is made." Esvar rubbed his face with the heel of his hand. The day's stubble rasped against weapon-hardened skin. His back hurt where the arrow had struck it. "*I* could marry one of Nasad's daughters," he said. "And stay there, in the Milayan court."

Tevin picked up his tea, sipped it, made a face. "Cold," he said. "That's not a bad idea. It gives us a hell of a hammer."

It could save Tevin's life. If he was killed, the kingdom would go to a man with the shah's army behind him. The potential for a Milayan conquest would keep the lords from doing anything that gave Esvar claim to the throne in place of his brother.

"Write the letter. If he's interested, I'll go." He had no expectations that marriage would be anything other than an affair of state, and this was better than resolving a conflict by marrying the daughter of a Vetian lord who hated him. The harshness of rule in Milaya was velveted with music and poetry and hanging gardens full of birdsong.

Tevin said, "If I write the letter, it's treason. If we ask, Karolje will see through it."

Each of them had a lifetime full of small defiances of the

king: a bribe to a prison guard, a kindness to a servant, a look the other way at a report of invective against Karolje. Defiances that could be explained away as errors or ignorance. There was no explaining away a deliberate negotiation with a foreign power. They approached the edge of a precipice.

"Tevin, he thinks you're weak. Show him you can be as ambitious as he is and he'll praise you for it. If he truly didn't want you to succeed him, he'd have found a way by now to name you traitor. If he's as worried about us as we think he is, we'd already be dead."

"Damn you, I don't want to be praised by Karolje." Tevin got up with enough force to push the sofa back a few inches. The legs screeched on the floor. "And you know that."

Tevin's conscience was the pivot upon which their plans always stuck. He tried to hold on to honor when no one around him did. Once Esvar had told Tevin that he could play the king's game without becoming like Karolje, and Tevin had shoved him hard into a wall, knocking him to the floor. Both of them had seen the bitter irony at once, and he had taken the hand his brother extended to help him up. But the line Tevin would not cross always lay on this side of the action that needed doing. He was not willing to dirty his hands even slightly. The fact of that restraint stood between them, immovable, unspoken.

Esvar said, more sharply than he would have if he had not been tired, "Is he your enemy or not? There's never going to be a good time to face him. You're going to be the king. You should want power."

"I'm no coward."

"I don't think you are." Esvar softened his voice. His brother wasn't close to breaking, not yet, but the fraying was starting to show. Had Tevin ever spent a sleepless night with a knife at his own wrists, considering the cuts? "Power accrues. If you marry me off to the Milayans, you'll be that much stronger. It's a better guarantee of support than flattering Lord Darvik."

Tevin stared at the floor a moment, then raised his head. His face was set. "Very well. I'll write the letter. I will offer myself but inform the shah that everyone is likely to live longer if you are the bridegroom instead."

"And in the meantime?"

"In the meantime we watch our backs, pretend to be loyal, and do politicking like hell. Start with the lords of the six southern cantons. You won't get anywhere with Lord Cosvar, but we need the others, however minor. I'll take everyone else."

Esvar grimaced. He hated politicking, and the lords of the south would want a renewal of war with despised Tazekhor in exchange for support. Most of them were older, too, not having displeased Karolje enough to be eliminated. "You're not giving me much to work with."

"Lead them to believe I'll reduce their taxes."

"You can't do that, that's over half the kingdom's revenue."

"Revenue that is then spent on maintaining those provinces. The lords will think it's a wonderful trade, paying less in taxes and having more control."

But, Esvar thought. He kept his mouth shut. Freedom from Karolje's oversight was the only coin Tevin had right now, even though most of the lords would govern abominably. If they ran their cantons to satisfy their own greed, they might still have a gentler hand than Karolje did. And their sons and grandsons were more malleable.

Tevin added, "If there's any conflict in the south, I'm going to set you down in it. If I do, these will be your people. You have charm when you want to. Use it."

That was a command. Esvar squirmed internally. He probably deserved the tone. He could hardly tell his brother to act like a king and then turn around and defy him in the next breath.

By conflict in the south, Tevin meant another Tazekh war. "Do your spies tell you something I haven't heard?"

"Korikos isn't arming for war. Not yet. But he's watching what happens here closely. If we have a civil war, I don't think it will be long before he invades."

Esvar had always imagined that whatever struggle there was for the throne, it would be settled in the Citadel, by duel or assassination or arrest. Soldiers would fall into line with the winner. Civil war was a different picture. A chilling one. Ruined crops, the lake and earth poisoned with death, the abandoned prisons from the Tazekh war filled again. Harpies feasting.

"Is it Goran you're worried about, or the resistance?" he asked.

"Both, but Goran more. He's stronger."

There seemed nothing to say to that. The rain drummed steadily in the courtyard outside.

Esvar finished the wine in three gulps that were more suitable for something much cheaper. "I'd better check that there are no lingering problems," he said. "Good night."

"Esvar."

"What?"

"I'm going to find a way to get you out of here."

I don't need to be rescued, Esvar thought. But Tevin could not cease the habits of a lifetime; he had taken on the burden of proving himself perfect to a ghost.

ANZA'S LEFT HAND slipped on the wet slates. Her right hand clamped down hard on the ridgepole and held. Wind lashed the rain into her face and cut through her soaked clothing. She reached again with the left hand and gripped. Her palm hurt; she must have cut it. She moved her left leg along the steep roof. Right hand, right leg, left hand, left leg. Again. The strain on her forearms was increasing. If she fell, it was a thirty-foot drop to the street, with nothing to catch onto. Water sluiced over her hands and under her body.

The Temple bells rang eleven, the first stroke startling her. She tried to pull herself higher on the roof. Her arms ached, and her fingers were losing sensation as the rain numbed her skin. She turned her head to see how much farther she had to go, but the dark and the rain made it impossible to judge distance. Gods, what she would give for a rope. Left hand, left leg. Her shoulders protested. She had always been good at climbing, but she had never had to go this far.

Finally she came to the chimney. It was wide and old and, like everything else in this part of Karegg, deteriorating. She reached for the bricks and found a gap in the mortar big enough to put her fingertips into. She tugged experimentally. The brick did not move. Gripping the brick with one hand and the ridgepole with the other, she brought her knees up under her and pushed with her feet. That raised her head over the ridgepole. Another push, and she was able to bring her left leg across and straddle the ridge. Breathing hard, she leaned her forehead against the chimney.

Her arms felt heavy as lead, and her hands were cramping. She touched her left palm and found the gash across the middle. Blood was warm under her fingers. The cut was not deep, or it would have hurt a hell of a lot more, but the blood wasn't going to clot until she could get somewhere dry and wrap it up. How was she going to explain it to Rumil? Maybe he would be asleep.

She flexed her hands repeatedly, trying to loosen the cramps. It was unlikely any of Karolje's soldiers would find her now; she had dropped the bow and climbed out the gable window onto the roof as soon as the flames went out. They would not have been able to see her through the rain and the darkness. Since then she had been making her way, building by building, along the block and away from the soldiers gathered at the other end. This house was on the corner; once she was on the ground, she would be able to run in three directions if necessary.

Lanterns shone at the far end of the street where the soldiers were. The noise had died down some time ago. They had searched the house thoroughly by now and taken or killed whoever they could.

She had thought she was prepared for death, whether at the soldiers' hands or her own. It was a necessary mind-set for a resister. Being captured was the worst thing that could happen. During the raid, she had been too busy shooting to think about death. Now, resting at last, she was suffused with fear. Her companions were dead, or would be soon, and she had barely escaped.

She did not fight the fear. It would fade. Fear to greater or lesser degrees belonged to Karegg. You learned to live with it, or you died. Nor did one grieve fallen soldiers in the midst of the battle.

There had been no time to prepare more than a cursory defense. Her resistance group had met there a few times over the last month—once too often, it appeared—and she had only had the bow and arrows because the house was being used to store them. Mink had brought the explosive to demonstrate how small he could make one.

Mink was dead. She had recognized his voice as he screamed. She would have to find one of the leaders and report, but not for a few days. There was nothing to be done about it. Let the soldiers lose interest. How had they been found out? A neighbor? A spy in the resistance? All six of them who knew about the house had been there, and none of the other five had acted like a traitor.

Her body shuddered with cold. If she did not get down now, she might not be able to later. She flexed her hands one more time, unstrapped her sandals, and tossed them to the ground. She grabbed the chimney and pulled herself to a stand. Hands on the top on it, she stepped around and felt at the bricks with one foot.

The bricks were coarse and cheap, the mortar cheaper. She found a toehold almost at once. She extended her arm and searched for a handhold in a good place. She gripped with her other hand. A steadying breath, and she swung her left leg off the roof. Her foot fumbled at the bricks, found a niche. She clung entirely to the chimney now.

Her right hand was the most insecure. She slid it down the chimney. A chink a handbreadth below was too close to be useful. Wind slapped her wet shirt against the bricks. An uneven bit of mortar dug into her left big toe. She brought her right hand back to where it had been and explored with her left. There was a handhold. She gripped, lowered her left foot.

She was over halfway to the ground when her right foot caught on a protrusion from the wall. She jerked with pain and surprise. The fingers of her left hand slid, and she clutched tightly, skinning her knuckles. She moved her toes over the chimney below the protrusion. It did not take long to find another toehold, but it was barely big enough. She put her right hand into the foothold she had just used and felt with her left foot. No holes, no chinks. Her arms trembled. Rain ran down the surface of the bricks.

Ten feet was a long drop, but not fatal. She set herself, closed her eyes, and pushed off from the chimney. Between the pain on the sole and the mud-slicked street, her right foot did not want to hold her weight when it touched down, and her ankle twisted. She was facedown on the ground before she could register the fall. Swearing, she got to her hands and knees. Her ankle throbbed, but not with the kind of pain that suggested serious injury. She groped around for her sandals and put them on. Then she got to a stand and tried to put weight on the ankle. It was bearable, but it would be a while before she could run on it.

She wrapped her bleeding hand into the bottom of her shirt and started walking north along the lightless street. The houses were dark. Even the stray dogs and the rats would be taking shelter. All she had to worry about was the watch.

✦ ✦ ✦

An hour later, she staggered tiredly into the house she had shared with Rumil since they finished at the College two years ago. She had only had to hide twice.

A lamp was on. The dim light would be enough to see her way to the stairs and up to the next floor. The servants were no doubt asleep by now. She wrapped herself in one of the cloaks hanging by the door and, shivering, climbed the stairs.

The bedroom door was closed but not latched, and yellow light shone around the edges. Damn. This had the potential to be ugly. Rumil had been short-tempered since winter, and their quarrels were becoming more frequent. It was a long time since he had softened her name to Anya. She tightened her grip on the cloak and opened the door.

Rumil, fully dressed, sat in a chair with his arms folded. He said, "Where the hell have you been?"

"Don't start this now, Rumil," she said. Their rows always left her feeling drained and hollow. Her clothing was dripping on the floor. She tossed the cloak over a chair. "I need to get dry and go to bed."

"You were late four nights ago. And a week ago. And two days before that. I can go on. Once, even twice, I could understand. But not over and over. Who is it?"

She was exhausted enough that it took a moment for the words to reach her understanding. When they did, she put down the towel she had been raising to her hair. "I'm not sleeping with anyone else," she said. "And not for lack of opportunity." She knew that statement to be a mistake as the words emerged. It wasn't even true.

"Then what are you doing?"

If she told him about the resistance, he would throw her out. The house was his. Well, his father's. His father was a well-off and influential wine merchant who sold to the Citadel steward and styled himself "Purveyor to the Crown." The king was corrupt, but the wines sold by Servos Tashikian were popular among the nobles, and that was all that mattered to Rumil's family.

"Radd kept me late," she said. "I got caught in the storm." She wanted to take off the wet clothing, but not with him looking at her as he was. She shivered.

"The storm came after dark. Radd wouldn't keep you that late. Something else did."

"I'm cold and wet and tired," she said. "Tomorrow."

"No," Rumil said, slapping his hand down onto the wooden arm of his chair. "Now. You're lying to me, and I've had enough."

Her shoulders hurt, and there were scrapes and bruises on her forearms that she had not seen in the dark. "If I tell you the truth and you don't believe me, what else can I do? I don't have any other lover. I don't want any other lover."

"What about Irini?"

"I've hardly seen her since we finished at the College. She's about the last person I would want to be with again. And she has her own lover, anyway."

"You're lying," he repeated.

"Stuff it, Rumil. If I were lying, why would I stop now? Not because you demand it, that's for certain."

He rose, rigid with fury. He had never struck her. There's a first time for everything, she thought. "You can sleep in the drawing room."

She stared at him. "Are you serious?"

"When you go out, I don't know if you're going to come back," he said. "If you don't want to be here, I don't see why I should accommodate you."

Oh, you pompous boy, she thought. Her own words were a knife stroke to the affection she still had for him. If that was how she saw him, she had no reason to stay.

"I'll leave as soon as it's light," she shot back. "I've never been unfaithful, but I won't stay with anyone who doesn't trust me. I don't need you."

"You'll be singing a different song in a week."

She wore the key to the strongbox where she kept her money around her neck. She jerked the chain over her head and flung it at him. It clinked on the floor. "There. Go on. Take what you want. Take it all. I don't owe you anything." She inhaled, trying to control herself. Two hours ago she had been afraid for her life. Rumil's anger paled by comparison.

He picked up the key and pulled so hard on the chain that the clasp broke. The key fell. "You're about to lose the only chance you have."

"Lose it? I'm taking it. I'm glad I never married you."

"You little bitch. I should have believed them when they told me you were a slut."

"I shouldn't have believed them when they told me you were a man."

"Half an hour," he said. "Half an hour for you to get everything you want to take with you and put it in the drawing room." He kicked the key back at her, then turned and tromped downstairs, each step booming in the stairwell.

Furious, Anza yanked the wardrobe open and threw clothing on the bed. She did not own much: clothing, a few books, some cheap hairpins, an elegant wooden carving of a mountain cat that was the only decorative thing she had brought north with her. A single, much-read letter from her father. A miniature of her long-dead mother. The queen's journal. She paused, holding that, and considered how lucky she was herself to be able to walk away from Rumil. Her money and one valuable ring.

Her father had kept some things for her, including the book of poems by Rukovili she had taken from the College. She had not wanted Rumil to stumble upon it. If her father had recognized the owner's mark as the queen's, he had kept silent. His belongings had all been confiscated by the Crown after he was executed. She hoped no one recognized the book. It would have been wise to tear the frontispiece out.

She left her wet clothes; the bloody shirt was ruined and the trousers were too old to be worth the trouble. When filled, her trunk was too heavy to lift by herself. She dragged it across the floor, smiling grimly at the scratch marks. The muscles in her sides and arms hurt. The cut in her hand opened again. The blood smeared on the handle of the trunk and dripped on the floor. Bracing the trunk's weight with one hand and pulling with the other, she brought it thudding down the stairs. The servants were surely awake by now. *Thud, thud.*

"I'll get it," Rumil said, not at all kindly. He picked the trunk up, carried it to the drawing room, and put it down with arrogant softness on the rug. When he released the handles, he noticed the blood.

"What did you do to yourself?"

She lifted her blood-smeared palm. "A cut. Nothing you need to worry about."

"I'm not worrying. Go clean up in the kitchen and don't get blood on anything. Go on, go do it. Now, Anza."

I killed three men tonight, she thought. She feared she had said it. He did not react, so she must not have. She turned her back to him and walked as slowly as possible to the kitchen.

She rinsed the cut with water from the kettle and bandaged it with a clean dish cloth, folded into a strip. To tie it she had to hold one end of the cloth with her teeth. She took the opportunity to look at her sore foot. Whatever she had scraped against had not broken the skin.

Anger still beat in her, but her voice was steady when she returned to the drawing room and said, "I'll be out of here faster with less embarrassment to you if you let Darish take me in the morning."

His face pinkened, but he said, "I agree. I'll tell him." He walked out.

Anza opened a bottle of raki and poured a glass of the clear fluid, spilling some. She took one hasty gulp. It burned. Then she loosened her shoulders and sat on the upholstered sofa. She sipped, enjoying the heat against her lips and tongue, the growing warmth inside. She would not sleep tonight, not as roused as she was with conflict.

Her days were spent as a clerk for the lawyer Radd Orescu; he would let her stay in his office for a few nights while she found somewhere else to live. It would be cheaper to live with one of her friends, but the risk of them coming to Karolje's attention was too great. Jance, whom she had once most trusted, had joined the Guard, and that had severed them.

She would not leave the resistance, not after what Karolje had done to her father. Her parents had never married, and after her mother died when she was eight, she had been raised by her mother's sister on the edge of a small mid-country village and tutored by an old man as though she were of noble birth. The summer she turned sixteen, five years ago now, the letter had come from her father, summoning her to Karegg and a place he had secured for her in the College. She had not seen him then for ten years, not since Karolje was crowned and he was assigned to the king's army, but the lure of a new city and the College drew her north.

He was a captain by then, but when he could he took her

out for an afternoon and an early evening dinner. They talked, each learning who the other was. She was now coming to realize she should have listened more. He had been a kind man, and a generous one, and once she had asked him why he stayed a soldier. She would never forget his reply, made over steaming black tea while winter flurries drifted down. *If the good men leave the army,* he said, *there will be no check on the cruelty of those who remain.* She said, *But you are ordered to do cruel things.* He touched her, which he rarely did, and said, *Karolje won't live forever. When he dies, someone needs to be able to set things right. And that is saying more than I should say, daughter.* She had already learned to be careful, and she nodded and changed the subject.

After that he taught her to shoot, to ride, to defend herself unarmed, to use a knife. She was competent but no more in all but shooting; in archery, she found her talent. Under Karolje, most weapons were illegal for commoners, and she practiced secretly, with her father or alone, in abandoned houses and weed-grown lots. No one, not even her lovers, knew about her father or her bow. She finished at the College, worked with Radd and lived with Rumil, and stayed well within the law.

Then, a few months ago, Karolje had her father executed. For what, she did not know. A week after she found out, she nervously entered a tavern that rumor said was crowded with resisters. She did not believe the rumor—if it was true, Karolje would have moved on them long ago—but she hoped it would signal her intent. She drank her beer and walked back to Radd's. Two days later the first message came.

She should have left Rumil then. It would have been better for both of them.

He might change his mind about her leaving in the morning.

She had to go anyway. She could tell herself she hadn't said anything about the resistance because she wanted to protect him, but the truth was she had stopped trusting him before then. She had not told him about her father's life, let alone his death. His father was deeply loyal to the Crown.

The air was still and silent, with that peculiar chill of late night alone. A night for ghosts. It was on such a night three years ago that she had stayed up late talking to Rumil, their conversation increasingly personal, until their hands touched. A passion born of long acquaintance and youth and need, which should have come to its end the next morning. They were too different, he the city-bred merchant's son accustomed to fine furniture and obedient servants, and she the farmer's niece who had come to Karegg to learn and expected nothing to be done for her.

Her wet hair hung in tangles down her back, dampening her shirt. She lit the fire laid in the drawing room hearth. The flames roared. She held her hands as close as she could bear to and tried to draw the heat into herself. The hot air felt splendid on her face.

Red and gold flames, not hot enough yet for white and purple tongues to lick at the logs. The flames from a broken lantern had caught one man. He had screamed. She saw the other soldiers rush to him, the fire ruddying their skin, and smelled the burning flesh. On the floors below her, heavy men hurried through the rooms. When she drew the bow, her hand trembled with nervousness, and she had to nock the arrow three times before she let it fly.

I killed three soldiers, she thought. On the roof, the fact had strengthened her. Now it was a kick in the stomach. She was a traitor. A murderer.

She drew back from the fire. Sweat was standing out on her

forehead, under her arms, dampening her palms. Was this what her father would have wanted? The men she had killed might have been good men, like him.

It's a war. There are always good men who die in war.

He had known what he was doing when he trained her.

You can't back out now, Anza, she told herself. You've killed. You've lied. You're committed.

She shut her eyes. The flames left their impressions on her sight. Flames lit the darkness, and a man died.

MIRANTHA

AFTER THE SECOND of her two sons is born and she has healed from the birth, she asks Karolje if she can take them south to see her parents. To her surprise, he agrees. She thinks that his father the king must have told him to assent. Her own father is the commandant of the Southern Share, which means his soldiers are the first line of defense against a Tazekh invasion. The king needs his loyalty. That was what the marriage was supposed to do, but Karolje's cruelty is eroding that support.

His cruelty does not bear thinking about. Beatings, always where the bruises will not show, insults, rape, the list goes on. Her only reassurance is that he is the same to many people; it is about him, not her. If she did not see his cruelty in so many other places, she would think she had failed, rather than been failed. In the first years he was sometimes kind and generous, convincing her that the violence was an aberration, but he no longer needs to do that. The trap has closed completely.

He is sixteen years older than her; she is the third wife, the other two each dying in the birth of a stillborn daughter. She at least has given him the sons he wants, with only one miscarriage between them, so she has value.

In Timor, in the only place she has ever seen as home, she leaves the infant Esvar with his nurse and takes Tevin to ride the border with her father and brother. It is summer, the days hot, the grapes swelling on the vines, the sky clear and intensely blue. Their road takes them past the lavender fields that she loves, the rounded bushes with their twilight and sunset purples. Lavender does not grow well in the north, but she has bunches of it dried, scenting her clothing, tied with ribbons and hanging from the windows and mantel in her bedroom in Karegg.

The border is a wide muddy river, and on the other side the Tazekh peasants toil in the fields. They stare at her father and his soldiers. She cannot see the peasants' faces clearly, but she imagines they are full of hatred. The river has been reddened with blood many times. There is a sliver of land ten miles wide between two rivers that has changed ownership repeatedly; right now it is in Vetian hands, and there is always the chance the Tazekhs will try to reclaim it. The new Tazekh king, Korikos, is reputed to be bloodthirsty and aggressive.

Tevin, who will be six in the fall, rides ahead with her brother. Her father says, "King Piyr knows he has done you wrong. He won't admit it, even to himself, but he will give me what I ask for you. What do you want?"

It is, she supposes, the only sort of an apology she will get from him either.

What does she want? No one has asked her that in years. Tevin loves her—it is the one grace of Karolje's disinterest. As the daughter of a soldier, she can be expected to raise a brave and disciplined son, and he has mostly left the boy in her care so far. She doesn't think she needs any other kind of love.

But she wants a friend. The wives of Karolje's closest companions sensed early by some alchemy of court that her friendship would be more a liability than an asset, and the other women are afraid of him. She is educated, intelligent; what she misses more than anything else is discussion. She reads poetry, politics, mathematics, often and deeply. And alone. Her mind is starved for nourishment.

She can't ask her father for a friend. She can, however, ask him for a tutor. Tevin is old enough. If she leaves finding a teacher to anyone else, the teacher will be a priest, who will be Karolje's servant and want nothing to do with her.

She says, "I want a tutor who is wise enough to teach my son and old enough that Karolje can't be jealous. I want someone I can talk to."

They jog along, blackbirds trilling from the bushes. Ducks paddle on the river. A Vetian fisherman standing on the bank takes off his hat and bows to her father as they trot past. Her father raises a hand in acknowledgment. Karolje would never do such a thing.

Her father says, "That I can arrange."

Ahead of them, Tevin stands in his stirrups and looks back gleefully at her. His fair hair is beginning to darken as hers never did, which increases his resemblance to Karolje. Her brother says something to him, and they turn off the road and ride across a field as fast as Tevin's pony will go. Her heart thumps a little with fear that he will be thrown or fall, but he can ride as well as he can walk, and nothing happens.

Her father says, indulgent, "He's a fine boy. When he's old enough, twelve or thirteen, send him to me for six months or a year, and I'll train him how to ride the border."

"Thank you," she says. There is no need to say it will require Karolje's permission. They both know that.

* * *

The tutor, Nihalik Vetrescu, is not clerk or priest or soldier or lawyer but a little bit of all; he knows history and law, can string a bow and gut a deer, and has more than once been her father's envoy across the border to the Tazekhs. No one can say he is an inadequate teacher for a king's grandson. He is at least ten years older than Karolje, of unassuming stature and poise, no threat. When they set off for Karegg at the end of summer, they go slowly because he has brought chests of books and other interesting things that weigh down the luggage cart.

The first night of travel, they stay at the home of one of King Piyr's lords. The lord himself has not returned from Karegg for the autumn yet, and the huge house has many empty rooms. Late at night she wanders through the mansion to the garden door and steps out onto a wide patio. She finds Nihalik there, sitting next to a strong-smelling candle that keeps the insects away.

She is too polite to ask him why he is awake. They talk for a while, quietly. He tells her about riding across the northern steppe with the Uzekh tribes and walking along the edge of the jungle in distant Eridia, about the ruined buildings in the far south of Milaya, about cities in the distant east that are built on hundreds of small islands. She is entranced.

Then the conversation twists and winds its way back to Vetia, and Nihalik is looking at her, saying, "What do you want your sons to learn?"

"Justice," she says without thinking. She takes a breath and speaks treason. "It would be better for Vetia if Karolje never became king. But if he does, Tevin needs to be able to heal the wounds Karolje leaves." She stares defiantly at him, chin up, feeling young.

"Children are inclined toward justice," he says. "Too much so, at times. They also have to learn to give. Especially children who will be kings."

She tries to imagine Piyr, for whom she feels affection if not love, saying that, and fails. She does not blame Karolje's father for Karolje, but the king is weaker than his son. A weak king is a man who takes, not gives.

"Yes," she says. "I want them to learn that they have a duty to their people. That Vetia is a small country amid many, that history is bigger than they are. That there are other ways of doing things."

"Tevin has the mind for it. He will need more than me to make that duty his own. The books I have, the lessons I can give him, are things Karolje too will have studied. The education of a prince is wide. You will need to show him what justice and compassion look like."

In his tone she hears not a warning but a hesitancy, a doubt. He is unsure of her. Perhaps not of her capacity but of her opportunity.

She says, "His father is not much interested in him right now. He is too young. As long as Piyr lives, there is time."

"I will do my best," he says.

The moon has risen, its misshapen disk casting shadows that flatten the vegetation. For a while they sit unspeaking, watching the shadows change as the moon moves. A cat pads softly across the patio, and an owl hoots in the darkness of a tall tree. Within the house her children are sleeping. So should she be.

"Mirantha," he says, breaking the silence. It is a familiarity she has not granted him, but she does not mind. He surely knows not to call her by her name in front of Karolje.

"Yes?"

"Do you know the story of the harpy goddess?"

She shakes her head.

"It is an old story, far older than Vetia, thousands of years old. There was a princess who had the gift of prophecy, and she foresaw that her father's actions would cause a war. She told him, but he did not listen, and the war started. The king lost battle after battle, and finally he asked his priests what to do. They did their divinations and told him he must sacrifice his daughter.

"So he did. It is to save the kingdom, he told her. You die as a soldier does. He laid her on the altar with his own arms, and the priests prayed to their gods. Then they slit her throat.

"What came out was not blood but shadow, dark as night and vast as mountains. It had the shape of a bird, and when it moved its wings, it smelled like death. Its face was the face of the princess.

"The priests and the king fell on their faces, speechless with terror. The goddess caught them with her talons and flung them away from her. They fell bloody and broken, and died. The king's enemies overran the country and made it their own. And ever since, the harpy goddess avenges women."

"Which women? All of them?"

"The ones who are not listened to. The ones who are killed by their fathers. The ones who suffer at the hands of men."

"All women, then," she says, unable to cloak the sudden bitterness in her voice. "Why did you tell me this?"

"Do you want a way out?"

"Are you speaking of divorce or of murder?" Pain she has pushed away threatens to leap forward. "I can't leave the boys."

"I know," he says, and the kindness in his voice nearly breaks her.

"I don't want escape. I want protection." She thinks of Esvar, with the swirl of soft dark hair on his head and his sweet, milky mouth. Of Tevin, laughing in delight while her brother chased him through the garden. "I want my sons to grow up safe in body and soul."

He doesn't reply. What reply is possible?

The shadows seem darker, the candle flame more intense. The air is rich with the scents of dried grass and sage and wax and distant water. The owl hoots again overhead, and she hears the rush of air through its feathers, the rustle in the grass as it swoops upon some creature.

She rises. "Good night," she says.

"Good night, my lady," he says, standing and bowing. She knows they will never again speak so directly of such things.

In her room, she changes into her nightclothes and blows out the flame. She goes to the window and pulls aside the linen curtain and looks out. Cicadas sing. The moon throws its light on the cypresses lining the long drive, their spiked shadows falling on the fields.

It strikes her, then, that she is once more leaving this southern land where she grew up, the graceful arcades of the buildings, the white walls and red roofs and blue sky, the peppery food and the shining leaves of the lemon trees, for the north. The north is cold. The land is fertile enough, but the fields are cut through with gullies and steep ravines. Instead of figs, there are apples. Streets are narrow, and the square, solid buildings are clustered around courtyards without greenery. Though the Citadel has gardens and fountains and splendid views of fiery autumnal hillsides ringing the lake, she is always aware of stone and cold and edges.

Her sons will be children of that northern land. She will do whatever she must to protect them from their father.

I WON'T ASK WHY," Radd said, "but what are you going to do next?"

"I'll find a place. I have enough money. Can you give me a few hours in the afternoons to look until I do? I'll work at night, since I'm here." Anza's trunk was stashed in the room in the back filled with Radd's odds and ends.

"You don't have to do that," he said dryly. He was a tall man, black haired, green eyed, dark complected, about twice her age. His children were being raised by his dead wife's parents in Osk. "I have a task for you this afternoon. When it's done, you can wander about Karegg as long as you need to. If you don't find a place this afternoon or tomorrow, I'll pay for a week or two at a lodging house. What happened to your hand?"

"I cut it. It's not deep." It had scabbed over already, but she had bought a clean bandage to wrap it for protection. It was not, fortunately, on her writing hand.

His face had on its skeptical expression. "Is Rumil responsible?"

"No. Not at all." She hated the obliqueness building within her. Would he know what she did not say? Absences, silences, truth in the interstices of speech. "You don't need to pay for lodging."

"I don't want you trying to save money and living somewhere dangerous. Take your time."

It was kind of him. Her pride rebelled, but she had decided a long time ago not to reject gifts in Karegg. A gift was its own kind of resistance against Karolje's constant taking.

"Thank you. What is the task?"

He gestured at a pile of papers. "Take the revised contract to Andrei Nikovili. I don't want to send a courier because he might want changes again. If they're small, make them. Leave as soon as he has signed all the copies, so he doesn't decide to insert a brand-new clause."

"And this morning?" She yawned.

"Did you sleep at all last night?"

"Not much," she admitted. She had seen her reflection in a mirror as she was leaving Rumil's house at dawn, and she knew she looked fatigued. Her entire body was sore from the work she had put it through on the roofs.

Radd took a coin out of a pocket and offered it to her. "I can't have you falling asleep on me while you're working. Go buy some tea and hot food."

It was still early, even for summer with its short nights. The rain had passed, and bright sun shone on puddles and wet streets. The main streets on Citadel Island were broad, and the open space as she crossed one afforded her a view of the western hill across the lake, gold light picking out the details of the craggy summit. The water would be blue, blue, blue.

The teahouse she liked was a few blocks away. Donkey-drawn carts rumbled by, and workers in drab and threadbare clothing hugged the edges of the street. When she first came to Karegg, the noise of the city had been overwhelming, and she had been reluctant to leave the relative quiet of the College grounds. Now the silence of the farmland she had grown up in seemed like a tale.

Inside the teahouse, several people were standing around a table, looking at a newsbill of some sort. The woman who brought her tea and a flaky meat pie seemed distracted.

"What's happening?" Anza asked.

"The king is offering an amnesty to any resisters who come forward before dawn tomorrow." She pronounced *amnesty* as "anmessy."

"They'll never believe him." The resistance was like a web or a honeycomb, groups separated from each other, and one confessor could not bring it all down. But it took only one, one doubtful frightened person, one woman who was sure she would be caught soon, one man who thought he had already been betrayed, to do damage.

The woman said, "That's not for me to guess."

The prudent thing to say. Anza nodded and sipped the hot tea. The amnesty might be bait for her; they would know by now that one person had escaped. No one knew each other's real names, so she could not be identified that way, but there were plenty of other clues. Short, young, dark hair and light olive skin, speech slightly accented, able to use a bow. Able to climb. She might have revealed other things to her companions without knowing it. Karolje's torturers and Truth Finders were expert at unearthing secrets that had been forgotten or overlooked.

Rumil did not know. Radd did not know. Karolje's soldiers could not scrutinize every young dark-haired woman. She was safe.

The pastry in her mouth tasted like wood anyway. She washed it down with tea, took another bite. A wain loaded with barrels rolled past the window. It was an ordinary day, and she had to treat it as such.

✦ ✦ ✦

By the time she walked to Andrei Nikovili's house, the sun was blazing down with full summer heat. Anza wrapped her braided hair around her head and held it in place with a pale blue scarf that protected her neck and forehead. As she neared the Citadel and the Old City, the condition of the roads improved. Houses were set farther apart; trees and lampposts sprang up to line the streets; the number of wagons decreased. She saw fewer people.

The gates had come down centuries ago, and all that remained of the old walls were ruined guard towers and fallen stones. Weeds and grass and wildflowers carpeted the broken battlements. A skinny stray dog watched her warily from a mound of overgrown earth, and a few harpies perched on top of the towers. They were ugly birds, with wrinkled pink featherless faces that looked almost human, sharp beaks, and vicious talons. Anza had only known them to scavenge, but in legends they flocked to attack, gave advice, and whispered curses. They were bad enemies and good friends. Her tutor had told her a story once about an avenging harpy goddess.

It was not far from the wall to Nikovili's house; he was not wealthy enough to live farther in among the mansions within the shadow of the Citadel. The house was colossal by ordinary standards, though. Anza was admitted into a large tiled room, empty but for a fountain bubbling softly. A glass dome occupied the ceiling above the fountain. Through the glass wall on the opposite side of the room she could see a flower garden, abloom with white and yellow and a dozen shades of red, extending back to a row of large and ancient laurel trees. She could not help being impressed. Then she thought of how cold the place would be in the winter.

The footman returned to lead her down a hallway with painted friezes on the walls. They passed several doors on each side before he opened a gleaming walnut door at the end of the hallway and let her into a large room. Three colorful Eridian rugs covered most of the floor, the flagstones showing around the edges. On the western wall, curtains, drawn over the windows now to keep out the afternoon heat, hung on rods from ceiling to floor; the opposite wall was lined with shelves in handsomely stained heartwood from a Milayan ambertree. A plump man of middle age with lips too thin for his round face sat behind an enormous desk. Wealth and vanity announced themselves in the form of a large oil portrait of the man (thinner and younger), his wife, two children, and a fluffy white dog.

Anza walked forward almost soundlessly on the carpet. She bobbed her head politely and waited for him to address her.

"So you've come from my lawyer, have you," he said, tapping the end of a pen against the wood. "Have you got the Milayan contract with you, or did he send you to tell me to my face that there's a problem with what I want?"

She took the three copies of the contract out of her bag. "These are ready for you to sign, sir. You will get one back after it's countersigned."

"Patience, patience," he said, reaching for the copies. "Let me read it first. Let's see, where were we? The third paragraph, I think. Yes, that's right. Here's the change. Good, that's fine." He read on, his thick finger moving down the page a line at a time.

The room was warm and quiet and dim, and Anza was glad he had not invited her to sit. She would have fallen asleep. A dog yipped elsewhere in the house. Through an open window she heard the distant sound of hoofbeats.

"What does this mean?" Nikovili asked, pointing at a paragraph near the bottom. Anza leaned forward and was glad to see that Radd had prepared her for the question. Nikovili had not understood it the three previous times either. She explained again.

"Humph," he said. "And Pashke Izr has agreed to it?" The question appeared to be rhetorical, because he picked up the second page of the contract without waiting for an answer.

The horse sounded closer. Quite a lot closer, actually. And more than one, galloping, much too fast to belong to a tradesman's wagon and probably too fast to belong to a coach driven by anyone other than a very reckless young man, if that. She couldn't hear wheels. She glanced nervously at the windows.

"Well, I suppose I'm wasting my money if I pay my lawyer and don't follow his advice, yes?" He dipped his pen in the inkwell and signed his name in an expansive flourish. He pulled the next set of papers to him.

Waiting, Anza feared he was going to compare the documents word for word to ensure that the copies were identical. Her hand ached in anticipation of copying the damn thing yet again. Then he signed them all and sanded the signature. The horses had stopped.

"Thank you, sir," she said, blowing lightly on the ink.

"Tell your master to come see me sometime," he said.

She put the contracts back in her bag, bobbed her head again, and started for the door. A large thud shook the room. In four fast steps she was at a window, pulling aside the curtain. Eight horses, their trappings bearing the royal seal. Booted feet tramped along the corridor toward the room.

They couldn't be coming for her, not that many. Which meant

they were coming for Nikovili and might leave as soon as they had him. The wooden wall panels in front of her had a crack between them. "To the right," Nikovili said, his voice shaking, and she saw the handle, cleverly built into the carvings on the panel. She pulled the door open and slipped into a closet. Nikovili had not moved from behind his desk. He held a vicious-looking knife.

She closed the door. The closet was dark and dusty and crowded. She felt about, found a chair and a few wooden boxes. She pinched her nose to keep out the dust. The back of the chair had a broken slat. It might make a weapon. Gods.

From the sound of it, several soldiers entered and crossed the room. Something heavy fell with a clatter. A man grunted.

"What are you doing?" Nikovili shouted. "Stop it, stop—" He screamed, fell silent.

Don't move, don't move, don't move, Anza told herself. Her mouth had gone dry. The dog was barking frantically.

"Get all his papers," one man said. "Tear the desk apart. Check the books. Check every square inch of this room. I'll send someone else in to collect the prisoner. What are you waiting for, girls? Get started."

A drawer slid open, and paper rustled. Wood creaked and splintered. As soon as the commander's footsteps faded away, one of the other men muttered something. A third soldier laughed.

Paper again. Drawers and cabinet doors. The sliding sound of books being pulled out on a shelf. Footsteps. A new voice said, "Here's a crate for what you find. I've come for the prisoner."

Nikovili moaned. The dull slap of a fist hitting flesh.

"Need any help?"

"Naw, I can lift him." She heard a grunt of exertion.

"I wouldn't want to have that lardy ass near my face."

They all laughed. A door shut.

Silence for a while. Then: "C'mon, you, we'd better look behind this fucking portrait."

"Ugly, ain't it? 'Cept the girl, she must be a nice piece now if this painting has any likeness. Heave on three. One, two, three." A loud thump.

"God on the tree, what the fuck is this frame made of?"

"Careful there, if the king takes this house, we're on the hook for anything we damage."

"Not the desk, lieutenant's on the hook for that one."

The search continued, punctuated by occasional sneezes and cynical comments. Anza waited, rigid with tension. She hoped they would not take the command to search every inch literally. The closet was hot, and her shirt was sticking to her. She had managed to tamp down her fear, but she was sure it would erupt again if they found the door.

At last one man said, "That's enough, don't you think?"

"We'd better roll the rugs up. Good thing it's stone underneath, or he'd have us lifting every floorboard. You take that one and I'll take this one, and then we can do the big one together."

"We don't need to do that."

"What's it—damn it, I hear him coming. Do it."

The lieutenant's voice said from the direction of the doorway, "Is that everything?"

"Just as soon as we check under the rugs, sir."

"Hurry it up."

There was a gap of about a foot between the edge of the rug and the closet door. Boots scuffed on stone. The soldier breathed heavily, coming closer. He must be right in front of her now. She closed her mouth. He moved on. A soft thud as he kicked at something, probably the rolled-up rug. He walked back noisily over the bare floor.

"All right," the lieutenant said an endless minute later. "Get that crate."

They left as loudly as they had come in. She waited. It would not do to stride out overconfidently and be caught by someone left behind. She let herself breathe more normally and relaxed her muscles and waited.

After a while the room was so still that she was certain she was the only person left in the house. She came out. The curtains had been pulled open, and the room was painfully bright after the dark closet. Gripping the slat had left deep red marks in her uninjured palm. No horses remained outside.

The desk itself was in one piece, but the drawers were good only for kindling. Books lay open on the floor and piled haphazardly on the shelves. The painting leaned against the wall. She smelled spilled ink. Between the ink and any of Nikovili's blood that had fallen on it, the best rug was ruined. Someone would cut it into smaller pieces and sell it on the black market to a merchant who wanted to look richer than he was. Nikovili would never see it again.

Radd was not going to get paid, either. And Pashke Izr's Milayan glassware would have to find another buyer. What had Nikovili done? It seemed unlikely that he was in the resistance, but he could easily have said something disloyal or cheated the wrong person. Most of the merchants cheated each other. The answer might be in the boxes in the closet, but she was not going to risk knowing anything more. Ignorance was safety.

The front door was shut. Locked, if the lieutenant was as experienced as he had sounded. She tried anyway. No good. She went in search of another way out and found a door in the kitchen.

It was unlocked. Doubtless they had been unable to find the

key. To her relief there was no blood anywhere. The servants must have yielded immediately. She went out into a sunny kitchen garden, the herbs arranged in neat rows, blossoms on the bean poles. A black and white cat lazed in the sun. She could almost have imagined herself in her aunt's garden, her feet bare and dirty, her hands smelling of onion and basil.

The resistance had taught her to be careful, and she peered around the corners of the mansion for any posted guards. Karolje would not want to take chances on looters. She saw no one. The gate was open as it had been when she came, the iron bars swung back against the brick wall. She edged carefully along the wall to the entrance. The trees on the street obscured all other shadows. She took one tentative step through the gateway.

A soldier caught her by the arm. She froze. Her heart raced in her chest.

"Got you," the soldier said.

She kicked at his shins, but he knew what he was doing and was at least twice her weight. He easily moved his leg out of the way of the kick and jerked her arms behind her. A second later she was shackled.

The metal cuffs were almost too loose for her hands. The soldier must have seen that too, because he struck her hard on the jaw, and she blacked out.

* * *

She woke curled on cold stone in the dark. The chilly air stank of damp and shit and fear. Her arm ached where she had been grabbed, and the side of her face was swollen and tender. The shackles had been removed.

For a long time she lay still. She was in the Citadel cells. Her mind kept twisting away from that fact, tossing up instead memories of the fight with Rumil, the rain, the woman in the teashop. If she thought about where she was, she would have to think about what might come next. Even in her village there had been stories about Karolje's dungeons.

At last the cold got her moving in both body and mind. She came clumsily to her feet and folded her arms across her chest. They had known she was still in the house. But it was Nikovili they had been after, not her. She had a chance, slim though it was, of being released. As long as they thought she was insignificant, as long as they focused on Nikovili instead of her, she could keep from betraying anyone. Taking her was a mistake.

Karolje didn't make mistakes. Tyrants never did. Anything that happened that should not have was soon recounted as deliberate. Accidents were transformed into intent. The people who Disappeared had never actually existed. She had known that before she came to the city. Without that knowledge, she would not have survived. The way to survive Karolje was to keep the past at your back and always march forward.

Had her father been kept in a cell like this, perhaps this very one? She explored cautiously with her hands. The stone was rough, the natural limestone of the place. The cell was narrow, not long enough to lie straight in, and so low-ceilinged that anyone much taller than her would have to bend. There were gaps between the door planks, but not wide enough to get even her thin fingers in. A metal grate at the bottom slid aside for food. She was in a hole. Better that than a torture chamber.

Leaning against the door, she listened. She heard outside the cell the nervous tap of finger on wood and a faint hiss that might have been a whisper. The tapping was rhythmic, obsessive. Otherwise she seemed to be alone.

She thought of the resisters who had been captured last

night. Was it one of them whispering in the dark? Or had they already been killed, bodies taken off the island and left in the pits on the lake shore? Common criminals were jailed on Beggar Island, and Karolje had a prison in the mountains for those he held alive. Wherever she was, it was transitory, a place between interrogations. The prisoners were probably all either suspected traitors or disobedient lords he wanted to punish. Executions usually followed a day or two after being captured.

She wondered what Radd would think if she did not come to his office tomorrow, how long it would be before he worried. Would he dare to look for her at all? It was a lonely, barren question. She did not want to be one of the Disappeared.

After a while the tapping stopped, but the whispering continued, the hiss of a snake, of a gas jet, of an arrow in the air.

✦ ✦ ✦

Much later, the darkness was shot with blazing light that hurt her eyes. The cracks between boards threw brightness into lines on the back of the cell. Flickering and the smell of smoke told her it was a torch. Footsteps, boots on stone again but with none of the reverberation of an open space. They slowed. A key turned in the lock of her door.

She squeezed her eyes shut in a futile attempt to hold back everything she knew of Karolje's torture chambers. He employed all the ancient methods of physical pain, and if that didn't break a person, he brought in a Truth Finder. They were priests of a sort. The stories said they could know all your memories and if they did a Minding the pain didn't leave for days and sometimes you went blind or deaf or mute. She had seen a victim once, a fellow student at the College. When he was released, he had been like a three-year-old, drooling and wetting his breeches and unable to read. His father's face she would never forget, a rigid controlled mask with terrifying anger blazing from the eyes.

He has had his Truth Finders trying to pry secrets from my mind. Mirantha had written that. She had not been driven mad. It was possible to survive.

I won't be afraid, she told herself. I won't. When she was target-shooting, she found a stillness at her core and rested there, the world motionless and meaningless. She reached for that stillness, that calm. She could go to pieces when it was over.

She found enough detachment not to panic when a soldier yanked her out and chained her hands again. Fear was an abstract thing, an idea, a word. Pain had no meaning. Her mind took in its surroundings, registered what happened, but found no reason to respond. Her heart beat in slow, majestic thumps with hours between them.

He towered over her. They walked up two levels, then turned onto a long gaslit corridor. The fourth door on the right was guarded. It was metal, blocking sound.

It led into a narrow, brightly lit white room. Inside were several soldiers, all but one in the familiar dark blue uniforms bearing the wolf's-head badge of Kazdjan's house. She was pulled in and made to stand in front of a fair-haired man with a thin face and narrow eyes dressed in dark grey. He did not carry a weapon, but others did.

The floor was stained concrete, in the center of which was a rusty grate. Anza knew what that meant in an interrogation room, and she drew more tightly into herself. The plaster on the windowless walls was perfectly even and glossy. Easy to clean.

"What's your name?" He was harsh.

Whips of varying sizes were mounted on the wall behind him. Two of the metal-handed stunning whips, a wire flail, a leather thong studded with brass, a rope divided into seven or eight strands with metal beads at the ends. A long, evil-looking whip that could wrap around a neck a few times. An ornate silver handle was attached to a thin woven cord of fire-twine that would blister the skin and corrode the flesh. Anza could endure pain, but a few lashes with any of those whips would have her blubbering and fainting.

"Anza Istvili." Her own voice was thin and weak. She had to squint because of the brightness. She was glad she had never carried her father's family name.

"What do you do?" he asked.

"I'm a clerk to Radd Orescu." It felt horribly inadequate.

"Nikovili's lawyer. Did Nikovili show you any documents?"

"No."

"Are you sure?"

"Yes," she answered, knowing with dread that there was no right answer to that question.

He stepped closer to her. "You're lying." His hand flicked, and the soldier behind her yanked on her hair and forced her to her knees. If her hands had not been behind her back, she could have grabbed the examiner around the thighs and pulled him down. He unbuckled his belt. It would be his trousers next.

I am the arrow, she thought. I am the arrow. There is no pain, there is no fear.

The belt came around her neck. He pulled. The edges cut into her skin. Tighter. Her throat compressed painfully. "Did he show you any papers?"

She had no breath left to deny it. She shuddered, trying for air. Pressure in her head made it hard to think.

The belt loosened slightly. She coughed, her body jerking forward. The soldier behind her grabbed the chain and pulled her arms up, bringing her erect and sending pain like coals through her shoulders.

"Did he show you any documents?"

"No!" she yelled.

The examiner pulled hard. Her cry of pain never made it out of her lungs.

This is it, she thought with a calm certainty. She knew she would pass out before she died, but she did not think the examiner would stop until her twitching legs had gone still and the room stank with her death.

The door opened. The soldier behind her took a step back. The examiner's grip on the belt slackened. When she coughed and fell over, no one stopped her. She gasped for air. The new arrival was a handsome dark-skinned man who had impressively strong arms. The badge on his sleeve beneath the rank markers was a silver wolf in profile. She had not seen that badge on any soldiers in the city.

The examiner said, "This is an interrogation, Captain. Your business can wait."

"He wants to see her. Now."

He. Who was *he*?

"When I've finished."

"Now," the captain repeated. "And send up anything you've confiscated."

"You exceed your authority."

"Do you want to test that?"

The man behind Anza breathed in at the question. If this continued, the captain might use force. He could lop off the examiner's head. The thought was sickening.

"Have her, then," said the examiner. "I'll put this in my report."

The captain unlocked her chains. Her wrists were abraded. Sitting, she was wracked with coughs again. The captain waited until the fit had stopped to raise her by the forearms, not touching the marks on her skin.

"Come." He held her arm, firmly but not too tightly, and pulled her out of the interrogation room. She went without fuss. Whoever this man was, the examiner had been afraid, of him and of his command. She did not want to know what power lay behind him.

They turned a corner and went up a flight of steps. At the top he halted and said, "I'm bringing you to the prince. Don't try to run, or it will go worse for you." He removed his hand.

Oh gods, she thought, her momentary relief crashing down around her. She had done nothing to rate being taken before either of Karolje's sons. They would not bother with anyone as lowly as her. Not even if they had traced her to the raid last night.

Unless they had found out who her father was.

4

ESVAR WAS NOT given to pacing. That was his brother's habit. To fidget he used his hands, rubbing a coin between his fingers or toying with a stick of sealing wax. Most wealthy men wore their hair shoulder length, tied back with a cord, but he kept his short, in part so he would not be tempted to touch it.

He had a chessboard on his desk, and while he waited for Marek to return with the prisoner, he played with a pawn. The pieces were metal, shiny new steel for one side and dull black iron for the other. He preferred having the first move, strategizing instead of reacting, so he often played black to make it harder for himself. To learn caution. To watch.

The door opened, admitting Marek. As soon as Esvar heard that someone not of Nikovili's household had been arrested, he sent Marek running to grab her away from the examiners. Ordinarily he would not concern himself with so routine a matter as the arrest of a merchant, but some of Nikovili's associates were powerful, a few having been guests of the chancellor at Citadel occasions.

He put the pawn back in place before looking at the prisoner. She was close to his own age, dark haired, dark eyed. Her skin was olive, marred by a huge swollen and purple bruise on one cheek. Without the bruise, without the filth of captivity, she might have been pretty. A dirty bandage over the palm of one hand looked new, though it had been soiled by the cell. She was short and slender, but he saw the muscles on her bare arms and knew she was strong and probably fast. She lowered her head as soon as they made eye contact, but not soon enough for him to fail to observe the utter blankness on her face.

He knew what she saw: a tyrant's son, a murderer, a man whose wealth and power could swallow her whole. She would consider herself lucky if she was only beaten. If he wanted her, he could have her with impunity.

He remained in his chair. This wouldn't take long. He said to Marek, who was standing against the door with his arms folded, "Did she have belongings?"

"I ordered them brought to you, sir."

"Make sure it happens. And have the examiner sent up too while you're at it. Who was it, by the way?"

"Mityos Lukovian, sir."

Damn and double damn. The man was one of the cruelest. It was unsurprising that he had claimed the Nikovili questioning; smuggling was a crime of property, not sedition, and technically within the chancellor's jurisdiction. Despite being under the command of Doru, Lukovian was loyal to Goran, and if Nikovili said anything that implicated the chancellor, the examiner would cover it up. He had probably already sent a report of Esvar's interference to Goran.

He waited until Marek had left to ask the woman, "Why were you at Nikovili's house?"

She coughed, touching her throat. He saw ligature marks. Her voice was hoarse and emotionless, her words slightly accented of mid-country. "I had brought him a contract to sign, my lord."

"Did he know you were coming?"

"He was told to expect someone to come with the papers, my lord. I don't know if he knew when." Careful, not about to assert anything that might be false. She had been trained to protect herself from power.

"Did you know him well?"

"My lord, I never met him before today."

"Did you draw up the contract?"

That triggered a slight reaction, a jerk of the shoulders. Surprise or fear, he could not tell. She coughed again and said, "I was the courier, my lord."

A disavowal of responsibility. Her clothing and accent suggested she was the child of a tradesman or crafter who had had money enough to keep a small home but not for leisure or books or travel.

"Do you know what he is accused of?"

She shook her head. Nikovili, like many other rich merchants, had tired of Karolje's excessive taxes and turned to smuggling. The evidence was genuine, and enough to hang him. The Crown was jealous of its revenue. But even a smuggler had to conduct his business with old customers and partners, had to have honest income to maintain appearances. There was nothing unusual at all in Nikovili continuing to sign contracts.

"Smuggling," Esvar said.

She looked up, face pale. The suddenness of the movement sent her into a fit of coughing. When she recovered, she said, "It was an ordinary contract, my lord. For Milayan glassware." Her eyes were watering from the coughs.

Karolje's tyranny had made fear a completely useless way to

measure guilt. He thought she was exactly what she seemed to be, a person who had been in the wrong place at the wrong time and was caught up in the arrest. An innocent.

He needed her. Needed her to go back into the city and recount an act of justice, needed her to say that Karolje's son had been fair. One of the few sharp memories he had of his mother was her telling him that justice was a lever; a small amount could move something very large if the force was applied properly. If enough levers were in place when Karolje died, he and Tevin could get the city to move in the direction they wanted.

He resumed questioning. "Did he ask you to carry any messages to anyone? Take any papers for him?"

"No, my lord." Another cough.

"Who did draw up the contract?"

She hesitated. "Radd Orescu, my lord. A lawyer."

He had heard of Orescu, whose clients included a few minor nobles. The man was said to be completely honest.

He took a gamble. "Were you taught at the College?"

"Yes," she said, barely audible. Why was that so frightening to admit?

Because with that and Radd's name, it would not be hard to find out most of her secrets. She had some. Everyone did.

"What did the examiner do to you?" he asked.

It was the wrong question. She shrank away.

"I'm setting you free," he said. "If I ask the examiner, he'll lie. What did he use?"

Her hand went to her throat. A smear of ink darkened the back of one of her fingers. She wore no rings, and her nails were short and blunt. A practical woman. She said nothing. Her guard was still up.

He had no reason to get her to lower it. He pointed at a

chair. "Sit down and wait until the captain returns with your things." To one side of the desk was the report he had been reading when he was told of the arrest, and he slid it back in front of him. He had learned young how to focus on one thing to the exclusion of anything else, and he was accustomed to the presence of waiting men while he read or thought.

The two men captured last night had talked, but essentially said nothing. They had followed orders and described only a vague plan for some sort of an attack at the docks. All they could say about the archer was that she was a young woman called Finch. The description of her could have matched three out of every ten women in the city. The woman captured with them had died before she said anything. Esvar hoped she had died quickly. Nothing in the report explained how the archer had acquired arrows of the sort used by soldiers, not by hunters.

He folded the report in thirds and put it in a drawer. The woman across from him had her hands clasped on her lap and her head bent. She might have been praying. He doubted she was. Her stillness had a patient strength to it that was not supplication. She wasn't expecting anyone to help her, not even the gods. He envied the calm.

Finally the door opened and Marek came back in. "Lukovian's waiting outside, sir," the captain said as he put a plain leather bag on Esvar's desk.

Esvar acknowledged the words with a brief nod and opened the bag. A few coins, a paring knife, an empty water flask. Papers. He took them out. Identical copies of a contract, signed by Nikovili. None of the provisions were unusual. The woman had not lied.

He refastened the bag and held it out to Marek. "Release her," he said. "There's nothing here."

"It's after dark," Marek said.

The Old City would be safe, but in the rest of Karegg she would be prey for criminals or the watch. A note from him would not save her from either.

"Have someone trustworthy take her home," he said. "Or to a shrine if she doesn't want to tell you where she lives. Send Lukovian in when you go out. I won't need you anymore tonight."

The woman took the bag from the captain and followed him out without a glance at Esvar. Esvar felt a twinge of emotion he was surprised to recognize as disappointment.

He had no time to think about it before Lukovian entered with as much defiance in his step as he probably thought he could get away with. On another night Esvar might have let it pass. Not tonight.

He stood and leaned forward, hands splayed hard on the desk. He needed Lukovian to feel the sting of the reprimand. "What the hell were you doing?"

"My orders were to question everyone, sir."

"Everyone in the household. It was pure chance that she was there. Did anyone else in the house know her name?"

"Sir, she had been hiding from us somewhere in the house. Innocent people don't hide."

"We both know that's not true. What do you mean, 'had been hiding'? They caught her later?"

"I don't know the details, sir," Lukovian said stiffly.

"It's your business to know the details before you start interrogating someone. If you don't know who they are and what they were doing, you don't know the right questions to ask. If you're more interested in killing people than doing your job, I can send you off to join the border guard."

Lukovian's color rose. It could have been either anger or shame. "I wasn't going to kill her, sir."

"Don't lie. I saw the marks on her neck. I heard her voice." It was tempting to goad the man, to abuse him. That was the language Lukovian understood. "Sit down."

"Sir?"

"In that chair. Now. Do you play chess?"

Lukovian sat as though he expected the chair to be pulled away beneath him. "No, sir," he said. He was wondering what the trick was. Good.

Esvar slid the board closer to the examiner. "A pawn," he said, demonstrating, "can move forward. Not backward, not sideways. One square at a time. It captures on the diagonal, like so. It's not powerless, but it's limited. The other pieces have more freedom. That makes them more dangerous." He positioned a black pawn to capture another pawn and a black knight able to check the white king on one move.

"I can take this pawn easily," he said. "Or I can let it go and threaten the king here. Which serves me better?"

"Threatening the king," said Lukovian. He was still suspicious.

"Yes. Threatening the king." He rearranged the pieces to a defensive posture. "And if I'm holding off an attack, I don't care about the pawns when I need to defend against the more powerful pieces. I certainly don't care about pieces that aren't on the board. If that woman was in the game at all, it was as a pawn. You aren't supposed to be putting all your time into the damn pawns, Lukovian. Let them go."

"It didn't hurt to question her. Sir."

"Do you think Nikovili is the only rich man who has broken the law? What do you think happens if word gets around that visiting a man for ordinary business can get you killed? What happens if the next time it's someone delivering a crate of wine? That's how things start unraveling."

"It wasn't me who arrested her."

The insolence tipped Esvar into sudden, violent fury. He had to pause to collect himself before he said, "That's irrelevant. You're experienced enough to know when there's no information to get from a prisoner. You don't get to kill them for your own fun." The words were thin and sharp as a knife.

Lukovian said, "Yes, sir," much more subdued. The message had hit home.

"Get out."

The examiner almost knocked the chair over as he rose. He left hastily. It was the guard outside who shut the door.

Esvar wanted to pick his own chair up and hurl it at the window. Anger was his demon, always. He did what he had taught himself to do: grip the edge of the desk and stare at his hands. He imagined the blood moving through each capillary, returning to his heart like waves to the shore. The force of his hold made his wrists ache.

Slowly, slowly, his fury eased. He released his hands and shook them, loosened his shoulders. He knew that if he thought back on what had happened, he would surge into violence again. Best to go outside, where he could be alone to rage at the stars if that was what he needed. He didn't want to hurt someone who didn't deserve it.

✦ ✦ ✦

The moon, a few days past the full, was bright. When he passed a lamp, his shadows fell at angles to each other. At the deserted exercise ground he paused. It was tempting to find a staff or a blunted sword and work out his anger. Without a sparring partner, it would be only fighting the air.

He avoided the barracks and took the path that led down the hill to the northern shore. The moon shone on the smooth grey stone, and he had no difficulty. He passed a guard post halfway down and noticed the familiar movement of a soldier moving forward to challenge and retreating as he recognized his lord. Someday, if Karolje ordered it, that recognition might mean Esvar's death.

A mosquito whined at his ear. He slapped at it and quickened his pace. Honey locust trees sweetened the air. To his left was the wall surrounding the Citadel gardens; to his right, moonlit grass, kept short and free of scrub. If an enemy took the docks, it would not advance unseen. Nor was there cover for escape.

Closer to the water, the hill got steeper, and the path became a series of stairs separated by ten or fifteen yards of leveled ground. The lightless towers of the Citadel protruded above the slope of the hill and the trees. The building was nine hundred years old and from here seemed to have grown out of the rock. It was immense, terraced and graded and trussed, rooms opening onto a courtyard on one side and looking over a steep slope on the other. In the oldest portions of the building, where walls were stone, the windows would be open, letting out light and sound. In the steel and glass sections, the walls acted as mirrors. One could not tell who might be watching.

He stopped walking at the top of the last flight of steps. Moonlight lay feathered on the calm, dark water. No boats were docked. The guardhouse by the dock was square and boxy, the flag on top limp against the pole. Light shone out of the open doorway. He heard laughter.

Four guards were on duty. It was a prize posting, saved as a reward. If you were on guard at the dock, you didn't have superior officers breathing on you, and the only work required was to check the cargo of the scheduled arrivals. There were men watching with spyglasses from Citadel towers who would be able to raise an alarm long before a suspect boat ever came close. The guards could sit around a table and gamble with dice or cards and not be caught in dereliction of duty.

They would be resentful if Esvar showed himself, authority intruding on their allotted freedom. He sat on the steps and tried to steady his breathing. He was much more agitated than he wanted to be. He should not have spoken to Lukovian. If things were going to unravel, let them.

A nighthawk swooped overhead. He flexed his hands. Westward, above the hills, a star brightened and went out. A meteor. There would be more over the next few nights; falling stars happened every year at this time. He wished he could be among the superstitious who thought the meteor shower presaged some great event. No gods had their hands in this world.

The water drew him. He forced himself to his feet and descended the steps, listening to the sound of his boots on the stone. A soldier came out of the guardhouse. Recognized, saluted, stepped back. Esvar acknowledged it and continued walking. This would get back to Karolje, the prince wandering alone when he should be doing his duty. Indulging in vices was understandable; seeking solitude was not.

He went past the dock to the narrow strip of stony beach, where he stood and looked at the water. When he was younger he had swum in the lake, diving off the dock, not for pleasure but for training. In summer there was the flash of warmth breaking through the sunlit surface and then, quickly, the chill of the water. Close to shore, the water was murky with tiny particles of silt and algae. Standing chest deep, he couldn't see his feet. Farther out was clearer and colder. Occasionally he would swim through a warm area where hot water from the underground springs rose upward.

He had almost died once in the winter, when ice fringed the shore and the chill water numbed his flesh at once. The dive was from a boat, not from the dock, or he would have hit the surface too hard to recover at all. He flailed his way back to shallow water, but when he tried to stand, his legs gave out and he fell forward. A soldier hauled him out, hacking and shivering, and wrapped him in a blanket and put him in front of the guardhouse fire. He was eleven.

The training had done what it was supposed to, toughening his body and inuring him to physical danger. And it left him feeling brittle, a blade of metal folded too often and too quickly cooled, sharp but breakable. Karolje had seen Tevin eluding his grasp by then, and he had tried to make a successor out of his younger son. If he had started two or three years earlier, he might have succeeded; but the king had been away too much in the south, fighting the Tazekhs, and some of the soldiers who remained in Karegg had treated Esvar with the sort of rough affection they might give to a stray dog. Women of the court took pity on him, the motherless boy. By the time the war was over, he had too many attachments to be twisted out of all compassion.

He bent down and felt among the stones for a flat one, which he skipped out onto the water. Seven bounces before it sank. His mother's body was on the lake bed, he was sure of it. The soldiers had likely killed her at the dock, then weighted the body and dropped it over the side of a boat a mile at least from shore. That was what would happen to him or Tevin if they resisted the king past his limits. They would die alone, and their bodies would be swallowed by the lake waters, and fish would swim among their bones while some other man was king.

A second meteor fell, a vanishing brightness. He was calmer.

I *will* resist, he thought. His anger at Lukovian was anger at himself. Anger at his own timidity, delay, weakness. He should find the strength and courage and resolution of the woman he had freed. The king's evil had gone on long enough. Waiting for Karolje to die was a coward's way out.

How to start? He skipped another stone. Whatever form his resistance took, it would have to be subtle at first, a sculptor tapping delicately at a rough form. He could not tell his brother. Tevin's struggle was in the Citadel, gathering strands of allegiance. Perhaps fighting. Esvar's work would be not with fire and blood and command but with small acts of justice. He would snarl Karolje's plans and try to make a city that was not diseased.

Stones shifting under his boots, he walked back to the steps. The lightless hill loomed over him, moonlight scattered among the darkness of the vegetation. The Citadel, obscured by the angle of the slope, waited for him in all its shadow and pain.

He thought again of his mother. She had resisted Karolje with every breath. He would do no less.

MIRANTHA

FALLING IN LOVE, when it happens, is unexpected.

She is in her public rooms, where she gives orders and performs her duties, when a man is admitted to see her. He is a priest, dressed in black, no more than thirty-five. She is accustomed to old men as priests. He is handsome, bronze-skinned, light on his feet, with black hair cropped close to the skull.

The king's servant who has brought him says, "My lady, this is Father Ashevi. He is to be the new priest in the Citadel."

"Welcome," she says. Since the old priest died last summer, there has been a succession of men sent by the Temple, all of whom stayed only a few weeks before moving on. She suspects that the Hierarch has been trying to find a man who will satisfy both King Piyr and Karolje, yet keep his loyalty with the Temple. If Ashevi is being presented to her now, he must have made all the men happy.

He kneels before her and says, "My lady, I am proud to serve you and counsel you, as you wish." His voice has an accent she cannot place. His voice is beautiful.

She has not felt passion for years. What she first felt for

Karolje died soon after the wedding, and she has protected herself since. At the sound of Ashevi's voice, desire rushes in.

"Thank you," she says, and the day continues. But it is too late. She is lost.

✦ ✦ ✦

He comes frequently to visit her. She makes careful inquiries among the servants and the courtiers, but they yield nothing more than a rumor that he had been a teacher in the College once before being dismissed for some impropriety. She is certain he is her husband's spy, and she speaks to him only as much as is proper. On holy days in the chapel, she kneels and avoids looking at him, staring instead at the rent limbs of the god sacrificed on the tree. The god looks down at her, the god she has lost all belief in. Her prayers have never been answered. Ashevi's voice rings with passionate faith.

At night, alone, she remembers his hands, the tilt of his head, the way the sun falls upon the plane of his face. He is dangerous, she says to herself. He cannot be trusted. He will betray me. And still her restless fingers find their way over her aching body, need driving her.

✦ ✦ ✦

Then, despite all the efforts both diplomatic and martial by her father to keep the peace at the border, war with Tazekhor starts, and the king sends Karolje south to fight. With him gone, the pall that lies constantly over her lifts. The king is busy with his advisers, and her sons are left to her keeping more than they ever have been. She takes them out sometimes, riding in the royal hunting preserves on the lakeside. They are always surrounded by guards because of the danger from Asps, the king of Tazekhor's assassins, who fight from shadows with explosives and cruelty. Esvar is five, fully out of the nursery, and his brother soon to be eleven. Nihalik usually accompanies them.

One day Nihalik has twisted an ankle and is not able to ride, and it seems natural to invite Ashevi in his place. The air is hot and dry, and the cool of the shady forest falls over them like water. The boys are full of energy and scramble up trees and chase each other over the slippery pine needles while their guards try to keep up. She sits on a rug beside a stream with Ashevi next to her, soldiers ranging around but not close at hand. A ground squirrel scampers over the rocks. The stream burbles softly.

There is food and wine and pleasant conversation. He tells her about his travels to the eastern edge of Vetia to see the Firefalls, the stories he has heard from Milaya about ancient heroes. His world is so much wider than hers. She eats and drinks a little too much and gets drowsy. Ashevi's voice is smooth and lulling. His eyes are a warm, inviting brown as he offers her a refilled cup. Her hands tremble as she receives it, and dark wine splashes over the brim of the cup and onto her skin and dress. "Oh," she says, and lifts the cup to her mouth with both hands. She drinks deeply.

She puts the cup down and dabs at the spots with a napkin. "That needs water," he says. He takes the napkin and goes to the stream. Reflected light makes his face shine. When he wrings the napkin, the drops fall like diamonds back to the water.

He gives her the damp cloth. She wipes her mouth. She has enough caution left to look around for any observant guards before she scrubs at the spots on her bodice. She is aware of her breasts moving with her quickened breath.

She folds the napkin and returns it, careful not to touch him. Somewhere distant, the boys are shouting. A jay squawks high up in the tree branches. The sky is a cloudless, shining blue, and the air is thick with the scent of pine needles and water. She feels light and faint with happiness.

✦ ✦ ✦

No words or gestures pass between them, but they know. It takes three days for them to find a way to each other. She comes to the chapel, an ancient room far removed from the busy places of the Citadel, purportedly to pour libations in prayer for her husband's safety. The libations are doubly a lie, because she neither believes in the gods nor wants Karolje to live.

The room is small, dim, hot. A single oil lamp burns near the door. The floor, the walls, and the dais are a beautiful, highly polished red-gold wood. The smell of incense has permeated everything in the room and is a faint harmony to the other odors, wood and wax and oil.

He waits for her in his ceremonial red robe. She shuts the door and walks toward the altar and the sacred water. The air is heavy with the past, with centuries of worship, hymns and invocation of many gods. Prayers repeated over and over are a faint murmur in her mind, like the crash of distant waves. People have come in fear and thanks and hope, in despair and triumph. Kings knelt, widows wept.

He takes the flask of oil from her and puts it on the altar. His hands come to her breasts, his mouth to hers. She feels the hardness of his teeth beneath his lips. He slides his fingers inside her bodice and slips her dress off her shoulder. He squeezes her nipple. It is painful and exquisite, and she draws in breath. She shivers and sinks to the floor.

Quick and urgent, neither of them undressing, he pushes hard into her. She bites her thumb to keep months of anticipation from releasing in a shout. The pleasure is immediate, dizzying. He holds her tightly while she jerks with the cascade of ecstasy.

He withdraws, and as she pulls her skirt down, she realizes he is unfulfilled.

"Later," he says, smiling. "It is enough for me to have pleased you, my lady."

"We can't keep on," she says. "Karolje will find out when he comes back."

"I am a priest," he says. He kisses her and pulls her sleeve back up. Then he steps back and smooths the fabric. "Priests are allowed secrets other men are not. The gods will protect you."

The gods are no protection at all. She remembers Nihalik's story of the avenging harpy goddess and wishes desperately that it was more than a story, that the goddess could free her from her husband and let her have Ashevi without fear. But no shadow fills the room, no wings flutter the air. Her hands are only hands that crave the feel of Ashevi's body beneath them.

She kisses him again. Then she turns, takes a steadying breath, and leaves without looking back.

THE ANCHOR WAS even worse than Anza had imagined. Narrow glassless windows set in bowed boards, an unconscious vagrant whose eyes were swollen and suppurating lying next to it, the door painted a dull peeling black. The roof of a warehouse across the street sagged. The stink of rotted grapes and urine underlay the greasy odor of fish cooked in cheap and repeatedly used oil. The lake water under the nearby bridge was still and scummed and vile. It was a hot, hazy day, the setting sun lacking any clarity of light that could have made the place look less miserable.

Just the sort of spot for the resistance to meet.

Anza pushed the door open and stepped into a dim room. Two pitch torches and a fish-oil lamp provided inadequate light. Years of ground-in dust greyed the floorboards. A creature moved under a table, and flies buzzed around congealed grease. Something smelled rotten.

The woman who must be Sparrow—the only other woman present was much too young—sat at a table in the back. She was dressed in men's clothing and had a yellow scarf tied loosely around her neck. A cap was on the table in front of her, next to a tin plate with chicken bones on it. Ignoring the glances of the few people in the room, Anza crossed and took a seat next to Sparrow.

"I hope you weren't the one who ate that chicken," she said before she could stop herself.

Sparrow grinned. Her teeth were good. She was about forty-five, with short hair that might have been silver or white-blond and a strong, slender build. The hard edge to her face suggested she would kill without a second thought.

She said, "I have a stomach made of lead. Spoiled food isn't going to be what kills me. You surprise me, showing up. I didn't think you would."

"It never occurred to me to do anything else," said Anza. She took a deep breath, which she then regretted as it brought the smells of the place more strongly to her. She said, "Why did you want to see me? Is this about what went wrong three days ago?"

The message had come that morning, a note delivered with a code phrase as she left the public baths. *The Anchor, Beggar Island by the bridge, sunset. Sparrow.* The tavern was four miles from Radd's office, and Anza had had to hurry.

"In part," said Sparrow. "How did you escape if they got hold of you enough to beat you?"

Anza touched her cheek. The swelling was going down, and the purple-black was beginning to fade, not that it was possible to tell in this place. "That was a different incident," she said. "They weren't connected."

"Did Rumil hit you?"

How much did Sparrow know about her? "No. And as it happens, I've left him."

"Are those marks on your wrists from the same event?"

"Yes. I work for Radd Orescu. A lawyer. I had the misfortune of being at a client's house when king's men came to arrest him. They took everyone. They didn't use a weapon on me, but I was knocked out." Radd had been furious when she told him, furious and ready to send her south to his wife's family for protection.

"And you were released?"

"Eventually."

"Who decided to release you?"

Prince Esvar, she was supposed to say, but the words would not form. "They didn't explain things to me. They were in charge. I must have been more bother than I was worth."

She had expected Esvar's face to show cruelty, inflicted upon him, inflicted by him. Instead she would have thought him attractive if she had not known who he was. He had been firm. Neither gentle nor vicious. And surprisingly deliberate with his words for a man who was accustomed to being obeyed. Why had he pulled an ordinary woman out of the clutches of the examiners? Her safety was not what had driven him. He wanted to see her for some other reason.

His voice, amber instead of stone, was clear in her head. *If I ask the examiner, he'll lie. What did he use?* The controlled anger had not been directed at her.

Her father had spoken little about things that transpired in the Citadel, but he had said enough for her to know one had to tread carefully among the different alliances and factions. The hostility between the prince's captain and the examiner had not been feigned. Esvar had not cared who she was; freeing her had been a strike against Karolje, a claim of authority superseding the king's. Did he want the crown himself? What about his brother? Rumor said that neither prince was as cruel as Karolje, but since the king hadn't killed them, she had counted them loyal. Perhaps she was wrong.

Sparrow broke into her thoughts. "Why was he arrested?"

"Who?" Anza said, startled. "Oh. The client. Smuggling."

"You're sure?"

"I'm sure that's what they said. I have no idea if that's true."

To her surprise, Sparrow laughed. It was not malicious. "Who was the client, and where does he live?"

"Andrei Nikovili. He lives on the Old Wall Road. His business is somewhere in the Teak District."

"Did they ask you about us? Or use a Truth Finder?"

The ligature marks on her neck had faded, but she could still feel the tightening belt. "No," she said. "It was to be quite ordinary torture, just for their entertainment. The examiner was going to kill me before even asking questions. That was how I knew he didn't think I was guilty of the smuggling. I was—I wasn't part of the household. I think he saw me as an unexpected treat." That was what Esvar had realized. She had been lucky.

"How did you survive?"

"He was interrupted by something more important." Why was she withholding the truth from this woman?

Because truth was the coin she had, and she did not want to spend it yet.

Sparrow considered this. "You're quite calm about it."

The cook slapped something on the griddle, which sizzled noisily. Anza shrugged and said, "I just pretended it was happening to someone else. It didn't go on all that long."

"That strategy works for a while," said Sparrow. "If you do it too much, you do become another person. Remind me why you joined us." Her tone changed; the conversation had become an examination. When Anza first joined the resistance, she had been asked similar questions by her contact and by the people in her group. Now Sparrow was making her own assessment.

"Karolje had my father executed."

"Executed. Not murdered? What was he to the king?"

Anza said, "A soldier. A captain. I don't know why he was killed." She could have said more, but she remembered Radd's words: *Answer the question asked. No more, no less.* He had said that when she told him about Nikovili's capture. She had not expected to use the advice so soon.

"A soldier. You know how to shoot. Did he teach you?"

"Yes. He brought me a hunting bow and arrows. Good ones, when I could shoot well enough." She had not asked him where they came from, because she knew he would not tell her.

"Why did he teach you?"

The smack of an arrow into a straw target, the shape and smoothness of the bow, the precise movement of her fingers when nocking, had all pleased her. The curve of an arrow in flight.

"I wanted to learn. He taught me other weapons too, he wanted me to be safe."

"Which of your friends knew about him?"

"None. They thought I had an uncle I visited sometimes." Her relationship with Rumil—and with her other lovers—had never reached that point of honesty. To protect her father, she had told herself. It was his secret, not hers.

She wondered now if it was shame that had kept her silent, shame that her father served Karolje. It would not have been a shameful thing to any of the people she knew at the College, except perhaps Irini, who flirted with defiance. Had she been embarrassed that her father was so common? Or was it just the instinctive fear that came with living under a tyrant, the hoarding away of any information that could make her vulnerable?

"When was he executed?"

"Three, almost four, months ago."

"How did you find out?"

"He didn't meet me when he was supposed to. When I hadn't heard anything two days later, I went to his house. It had the king's Mark on the door." She had suspected by then but had hoped his absence was something else, sickness or forgetfulness. When she saw the Mark, those fantasies vanished and a painful nausea settled in her stomach, there for days. Just thinking about it brought it back.

"Where is his house?"

"Near the Citadel. We didn't usually meet there, but I knew where it was."

"What was his name?"

"Alcu Havidian."

"I can probably find out the reason he was executed," Sparrow said. "Do you want to know?"

Did she? What if it had been for some reason dishonorable? Or worse, stupid? If she didn't know, there would always be a place on the edge of her life like an unhealed wound, scabbed over perhaps but tempting to pick at.

"Yes," she said.

"And if it turns out to have been one of Karolje's rare acts of justice?"

"There are a thousand other reasons to fight."

Sparrow said, "Can they get at you through any of your father's friends? Other soldiers?"

"He never told anyone about me. He didn't marry my mother, and she died when I was eight. That was near Mirsk. My father came north when I was six, and I didn't see him again for ten years." Mirsk was four hundred miles away; there had been no visits, not even when her mother was alive. Anza herself had gone back only once to see her aunt, three years ago.

"Who else can Karolje use to hurt you?"

She had drifted from most of the friends she made at the College. They had all scattered to different places in the city, and though she saw them occasionally, they were not confidants. Nor were Rumil's friends, boisterous rich young men who had no interest in her. She had not talked to Irini for over a year. Without Rumil, the only person she cared about was Radd.

"If they did something to Radd, I would feel as if I had betrayed him. It wouldn't break me," she said. "I don't have any other family."

"How did you come to work for him?"

"One of the masters at the College sent me to him."

"How did you come to be at the College?"

"My father arranged it."

"Soldiers don't usually have that kind of pull."

"That's all he told me."

"You never questioned it? You assumed that whatever came to you, you were entitled to?"

Anza knew she was being goaded. The other students had been the children of nobles and wealthy commoners. She had no name, no wealth, no family to match theirs, nothing but a letter from her tutor and a promise from her father. Within a few weeks her awareness of her poverty had faded from her consciousness. She was good at what she did.

She said, "I succeeded."

"Your place—both of them—resulted from a bribe, most likely."

"My father was an honest man!"

"An honest man who taught his daughter illegal weapons?" Sparrow said sardonically. "So Radd is a weak point. On the other hand, if you need help he's trustworthy."

"You know him?" The thought made Anza uncomfortable. She wanted to keep the parts of her life separate.

"I have observed him," said Sparrow. "I won't go into details."

"Did you observe him taking a bribe from my father?"

Sparrow blinked. "No. The customary way to get a clerk is to send to the College, and the College makes the selection. It will be one of the masters who did the dealing with your father. It won't have been the first time it happened. Their pay comes from the Crown, and it's not sufficient."

"I thought—the students—they pay to be there. Where does it go if not to the masters?"

"They get a small stipend. Much of the rest goes to pay the tax the Crown requires. The College paid a high price not to be shut down entirely. Not all the masters who left were expelled, you know. Some of them refused to teach with Karolje breathing down their necks and left on their own before he was crowned. You can be sure that the ones who did not make it safely to Milaya are still under close watch."

Anza had known the College was observed by Karolje's soldiers. She had seen them at the gates and squares every day. Sometimes the classes had been visited too, by quiet grey-clad men who she realized now with a shock must have been examiners.

Sparrow stood and put on her cap. "Let's leave while there is still some light."

Anza followed Sparrow out. She had passed the first test, it seemed.

The sun was down. Color had not completely faded from

the sky yet, but the haze had lifted, and there were stars in the east. The streets were unlit.

Sparrow walked quickly despite a slight limp that must have been from a long-healed injury. She led them east past more dingy taverns and faceless warehouses, then turned south into a narrow alley. Anza smelled old garbage, years of it, the brick walls and dirt alley so odor-impregnated they would never smell clean. The increasing darkness put her on edge. Beggar Island was said to be thick with cutthroats.

The alley went straight south for perhaps half a mile, terminating in a square. On Citadel Island it would have been patrolled and empty after dark. Here, people sat next to fires or stood, most in clusters, a few alone. After a moment of staring, Anza realized the strange shapes scattered about were low tents made with a blanket propped up on a stick. She had brought nothing except the key to Radd's office and a little money, thinking not to tempt thieves. It might be a lot of money here. She wished she had a weapon.

They turned left onto a street, narrower than the alley, that wound its way up a low hill into a slum. Anza's back tightened with wariness that someone might be watching them. The buildings were shacks, crowded together, curtains hanging in the doorways, roofs flat. Most were dark. The street was rutted, and Anza stumbled once. At the top she paused to wipe her hands on her trousers. She knew not all her sweating was from the exertion.

The road descended, steeply this time, and they went cautiously. When they reached the bottom, Sparrow made two rapid right turns, a left, another left, a right, and a final left among more shacks. Several blocks on this route took them to the first wide street they had been on since they left the Anchor. The houses were actual houses. Sparrow walked to the fourth one on the right and opened the door.

Anza stepped in behind her and exhaled in relief. It was darker than outside. She shut the door as Sparrow lit an oil lamp. In the flaring light, Anza saw a small square room with a steep stairway against a wall and an open door in the back to another dark room. Spacious, compared to the rest of the buildings she had seen so far on Beggar Island. The furniture consisted of two splintering crates, a stool, and a battered armless chair.

"Do you live here?" Anza asked, slightly appalled.

"Only sometimes," said Sparrow. "Rarely more than a week at a time. Often enough to discourage squatters. There are two pallets upstairs. Nothing is illegal except what's in my head. Tell me what you observed on the way here."

She shook off the last remnants of tension. "It would be easy to get lost. People must die of cold in winter. It's not as dangerous as rumor has it, but there's no place to hide if you have to run. Those roofs would not provide any cover and are dangerous to be on anyway." As the recitation ended, Anza realized that her father had trained her more than she knew. To observe, and to report.

"If you got cornered in there, how would you get away?"

A much harder question. The shacks provided no shelter or escape path. "They'd have to kill me," she said. "I could get by one of them, I think, if he wasn't expecting it, but not past two of them. I'd fight."

"If you were attacked by soldiers and not by common criminals, they wouldn't kill you. They would capture you. Karolje always wants prisoners. Can you kill yourself?"

A week ago, she would have unhesitatingly said she could. She knew how much better death was than an interrogation.

Now she remembered the cell in the Citadel, where she had never once thought of suicide. She had clung instead to a hope that innocence would be enough to free her. When the examiner tugged the belt around her neck, her only thoughts had been of breath.

"I don't know," she said. She and the resisters with her at the raid had known they were surrounded and had decided to fight. In the chaos the soldiers had not made it to the attic before the rain started and she fled. "I thought I could. But I might be too much of a coward. I'm sorry."

Sparrow gave her a long, unsettling look that made Anza's insides squirm. Then she said, "It's not cowardice to want to live. That's why you're fighting."

"I don't want to ever give away resistance secrets."

"The resistance doesn't depend on any one person. Not even me. Sit down." She pointed at the chair. "I'll bring us some wine. There's no food, unfortunately. If I leave any when I go, the rats get at it." She disappeared into the back room.

Anza sat gingerly and toed her sandals off. Her feet were dusty. She was still being tested. It was not unlike the questioning by the prince. Sitting, waiting for judgment.

Sparrow came back carrying two glasses of wine and offered one to Anza, then seated herself on the stool. "Do you obey orders?"

That too required an honest answer. "I always have, if you don't count some of the College rules. But no one's ever told me to do something unconscionable."

"You believe in something besides vengeance, then. The gods?"

"They aren't why I have a conscience," she said. She tasted the wine. If Sparrow could buy wine of this quality, she definitely had more money than the poverty of the building suggested. "There would be no point in fighting Karolje if I didn't think there could be someone better."

"Are you good enough to pick your target out in a crowd and not kill the wrong person by accident?"

Anza looked at her hands. The cut from the roof was scabbed over and no longer required the bandage. She pictured herself holding the bow, pressing the arrow to the string, the movement of the muscles in her shoulder as she drew back.

"No," she said reluctantly. "I'm good, but not that good." She would keep to herself her other thought. It had been easy to shoot the soldiers at the raid because she was afraid for her own life. Because it was dark and she did not have to see their faces. In cold blood was different. She would have to learn.

"If you are skilled enough with the bow, we will find a way for you to use it. Don't doubt it. Now, tell me what happened three nights ago."

At last they were getting to the meat of the matter. The present, not the past.

"We were caught. I have no idea how they found us. They set soldiers at the front and the back and waited until after dark to break in." Thuds against the door, screams of pain, the thunder of many booted feet on the stairs. "Mink had brought an explosive, and he threw it at the soldiers on the street. I shot at them and killed three before the rain started. I was in the attic, and they hadn't got there yet, so I went onto the roofs."

"Mink should have discharged the explosive in the building."

"If he had, the whole block would have been damaged. It wouldn't take much to start a fire. The houses there are all wood."

"Did they capture everyone else?"

"I don't know. Mink died. There was fighting. And screams." Her voice shook a little.

"What had your group been planning?"

"Hare said we were to cause general disruption. That's as much as I knew. But Mink was making explosives. Not in the house, he brought them with him to show us. We were trying to decide where to use them. At first Hare—he was our leader—wanted to destroy a bridge, but Mink said they weren't powerful enough for that and we should use them to put holes in boats. Then there was the question of what boats to sink, and when. Hare said he would get names." Saying it, Anza heard the absurdity. Sinking boats would have made merchants lose money, but in the long run all it would have achieved was more soldiers at the docks.

"It's an awful plan," said Sparrow. "Not in its aim. Getting merchants to turn on Karolje is a good move if it's the right merchants. But not by putting holes in their ships with explosives."

"Why not?"

"If you heard explosives were used, would you think it was the work of the resistance?"

"No," Anza said, understanding. She had known something about the plan was wrong but had not been able to say what. "I'd think it was the Tazekhs."

"Precisely."

Tazekhs were good with mechanical things, and they used incendiaries and explosives for everything from blasting rock to killing people. Anza had heard stories of explosions that had brought down entire buildings. A few thousand Tazekhs lived in Karegg, some as sellers of the fine wool made from the hair of Tazekh mountain goats, others as clockmakers and locksmiths and tinkers. The women never left the Tazekh area of the city. A handful were wealthy; most were not. In the war, after the queen vanished, they had been taken by force and confined to a prison in the hills. Radd had told Anza that many had starved to death.

The Tazekhs were more hated than Karolje. The king was a tyrant, but he was Vetian. He had lawfully inherited the throne, been anointed by the priests. The Tazekhs dined on the flesh of their dead and sacrificed infants to their gods, according to the stories. They kept witches at their sides instead of burning them, skinned their captives alive, and worshipped a three-headed dragon that was a monstrous creation of the wizards in an earlier age. If a woman lay with another woman or was adulterous, she was buried to her waist in the desert and stoned to death. Anza thought that was probably the only one of the rumors that was true.

If attacks were blamed on the Tazekhs, the Vetians frightened of Karolje would slaughter the Tazekhs in the city and turn their anger south. Karolje could ride that rage to another war. The resistance would fall away in disregard or be crushed altogether.

Sparrow went on. "The resistance can't survive another Tazekh war. Karolje will clamp down harder, and more and more people will choose to become collaborators. It would not surprise me if Karolje were to start rumors that our attacks were directed by Tazekhor. We have to claim our struggle."

"And that means no explosives."

"It means no explosives that aren't discharged publicly by one of us. Hare should have known better. I'll have to send someone to Mink's house to get any that are still there. I don't want them used."

"Publicly means innocent people get killed."

"Yes," said Sparrow. "Which is why we haven't done it, and

won't. It's no use killing ordinary citizens to put pressure on Karolje. He doesn't give a damn. We have to strike directly at his soldiers and his supporters."

Anza tried to conceal a shudder. Sparrow's voice was so cold, so methodical. Her objection to killing innocent people was one of utility, not morality. If it would get her what she wanted, she would do it. I'm in, Anza thought. I can't get out.

"If explosives are no good, what weapons do we have?"

"We have two. The first is fear. Karolje's aides, his soldiers, his men who keep order, are vulnerable. Magistrates and tax collectors. The merchants who support him. We have destroyed the supplies meant for the Citadel and killed soldiers in their guardhouses. We've smashed windows and ransacked offices. We leave handbills that claim responsibility and make threats."

Anza was surprised they had a printer. A press was a hard thing to keep hidden.

"Who are we trying to frighten?" she asked. "The king's supporters, or the citizens of Karegg?" It would have been a useful question to ask when she first joined, but she had been so bent on action it had not occurred to her.

"The king's supporters. Unfortunately, it went sideways at the raid you were in. That can't happen again." She took a coin out of her pocket and flipped it in the air, caught it neatly. "The second pincer is money. We have to hurt the right people. It won't be Karolje, that's a given. But we can make sure that Karolje's supporters lose income. We don't have to know where every lord is aligned to hurt the ones that matter most."

"Soldiers aren't paid well. You might be better off bribing them than killing them."

"It's been considered. The problem is that the ones who aren't bribed will rat out the ones who are. So for now we will aim at the lords. There are two in particular I would like to bring down. The chancellor is one. Lord Doru Kanakili is another."

"I know his wife," Anza said. She and Thali had been lovers for a few months several years ago and had parted in bitterness, not speaking to each other at all Thali's last year at the College. When Anza heard about the marriage, she wondered if Thali and Doru had each made it to spite someone else. "But he doesn't have any position in the Citadel."

"No named position. In practice, he's Karolje's spymaster. He has his hands in everything and can order an assassination whenever he wants. The chief interrogator reports to him. Is there any chance you were released as a favor to his wife?"

"Ha!" Anza said. "If she knew they had me, she would have come down to watch the torture." She did not really believe that; Thali had been a selfish woman with a vindictive streak, but not cruel. It made Anza feel a little sick, imagining Thali in bed with a man so evil. Thali could not have known when she married him, could she?

"I see," said Sparrow. "In any case, both the chancellor and Doru have entrusted their money to banks that can be brought down. Once we do that, anyone who has dealings with the men will be nervous about their own funds. When the lords in the Citadel start turning on each other, Karolje's power will ebb."

"What about his sons? Will they be our targets too?"

"If they support him, which we will have to assume they do unless they act against him."

Anza did not respond immediately. She wished she knew what the prince had been thinking. Now was the moment to tell of his involvement in her release, if she was to tell of it at all. It seemed too improbable to be believed.

Overthrowing the Crown could send the country into war.

Someone who thought he had a right to rule would acquire more soldiers, more wealth, more resources to claim the throne for himself. The house of Kazdjan might die, but the house of some other man would take its place.

She said, "If the lords start turning on each other, then what?"

"We have people in more places than you can imagine. Many of them watch and wait now, but when the time comes they will act." Sparrow bent forward and traced a pattern in the dust on the floor. A spiral. "We will place this symbol throughout the city. Throughout the Citadel, even, if we can. And our people will know to prepare to rise."

"What will they do? Is the resistance large enough? Most people aren't good with weapons."

"Once it starts, people will follow."

"That's an awfully big risk," Anza said, thinking. Karolje was hated, but he might be feared more. There was no way to tell. If the resistance failed to start a revolution, it would be crushed and have to begin afresh.

"We aren't here just to inconvenience the king," Sparrow said dryly. Anza realized the argument must have been had among the resistance leaders many times. Her own criticism was neither insightful nor earned. She was embarrassed.

She looked at the spiral again. Sparrow had started at the outside and drawn it inward, a tightening, a coil. "Why a spiral?"

"It's easy to draw, recognizable, and unlikely to be made by accident." She tugged the scarf. "Get something yellow to wear when it's time. It is one way we can recognize each other."

Anza nodded. She had a head scarf of her own that would do. She said, "And afterward, if we win? Who rules? You? Someone has to lead." Even if she knew nothing of politics, she would know that; humans needed leaders. She had seen it with village children, with students at the College, with those of Radd's clients who anxiously deferred to him.

"Not me," Sparrow said. "Never me. Nor anyone in the resistance, I think. We have to find people like Radd, who are thoughtful and strong without being overly ambitious. And we need several of them, to check each other."

Radd would be a good ruler, though he would hate it. How many people like him were left? Had Karolje's corruption spread far beyond the Citadel?

"There might not be enough good people," Anza said. "It could be chaos."

"It's a risk we have to take. The gate to power is locked by accident of birth or by force or both, and it must be unlocked. This isn't a battle we fight just for ourselves, for now. We're fighting for our grandchildren's grandchildren. Our enemy is not just Karolje, it's the idea of Karolje. We can't let kings have such power ever again."

"Let?"

"Kings only have the power that is given them. They need our consent, even if we don't know it. That is what will eventually undo Karolje."

Anza nodded. It occurred to her that the resistance was not about deposing the king so much as it was about restoring power to those who thought it lost. That was what Esvar had done in freeing her. He had given her back her power over herself. She wondered if he knew.

The house grew fuller and fuller of silence. In daylight, it would have become uncomfortable. In the heat, the shadowy lamplight, the lateness of the hour, the silence took on a soporific quality. Dense, thick, slow. Sparrow's back was to the lamp, her face unreadable. The muscles in her forearms were relaxed.

"Well," Sparrow said. "I need to decide what to do with you. You're of more use than for things like breaking windows. If you had a teacher who put you at the same level as the other students in the College, that must have been costly to your father since you were small. Why did he do it?"

Because he loved me! was hardly an adequate answer. Anza recognized Sparrow's tone—it was probing, not accusatory. Sparrow was right about the tutor; the old man, Nihalik, must have once been a teacher of lords' sons. He had appeared one day in her life, and she had not questioned it. She vividly remembered those hot afternoons in his cottage, when she sat across the table from him while he taught her things no farmer's niece needed to know. Languages, mathematics, and above all history. Histories of countries that had no kings, essays on the origin of laws. Dangerous things, which had prepared her to fight Karolje.

Thinking as she spoke, she said, "I was his only child. He had no wife, no other person to give money to."

"He didn't have to bring you here to support you. You would have been safer back in your village. Did he want you to marry up, to marry someone like Rumil?"

Her father had never met Rumil and had never criticized her for living with him. But he had not pressed her to marry either. There was no ordinary reason he would—many people without property did not marry at all—but if he wanted a rich husband for his daughter, he had been silent on the subject.

"No," she said. "He never said anything about marriage. I don't know what he wanted. He was a quiet man." The one time she had confessed awkwardly to him about the end of the affair with Thali, he had given her an embrace, but no advice.

"I can't know why your father did as he did. But I doubt he was unable to see what would result. With the right clothing, no one would guess you were not a well-born woman. I think he wanted you to have power, perhaps even to get into the king's court."

"Why would he want that?"

"Perhaps he saw a future for you as a spy. Bringing you into the Citadel would have opened a door."

"Bringing me into the Citadel would have been dangerous. He'd have made sure I was better with a knife," Anza said. "And he wasn't a traitor."

"It's not a bad thing to betray Karolje. Karolje has betrayed his own people."

"Yes. No." She shook her head fiercely but had no words. The picture of her father that Sparrow painted was of a man who was sly, disloyal, and manipulative, and she was sure her father had not been those things. But did she want to believe he had been loyal to a tyrant? That he had not had the courage to oppose what he knew to be wrong? He could not have opposed Karolje directly.

Perhaps he had. Perhaps that was what he had been killed for.

And here she was herself, an undisputed traitor. A murderer. What right had she to question her father's actions? Were evil acts in the service of good still evil? Could good people do evil things?

Sparrow's question about the gods had been pertinent after all. Anza was not sure right now where her moral center was. It was not a question the College had ever wanted to discuss, because it would have inevitably led to an examination of the state. She had had such conversations with Nihalik often, but her conclusions, her beliefs in her own behavior, had never been tested.

Sparrow said, "You don't have anything to be ashamed of, Anza. Life is compromise. Not at the core of our principles, but it can be a long time getting to them, especially if you are trying to keep other people from getting hurt along the way. The opposite of abasement is fanaticism, and the strong, decent, principled people fall somewhere in the middle. When you make your choices, you get shunted in one direction or the other, and sometimes at the end you find yourself in a box without knowing how you got there."

"Are you saying that's what happened to my father?"

"He had the courage to train you to fight back, with weapons and with your intellect. That's no small thing. Honor him for it."

The words brought back grief she had thought vanquished. She swallowed and said nothing.

"I'm not going to make you a spy, at least not yet," Sparrow said. "And I won't ask you to do anything that endangers Radd. For now we will start with the bow. You will need to learn the codes and signals. Kanakili's spies might be able to connect things, but there's no reason to make it easy for them, so you need a new name for messages and the people who don't know you. What should we use instead of Finch?"

"Harpy." It took hardly any thinking at all. She remembered the birds sitting on the ruined city walls. The vengeful goddess.

"Why the harpy?"

"When Karolje kills everything else, the harpies will still be here."

A slow smile curved Sparrow's lips. "I like that," she said. "I like that very much."

TEVIN POURED THE tea, a dark stream. He said, "Let me set a problem before you. This problem is named Interrogator Mityos Lukovian."

The sky was cloudy, and though the air was muggy, the tea was a comfort. The window looked north, over the garden to the iron-grey lake. Esvar's blood felt sluggish and cold despite the heat.

He sipped the tea, which was dark and bitter as both he and Tevin preferred, and said, "Has he complained about my interference with his work? Because if he has, I don't regret it and I'll do it again." Thus far, Karolje had treated his second son as loyal. Defective, but loyal. It was a flimsy shield but should be strong enough against one of the king's minions. An examiner's power did not penetrate Karolje's own defenses.

"Worse than complained. He's saying that you conspire with the smugglers for your own gain and bank the proceeds in Milaya. In essence, that you are traitorously defrauding the Crown. I've had him arrested."

The allegations were utterly absurd. Someone could still

twist facts to fit the story. Forged documents, false confessions. Esvar had seen too many men brought down that way to believe he was immune. Karolje was unlikely to believe it—that was a little less certain these days—but the king wouldn't hesitate to make use of the story if it suited him.

And perhaps it was not quite as absurd as Esvar wished. "If that letter you sent to Milaya is discovered, this rumor could get teeth," he said.

"That's one reason Lukovian needs to be silenced."

Silenced. How far would Tevin go? Well, this was the kind of challenge he had asked Tevin to make.

Esvar tilted his chair back. The ceiling plaster had been patched and painted in the spring, and it was a smooth expanse of warm gold. He said, "Lukovian was angry at me, no doubt of that. But he wouldn't do something like this on his own. Goran must be at the other end of the rope."

"I agree," said Tevin. "Lukovian's his man, and this is exactly the sort of meddling and slyness Goran loves. That doesn't make it less effective."

"Does the king know about the arrest?"

"Yes. I told him with three other men in the room, including the chancellor, and Karolje listened to me, which made Goran unhappy."

"Why did Karolje listen?" Esvar asked, baffled. The king had let darker rumors flourish many times.

"Not for my sake. This business about Lukovian is Goran moving to consolidate his own power. He moved too soon, and Karolje didn't like it. If we're going to be taken down, he wants to be sure he's the one behind it. I think it likely that he Disappears Lukovian and the whole story vanishes."

"Better he Disappears Goran."

"He won't do that. He needs Goran to balance Doru and keep us in line."

If only the two men could battle each other to the death, and their supporters with them. "What happens next?"

Tevin said, "I need you to be patient and not push anything for a while. Don't do anything unconventional. You shouldn't have talked to that girl, now they're going to be convinced she had something to do with it. I'm considering having her watched, for her own safety."

"That would draw attention to her," Esvar said, slightly queasy. He had not screwed up that badly, had he? The sweltering, colorless air hung around him, heavy, confining. "Don't try to fix things, that never works. It will be too tedious for them to follow her for long. She's not any sort of threat."

"You know that and I know that, but they don't believe anyone is innocent. Whatever possessed you to get involved in the first place?"

Justice. A word full of righteousness he did not have credit for and never would, no matter what he did. He was too tainted.

"It must have been something I ate," he said. "It won't happen again."

Tevin glared at him. "It had better not. Do you remember Piyr dying?"

What was that about? "It's hard to tell what I remember and what I've filled in since. I remember him lying in state." That was vivid in his mind. The bier, edged in gold and covered with blue velvet. The dead king, grey-white hair and beard trimmed, fully uniformed, hands on his chest. In the memory Esvar looked down at him; he must have been lifted up to view. The silver wolf's heads on the tops of the posts at each corner of the bier had been frightening, their black diamond eyes gleaming and alive.

Tevin said, "If Piyr had lived longer by a few years, he might have had Karolje killed to make space for me. Or if we hadn't been at war. He knew what his heir was like. He didn't think he could leave a regency, though. There would have been too much quarreling. Piyr was weaker than he seemed."

"Who told you this?"

"He did. They took me to see him before he was too sick to talk. Everyone else was sent out of the room, even the doctors. It was just me and the old man. He made me sit next to him, on the bed. He told me who I should go to if I needed help. Five men, two women. By the time Karolje dragged me south for the next campaign, they were all either dead or had withdrawn from court. I made a mistake with one of them at the coronation, listened to him for too long or smiled too much, I don't know, and before a month was out he was killed for treason. His ghost and Piyr's ghost were in my dreams for a long time after that, blaming me."

"Gods," Esvar said. He had been just six, his brother eleven, when their grandfather died after a long gradual decline. There were times he envied Tevin, who remembered life without Karolje as king, who had known their mother and grandfather longer. And then there were times like this, when he was glad he was the second son, unburdened with expectations.

"The lords remember who was killed or exiled those first few years. They're all wondering if I will be as ruthless. Goran will be my example. If I play things right, he'll retreat swiftly."

Esvar thought it over. "Blackmail," he said. He had not expected such a strategy from his honorable brother. "You have something dirty on him."

"Something very dirty. Which you are better off not knowing right now. I've only told you this much so you won't crowd me. I have to find the exact moment to spring it on him, and that depends on Karolje's health."

The sudden steel in Tevin's usually warm brown eyes took Esvar aback. Turn those eyes on the court and they'll obey you, he thought.

"You're up to something," he said.

"I intend to be the king." Tevin's voice was newly edged.

This time he means it, Esvar thought, warming with grim joy.

◆ ◆ ◆

His new lieutenant, Jance Mirovian, had the erect carriage of a soldier but none of the plod of the ordinary guards. A slenderness to his build, not unlike Esvar's own, indicated he had spent his life in some comfort before coming to the Citadel. He had hazel eyes, light skin, and hair that would have been dark gold if it had been allowed to grow. The resemblance to Lord Darvik was noticeable.

Esvar had decided to test the man's intellect, so he took him to the house where his own raid had failed. Three thick boards had been hammered roughly across the doorframe. The guards wrenched them loose with a crowbar. The king's Mark burned into the door would be enough to keep the curious away, but there were always fools. A door opened in the neighboring house long enough for a head to peep out, see the soldiers and horses, and retreat. Esvar wondered if the head belonged to the person who had tipped off the watch about the meetings. Spies were good, but frightened neighbors were better.

That was thinking like the king. Like a soldier, damn it, and a loyal one. It was so easy to do. All the forces around him pushed him in that direction. No wonder Tevin tried so hard to set himself apart from Karolje.

Nothing showed there had been an explosive unless one knew to look. The rain hadn't managed to fill the crater with mud or melt all the lumps of thrown earth, but the potholes appeared ordinary. One of the lower windows in the house had been broken.

The soldiers had left the door open when they went in, and he heard the thump of their feet on the stairs like beats on a drum. It was not long before a man opened the gable window and gave the clear sign.

Esvar said to Mirovian, "What do you know about the resistance?"

"What everyone knows, sir. They've killed some soldiers and damaged property. They're scattered and ineffective."

"Not as ineffective as you think. I've been leading the raids on the resistance since Captain Havidian was executed, but it's soldiers' work, not a prince's. Unless you prove yourself a fool, I'm handing it over to you. Did word get out to everyone in the Guard as to why he was executed?"

"Because his men killed the resisters instead of capturing them," Mirovian said.

The raid had been planned for weeks in the hopes of capturing a leader of the resistance, Ivanje Stepanian. Once Stepanian died, the captain's execution had been a foregone conclusion, along with that of the man who had actually killed him. Stepanian's secrets were sealed forever. Several soldiers had died too, bitten by one of the king's hellhounds that had gone wild. Havidian had always been loyal, and there had been no reason to assume it was anything other than bad luck, but an unlucky soldier was as much a weakness for Karolje as a treacherous one.

"Just one. But it was the wrong one. And one got away."

"Is there any chance the leader was killed intentionally, sir?"

"For mercy?"

"Or to keep the secrets."

The possibility had been considered, of course. Nothing had been found in the lives of either Havidian or the soldier to indicate sympathy toward the resistance, let alone treachery.

"It was unintended," Esvar said.

Mirovian's face had the intensity of expression belonging to a man about to descend a narrow path on a steep cliff. He had to be calculating whether there was a way to honorably avoid the mess he was about to be ordered into. Alas for him, there wasn't.

"Was it here, sir?"

"No. The failure here was not the late lamented captain's. It was mine. Two resisters died, and another killed three soldiers and escaped." Esvar pointed up at the gable. "There was an archer there. She got out somehow, over the roofs I imagine. One deduces that she was able to climb. It was a dangerous thing to do that night."

There was a brief silence. The soldiers who had searched the house had come out and taken up guard positions to either side of Esvar and Mirovian. The horses' tails flicked loudly at the flies.

Mirovian said, "What happened, sir?"

"They threw an explosive," he said, "a small one, but enough to make a mess of the road, and shot my men. The raid had just begun."

"They had explosives?"

"Yes. And we know they weren't Tazekhs. The three we captured told us about the woman who escaped. Fortunately, the two who died were as young and unimportant as the others."

"Do you know anything about the one who escaped?"

Esvar said, "She was described as small and dark-haired, which could be anyone. She used a plain hunting bow and soldiers' steel-tipped arrows, which is a failure on someone else's part. If you had been in command, what would you have done to keep her from escaping?"

Mirovian thought, a wrinkle of concentration on his brow. "It would have been impossible for armed men to be quiet. Too heavy on the stairs. If she was waiting in the attic, I don't see how you could have prevented it, sir. Not unless you had archers yourself, and light to show up anyone leaving." He glanced up at the gable.

"So on the next raid we bring an archer. What surprise will the resistance have for us that time?"

It was an impossible question, and Mirovian ignored it. "How'd they get explosives, sir?"

"The man who had brought the explosive was killed. We have no idea who he was or where he lived. There could be—probably are—dozens more of the things hidden somewhere in the city. Let's go in." He swung off his horse.

The floors were smeared with dried mud from the passage of soldiers who had searched the place. A stool lay on its side in the front room. A spider had built a web between the rungs. Beside the stool was a large bloodstain.

Esvar pointed at the stain. "Someone died here, to leave that much blood. That's not supposed to happen. What went wrong?"

"Plenty of room to disarm him," said Mirovian. He squatted and righted the stool. "Especially with a whip. If the resister used the stool as a shield or threw it, say, that could have worked to hold someone off. What do the soldiers remember, sir?"

"The ones who weren't killed themselves deny doing it,"

Esvar said in as matter-of-fact a tone as he could manage. He did not want to imply that he thought he was being lied to, but he did not want to foreclose the possibility either. "They went in without a light," he added. "They were relying on a lamp outside. Was that the error?"

Mirovian looked at the unplastered wall, where boards were darkened with rot and splinters protruded. "If an oil lamp had spilled during a fight, this place would have gone up like kindling. That's a hell of a risk. It seems to me that two resisters dead and one missing is better than all the soldiers and the resisters dead and fire running through this part of Karegg."

"So I judged," Esvar said.

The other two rooms on the first floor consisted of a kitchen in the rear of the house and a windowless room with a table and a few chairs. There was nothing to remark on in either. Esvar led Mirovian up to the attic for the next stage.

The top floor was one large room with one window each on the street and the back. It was very hot. The ceiling was low and slanted sharply down so that both men had to bend. Soldiers' footprints tracked through the dust. The soldiers would have been handicapped by the darkness and the ceiling.

Esvar crouched by the window as though preparing to shoot. The archer had been in a tricky position, and killing three men had not been nearly as easy as it looked. She must have leaned halfway out the window to shoot. Her aim had been damn good.

He rubbed his shoulder, remembering the arrow that had grazed it, and said, "What do you see?"

"Are you sure only one got away?"

"Yes." Esvar moved aside. "Could you climb out?"

The lieutenant eased his upper body out the window, which

was barely wide enough, and reached up to grab at the gable roof. He swore. Esvar heard a crash, probably a slate striking the ground.

"She had to be small," Mirovian said when he had managed to get back in. His uniform was smeared with dirt, and there was blood on his hand where he had cut it against a slate. "She must have waited here as soon as the resisters knew they were trapped, but getting out that window and onto the roof, in the rain . . . That took nerve." His tone was almost admiring.

"And ability," Esvar said. He led the way back to the stairs.

On the second floor were three bedrooms. The one in the front held a narrow bed with a thin mattress and an empty bookcase. The second room was empty. In the rear room a bed with thrown-back sheets occupied most of the space, but Esvar's attention went straight to the window.

The glass was broken. A few jagged, dangerous-looking shards protruded upward from the bottom of the frame. Smashed glass on the floor had been broken into smaller pieces by booted feet tramping on it. The wood was blotched with water stains and blood.

Avoiding the glass, he examined the wall around the window and saw what he had hoped not to see: faded blood marks in a spray pattern that spoke of a cut artery. The resister had broken the window and used the glass to slice his throat open. Esvar turned around and looked at the bed. A large brown stain lay over the crumpled linens.

His stomach tightened painfully. He threw his hand to the windowsill for support as the world rocked.

Blood wet and red on the coverlet, the floor, the overturned table. A crack in the mirror, books in disarray on one shelf. A bottle of spilled lavender scent perfumed the room. "Get him out of here," said Tevin. The king said, "No. Look at this, both of you. Look long. This is what the Tazekhs did. Remember this. Kill them for this." The guard behind Esvar put a hand on his shoulder, holding him in place.

"Sir? My lord?"

He felt unsteady in the knees, but he kept his breakfast down and said, "Here we had a suicide. I don't think that could have been prevented."

"The resisters will do that?"

"When it's a choice between taking a knife to their own throat and keeping their secrets, or facing what's waiting for them back at the Citadel, it's not a hard decision to make. Have you ever watched an interrogation?"

"Um, no, sir."

Count yourself lucky, Esvar thought. He considered ordering Mirovian to observe, so the man would know what happened to his prisoners, and decided not to. It would either ruin him or drive him into the arms of the resistance. And would that be so bad a thing? he asked himself.

The thought was almost as much of a shock as the memory had been. He had committed himself to opposing the king more deeply than he had realized.

He said, "It's not a necessary part of your training. But the stories you've heard are probably all true. Many of the resisters can't screw themselves up for suicide, but some can, especially the older ones. The raids help us reduce their forces, but we don't get a damned lot of information from them." *Us. Their. We.* He hated it. I'm glad she got away, he thought.

"Is that what happened with Captain Havidian's raid, sir?"

Perceptive question. "A suicide? No. One of his men got caught up too much in the heat of things and botched it."

"Botched it like—" He broke off.

"Like one of my men did downstairs? The circumstances were similar. My man didn't kill the leader of the resistance, though. One of the leaders. They've been even fiercer since."

"Who are their leaders now?"

"There is a woman named Sparrow, about whom no one knows anything except that she seems to lack neither money nor ingenuity." He looked at the broken glass again. "We've seen enough. You'll come with me on the next raid, and if all goes well, I'll turn you loose after that."

Mirovian's hand was still bleeding, and he cut a strip of cloth from the bedsheet to bandage it. Esvar tied it for him, thinking vaguely as he did that he had seen a cut like this on someone else's hand recently.

They went out and mounted. Mirovian got up more slowly than usual and stared up at the gable. Esvar couldn't read his face. Perplexity? Concern? There was something going on in that College trained mind. Was he still puzzling out the resister's escape?

"How do you know where to raid?" Mirovian asked. It sounded like an afterthought.

"That's the spymaster's responsibility. He takes his orders from the king."

Mirovian opened his mouth, thought better of whatever he was going to ask, and nodded. "Yes, sir," he said, his voice as crisp and soldierly as any commander could want.

Damn, Esvar thought. The man was holding something back. If he asked now, all he would get was bluster. He would let the secret sit within Mirovian long enough to be uncomfortable.

* * *

At the Citadel, he went to his mother's rooms. They were unguarded, the corridor empty. A fireplace was set in one wall, its hearth empty and clean. Mirantha had kept things on that mantel, a vase of flowers in the summer, a thick candle nested within sprigs of holly in the winter. There had been a little wooden cat, narrow-faced, sitting upright, tail curled around its feet. And lavender, bunches of it hanging dried from each end of the mantel. The tiny blossoms sometimes fell onto the hearth and dotted the stone with color.

Servants swept the floors and cleaned the windows as they did everywhere in the Citadel, but the furniture was covered against dust, and the walls were bare of any ornament. The queen's jewels, her books, her clothing, all had been packed away, waiting for a return that would never happen. The air did not smell of lavender anymore. The glass in her window had not been broken. Not that escape for her.

What if she had found some way to flee? Blood without a body proved nothing.

It was a childish fantasy. She would not have abandoned him or his brother, especially not then, when her lover was dead and Tevin was being pulled closer and closer to Karolje. The guards had been found killed, all four of them, and her two maids. Esvar could not remember their names. The queen was gone, abducted, and two months later Karolje broke the treaty and invaded Tazekhor in revenge. Tevin had told him before the army went south that it had been Karolje's own soldiers who took Mirantha.

Why? Esvar had always thought Karolje killed her because that was what Karolje did. She had been unfaithful; when her lover was executed, everyone expected her death to be next. He saw now that Karolje would not kill a tool as useful to him as a queen without a good reason. If he had wanted an excuse to start a second war, he could have found others. Mirantha's death was not a matter of impulse, as beating her or strangling her in bed might have been. It had been ordered by a man who excelled at strategy.

The only possible explanation was that she had been a threat. She had been a warrior's daughter, tall and strong and skilled with weapons. Karolje was sixteen years older than her. It would have been possible for her to kill him if he was drunk or sick or sleeping. The king had moved first.

MIRANTHA

WHEN SHE FINDS out she is pregnant, she finds out that Ashevi too can be cruel.

It is four months since the first time. They have devised ways and places to meet, never twice the same, never without the sense of danger. She has grown to crave that alertness. The act is not lovemaking, not with such speed and silence, but it is not animal rutting either. She is learning what pleasure is as well as desire. He shows her small tendernesses and brings gifts, a book or a flower or a velvet ribbon. Once he gave her fresh lavender, but she did not dare keep it. She asks him why he breaks his vows, and he tells her that priests' strictures were made by men and love was made by the gods. Because it is not at all unheard of for priests to have bastard children, and because what he says is what she needs, she accepts it. She never asks him why he dares to go behind Karolje's back. Asking that would be sure to make someone notice.

Then she misses her bleeding and her breasts grow sore. She tells him while they stand on a courtyard balcony, watching Tevin shoot his bow on his eleventh birthday. The demonstration is attended by many observers, but they have the balcony to themselves. King Piyr, who should be with her, has been advised by his doctor not to spend so long in the cold. He is weak and frequently ill now. She stares at her son, hoping he will make a better man than her husband, and says, "I'm pregnant."

"You have to get rid of it," he says at once.

She already knows that, but she wanted more kindness from him. Her hands pressing into the rail of the balcony, she stands silently while Tevin nocks and draws. The arrow hits the center of the target among a thicket of other arrows. He has missed by a few inches only once. She was a good archer as a girl, and watching him, she longs for that past. The autumn wind blows bits of straw loosened from the target around the courtyard.

She says, "You might act a little more unhappy about losing a child."

He looks at her, and the pressure of his gaze makes her glance away from her son. The pupils of his eyes go on forever into a great darkness. "I don't want a child. And certainly not with you. It's much too risky. Get rid of it, and make sure you don't conceive again."

She wants to strike him. "You sound like Karolje," she says.

Another arrow hits the center. He claps. He says, "Don't come near me until it's taken care of. And if it gets found out and you cry rape, I will deny everything."

On the balcony opposite, Esvar stands with his tutor. The boy watches his brother but Nihalik is watching her. She is sure he knows.

Tevin has used up all his arrows. One of the armory boys runs to pull them from the target. She leans over the rail and calls to the prince.

He looks up. "Lady Mother?" She sees his father in his face, and also a line of his jaw that belonged to her family. He is beautiful and healthy and untainted.

"Split an arrow for me," she says.

On his third shot, he does. As the applause echoes around the courtyard, she looks at Nihalik and asks him with her eyes to come to her.

✦ ✦ ✦

That evening, he brings the books in which Tevin has done his lessons and the pile of paper that is Esvar's work, handwriting large and awkward. Any soldiers or servants who glance at the papers and books will know exactly what they are and think Nihalik has come to discuss the boys' studies.

Night falls early this time of year, and though it is not late it is quite dark. The lamplight only brings out shadows. She says, "Tevin will be treated more as a man now that he has turned eleven. The king sent to speak with him this evening. Is he aware of what it means that he will someday be king?" She hopes he knows what she is asking. Even here, in her own room, she is guarded with her words.

"Yes. And he knows what is needed for his own safety."

"Piyr is ailing and old. When he dies, Karolje will replace you with someone loyal to him. I am afraid Esvar will be too impressionable. What do you suggest I do? Anyone I put forth, Karolje will reject out of hand."

"There are men at the College who can be nudged to put forth their names without you having anything to do with it, Mirantha. But I would have expected you to propose Ashevi."

It is a challenge. The two men do not like each other. Until today, she has thought it a natural antipathy between them, groundless.

She says, "I don't doubt either his learning or his capacity to teach. But . . ."

"I can't tell whether you want me to convince you he is the right man or the wrong one."

It stings. She wants to love Ashevi with the same simplicity she did yesterday. "He would never hurt the boys," she says.

"He might well hurt you."

The days—the years—have stretched her to a breaking point she was unaware of. She snaps. Her hand comes down hard over his on the table, and she says in a fierce voice that seems to come from outside herself, "Do you know what I have endured since I married? Ashevi cannot hurt me more than Karolje has."

"It is the ones we love who hurt us the most," he says. He presses her hand. "Always."

She whispers, "Is it so obvious?"

"Send your maid away for ten minutes," he says after a long silence. "Tell her you have a headache and need medicine. And strong wine to drink it with."

As soon as the door closes behind the maid, Nihalik says gently, "Has he got you with child?"

It was why she sent for him, but she can't bring herself to say the words. She is ashamed it has happened, ashamed to ask for help, ashamed he guesses. She feels herself flushing and can't meet his eyes.

He goes to her mantel. She hears the soft brush of paper against wood and knows he has left something for her. His movements have disturbed her bunches of dried lavender, and the scent wafts through the room. Outside the window is a wall of darkness. She is afraid and cold and lonely and wishes she were home in the south.

Nihalik returns to the table and, taking his seat, pulls one of the books to him. He says, his voice a little too loud, "I can write out a course of study for each of the princes, my lady. It might be of help."

It might also be dangerous. "When the time comes," she says. "I am satisfied with things as they stand now."

They speak of safe subjects until the maid returns with the powder from the doctor. Nihalik gathers the boys' work and says, "You can be proud of them." He bows and departs.

The maid mixes the drug with the wine, sees that she drinks a little, and helps her out of her dress into a night shift. Mirantha dismisses her. She adds the powder that Nihalik left and drinks again. This time the wine is bitter and makes her mouth tingle.

Her head is hurting in truth now, and the candle is unbearably bright. Her abdomen and lower back cramp as though she is being knifed. She blows out the candle and lies down, pulling the darkness around her. The world spins a little.

Merciful sleep comes soon.

✦ ✦ ✦

In the morning, the pain is gone and her bleeding has started. She feels light-headed and weak. Just a little late, that is all the servants will think if they notice. She will make sure it does not happen again.

The only way to be sure is to avoid Ashevi.

For a long time she sits by her window, thinking. Overnight, autumn has turned to winter. Snow is drifted on the sill and falls onto the ground twenty feet below. The garden is white and the lake only a distant blur of grey. The air next to the window is so cold she should pull the drapes, but she wants the light.

At last she rises and writes a message to Ashevi that says only, *It is done.* She folds it and seals it, then stands by the hearth and considers throwing it into the fire. The message is an invitation of sorts. If she tells him nothing, he will stay away from her. Snow whisks against the window glass.

Then, despising her weakness, she gives the maid the message to deliver. He will see her tomorrow, the next day. She can't give that up yet.

ANZA SHUT THE door behind her—Radd was still working inside—and halted. Rumil leaned against the corner of the building, waiting for her, handsome as ever.

"Hello," she said coolly. She was tired from a day of work and wanted to go home.

He smiled. That charming smile. "Hello, Anza. Can we talk a bit?"

"About what?"

"Come and have a drink. It won't take long. I'm buying." His voice was friendly, persuasive.

She was much angrier at him than she had thought she was. She should just swear and walk away. "I'll give you a quarter hour," she said. "Including the time it takes to get to a public house." She started out without waiting.

He caught up quickly with his long stride. Their shadows stretched out before them. "My father is selling my house. There isn't room to store everything. Do you want any of the furnishings?"

He wanted her to ask why. "Not even to borrow," Anza said.

She had been sleeping on a pallet on the floor of her new flat, but she would not trade that for Rumil's softest bed.

He winced. "I said some things that night that I'm not proud of. I'm trying to apologize."

"You accused me of infidelity. That didn't come out of nowhere. You had it in your mind long before you said it." She planted her feet firmly and waited for him to stop walking and look at her. "We aren't good at being lovers. My leaving was the best thing for both of us."

"I know you weren't unfaithful. I was angry. I—"

"Stop," she said, speaking over him. "Let it go. If you keep talking, you'll say something else you regret." She started walking again.

He blocked her way. "Anza, we've known each other for years. You're not going to let one argument be the end of that. I still love you."

"You're the one who threw me out."

"It was a mistake. Just listen to me. We can fix this."

"I don't want to fix it. And you don't either, not really."

"Don't tell me what I want," he said, his voice sharper.

"Rumil, you can't buy trust back. You can't. Or forgiveness."

"If you weren't unfaithful, what were you doing those nights?"

"Working." She jabbed her thumb over her shoulder. "Go back and ask Radd. I'll wait."

"Never mind," he said. He spun and stalked off.

* * *

Anza's new flat was in a neighborhood that was neither poor nor prosperous; the stone buildings were constructed well enough but stood shabby and disheveled, the faded paint on the doors indistinguishable greys and the roofs missing slates. Nothing remarkable. The street was steep and narrow, like most other streets in that part of the city. Sometime far in the past there had been money to cobble it. The courtyard of her building was weedy, and the entrance and stairwell, where the sun rarely hit, were damp. There was a well that reached down to one of the city cisterns and a foul-smelling sewer outlet for emptying the chamber pots. Across from the entrance was a narrow tunnel, which led to an adjacent courtyard and thence to a street. There were dozens of such wynds in Karegg, designed to make it easier to pass from one street to another on the long blocks.

She had a meal and took her tea outside to drink on the balcony that circled the courtyard. Sunlight still struck the upper side of the building opposite her. The floor and supports of the balcony were stone, but the rails were only rusting iron bars. Her neighbors were busy with evening things: taking down and folding the sun-dried wash, filling pails from the well, cleaning dishes. The air smelled of kenna smoke and tea. Two cats crouching near the well glared at each other. A flock of harpies flew east overhead, going to their roosts.

The house she had lived in with Rumil already seemed not quite real. As Sparrow had said, with the right clothing she could have moved easily among nobles. She knew how to disguise herself with finery and manners. Rumil's house had been a costume of its own, worn and now put aside. This flat, stone and city-bound though it was, was more like the farm cottage she had grown up in than Rumil's house and its garden and greenery had been.

Footsteps sounded on the stairs. Anza turned her head, expecting a neighbor. Instead, surprisingly, she saw Jance. She had not seen him since they left the College. He was a soldier now, much too close to the king's eye for comfort even before she joined the resistance. He wore a loose silk shirt and neat brown trousers tucked into expensive boots. The leather was dusty. His hair was short, and his face was thinner than it had been while they were at College; it had changed from a boy's to a man's.

"Jance!"

"Hello," he said. "I've been looking for you."

They hugged briefly. Anza said, "How did you find me?" She viewed the courtyard through his wealthy eyes: old, stained, blocklike, and ugly. He would try to talk her into moving someplace else.

"I asked Rumil first. He told me you had gone back to Irini. Is that true?"

"Hell no. I need some time with no one else entangled in my life." That should be a direct enough statement to fend Jance off if he was having any lovesick thoughts. They had been good friends, nothing more, but there had to be a reason for him to have appeared now.

Jance said, "Did you get tired of him, or did you leave because of his money problems?"

"Money problems?"

"Yes. Through his father, I gather. It's been going on for months."

"And he accused me of keeping secrets!" It was hard to feel much rage against Rumil now, though. "He never told me. How did you find out?"

"We were drinking. At one of the taverns near the College. He didn't want me to come to his house. He said I should ask Radd where you were living, so I did."

"You really wanted to talk to me, didn't you?"

"Yes. Can we go in?"

"Yes." They were quiet while she made him tea, served in an earthenware mug that had come with the flat. She put it before him and sat on the other stool by the table and said, "How is it being in the Guard?" She hoped it hadn't made him brutal.

"Tedious and low-paying," he said, "but it has its moments. It keeps me active. I was just promoted, so I will be getting more responsibility." He sipped his tea. He had a bandage around his hand like the one she had needed after the raid. His eyes had darkened.

"Doing what?"

"I'm being trained to lead the raids on the resistance," he said.

And you're doing it? she thought. But Jance had no choice. If he didn't obey orders, he could be executed. As her father had been. She could not keep herself from glancing nervously over her shoulder at the window. What if he wasn't alone?

He followed her thought. "No one knows I'm here, Anza. I made sure of that. I may as well ask you now. Did you know a captain at the Citadel named Havidian?"

She had never expected Jance to be the one to ask that. What did he know? "Why?"

"I take that as a yes. What is he, your uncle?"

"My father."

"Get the hell out of Karegg," Jance said. "The king's soldiers are looking for you."

Terror she had thought she was done with ran through her again. "They can't be," she said. The cell had been so cold. When she was back at Radd's that night, she had huddled under a blanket despite the summer heat, shaking and shaking. Whenever she closed her eyes, she saw the examiner's pale hands holding the belt while his trousers bulged close to her face. She smelled her own fear-sweat and the leather of the belt and the metal of the chains. She remembered the fouler odors in the dungeon, and the whispering, endless whispering.

"You look like him, Anza. I trained with him. I knew he reminded me of someone, and I couldn't think who, and I figured it out a few days ago. I got sent to a house where there had been a raid. An archer got away. An archer who was small and good at climbing and able to get military arrows. She was described as young and dark-haired."

She leaned over to sniff the tea. Its clean fragrance helped calm her. They didn't know anything about her.

"Many women in Karegg look like that," she said, trying to reassure herself.

"But how many of them know someone who could teach them to shoot?"

She shrugged. "The resistance can teach people. Are they looking for a member of the resistance or for Captain Havidian's daughter?"

"A member of the resistance, now. Right now they don't think your father was a traitor. But they'll wonder if they haven't already how a woman could shoot well enough to kill three soldiers, and they'll start looking for soldiers who might have trained someone. Prince Esvar already has suspicions about the arrows."

"That won't lead them to my father," she said. "Why should it? He never stole any arrows. And why would I join the resistance when my father was a soldier? Why would he train me? Neither of us would risk killing the other."

"Someone will remember his short, dark-haired daughter. Soldiers notice things, and there's nothing for spurring memories like being questioned by a commander or higher."

She got up and brought down two glasses and a bottle of raki. Drinking with Jance was not the smartest thing to do right now, but she needed to blunt the anxiety mounting in her. She poured them each a full glass. The burn and sting in her mouth was clarifying, even clean.

"No one knew about us. We were careful. I don't see how they can find me, unless you tell them. Anyway, I'm not guilty of anything but being his daughter."

"I don't believe you," he said. "I'm sorry, Anza, but it's obvious. You fit the description perfectly. I tried to get out the window onto the roof, and it took a hell of a climber to do what you did."

Esvar had seen her. If she resembled her father as much as Jance thought, he could make the connection too. Her hand went to her cheek. Her face had been bruised and swollen then, which might serve as some disguise.

She gave in. Jance knew her too well for her to lie convincingly to him. If he was questioned by a Truth Finder, his suspicions would come out and they would look for her anyway. "It's only obvious because you already know me. Are you going to tell anyone?"

Jance drank, coughed. "Gods, that's going to make my eyes pop out. Of course not. But Thali can figure it out if she puts her mind to it, she knew what your father looked like too. And she's married to the spymaster. You need to leave."

"I don't have anywhere to go."

"What about your aunt? Was living with her so terrible?"

"Her, no. The area, yes. Nothing new ever happened. People talked about the same things their grandparents talked about fifty years ago." It had been a life of routine, of mindlessly pulling weeds or sorting beans, of repairing thatch, of discussing the crops and the weather and who had argued with whom. She had wanted more for herself as far back as she could remember. Her aunt had been a kind woman, but not one given to thought beyond the tasks of living.

"Go to a city, then," Jance said. "There are lawyers everywhere who need clerks. I can loan you money if you need it."

Jance was risking himself by coming here to warn her. He was owed a better explanation. "Karolje's here," she said. "He's evil. I have to fight him."

"The resistance can find someone else."

"It's not about the resistance. It's about me. I can't turn away from the things he's done. I don't have children to protect. I can take risks other people can't."

"You don't know Prince Esvar. He's very competent."

She considered telling Jance she had met the prince once, that he had set her free, and decided not to. She didn't want Jance to have to conceal anything more than necessary. If a connection between the missing resister and Havidian's daughter was made, a further connection to Radd's clerk would lead straight to Radd.

"Has Esvar said anything about my father?" she asked.

"No. But I wouldn't expect him to tell me everything he thinks."

"How did you get picked to work with him? Does he want to go to bed with you?"

Jance had just taken a drink, and he spluttered violently, spraying raki into a napkin. When his face had returned to a more usual color, he said, "Not him. He prefers women, there's no question about that."

"Well, soldiers . . ." she said, spreading a hand.

"Some soldiers. Not all of us." He sipped the raki. "My cousin's a lord, you know that. I assume I was chosen as some sort of favor to him."

"What's the prince like?"

"Perfectly civilized," said Jance. "But I wouldn't want to get on his bad side."

"Cruel like Karolje?"

Jance spun his glass in his hand, drained it and poured another. "No. He tries to be fair. I don't think he's forgiving of much, though."

Esvar had released her. That had been fairness.

"I haven't done anything that needs his forgiveness," she said. She finished her own drink. When she refilled the glass, she spilled a little.

Mirantha had been desperate to save her sons. Karolje had surely killed her. What had that disappearance, that death, done to her children? Tevin had been fourteen. Esvar had been eight. What would Anza have felt if her anger and grief about her father had had twelve years to harden? Her own mother's death had come when she too was eight, and now it was only a softness in her memory. But her mother had died of illness, not of murder.

How would she feel if one of her parents had killed the other?

Vengeful, terrified, ashamed. She tried to imagine what it might have done to her soul and failed. She would seek justice, but Karolje's sons did not have that chance. Or they might have been fed lies about Mirantha for so long that they had sided with the king.

"Does Esvar *want* to find me?" she asked, inspired by the raki.

"Why wouldn't he?"

"I'm not worth much."

"Don't count on that. That just means they won't try to be subtle about things." He wiped his mouth and stood. "I'd better go. If you see me at a raid, try not to shoot me."

It stung. "Don't do that."

He flushed. "There's another raid in a few days, but I won't be told any of the details until shortly before. I won't be able to warn you. If you're there, I'll have to arrest you. Even if you don't leave Karegg, can you lie low for a while? Please."

"I'll try," she said. She got up and went to his side, held out her hand. "Thank you. I think you'd better not come here again. Nor talk to Radd or Rumil or anyone else. I don't want you to put yourself at risk."

He squeezed her hand and bent down to kiss her cheek. "Be careful," he said, and let himself out.

She watched out the window until he had walked out of her view on the street. The rooftops were red with sun. A woman hollered her children home. Everything seemed peaceful.

"Damn," she muttered. She returned to the table and drained her glass of raki.

• • •

The warning peal of the Great Bell of the Temple was said to be able to wake the newly dead. Anza roused to its sound rolling through her body. The vibrations shook her teeth and breastbone. Her first confused thought was of war, and she rolled groggily out of bed and dressed as fast as she could. In the street below her open window, people were talking and shouting. She smelled smoke.

Inside the dark courtyard there was nothing to look at, but

from the street she saw the firelit pillar of smoke in the southwest, sooty black framed by orange light. She half expected demons or hellbats to fly out of it. The air smelled of burning oil and creosote. The bell gonged again. Dogs howled from all directions.

Whatever was burning was big. It was a strike by the resistance, it had to be. Gods, she hoped no one had used explosives.

Or, horrible thought, what if Karolje had set it himself? Perhaps he was punishing someone or wanted to stir up feeling against the Tazekhs. His soldiers would rush in to put the fire out and be treated as heroes. That was exactly the sort of deviousness Karolje was capable of.

For an instant the world skidded out of control. Would her father have wanted her to take the risks she had? He could not live again no matter what she did. Perhaps she would serve his memory better by staying safe.

No. He had trained her. He had intended her to fight. He had brought her here, into the heart of danger, and she wasn't going to waste that gift.

✦ ✦ ✦

In the morning, the smoke haze lingered. A yellow sun cast smoldering light. Stony-faced soldiers walked the main streets, hands on their sword hilts. Some of them led the chained hellhounds, large black dogs with venomous bites. If the dog chose to use its venom, you died fast, but not fast enough.

Anza did not know her new neighborhood well enough to avoid the checkpoints. Armored soldiers stood with pikes and bows and swords and whips, ready for any kind of violence they needed to inflict. At two of the checkpoints she was waved through, but at the third, near the cloth sellers' market, she had to stand in a line. Her bag was searched. She waited, head lowered, obedient. The soldier who questioned her was only of average build, but his mouth was thin and cruel. No, sir, yes, sir, of course, sir. He sent her on her way with a hard push on the back. At least he hadn't taken the opportunity to feel her breasts.

At the office, the window was open and the curtains pulled clear so Radd could see anyone passing by. His desk, dark oak that still managed to show stains and nicks, was unusually tidy. He's leaving, she thought.

"The fire last night," he said, "that was arson, Anza. It destroyed most of four warehouses before it was put out. The owners of three of the four have influence in the Citadel. Karolje's going to come down damn hard. He's set a curfew for sunset, and they're not letting most people leave the city."

"Did anyone die?" she asked.

"Three of the men trying to put the fire out, and another two are gravely injured. It's said to be still too hot to look through the ruins."

"Who was responsible?"

"Sit down," Radd said. "Listen to me very carefully. I lived here when the last Tazekh war started and Piyr died. It feels much the same now. Things are about to break. Don't ask questions, of me or of anyone else. Don't go looking for old friends or start spending nights out. Go from here to home to here, and nowhere else except the places you absolutely need to. Don't talk politics with anyone. Or history, or Citadel gossip."

She nodded. It was good advice, and in other circumstances she would have taken it.

"They might come after me," he said. "I was arrested in the last war. My wife was half-Tazekh. If you come and I'm not here, get the hell out. Go as far south as you can."

"What if it wasn't the Tazekhs? What if it was the resistance?"

His sigh was as expressive as an oration. He said, "Karolje's going to tear this city apart looking for those arsonists. It doesn't matter who set the fire, he needs someone to target and he'll take anyone who crosses his path. It's far better for you to err on the side of caution. Do you want to find out what other things king's men are capable of besides that bruise on your face? Someday they are going to search you, and whatever you are carrying, even if it's nothing, will be enough to put you to the question."

She wished she could confide in him. "I'll be careful," she said.

Then she went into her windowless side room, lit the lamp, and started on routine tasks. There were letters to write, accounts to manage, papers to sort and file. The language of contract and bequest, dispute and appeal, demand and rejection, flowed from her pen with a comforting familiarity. The smell of fresh ink was stronger than the acrid scent of smoke.

As she dripped wax on the flap of an envelope, she remembered Sparrow flipping the coin. Every loss had to be borne by someone. If Karolje wasn't crushed, the people of Karegg would be.

✦ ✦ ✦

It was twilight by the time Anza and Sparrow arrived at a large mansion on the eastern edge of Citadel Island. The mansion was surrounded by a wall at least eight feet high with an ostentatious gate, which was flanked by a pair of tall, narrow boxwoods. A uniformed servant opened the gate for them. The house was pale stone, features indistinct in the dusk. Sculpted bushes loomed around it. Lights were on in all visible windows. Sparrow used the heavy knocker on the door, and they were promptly admitted by another uniformed servant. Standing in the large foyer, Anza heard voices upstairs.

"This way," said Sparrow, leading her out of the foyer and into a wood-paneled drawing room where sat three men and two women. Anza froze in the doorframe. One woman was Irini, her chestnut hair gleaming.

They looked at each other in consternation. There was no animosity between them, but Anza didn't like the thought of someone who knew that much about her being in the resistance. Irini probably felt the same way.

Sparrow said, "We have a new member. Harpy, come forward."

Anza did, trying hard not to bite her lip. She felt about three inches tall. The last time she had been this nervous had been when she first walked onto the College grounds.

Sparrow introduced the others. Irini was called Moth. The men were Jasper, River, and Miloscz, the second woman Apple. Then she said to Anza, "Tell them what you've done."

"I—" She cleared her throat and started over. "I killed three soldiers during a raid. I got away."

Miloscz said, "Prove it." He was dressed expensively, hair pulled back in a rich man's tail. His manner said that he was used to power. She wondered why he used a real name.

"I can't," she said, her nervousness dropping away as she engaged. "But I will swear by anything you like."

"Cocky, aren't you."

Sparrow said, "Are you challenging my decision, Miloscz?"

The silence lasted long enough to be uncomfortable. Then the man said, "No."

"Good." She looked at River. "She's your student. Leave your bag here, Harpy. Go with him."

River stood. He was in his middle thirties, tall and lean with reddish-brown hair tied back with a blue cord. A scatter of freckles across his nose and cheeks gave his face a mischievous charm. He shook her hand.

They left the room and descended a narrow staircase to a wine cellar. The air was cool. River reached up and moved his hand at the top of one of the racks. The rack swung open, revealing a closet bristling with weaponry. Swords, bows, a few pikes. Anza drew in breath. He took a quiver and bow from the closet and handed Anza the bow. It fit her well and was much lighter than the bow her father had given her. The wood was well carved and beautifully polished.

"This isn't a hunting bow," she said.

"It's the same as is used to train the lords' sons for war when they're boys. The range is longer and the arrow faster. Get comfortable with it here before we go outside."

"Shooting in the dark?"

"That's when you're most likely to be working," he said.

The reality of what she was undertaking bore down on her. She spent ten or so minutes holding the bow at various angles from various positions, checking the tension of the string, nocking the blunt-head arrows. She practiced tossing it from hand to hand, slinging it over her back and shoulder, stringing and unstringing it.

"You know what you're doing, I'll grant you that," said River after a while. "Come along." They went back up and along a corridor. He removed the heavy bar from a door at the end and swung it open inward. Rivets on metal bands caught the light. It had gone full dark. The air drifting in was sweet with night blossoms and grass.

At the back of the house, a long lawn sloped gently downward. Garden beds and hedges were dark features to either side. A stone path split the lawn lengthwise, ending in a small round pavilion with a stand of trees behind it. The lake lay beyond, a sheet of black. Frogs croaked near the water. The only light came from the stars.

"There's a statue in the center of the pavilion," River said. "Can you make it out?"

"Yes," Anza said. It was too dark and distant for her to tell whom it was a statue of, but the stone was light-colored, and she saw the head, the bent arm, the angle of the hips.

River handed her the quiver. She adjusted the strap and checked her reach. She had no hope of hitting the statue. River had to know that. It was not her ability to hit the statue that was being tested.

"There are ten arrows," he said. "Shoot them as fast as you can without stopping between them. On my mark. Go."

Her first two shots were clumsy, her third smoother. With the fourth she found her rhythm, and the last six arrows left the bow cleanly and forcefully.

"How are we going to find them?" she asked. River hadn't brought a light.

"Not so fast. Your speed was good, but you drifted. Your shoulder turned in and your elbow out on those last two." He put one hand on her shoulder and the other around her forearm. She tensed at the first touch, but relaxed herself as he adjusted her positioning. "Feel that?"

"Yes." She did, an uncomfortable tension as her muscles

aligned unfamiliarly. She remembered her father saying, *Bring your shoulder back.*

"Draw and release ten more times. Keep the elbow where it belongs."

She obeyed. Twice her elbow moved outward and she corrected it.

"Now," he said, "put the bow down, then take your stance and hold it while I get the arrows."

It was easy at first. She watched him moving smoothly through the grass, bending now and then. He had three arrows in his hand when the strain started in her extended left arm. Then her right shoulder. She evened her breath. In, out. In, out. Her bent elbow was shaking. She tightened her leg muscles. Breathe. She imagined the air spreading beyond her lungs to the rest of her body, strengthening the tendons in her wrist, buoying up her arm.

An itch developed below her shoulder blades. This should not be so hard, damn it. All she was doing was standing still. Breathe. Her right shoulder twitched. Her jaw tightened with resolve, and she forced herself to relax it.

Grass beneath her, and dirt, and below that rock. Rock would hold her up. The earth pulled relentlessly at her. Lifting a foot was like separating iron from magnet. When she fired an arrow, the same forces pulled at it. There was no escape, not even through speed. The arrow would strike anything in its way, but it could not win the war with earth.

She wanted to shake her head to clear her thoughts. Doggedly, she kept to her position and started counting with her breath, letting the numbers become meaningless words.

"Good," said River from her left, and she started. Her arms trembled and fell. He continued, "You didn't hold that as long as you think you did, though. You have to get stronger. I have the arrows. Your aim was decent, but your range needs work. Let's try again."

✦ ✦ ✦

He let her quit when she could no longer close her fingers around the bow. Inside the house, bow and arrows put away, she saw that her fingertips were chafed and swollen. It was going to be miserable to use a pen tomorrow. Her arms seemed to weigh as much as she did.

A single lamp lit the unoccupied drawing room. Anza slumped into a chair. After a few breaths she leaned forward to unfasten her sandals. River opened a drawer beneath the window seat and tossed a blanket at her. "I suggest you lie on the floor," he said. "If you fall asleep in that chair, you're going to be stiff as hell come tomorrow, even if you are only about twenty."

"I suppose you get a bed," she said, trying to gather the fortitude to move out of the chair.

He grinned. "If you were a real soldier on campaign, you'd be on the bare ground with hard lumps under you every way you lay."

She was abruptly quite awake. "What the hell do you mean, 'real soldier'?"

His voice went icy. "What do you think I mean? Conscripted, worked to the bone, having watched your comrades get injured, even killed in training, your own body scarred, your superiors insulting you with every breath . . . You're soft, girl, you always will be. Doesn't matter how well you shoot, you're never going to be able to endure a tenth of what a king's man does."

"I know it's not a game!" Anza said. He ignored her and left the room.

She made an obscene gesture at him under the blanket and rearranged herself in the chair. She glowered at the lamp.

"He's right," said Sparrow from the doorway. "And quite wrong, too. There's more to soldiering than brute force, which River knows perfectly well or I wouldn't have him with me. We're not going to get anywhere by hurling ourselves at the Citadel gates. That doesn't mean you don't need a great deal more training."

Anza flushed. "I'm sorry," she said.

Sparrow left the doorway and seated herself in a chair opposite Anza. She leaned forward, elbows on thighs, hands clasped together between her knees. She said, "My father fought in the Tazekh war. He died as the result of an utterly dishonorable decision Karolje made. Many other men died with him. I'm not going to risk everything I've worked for since by trusting any of it to a hotheaded girl who lacks discipline. Moth told me you were once her lover. Is that true?"

"Yes."

"She also said the two of you split because you wouldn't settle into it. You thought she was boring."

"That's not—" She stopped. Her rapidly growing shame said that Sparrow was right. She and Irini had stopped being lovers after only three months because of dissatisfaction Anza was unable to articulate at the time. All she had said was that she didn't think they were giving each other the happiness lovers deserved. She saw now, painfully, that as much as happiness she had wanted novelty.

"I suppose that's true," she said. "I hadn't thought of it that way."

"Do you understand that there is nothing about what we are doing here that is exciting? We spend twenty hours planning something that takes five minutes but has to be done perfectly. With discipline, without spontaneity. There's only room for improvisation if things go wrong. Pray that you never have to improvise. That's what it means to be a real soldier, and it has nothing to do with how many people you've killed or what you want for yourself."

"I see."

"If you have any fantasies that I am going to slip you into the Citadel to put an arrow through the king's heart, get rid of them now. That's not how this is going to work. Clear?"

"Yes."

"Good." Sparrow relaxed. "Now, River said you have a good eye. I can't have you come here every day to practice, so on the days you don't I want you to practice your stance. Make yourself stronger, quicker. You might have to get yourself over a wall or into a coal bin to escape."

"Who are going to be my targets?"

"Karolje's soldiers, for the most part. Occasionally we may need you to do something else in the way of causing a distraction. It won't be for a while yet. We have to be sure you're ready. Come back here the third evening from now. We'll try to get you here every two or three days. Don't come unless you've received a message confirming when to meet. If Miloscz—he owns the place—gets found out, we will have to scatter fast."

"Why do we use his name, then?"

"No one in the resistance works with him except those of us here now. And it's convenient to have one person who can present their real face to the world for tasks involving money. He's too well known in the city to get away with a false identity. Ivanje was the same when he led us."

The lamps, the furnishings, the carpet all spoke of old

wealth. On a side table a porcelain vase held an arrangement of red and yellow hothouse tulips. The room the prince had talked to her in had been sparer than this.

"You said one of our weapons was money," Anza said. "What is gained by destroying warehouses? Who gets hurt?"

"Men who are going to want money from the Crown as soon as their insurers deny the claims. Karolje won't want to pay it. That will set off a round of squabbling. And in the meantime we look stronger." Sparrow looked at the doorway and stood. "Come in, Moth. Teach her as many of the codes as she can remember, and the names."

When she was gone, Irini plopped down cross-legged on the floor. She was thinner than Anza remembered her, her jawline pointed. Her eyes were still the blue-grey that Anza had fallen into years ago. She rested her shapely hands in her lap and said, "Well, here we are. Is it true Rumil threw you out?"

"I'm surprised anyone is gossiping about me. Or is it about Rumil?"

"I still know people from the College who wonder about you. It is mostly about Rumil, though. You could hardly expect people to be quiet given what's happening to his father."

"I suppose not," Anza said. She did not want to admit Rumil had not confided in her. "Anyway, it's true we aren't living together. I didn't want to stay on the conditions he offered. He thought my absences were because I was having an affair. With you, as it happens."

"I trust you set him right?"

"I tried. He wasn't paying attention. If you see him, you have my permission to slander me if he makes things difficult."

"He would think I was angry because you had left me again," said Irini.

Anza said, "He lacks imagination. Not in bed, in life. I stayed about six months too long. I'm ready to swear off all lovers for a while. I hope you aren't having troubles."

"Didn't you know? Soldiers took Velyana. She's Disappeared." A hardness to her voice that was the covering for pain.

"What?" Anza said. "When did this happen?"

"Eight months ago. I came home one day and she was gone. The neighbors said she had been taken as a traitor. There was blood on the floor. That's why I joined the resistance. The house of Kazdjan is an evil thing that ruins everything it touches, and we have been living under them for far too long."

"Oh gods, Irini, I'm sorry." Velyana was either dead or locked away in the king's prison in the mountains, suffering. "Do you need help with the business? Radd is very good at contracts."

"It's not the contracts, it's the bribes. I have to pay the watch, and the docking fee collectors, and the wagon drivers. There's a new tax on some of the things I use for the scented candles, and I pay twice, once in taxes to the Crown when I buy and once in bribes to the merchant I buy from to keep the ingredients in supply for me. That goes to the Crown too, I suppose. The sellers don't seem to be as wealthy as they should be if they're charging everyone this much. They have to find ways to make money too."

That explained Nikovili's smuggling. Anza wondered what Karolje did with the money. It was not being put toward the upkeep of the city, that was evident. Did the king use all his taxes for his army? Did he hide the money away like a miser so that he could dribble out royal largesse when he needed to? Or was it spent on pleasure, golden plates and the best musicians and bottles and bottles of Tashikian wine?

"At least I'm not Tazekh," Irini added. "They have to pay a

tax just for living in the city. It's getting harder for any of them to have a business at all."

"You would think they'd want to be part of the resistance," Anza said.

"It's much too dangerous. They wouldn't trust us, and we wouldn't trust them. Our fight isn't theirs."

"What do you mean?"

"We're his people. They're outsiders. When we knock Karolje from the throne, they still will be." Irini shifted her position. "I used to think I could never kill anyone. But if you gave me a knife and a chance at the king, I'd do it. Not just for Velyana's sake. He's rotted the entire country. Before I started at the College, my grandfather told me how they used to come into Karegg for a few days, him and my grandmother, and they would shop and go to the theater and pay for a pleasure ride on the lake, and that was how things were. They trusted the soldiers they saw. I can imagine it, the actors and the boat and the ridiculous hats my grandmother liked to wear, and I feel like that's a dream we'll never get back. So I would kill him for that too."

Anza had seen engravings of Karegg fifty years ago, men and women in splendid dress outside theaters and concert halls. Now the theaters staged dull plays approved first by the Crown, their audiences scant and subdued. Irini was right. That was a loss. Like Rukovili's poems, which had nothing to do with sedition but were banned because of the poet's other words. Karolje forbade art and beauty because they invoked a world that was better.

She was getting tired. She rolled her shoulders back, trying to loosen them, and yawned.

Irini said, "There's a room upstairs for late nights. I'll be sleeping there. You can use one of the empty beds if you want. No one will bother you."

The rug was thick, and there were cushions tucked in the corners of the small sofa. "I'll be fine here," Anza said, rising to collect the cushions. "I think if Sparrow wanted me to have a bed, she would have offered one."

"On the other hand, she didn't tell me not to offer." Irini stood. "Come on. You can learn the codes in bed as well as you can sitting on the floor."

"Does Sparrow sleep there?"

"No. She has her own room. So does Apple. We all do, this house is huge. Don't worry."

"What about the servants?"

"They know what's happening," Irini said. "Serving Miloscz here is how they have chosen to help us. People don't all fight. They do what they are suited for."

"All right," said Anza, conceding. Then she stopped and swallowed her pride. "Rumil never told me his father was losing money. Everyone else seems to have known. What have you heard?"

"The story is that he is heavily in debt. There's nothing dishonorable about it—he spent too much and had a run of phenomenally bad luck. And I suppose some ignorance. He didn't know what he was doing when he bought the vineyards. The harvest failed."

Her eyebrows went up. Bought the vineyards? Rumil had said nothing about that either. How long had he been keeping secrets? Not that they were any greater than what she had kept from him.

"Rumil came to Radd's to speak to me yesterday," Anza said. "I hope he didn't follow me here."

"It's pretty well guarded. And he was never the kind to climb over the walls, that was you. Did he—Anza, why did you join us? How long have you been in the resistance?"

"Karolje executed my father a few months ago."

"I thought your father was dead."

"We kept it a secret. He was a soldier. He didn't think anyone should know."

"Did Rumil?"

"No. And he has no idea about the resistance. I don't think he was interested enough in me to collect any clues."

No, that wasn't fair to him. Early on there had been many nights where they stayed up late talking, listening, drinking his father's wine. They had loved each other once. That had begun to change last autumn. She had attributed it to the bloom coming off the romance, but that was probably when the money troubles had started. A crop of withered grapes. He had likely been ashamed to tell her.

"Not by then," she amended. "I suppose I wasn't paying much attention to him either."

"At least you could leave."

At least she could leave. That was a grace.

MIRANTHA

HIS FATHER DEAD, Karolje returns from the south after only a year of war, a handful of new favorites with him. The battles will continue in his absence. He comes to her bed his first night back. He is drunk. She has expected it, and she lies quietly while he thrusts into her. His rhythm is nothing like Ashevi's when he is in passion; for Karolje, with her, the act is not about pleasure. When he has finished and she lies sore and silent, he kneels over her and presses her wrists hard into the mattress.

"I'm done with you," he says. "Do you understand? Do you?"

"Yes, my lord."

"You will ask me nothing and obey me in everything. You will come when you are called for and at no other time. When you are with me in public, you will look happy. You are my devoted wife, and if you anger me, I will whore you out to my generals or lords. And if I do that, what will you do?"

Despite herself, she is weeping. "Yes, my lord," she says.

"*What will you do?*"

"Whatever they ask, my lord."

He releases her wrists and gets off the bed. "And you've

been coddling the boys. You're not to be alone with them again. Ever."

She still has enough pride left not to beg. I will kill you for that, she thinks.

He leaves the room. The silence from the antechamber after he shuts the door is ominous. She imagines he is forcing himself on the maids. Then she hears the outer door close, and where the weight of his presence had not crumpled her, the relief of his absence does.

✦ ✦ ✦

Two nights later, she lies in bed waiting for her clock to strike the first hour after midnight. At last she cannot bear the waiting any longer, and she gets up. She puts a robe on over her shift. Sandals on her feet. She lights a candle in a holder and puts out the lamp. A sprig of lavender has fallen from the bunch above the window, and she treads on it. The bitter sweetness of its scent rises.

The maids are asleep in their room. The guard outside her door wants to follow her. She tells him firmly not to. She can see him considering refusal, but something in her face changes his mind. What would he say if he dared to argue? That the queen—because she is the queen now—is not safe in her own Citadel?

Esvar's room is above hers. She walks along the corridor and up the stairs. His door is guarded and unlocked. Inside, his nurse sleeps in her alcove. The boy lies on his own bed, covers a tangle, face smooth, lips pouting a little. He is still so young.

"Esvar," she says. "Vasha." He rejected the childhood nickname a year ago. She leans over and kisses him. He doesn't stir.

Through the Citadel and out to the gardens. She takes her sandals off and carries them in one hand while her feet enjoy the cool flagstones of the path. Bright stars shine down. In the distance, far away but clear in the night's quiet, the Temple bells toll one.

She passes under a trellis into the inner section of the garden. The fountains are shut off for the night. In daytime she can see the reflection of a nearby gazebo in the garden pools, but tonight the water is black and still, throwing nothing back. She stands a long time looking at the silky surface. That would be another way out, but she is not in enough despair to take it.

She hears a movement in the grass, and then her name. Tensing, she turns and sees Nihalik. This meeting was his idea, and the suggestion of it left a taste of fear in her mouth. Karolje has forbidden them to speak. She is safe from Asps or traitors, but not from her husband. Karolje has chosen Ashevi to replace him as the boys' tutor, and Nihalik has been sent away. He will leave at dawn.

He is not usually courtly, but this time he bows and says, "My lady." His silvered hair looks ghostly in the starlight.

Bitterly, she wishes it were Ashevi who had been dismissed. Not Nihalik, who has been her safety. She is afraid of what Ashevi will teach her boys instead: harshness, arrogance, domination. He likes power. She hates herself for being drawn to him.

Nihalik offers her a small book, a sealed packet of papers, and a letter. She slips them inside her robe. He says, "After you read these papers, destroy them. The book is for you. The letter is for Tevin. Tell him to wait until he is alone to read it. It is better if you do not know what I have told him."

"And Esvar?"

"Tevin will watch him where you can't. And teach him. They are both clever."

Above, an owl hoots, reminding her of that first night she spoke to him after they left Timor. It seems a very long time ago.

"Mirantha, I must warn you. If you continue to have Ashevi as your lover, you will be hurt. He has more influence than he has let you see."

"It's over," she says, dry-eyed. "It must be, with Karolje back."

"He will try to convince you otherwise. Be careful."

It is advice she does not need. She has known since Piyr began to weaken that the affair with Ashevi must end. It would be better if he were not the boys' tutor, but she dared not argue with Karolje. She wondered what he gained by giving Ashevi the post and concluded it was control over his sons. And, because they are her sons too, it is another hold on her.

"Will I see you again?" she asks. She feels as forlorn as a small child.

"If you need to find me, you can. But I won't come back to Karegg while Karolje lives. My queen, don't let anyone convince you that you are not strong." He bows again and turns.

She should say farewell but can't. She watches him walk under the trellis, summer flowers massed and untidy over it, and move out of sight. His footsteps show in the dew. Beyond, the bulk of the Citadel looms. It is all Karolje's now.

In her room, she opens the papers. The first of them is a list of names of people she can call upon for help if she needs it. She wonders about these men and women, lawyers and shopkeepers and carpenters. One is a master in the College. She memorizes their names and addresses, then burns the list. The second paper is a set of instructions about how to reach Nihalik if she needs to. That also she memorizes and destroys.

The book is a small volume of poetry. She pages through it. Lines catch her eye, here and there a stanza or whole poem. The language is beautiful, precise and vivid. The book contains love poems, and reflections, and poems of despair. Sunset-gilded waterfalls and kisses that taste of wine and happiness.

A single phrase strikes her in the heart: *Where lost breaths are swallowed breath by breath*. She reads the poem in whole twice, three times. *Harpies own all twilights*. Yes. The birds of death and loss and vengeance. The twilight realms where shadows might be real, where the eye slips on what it sees, where nothing is certain. The border, the edge, unfixed. That is where she must hide herself. She frees a sprig of lavender from the bunch on the mantel and uses it to mark the page.

She puts out the light and slides back into her bed. Her feet are still cool from the grass. She remembers again that night six years ago. Longing for her home swoops through her painfully, and she closes her eyes. It takes a long time to fall asleep.

✦ ✦ ✦

Karolje apparently issued no other orders regarding Nihalik, because in the morning she gains entrance to his rooms without trouble. She looks at the boys' workbooks, which are all that remain on the shelf. Nihalik took his own books with him.

The books are identical, bound in green leather and stamped in gold with the royal crest. Because of the war, Karolje intends to crown Tevin as his heir during the coronation in a few weeks. She imagines that Ashevi will continue to teach him, but not in the same manner. She opens a drawer and finds another book in Tevin's hand, half of it at least still blank.

With Nihalik gone, there is no one she can say things to. She needs to write, dangerous as it is, to keep herself from festering. If the book is missed, they will think Nihalik took it by mistake. In her room, she puts it on the shelf with her other books. It sits, innocuous, full of potential. The keepsake of a sentimental mother.

The books shelved with it are ones Karolje has said he will ban outside the Citadel. He has already begun to purge the College of the masters he thinks will oppose him. Language is a weapon, learning is a weapon, and he knows it. He can't do anything in the Citadel, where the courtiers have already read the books he wants destroyed, but he can control the rest of the city and much of the nation. He is requiring tutors and clerks and lawyers and the like to have licenses, their books inspected and approved by the Crown. His censors are busy at the College library, separating the approved books from the others.

That afternoon, she is called to a meeting to plan the coronation. Karolje's cousin Goran is there, and a cold-eyed lord named Doru Kanakili, who attached himself to Karolje in the south, and the Hierarch, and Ashevi, and half a dozen others whom Karolje intends to build his reign upon. She would warn them, but they won't listen. She is the only woman.

She looks at Ashevi, not far from Karolje, and sees a pleased smile on his handsome face. He feels more powerful now. She wonders if Karolje knows. She imagines Ashevi quarreling with him, telling him in triumph, *I fucked your wife.* She despises herself for thinking it, for not trusting her lover to keep the secret, for imagining him to be as selfish a man as her husband. Once she has the thought, she cannot get rid of it, and the words beat a constant counterpoint in her mind during the meeting. *I fucked your wife. I fucked your wife.*

* * *

The king replaces all her maids, and she is accompanied everywhere by the gossipy, sharp-eyed wife of Karolje's favorite general. The night before the ceremony there is a celebratory banquet. The food is plentiful and exquisite. Meat sliced almost paper thin, fruits from the far south that must have cost an exorbitant amount to ship without spoiling, four kinds of delicately flavored soup, eight kinds of cheese. Wine, including the rarest pale blue. The plates are gold and silver, and the glassware sparkles and shines.

Twelve years of banquets have given her experience enough in dissimulating, and she laughs at Karolje's jokes and is interested in everyone's conversation. She wears a beautiful flame-colored silk gown and a golden torque that cannot be grabbed and twisted around her neck. As the night wears on, the din becomes overwhelming, and all she has to do is sip wine and nod and smile. None of her family are present; her father is at the front and her brother is in Timor, recovering from a wound. Their mother is caring for him. Or so Karolje said.

When the dancing starts, she asks for and receives permission to leave. Tevin is still at the table. She expects it to be the first of many such nights. There is no keeping him out of Karolje's corrupting influence now.

◆ ◆ ◆

On the way back to her rooms, she encounters Ashevi. He bows. She imagines his mouth on her breasts and is almost felled by the strength of the desire that shoots through her. Her legs are wobbly. She can blame it on the drink.

A guard stands thirty feet or so away, well within earshot. There is nothing to say. She greets him politely and walks on. *I fucked your wife.*

8

DRESSED LIKE A prince instead of a soldier, diamonds sparkling on the collar of a silk shirt, Esvar studied Servos Tashikian while the clerk went through the formalities. They were in the receving room where small private audiences were held. It was carpeted and curtained, softer by far than the throne room. The dais was only a step high, and the gilded ornate chair on it was upholstered with velvet. Several plainer chairs in the room allowed the prince to invite petitioners to sit, but he had no intention of offering one to Tashikian.

Tashikian was a wine merchant of about fifty or fifty-five. His clothes were expensive and well-cut, his greying brown hair sleek and held at the neck with a bronze pin. His eyes were green-gold in an ungentle face, the sort belonging to a man who preferred trampling his opponents to compromising. It must gall him to have to ask anything.

Esvar said, "State clearly your petition or complaint."

Tevin had foisted the hearing off onto him, and he wanted to be done with the business quickly. It was a routine afternoon ritual, and he had already adjudicated the other matters, settling a small part of an inheritance dispute between the two daughters of Lady Katina and issuing a formal order to Lord Nirik to leave the lady he was enamored of alone. It was unusual for a commoner to have been allowed to petition directly; the man must have bribed several people well.

"Your Highness." Tashikian stepped forward to the proper spot and bowed. He said, smooth as a hot knife through butter, "I beg your pardon, my lord, but I had hoped for private words with Prince Tevin."

Of course he had. Tevin would be king. He had seen battle and commanded troops. He brought every eye to himself when he entered a room.

Esvar said, "Not the king?"

"I should be glad to see the king were I invited, but I do not presume to expect it."

You presume a hell of a lot, Esvar thought. He chastised himself for a short temper. He and Jance Mirovian had raided a house the night before, and nothing had gone wrong. At least not from Karolje's point of view. Esvar had sat quietly in his room afterward, drinking one glass after another of good wine. He was not sure how much longer he could keep up the pretense of obedience.

"I sit in His Highness's place with his full authority."

Tashikian inclined his head. "As you know, the warehouse fire destroyed goods worth thousands of marks. Mine were insured, but the insurers are refusing to honor their contracts. Nor am I the only man in this position. Therefore I have come to seek compensation from the Crown."

He was not the first man to come forward about the fire in the two days since it had occurred. The curfew and the soldiers in the streets, the arbitrary searches, the delay in goods entering Karegg, had brought lords and merchants full of complaints to the Citadel. Tashikian was the first man Esvar was aware of, though, who had asked for money. It explained why he had demanded a royal audience.

"Do you speak for the others or only for yourself?"

"Only for myself, my lord. But much of my inventory that was destroyed was intended for the Citadel." Tashikian bowed. "I count the steward here as one of my best customers."

"The problem, sir, is that while the treasury would bear the loss had the wine already been purchased by the Citadel, the risk remained yours. How much was the damage?"

Tashikian told him. It was substantial, but not enough to ruin a man unless he were significantly indebted in other ways. A man who dressed and carried himself like Tashikian did should not be hurt much. Especially if he was selling to the Citadel; the steward was a lavish spender. Good food and good wine kept the nobles happy.

Esvar said, "Do you have a ruling from a magistrate?"

"No, my lord."

"You don't have the standing to petition directly without one. You need a magistrate's ruling against you first." Any lawyer Tashikian consulted would tell him the same. "And in any event, this is a matter for the chancellor. Why are the insurers refusing?"

"My lord, they say the fire was an act of war and therefore outside the contract."

That caught his attention. "Vetia is at peace. What are the grounds for their claim?"

"This." He withdrew a paper from a pocket and held it out to Esvar.

It was a handbill, printed on cheap paper in a mixture of type sizes and artistic flourishes. A rip at the top showed where it had been pulled roughly from a nail. *THE FIRES OF RESISTANCE GROW EVER HIGHER!* it shouted. In smaller print it said, *We will not rest until the traitor Karolje is dead. Join us, or watch Karegg burn!* In the center was a drawing of a sun on the horizon. Rising or setting, it could be either. The rise of the resistance, the fall of the king.

"It was nailed to my door," Tashikian said.

Things are moving, Esvar thought. These bills must have been reported by soldiers and Doru's spies, but no one had seen fit to inform him. Was he under suspicion? Or had the bills been deemed unimportant? If he didn't give an order to go hunt down the printer, would that be seen as incompetence or as treason?

His brother must be beset with such questions, frozen by choices. Esvar was ashamed of his own earlier resentment. Tevin had seen battle, yes, but the cost had been spending all those years at Karolje's side.

He was tempted to theatrically crumple the handbill. All his training told him to send Tashikian away happy with him and furious with the resistance, or to frighten the man enough that he would slink into a corner and lick his wounds. Neither of those impulses helped fight Karolje.

He returned the bill and said, "The Crown bears no responsibility for the acts of vandals. Be glad it's me you're seeing and not the king. I can't award you any compensation. I can set the matter before a magistrate for a prompt hearing so that you don't have to wait months. Nothing else is within my jurisdiction right now. If he rules against you, you may petition again. The chancellor, mind you, not me."

"Yes, my lord," said Tashikian, sounding displeased.

Which was absurd. He would get his money. No magistrate in his right mind would declare a war where the king had not.

Esvar dictated the order and sent Tashikian away with three copies. He dismissed the clerk and guards and leaned back in the chair.

The destruction of a few warehouses was not going to bring down the throne. But the next arson attack might be a mansion or a wharf. Enough arson and other destruction would bring the more influential merchants and their insurers and bankers clamoring to the chancellor. They could not be got rid of so easily as a group as Tashikian had been by himself. Goran would complain of the resistance to the king and the guard captains, who would crack down harder on the citizens of Karegg. What else would happen?

Destruction was costly, both in expenses and in trust. Karolje was good at squeezing blood from a stone, but at a certain point the stone was drained. The minor nobles who were kept placated with generous gifts and lavish feasts would be the first to feel the loss. Something would have to yield to the pressure. And Esvar would damn well take advantage of it when it did.

✦ ✦ ✦

That night, Esvar entered the Citadel's chief salon to the usual minor commotion occasioned by his presence. He settled it with a genial wave and filled a glass for himself with wine. His dark clothing contrasted with the bird-bright finery of the others. Sipping, he looked around. The door to the outside terrace was open, but that had not cooled the room much.

The salon suffocated him with opulence, the parqueted floor made of expensive wood, the furniture gilded, the walls papered with silk. The chandelier contained hundreds of crystals, which winked brightly in the light from beeswax candles. At times when he was a boy he had come into this room alone and lain on a divan, looking up at the plastered ceiling. He had tried to count the thousands of tiny roses that made a border and always lost track.

Several young men moved in on him. Younger sons doomed to living off generous allowances and small inheritances, they glittered with loyalty and obedience while their eyes shone with poorly suppressed ambition. Like Esvar, they were too young to have fought in the Tazekh war, and he doubted any of them had ever killed anyone. These were men he had been a boy with, men whose parties he attended and requests he listened to, but they were not his friends.

He let them talk. That was what he was here for. Every bit of loyalty he could gain mattered. They had fathers and uncles and cousins to be won. And sometimes Citadel gossip was informative.

The women came too, their shoulders bare and smooth, their hair braided and pinned and netted with jewels, their fingers flashing with rings. The younger ones flirted and the older, married ones dropped hints about things they wanted for their husbands. He remembered the woman he had freed from Lukovian, her face bruised and her hands unornamented. At the moment she seemed infinitely more real than the women in the room.

He offered nothing and made no promises. He talked to the nobles Tevin had told him to talk to and tried to find out their allegiances. When Goran's wife, Tahari, came in, he chatted politely with her and mentioned oh so casually that his brother was in need of a wife. Let Goran face the possibility of moving down a step in the succession. Or perhaps she would not pass word on to her husband. She was a particularly hard woman for him to read. She had been one of his mother's handmaids, years ago, and she had taken lessons from what happened to Mirantha. He could tell that her cheerful friendliness was an act, but he had no idea what lay beneath it.

He had been in the salon, which was increasingly loud and stultifying, for about an hour when he saw Lord Darvik making his way determinedly toward him. A memory of Jance Mirovian staring at the gable of the abandoned house flashed through his mind. Whatever the lieutenant was hiding, Darvik might know.

He greeted the lord and said, "Let's step outside, where it's not so beastly hot." He knew this would bring some attention to Darvik from people who wondered why the prince had withdrawn with him. It could not be helped. He needed to be able to think.

The terrace was on the north side of the Citadel, overlooking the black waters of the lake. The surrounding mountains were a different shade of darkness against the starry sky. Esvar turned his back on this romantic vista and stood in front of the terrace wall, which rose to his waist. His eyes moved left along a row of dark windows until they came to one that was lit with the flicker of a fire in a hearth. Karolje was cold even in summer.

There were other people on the terrace, talking, laughing, but Esvar and Darvik had room enough to be private. The stone had released the last of the day's heat, and its coolness was a sweet breath after the crowded salon. A moth fluttered around the lamp by the doorway.

Esvar said, "Is Jeriza here, Darvik?" He kept his voice low, even though it was unlikely they could be overhead.

"No, my lord, she stayed home. She was unwell." There was a hint of question in the words. Esvar could imagine the rush of fear; what did Karolje's son want with his wife? Like her husband, Jeriza was popular with the younger nobles.

"I hope she improves," he said. "There's a matter I want to speak to you about, but you had something to ask me?"

The lord visibly took a breath. He was broad-shouldered,

bearded, and thirty. He said, "It's a passing thing. She will be lively as usual by tomorrow." He reached into a pocket and withdrew a piece of paper. "I wondered, my lord, if you had seen this."

It had to be the handbill from the resistance. Esvar unfolded it enough to see that his guess was correct. "I have. How did you come by it?"

"A man I know brought it to me. He said he had seen dozens of them."

Esvar refolded it and put it back in his own pocket. "If anyone else brings you one, destroy it," he said. "Though I expect word is all around the city by now. Has your friend lost money from the fire?"

"Not him. But I've heard of others. Everyone is blaming someone else. The magistrates and lawyers will be busy."

"The Crown's not going to pay."

"So I imagined," said Darvik. He paused and looked lakeward. Then he faced Esvar and said, "It has me wondering if my money might be more secure in Mirsk or Traband, though. Even if only a quarter of the items stored were insured, that might be more than the banks have to pay out." He could not be the only person having such thoughts.

If the banks in Karegg failed, the lords would turn on the chancellor and the king. The Crown had no legal responsibility for the banks, but it would be blamed, because kings were always blamed, because the resistance had not been suppressed. The merchants would follow in discontent. Behind them, the workers who were no longer paid. Debts would be called in for collection from people who could not pay. The already high tension in the city would escalate.

Someone in the resistance had a good understanding of both

politics and economics. But had they thought through to the next inevitability, in which Karolje increased his force against the people of the city? In which trust between citizens degraded even further?

"How much money do you have in banks in Karegg?" Esvar asked. "Including what is not in the tax records."

Darvik hesitated, looked around, answered. He was wealthier than Esvar had thought.

Esvar said, "Withdrawing money from your bankers in Karegg is one of the things the resistance wants. It might be made illegal if these attacks continue. If you're going to do it, you had better do it soon. You should make sure your friends know the situation before they make a decision on whether or not to do the same." Anyone who got money out before the banks failed was at a great personal advantage, and that could easily be reframed as treason.

"Some of them are anxious, merchants and nobles both. Very anxious."

A woman shrieked with laughter in the group of people at the corner. Their voices were loud. Esvar was torn between anger and envy at the frivolity. He hadn't been so carefree in months. Beside him, Darvik shifted his weight.

Esvar said, "If your friends need any reassurance about their funds, they should approach the chancellor, not me. My immediate concerns right now are military, not financial."

"I don't think my friends will be expecting reassurance. They can see the landscape as well as any of us."

A landscape in which violence spiraled outward, growing more powerful as it went. In which the best policy was escape. Quite abruptly, Esvar could not endure any more pretense. Tevin trusted this man. He would do the same.

He said, "I'm not going to try to persuade you that your fears are groundless. I do suggest you be very careful. My brother needs loyalty. Does he have yours?"

"Yes, my lord."

"Even over Karolje?"

Darvik's silence lasted longer than any yet. Esvar firmly kept his eyes on the lord's face instead of letting his gaze go to the water, the other people, the king's window. A loon called from somewhere out on the lake.

"Yes," Darvik said.

The words hung a moment, weighty. A pact. What a strange and twisted world it was where avowing loyalty to the heir to the throne could be dangerous.

"When Tevin's king, he won't forget who helped him," Esvar said. "Nor will I. But he can't rescue you if you jump ahead of him. Don't do anything precipitous. He's got me tied down too."

"That's probably what my younger sister used to think of me," said Darvik. "What was the other matter, my lord?"

"I'm about to rely heavily on your cousin. If that's a mistake, I need to know now, before he gets into a situation he can't get out of. I won't tell him anything you say."

"He's bright, and when he makes a promise, he keeps it. He's not slipshod."

"Is he truthful?"

"So far as I know, yes," said Darvik. "But he's my cousin, not my brother. I haven't lived with him."

"What was he like when he was at the College? Did he do well?"

"He did well in his studies. Early on he had a tendency to break the rules and got in a few scrapes, but he settled. He always had friends."

"He's hiding something from me. Do you have any idea what it might be?"

Darvik looked surprised. "Not at all, my lord. It likely seems much more important to him than it actually is. He wouldn't be doing anything disloyal."

But with whom do his loyalties lie? Esvar thought. It was no use asking Darvik that, so he said only, "Thank you."

Darvik nodded. Esvar dismissed him with a gesture. He looked at the lake and then, with deliberation, back at the Citadel. If Karolje died tonight, he would be the heir, one knife stroke away from the throne. He still could not see how things would play out. Would Goran let Doru move first, then claim the crown himself when the princes were eliminated? Would Doru try to remove Goran before going after Tevin? Were there resistance spies in the Citadel who would do something utterly unexpected?

He stood for a few moments longer, readying himself for the crowded room, then went back into the salon. It was as noisy and bright as it had been earlier, and he went to get another glass of wine. While he was waiting for the servant to pour, he looked around and saw Doru. The spymaster was watching him.

Esvar had no intention of provoking Doru. But he could not let the man get away with witholding information from him either. He took the wine from the servant, had a deep enough swallow that he was unlikely to spill anything while walking, and made his way through the crowd to Doru.

When Esvar was close enough, the spymaster said, "My lord." His voice was just on the acceptable edge of mockery. The people standing nearby quieted. They smelled blood.

Esvar switched the wineglass to his other hand and removed the handbill from his pocket. He slapped it against Doru's chest and let go of it.

"Next time, tell me," he said, and walked away.

He did not look back. Doru was much too disciplined to follow. His response would come later, in some more subtle form. In the meantime, enough people had now seen the handbill that it could not be kept a secret. The resistance's growing strength was no longer invisible.

✦ ✦ ✦

He returned to his workroom and, late though it was, sent for Jance Mirovian. The time had come to confront the man about his secret. While he waited, he read the routine reports that his clerk had left for him at the end of the day. He paused over the list of arrests by the watch, read it carefully instead of shuffling it aside as usual.

With the sense of bringing doom upon himself, he circled three of the names and wrote beside them *RELEASE*. A woman who had no charges laid against her, a man who had lingered suspiciously near the docks, a man who had been staggering drunkenly and railing against the king. For all Esvar knew, the three were vile criminals and deserved to be arrested. But not based on what the report said. Justice was not justice if it was applied only to the people one approved of or liked.

He wrote an order laying out the same names, confirming their release, and requiring the other arrests to be set before a magistrate within three days. He put his seal below his name and set the documents aside for the clerk to copy in the morning.

Then he closed his eyes and breathed deeply. He did not

think the act made ripples big enough to come to anyone else's notice. He felt small and terrified anyway.

When the lieutenant arrived, Esvar gestured for him to take a seat. Mirovian obeyed with the attentively blank face of a soldier awaiting orders. He was good at it.

"You were hell on your minders as a child, weren't you?" Esvar said.

"Sir?"

"You broke rules and played pranks and got away with it. How did you end up in the Guard?"

"I didn't want to take orders from my father about bales of cloth and bills of lading."

"Understandable. You did well last night." He tipped back slightly in his chair and folded his arms. "The resistance is getting stronger, and that means the raids are going to get more complicated. I can't let you lead them on your own if you're keeping secrets. I have to be able to trust you. You aren't telling me something you thought of when we went to the house where my raid failed. Out with it, even if it's speculation."

"There's nothing, sir. There was a lot to think about."

Mirovian's voice was steady, his gaze direct, but his body had tightened. He was lying. He was protecting someone.

The only person to protect was the resister who had got away. Esvar wanted to let her go. But he couldn't let Mirovian lie to him. And if Mirovian knew her identity, was he tied to the resistance? This had to be untangled.

"You're lying," Esvar said softly. "Who was she? I'm not going to send the hellhounds after her."

"Not a resister, sir." He swallowed. "We talked about Captain Havidian, sir. I knew his daughter."

Esvar had expected anything but that. Havidian had not

been married. Bastard children were not uncommon, but the captain had never played the rake. It was an incongruity in Havidian. Incongruities weren't supposed to happen. When they did, if you pulled at them you often learned interesting things.

"Tell me about her."

The man's lips formed but did not say *Why?* "He brought her here to study at the College. That's where we met. I think the captain must have had hopes that she would be able to marry up. Her family was too poor for her to meet wealthy men any other honorable way."

"Too poor to marry up but not too poor to attend the College? Never mind." That explained why Havidian had lived with much less luxury and entertainment than other men of his rank and pay. "Did it work?"

"I don't think it's what she wanted, sir. She wasn't married the last time I saw her."

"What does she do?"

"I don't know, sir. I haven't seen her since we left the College."

That was an evasion, and not a very good one. "And you thought of her when we were at the house because we were talking about her father? No other reason?"

"None, sir."

"Why didn't you tell me this then?"

"It didn't seem relevant, sir. She wasn't there. He's dead."

True, but . . . Mirovian was saying *sir* too much. Havidian's daughter mattered to him. Was he in love with the girl? Havidian had been a handsome man; his daughter was likely pretty. Or perhaps not. Mirovian's air had a tinge of nervousness to it that Esvar associated with guilt rather than uncertain love affairs. Why the hell did the man feel guilty about knowing a soldier's daughter?

Havidian was safely, quietly dead. Investigating him served no purpose. Any information that did turn up was much more likely to strengthen Karolje than Tevin. Let the dead lie.

He failed to convince himself. "It might not be relevant to us," Esvar said, "but it is to her. The Crown took his money, thinking he had no heirs. She's entitled to it."

The first surprise on Mirovian's face. "But he was executed, sir! And she's illegitimate."

"He was executed for error, not treachery. There's no attainder. The legitimacy, yes, that's an issue, but not a large one. She's not dispossessing anyone but the Crown, and what the Crown takes, the Crown can return."

Mirovian said nothing.

"I'll give it to her myself," Esvar said, to see what happened. "Find her."

"That will take a while, sir, unless I'm released from other duties."

"If she was at the College, the College will know where to start looking. Don't let them make you into a spy, Lieutenant. Your face is much too expressive."

There was an awkward silence. Then Mirovian gave in, but only a little. "I don't think she will come to the Citadel willingly. I can bring her the money." That had taken courage—or desperation—to say. The fiction that the Citadel was safe for the innocent was one of the things that kept the kingdom running smoothly.

Esvar had no desire to frighten the woman further, or to call attention to her. Let her home stay unrevealed. Doru's spies didn't need to know more than they would through following Esvar. Giving the money to Mirovian was the best thing to do.

But by now his curiosity was aroused. "Her father's house,"

he said, drawing a sheet of paper toward himself. "In two days. If I give it to her, I can swear to its provenance if she's questioned. I'll send you off with her afterward, to ensure that the money gets safely where it should. What's her name?"

"Anza Istvili."

The name tickled him with familiarity he could not place. It was ordinary enough; perhaps he had met some other woman who shared it. He wrote quickly, just a few sentences, signed and sealed it, and handed the note over to Mirovian. The soldier held it carefully, as though it were breakable.

Esvar said, "Take that to her tomorrow, first thing, and get her response."

"What if she refuses?"

"You would be surprised at the amount of fear money can overcome."

"Sir, she's one of the least bribable people I've ever met."

Esvar said, "This isn't a bribe. There's not a damn thing I want from her." He picked up one of the chess pieces and turned it in his hand. "If you are anything less than honest with her, or misguidedly try to keep her from coming, I will be displeased."

Mirovian hesitated. "I understand, sir."

The hesitation might mean he was tempted to disobey. It would be easy enough to lie, to say he couldn't find her or that she had left the city. Deliberately, Esvar dropped the pawn. Mirovian's head snapped up at the noise. He looked alarmed.

Esvar said, "I give you my word that I won't hurt her. If she truly won't come, don't force her, but I'm not going to make the offer of her father's money again. Send the guard in on your way out."

He gave orders, and soon a servant brought him a box containing Captain Havidian's personal belongings. There was not much: a miniature painting of King Piyr, a handsome glass vase, a pocket watch, a bone-handled razor, finely carved. Three books. Curious, Esvar removed them from the box.

The first was a well-known treatise on the art of war, the second a collection of holy writings. The third was small, fitting easily in one hand. Sickening recognition of it rose through Esvar like a bubble and broke the surface of his denial. It had been his mother's. He remembered the golden symbols tooled in the cover. They had always been mysterious.

Another copy, he thought. That's all. Rukovili had been a popular poet before he was convicted of treason and his works destroyed shortly after Karolje assumed the throne. He opened it.

On the first page was the inked impression of the queen's seal.

Had Havidian been one of the men who killed her?

The thought shook his faith in his own judgment. If he was wrong about Havidian, how many other things was he wrong about?

No. If Havidian had killed her, he would not have been stupid enough to steal a book from her that was unlawful to possess. For the same reason, Mirantha would not have given it to him. It had come into his hands some other way.

His daughter had been at the College. The queen might have sent her books there for safekeeping. A master at the College might have been the one person Karolje allowed to retain control of forbidden texts. Karolje knew how dangerous ideas were, but he was not foolish enough to destroy everything he prohibited. One needed to know what the dangers were.

He traced the circle of the queen's mark. Even if the book had been at the College, what had Havidian's daughter done to acquire it?

What would she do if he gave it back?

Esvar closed the book. He had stepped into something older and perhaps deadly, a tangle of connections that made a shape he could not see. He could let it go—it had no bearing on his other concerns—or he could dig more deeply into the past. There was no question what his brother would say; Tevin's attention was focused on the future.

Damn it. He had to ask her. Likely the girl would know nothing, and that would be the end of the matter, but the puzzle would nag him to the end of his life if he ignored it.

He slipped the book into his tunic pocket. He left the workroom for his private rooms, where he sat in bed and by the light of a single candle read the poems in their entirety. A dry sprig of lavender was placed between two leaves near the end. He left it there. Its faint scent clashed with the poem, which was about loss. An undefinable sadness settled in his body. He did not want to think about what the poem might have meant to his mother.

Finished, he put down the book and blew out the candle. Anza Istvili, he thought. Who are you and what do you have to do with a queen?

9

IT WILL BE fine," said Jance. "If I thought he was going to trap you, I would have told you."

I know, Anza thought in nervous irritation. It was the third time he had said it. Jance was trying to reassure himself, not her, though, so she stayed quiet while he tied the horse. When he had come to Radd's the day before to tell her, he had been furious at himself for having been so transparent to the prince. *I'll go,* she had said, remembering Esvar's face across the desk. She wanted to see him again, to find out if he was the man he had seemed to be when he freed her from the interrogator. She knew she was taking a risk in trusting Karolje's son. But he was also Mirantha's son.

The door to the house fronted the street with only a small stoop. Jance pushed it open and led her in. A thin coat of dust dulled the surfaces. The furniture had all been taken—sold, she presumed—and the cupboards cleared of anything valuable. Her father had kept it tidy and uncluttered, and the only things left to possibly sit on were a wooden pail and a step stool. She doubted the pail would hold her light weight. Dried beans spilled out of a burlap sack that the rats had gnawed into.

The place already had the smell of abandonment and was

uncomfortably hot. Anza opened two of the dirt-dulled glass windows, which helped. Then she went back out to wait on the stoop. Beside her, Jance tapped his fingers on his thigh. The stoop was in the shadow of the house, cooler yet than the air. Across the street, the sun struck gold on the small, well-made houses. A few large and ancient oaks towered over the buildings on either side.

"Here they come," said Jance. Horses trotted loudly on the cobbles. Five of them, sleek, beautiful beasts. She knew next to nothing about horses, but even she could tell that these were well-bred and costly. One might be worth more than her aunt's cottage. The riders, including the tall young man in the center, wore uniforms with the same badge she had seen on Esvar's captain, a silver wolf on the sleeve. The dark-skinned captain himself was one of the riders. Somehow that was reassuring.

They pulled up a short distance away, and the prince dismounted smoothly. "Sir," Jance said in a deferential tone she had never heard from him.

She had time to observe the startled recognition on Esvar's face before he schooled his features. "You," he said evenly to her. She heard Jance's intake of breath, quickly cut off. Doubtless he would lay into her afterward for not telling him she had met the prince before.

"My lord," she said, wary. She was unsurprised to be known, though she had hoped the prince would not remember her well enough.

In daylight he was extraordinarily handsome. Dark-haired, dark-eyed, skin fair under its sun-browning. Taller than she had thought from seeing him behind his desk; the top of her head did not come to his shoulders. He wore a knife but otherwise was not openly armed.

"Mirovian."

"Sir?"

"Stand guard out here. We'll go in. We might be a while."

Jance's eyes flicked to Anza, and she nodded very slightly. She hoped the prince did not notice his soldier asking her for permission. She would not have said that she felt *safe* with Esvar, because he was not a safe man, but she did not fear physical violence.

Jance held the door open and closed it behind them. The room became much dimmer. Esvar said, "Why didn't you tell me you were Havidian's daughter?"

"I beg your pardon, my lord, but it didn't seem wise to admit to being related to a man who had been executed."

His hand curled into a fist, then opened, fingers spread. His only jewelry was a seal ring on his ring finger. "Of course. I withdraw the question."

She wanted to say, *Give me the damn money and go away!* She wasn't that reckless yet.

"Did you lie to me about Nikovili?"

"If I had, I wouldn't be here."

He took two measured steps toward her and stopped. They were not close enough to touch. He could have sent Jance with the money. Esvar wanted to see her himself, and it had nothing to do with their prior meeting. What was it?

He said, "I know you would rather have your father than his money. If I had been able to prevent his death, I would have. He was a good man and a good soldier."

To her shame, tears filled her eyes. Her heart hurt. She blinked the tears back and said, in a voice she was pleased was steady, "Thank you, my lord."

He had a leather pouch slung across his chest. He removed it and laid it on the floor. "He never owned this house," he said, "and the money from selling his furniture was not accounted for. But in here is all the money he had saved and the pay he was owed when he died. I have also included the cost of his commission."

Cost of his commission made it all final. Looking at the floor, she bent over to pick up the pouch. It was heavy. In one graceful motion she stepped backward and straightened. She sniffed mightily.

He produced a handkerchief from a pocket. "It didn't occur to me that it would be so dusty," he said, offering it to her.

It was silk. The tips of their fingers brushed as she took it. She blew her nose and dabbed at her eyes. Then she did not know what to do with it. Returning a used handkerchief to a prince was vulgar. Dropping it would be an insult. His hands were long-fingered, graceful, the nails neatly trimmed. She was sure they had been bloodied in many a killing.

"Keep it. Open the pouch, please."

The coins at the bottom were obscured by a book. She removed it, knowing what it was. The book of poems she had stolen from the College library. The book that had belonged to the queen. She could not help also looking at the money, much more than she had expected. Enough to leave Karegg and live comfortably for a year before she had to find occupation.

"Rukovili," she said. "It's banned, my lord. I can't own it." She held it out to him. It had been his mother's. His mother's. He had to know that. What did he mean by giving it back to her? It was a message she did not have enough clues to interpret.

"Your father had it. You've seen this before. You didn't even have to look inside to know what it was. Where did it come from?"

"It doesn't matter. It's not mine."

"I want you to have it."

"If I am arrested again for possessing it, will you release me?" Her voice was raw with sudden resentment, and she half expected him to strike her.

He stepped forward and took the book out of her hand, slipped it back into the pouch. His eyes slid briefly over the healing cut on her palm. "Destroy it if you feel unsafe. I think it has value worth the risk."

It's not your risk, she thought. He didn't know what risk was. She bowed. She wasn't brave enough to oppose him. Submit and wait to be dismissed.

He went to the nearest window and closed it. "Sit down," he said. "I'm sorry all we have is the floor."

She obeyed, irked. He wasn't the host. This was her father's house. He closed the second window and sat opposite her, legs crossed. Seated, he did not seem so tall. The disturbed dust made her sneeze.

Esvar said, "Do you want to know about your father?"

That was what Sparrow had asked. "Yes."

"He was assigned to capture one of the leaders of the resistance, a man named Ivanje Stepanian. In the process, Stepanian was killed. That was an error Karolje could not tolerate."

"Did my father kill him?"

"No. It was one of his men. But a captain is responsible for the mistakes of those under him."

A mistake. Another man's carelessness had killed her father. She felt as sick as she had when she had come to this house and seen the king's Mark on the door. It was more painful than if her father had deliberately defied the king. At least then his death might have bought something.

"Was there anyone who might have wanted my father dead?"

"If you're asking whether he was set up, the answer is no. The soldier paid with his life too. Nor was anything found giving either your father or the soldier a reason to want Stepanian dead. They haven't been tied to the resistance. It was an accident."

"It's not just," she said, like a child.

"Justice is not much valued in the Citadel," he said, which sent a shiver down her back. Those were treasonous words.

She looked at the closed door. They were sealed in against the rest of the world. Against the Citadel. Against the king. Her anger slid aside. They weren't allies, they could never be allies, but he was resisting Karolje in his own way.

She had not intended to tell him, but the words fell out. "My lord," she said, "you asked what the interrogator did to me. He tried to strangle me with his belt." Her hand tugged at the neckline of her shirt as she remembered the leather pulling against her neck.

"He's in prison," Esvar said, grim-faced.

"For that?"

"I reprimanded Lukovian for his treatment of you. He turned the reprimand around by starting a rumor that I collaborated in and profited from Nikovili's smuggling. That was treason."

"Was he really that stupid?" she asked.

His eyebrows went up. She supposed it had been an unusually bold question. He said, "He misjudged a political situation. In other circumstances, he might have come out on top."

"Accusing you?"

"When there's room for only one, the competition can get fierce. What is said in the city about the king's health?"

"Nothing, my lord," she said, startled by the turn in the conversation.

"He's dying."

Her first thought was that the resistance needed to know. Her second was that Esvar had a reason for telling her. It couldn't be to win her to his side; she had nothing to give him. Had she somehow become the empty vessel into which he poured his secrets? Or was he playing some more layered game she couldn't comprehend?

She said, "So your brother will be king?"

"Not easily. The men who have power under Karolje are not going to yield it. Lukovian was trying to leap ahead, that's all. When the king dies, all hell is going to break loose in the Citadel. From there, it will spread. There's a good chance of war."

"War? Not a quick bloody battle in the Citadel?"

Another surprised glance. "They didn't teach you to ask that kind of question in the College. But yes. Whoever wins, someone else will try again. It could go on for years."

The thick, breezeless air was stifling. She would take this back to Sparrow, and Sparrow would do what? Call for an uprising? Go to ground and wait to see who won?

He said, "When this happens, I will be in no position to offer you or anyone else protection. I'd advise you to leave the city, but I think I would be wasting my breath."

"I don't need protection."

"Oh?" His tone mocked her.

She held back her own bitter response. He was right, of course; she would be dead without him.

He said, "If Karolje finds out about you, you'll be in danger."

"I'm not a threat, my lord," she said. Not yet. "My father

told me very little about what he did. There is nothing I could use against the Crown."

"You were your father's secret. That is inherently a threat. It's disloyalty. Even if no one knows it but you, me, and the king. He won't arrest you or harass you, but you'll open your door one evening and a man with a garrote will be waiting inside."

"But why?" They had leaned closer to each other, lowered their voices in conspiracy.

"Once Karolje takes it into his head that someone has hurt him, opposed him, lied to him, he will drive that person into the ground, even if it is someone so insignificant as a baker's apprentice. I've seen it many times."

The statement chilled her more than anything else he had said so far. His brown eyes were dark, intent. Not angry or frightened, some other emotion she could not identify. She wanted to trust him, but she had been in Karegg too long. Five years of shrinking away from soldiers, five years of seeing accused traitors hung, stood between her and the prince. Locks and swords and chains everywhere. The constant sound of soldiers patrolling the College grounds. The knowledge sealed away in the library. Once the man who kept a shop across the street from Radd had been taken away and was returned missing a hand.

With his finger, Esvar drew a triangle in the dust, circled it. He said, "Karolje hasn't succeeded in vanquishing everyone who hates him. He has driven their hate into deep hiding, though. He's been king for fifteen years. Opposition from the nobles sputtered out within the first year of his reign. Living in the Citadel is like picking your way through broken glass, day after day after day. It's exhausting."

His eyes were fixed on her. He knows, she thought. He has

put it together. There was nothing of proof, unless he brought her to the Citadel and confronted her with one of the resisters who had been arrested. They would keep one alive for that purpose.

"My lord," she said, "you had no reason to keep me from being questioned. You had no idea who I was. Why did you interrupt it?"

"Because I'm not him, damn it."

The intensity frightened her. She had touched a raw wound. "I'm sorry," she said, and then thought how *odd* it was to apologize to a prince, to have an ability to hurt him. He was only a few months older than her, but he wore power confidently. She had not guessed the shield had a crack.

"Let me tell you something. I warn you that it's ugly."

I don't want to hear it, she thought. Her mouth would not say the words.

He said, "The first time I killed a man, I was thirteen. They told me he was a Tazekh spy and gave me a spear to run him through with. He was chained to a wall. I was tall then, but not as strong as a man. I didn't think I could do it cleanly. But I had to. He was a traitor and the king was watching, along with all his generals. So I ran at him and speared him in the gut and then cut his throat with my knife. They cheered, and took me away and got me drunk. I don't remember much after that." He was calm. "The next day Tevin told me the man hadn't been guilty of anything. He'd been an ordinary Tazekh plucked off the streets to be my first kill, and I was an ordinary murderer."

She knew he had killed, but this was real. Specific. She felt dirty. "Then what happened?"

"Nothing. Everyone had what he wanted. Tevin was starting to push back against Karolje by then, so the king was hoping he could train me to be his replacement. That was the first step. Unfortunately for the king, I didn't prove to be any more pliable than my brother. But that's the kind of deceiver Karolje is. He finds a lie that will make the hideous more palatable. You have to remember that when you're talking to anyone in his sway. No one wants to hear the truth."

"And you?"

"I don't like being lied to," he said. "Or used. Neither does my brother. My goal is to see Tevin on the throne. It would be easy were I to imitate Karolje. Do me the courtesy of assuming I still have a soul." He stood.

Flushing, she scrambled to her feet. There were a dozen things she wanted to ask and did not have the courage for.

"Mirovian will take you home," he said, "or to wherever you want to put the money for safekeeping." He turned and in four long paces was at the door. He put his hand on the knob, paused, looked over his shoulder. "Your father served me better than he knew. Don't ruin it by being careless." He jerked the door open and went out. Light flooded in behind him.

Jance stepped in, much too soon. "Are you all right?"

"Yes," Anza said. She felt knocked on the head by the last things Esvar had spoken. "It was not what I expected."

"He knew you." He was not able to keep all the accusation out of his tone.

She touched her face where the bruise had been. "I was arrested with one of Radd's clients. The prince freed me. That's all."

"That's all? Anza, that never happens. How the hell did he get involved?"

"I don't know. I think it was Citadel politics." She looked at the triangle the prince had made in the dust. "It was a power move; it didn't have anything to do with me." Esvar's *Because I'm not him* was an answer but an insufficient one.

"You should have told me."

"Would it have changed anything? If he found out you knew about the arrest, he could have found me at Radd's. It was too chancy."

"I would have felt a little safer about the whole thing," he grumbled, without much force. "Did he try to tie you to the raid at all? Or to the resistance?"

"No. He hardly asked me anything." Her thought that he had connected her to the missing archer must have been her fear talking. She had better give Jance enough substance to satisfy him. "He told me some things I did not know about my father. He was kind, considering."

"Considering what?"

"Considering he held all the power. He could have used it as an opportunity to terrify me."

"He's taking a risk, giving you all that money," said Jance. "I'm sure it's legal, but I don't think it was approved. It comes with some damn long strings. If you want to change your mind, I'll take it back."

"If I was going to refuse it, I would have done that to his face. I'm capable of making my own decisions, Jance."

"But are they good ones?" he shot back. "I'm sorry. I'm worried."

"You don't need to be. Not about this, at least. I've been with Radd for two years. I do know something about how the world works."

"Well, for the gods' sakes, don't get reckless."

A board in the house creaked. She bent down and picked up the bag. "Let's go," she said.

They rode to her flat without speaking. Outside the building, he said, "I don't want this to be the last we see of each other, Anza. It's been too long as it is. I'm not on duty all the time."

"It might be dangerous for you," she said.

"I'll take the chance." He wiped sweat off his forehead. "There are times I want to talk to someone about something other than weapons or women or Citadel gossip."

That was as close as he would get to saying he was lonely. "All right," she conceded. "But we have to be careful. And neither of us has much time."

He nibbled on his lower lip. "I'll think of something."

✦ ✦ ✦

Home, she locked the money into her strongbox and sat at the table, head down. She should report to Sparrow. Tell her that there were tensions in the Citadel, that Prince Esvar at least was not aligned with the king. She did not want to. Sparrow would decide he was a weakness to exploit, which was an unfair exchange for the respect he had shown to her.

Damn it, that was what Jance had meant by strings. She was supposed to use anything she could against Karolje. She was letting herself be swayed by a false intimacy, by the respect Esvar and his power paid to her father. If the situations were reversed, Esvar would not hold back. Taking the money that had legitimately been her father's did not count as resistance.

A wisp of thought floated upward. Would Esvar fight against the king? Could he be used not as a flaw in Karolje's rule but as an ally?

If she told any of this to Sparrow, Sparrow would conclude it was too dangerous for the resistance not to cut Anza off. If it got found out and she had not told, Sparrow would think she was a spy. A hint to Irini, perhaps? Vague word of a rumor?

Esvar might be lying about everything. Perhaps he did intend her to be a spy, gullibly passing on information in order to weaken the resistance. She would have to be truthful and let Sparrow judge.

She swore aloud this time. Esvar was likable, that was the problem.

The Rukovili was beside her on the table. She picked it up. Mirantha had marked one poem with a sprig of lavender, and Anza had read it a dozen times. It was about harpies. And loss:

Songs of ugly hunger, early death
Where lost breaths are swallowed breath
by breath.

The sonnet ended with a line that sent a thrill of pleasing fear up her back: *The wicked tooth, and harpies own all twilights*. The bird of darkness, of death, of secrecy. Of hidden power.

What had the queen thought, reading that poem over and over, all the years before she died? Had it been a shelter, or a painful reminder? It had mattered enough for her to mark it. Had it said the things she could not? Anza tried to imagine what Mirantha had felt when Karolje killed her lover. Grief. Fear. Rage. Anger could shred you into pieces. She must have been so terribly lonely.

Lonely and frightened, with no one to support her. Voiceless. Yet Karolje had considered her enough of a threat to kill. That was a perverse sort of triumph.

What reason had Esvar had to return the book?

It was a move. Anza did not think she was his opponent, though. It was his father he fought. How did giving her the forbidden book strike against Karolje?

Perhaps not a move. Perhaps a symbol, sending this thing that had been the queen's away from the Citadel. A defiance of the past. An effort to protect what he had not been able to protect.

She went to her chest and dug through it. Mirantha's journal fit familiarly in her hands.

She had it nearly memorized. She opened it anyway. The air in the room filled, as it always did, with the scent of lavender. She read again, slowly, the few passages that described Esvar.

> *I am proud of Esvar, and worried too. I don't know what will happen to him when his father comes back. He is clever, and brave, but he likes to fight. He is encouraged in it by the soldiers and servants. I ordered his guards to break it up if he fights unfairly. I won't have him be a bully. He still listens to me, and I have told him to save the fights for the exercise yard. A good leader doesn't need to knock people over to command.*
>
> *But if the war drags on long enough for him to be sent south, or if Karolje comes back and takes him in hand, I fear the king will manage to use the violence to twist my beautiful boy into his own image. I am afraid this may already be happening to Tevin. I have written to my family and asked them to watch over him, but I have had no response. Karolje may have intercepted the letter.*

Which man had Anza seen today? The beautiful boy grown up as his mother wished or as his father wished? If the real him was hidden and hidden and hidden, how was what he showed not the real him? She touched the paper, thinking of how much was missing. What Mirantha had not dared to write must be recorded somewhere. In the stones of her room, in Ashevi's bones, in her sons' memories.

She should send Esvar the journal. He had a much better right to it than she did.

While I was at the execution this afternoon, my room was searched. Nothing was taken, but they didn't bother hiding the search. I don't understand why. The trial and all its spurious evidence were done a week ago.

Impalement. He was staked, not ganched. They cut his hands and feet off first. I thought they would blind him, but Karolje must have wanted to see horror in his eyes.

It was done publicly, in the center of the city. It looked like it would rain the entire time. Karolje stood between me and Tevin, where he could watch us, so we could not look away or touch each other. He made Esvar come too. I am afraid that alone will be enough to ruin him. Ashevi screamed. I thought he wouldn't, but at the very last he did. He couldn't help it. I have arranged his burial.

I have no tears left. I have not had any since that night.

I have said that Karolje did not hesitate at all before pronouncing sentence, but I don't know that. I don't remember anything of the trial. A woman went each day and watched, but she was not me. She watched, regal and emotionless, a queen, and I lived outside of time and light. If I had gone in with her, I would have wept and cursed and raged.

I am a danger to my sons now. Anytime I see them, speak with them, Karolje will think I am corrupting them. There is no way to leave.

I have walked in terrible places and done terrible things. Karolje would have driven me mad if I had not had my sons to protect. But he will kill me soon. I can see it in his eyes. He has had his Truth Finders trying to pry secrets from my mind. But what they want to know is not held in words or thoughts, and they cannot understand that.

When I am gone, Karolje will pay.

Then empty page after empty page.

Feeling hollow, Anza closed the journal. She had been so immersed in what Mirantha wrote that for a moment her surroundings seemed alien and strange. Poor Esvar. He had survived, at a cost she could not imagine. The queen had been Disappeared, into a twilight not of her own making, with no goddess to avenge her. Only her sons. He would not be able to do it alone.

Anza was not sure she would be able to help him.

MIRANTHA

It has happened. We are lovers again. I was so afraid.

There was an Asp attack in the city that did a great deal of damage, and the men were meeting until very late. I went to the chapel to offer libations for the dead, and he was there. He took me to a room where we used to go, and we gave each other pleasure, though for so short a time. When I think of it I can still feel the desire in me. I worried that the happiness of it might show on my face when I came back here, but I am certain it didn't. When I returned, my maid asked what had upset me. I told her it was the attack.

It was a terrible attack, so there was reason to be upset. Nearly fifty people were killed, many of them children. It was a Naming in the Temple for the new son of one of the lords, and the building was crowded. An Asp found his way in and set off several explosions. He was killed too, but Korikos has as many Asps as he could ever want, so retribution will not stop the war. At times I think that the war will not be over until every young man in both countries has died and the blood has so soaked the earth that it will never come out.

In the spring, Karolje returns to the war in the south, and this time he takes Tevin, who is twelve. He has appointed a cousin as his chancellor and named him co-regent with Mirantha if he dies. Goran is third in line to the throne, and she is afraid that if Karolje dies, neither of her sons will live long under a regency. She is sure Karolje has planned this to keep her from trying to kill him. He came to her every night for a week before leaving, and she knows he wants another heir.

She goes to the Temple to pray in public for the army's success. For her husband's life. There are three priests. The Hierarch pours the oil into the bowl and leads the prayer for the army. Old words, familiar words. Chants, a hymn, a prayer by each priest. At last it is her turn. A ritual for the god she does not believe in. More than anything she would like to summon the harpy goddess, to become the harpy goddess, to be winged and taloned. The darkness of the Temple feels like twilight.

She kneels, and the Hierarch dips his fingers into the bowl. He puts a hand on each side of her head, the oil and water running in droplets across her skin, and blesses her. She rises, a queen, a supplicant, and turns to the audience. Esvar is seated in the very front, next to Ashevi. Incense smoke swirls in the still air. She brings her hands together, palm to palm, and touches her thumbs to the center of her chest. Then she spreads her arms.

A priest strikes a bell. The gong deepens and resonates as it spreads through the room, and she thinks the sound will lift her from her feet. It ceases, and she walks alone down the long aisle of watching people. The smell of incense and oil is ingrained in her skin and hair. She wishes it was lavender.

Her carriage waits for her outside the Temple grounds. Her servants come, and Ashevi and her son. She wants to take Ashevi's hand but is aware of Esvar, silent as always, his dark eyes observing everything. He is very still for a child of his age, just turned seven. She must shape him while she has the chance.

In the Citadel she retires to her rooms and has her maids undress her. They banter cheerfully, as she has encouraged, and she does her best to draw them ever further out without losing her dignity. She puts on a long blue dress that brings out the blue of her eyes and the shine of her hair. Her heart and body tell her to go to the chapel, to wait in false prayer until she can embrace her lover in unholy passion. Her mind tells her to be wiser, and she obeys her mind.

She sends for Esvar and goes to the pools in the garden to wait, to sit in the gazebo and sink into the sun and the rose perfume and the splashing water. Two guards stand at the entrance to protect the queen's meditation and, more significantly, to watch for Asps.

Esvar comes, accompanied by a single guard who waits at the trellis with the others. Karolje's edict that she is not to be alone with her sons is enforced inconsistently in his absence. The boy sits on the bench beside her. He is tall, all arms and legs, and his toes touch the ground where another child's wouldn't. She takes his hand and holds it between hers. His brows and hair are as black as Karolje's.

"You and I have only each other right now," she says.

"I wanted to go."

Esvar had made no secret of his desire to be a soldier with his brother. "I know. You're brave, but it's your work to stay here and learn what you need." She takes a breath. She should not be this tense talking to him. "Do you know how a lever works?"

"Yes. Nihalik explained it. It spreads the force over distance to move something heavy."

"Show me."

He looks around. There are no loose sticks or rocks for him to demonstrate with, but he is wearing a small knife. He draws it and removes his shoe, which he puts on the bench. With the tip of the blade he lifts the shoe.

"That's easy," he says. "The shoe doesn't weigh much. I could show it better with something heavier."

"The shoe is sufficient. I see that you understand. What is a lever used to lift?"

"Stones," he says. "That was how the Citadel was built. A catapult is a lever. Tevin showed me how to build one."

"Good. I need you to understand something else, Esvar. Vetia is like the Citadel. It has been built too. I'm not talking about the cities and towns, I'm talking about laws. Ideas. It is a country because people have worked for hundreds of years to make it one."

He picks up the knife and lunges at the air. His form is excellent. "By keeping out the Tazekhs."

"No. Savages can fight each other. We make a nation by living peaceably together. That's what laws are for. Do you remember the oath your father swore when he was crowned?"

The words catch him. His face is puzzled. Across the garden, a tree with bright new leaves bends in a soft breeze. "To protect and defend from enemies within and without," he says rotely, lunging again, "to uphold the law, to rule justly, and to serve the gods."

"To rule justly. Justice is a lever, Esvar. It is a force that gives people power to move things much bigger than themselves."

"I don't understand."

"Try," she says urgently. "Justice is how you build a country. And it's what you use to pry away things that are ill-built. It is a king's work to be just." She stops, frustrated. He is too young to understand. Everywhere around him he sees force. How can she explain that justice is a form of power when he has been taught that his birthright rests on war?

"Esvar. Your father and brother have gone to war. If they are killed, you will be the king. It is unlikely, but I need you to remember this: if you are ever a king, you must be fair and brave and wise. Those are your tools. Not swords, not dungeons."

Something—her tone? the mention of his brother?—gets through to him, and he sheathes the knife, turns around to face her. Whatever he is thinking is too big for his words. Slowly he comes forward. He presses his forehead against hers. There is no way to warn him against his father.

Perhaps he does not need a warning. She kisses his cheek. "Go on, love," she says cheerfully. "Back to your guard."

He grins at her, her beautiful boy, and runs off with all the vigor of childhood. She watches him go under the trellis, then turns her head back to the pools. The sun reflects blindingly on the water.

Almost immediately after, Ashevi comes. He was probably waiting. He kneels at her feet. The priest yielding to royal power, acknowledging her Temple prayers. It is deceit, as all their interactions are bound to be.

She bids him rise and stands herself, so that they face each other. The fountain will cover the sound of their voices. Sun falls bright on his face, emphasizing the fine shape of his mouth. It seems an eternity since she has been touched with any sort of tenderness.

She had not intended to speak to him. But this seems to be a day for telling difficult truths. "We have to be done. Forever. This can't go on."

"I still love you. In my dreams I taste you."

"You must go," she says. "Leave the Citadel, leave Karegg."

"Is that a royal command, my lady? Because if it is, I will obey it."

"No," she says, holding back tears and anger. "But don't come to me alone again. And I will not come to you. It's the only way."

He says, "What happens to you if Karolje dies in the war?"

"I would have to battle Lord Goran for Tevin's regency. You know that."

He waves an impatient hand at the water. "That's not what I meant. What happens to you, to Mirantha? When you are free of the beast, will you open your heart? Will you rage and despair? Will you fall in love with one of his lords? What happens?" He is full of intensity.

It is as impossible to imagine as death. She will never be free of Karolje.

"You're a priest," she says. She wonders for the first time if he believes in his god. "No matter what, I can't be with you."

"When I pour the oil, I see the smoothness of your thighs. When I light the incense, I smell your body. When I move my hands in prayer, I stroke your breasts. It's you I worship, Mirantha. I can endure this parting now, but not forever. I will forsake the priesthood and you will forsake the regency and we will leave together."

She wants him, how she wants him. It takes all the control she has to leave her hands dangling at her sides. She says, clinging to the fact that will save her, "Karolje isn't dead. And he won't be killed in battle. He will come back."

"Do you want him to live?"

The bitter truth bursts from her. "Gods, no."

"Do you hate him enough to kill—"

"Stop, stop! Don't go there. I love you. Let that be all."

"He's not your husband, Mira, beautiful Mira. He's your jailer. He keeps you from joy, from your children, from—"

"Stop!" she cries again, and runs from him.

* * *

That night in the bath, she thinks what an odd question it was. *Do you hate him enough to kill him?* not *Do you love me enough to kill him?* And how easy to ask it, now, when the king is not at hand. What if she had said yes? What would Ashevi do? Would he arrange an assassin or would he report her as a traitor?

How little he knows her, suggesting that they leave when she still has her boys to care for.

She says to the maid, Tahari, "Have you ever been in love?"

The girl turns pink. "I can't say, my lady. There are men I've fancied, but they haven't returned it."

"Really? That surprises me, a pretty girl like you." Both her maids have wavy dark hair and large white breasts, and she is fairly certain Karolje had them in his bed when he was here. Perhaps she should arrange marriages for them now that he is gone.

She lets Tahari dry her and robe her as usual, but instead of going to bed, she sits in front of her mirror and brushes her damp hair, the gold now darkened with wet. Ashevi is too dangerous, she has to face that fact. If she sends for the Hierarch in the Temple and tells him Ashevi has to go, that will take care of matters.

Coward, a voice inside her says.

She takes the Rukovili off the shelf and opens it to the harpy poem. The scent of lavender is the scent of loss. The words—*the idylls of we who pretend*—hurt. She is sick of pretending. She wishes she had had the courage years ago to ask Nihalik if the harpy goddess was real.

The answer, no matter what it was, would have been too hard to bear then.

✦ ✦ ✦

Six weeks later, she sees the swelling of Tahari's body and knows the girl is with child by Karolje.

ALL THE WAY back to the Citadel, Esvar thought about Anza. The soldier's daughter who had attended the College, who had sat in his workroom with her head down and waited calmly. It must have taken immense courage to come back into his presence, even in her father's house. Especially in her father's house, where everything would remind her of his execution. She had no particular reason to trust a prince's word. Her movements had been quick, her small body coiled with energy, ready to flee. But she had never flinched.

He had said far more to her than he had intended. He should have sent Mirovian with the money and left it at that. But curiosity had impelled him there, and something about her had loosened his tongue. Perhaps the plain honesty of her grief. He was not accustomed to people being honest with him. And perhaps, he admitted coldly to himself, he was still trying to find a way to use her as a lever.

Another thought tugged at the back of his mind but vanished at the Citadel gate. A soldier waited for him, mouth set.

"The king wants you," the man said with no courtesy at all.

The old, ordinary terror pricked Esvar. What had he done

wrong now? He washed and dressed in clean, formal clothes. Then he went.

Karolje made him wait. It was no use chatting with the four guards, who kept strictly to the rules this close to the king. Esvar knew how to stand, too, which he did instead of sitting. That made the page on duty stand. The silence and stiff formality locked around them like a tower without a door, nothing to do but repeat one's steps over and over. Esvar turned his mind to minor problems needing his authority but not much attention.

Eventually the door opened. The chancellor and the spymaster came out, Goran looking pleased and Doru neutral. Whatever Karolje was up to, it was in Goran's favor at the moment.

He went in, and a guard shut the door. The king was alone save for his physician, a thin-faced, sharp-edged man who was possessed of more nerve than nearly anyone else in the Citadel. If Karolje's illness took a sharp turn for the worse, the man might be impaled as a traitor.

"My lord," Esvar said, bending his head as little as he dared. When he looked up at the king's face, he was shocked. The illness had redoubled itself. Several red sores had broken out on Karolje's cheeks. His eyes remained as alert and vicious as ever, and he sat erectly in a chair.

"Where have you been?"

His first thought was that Doru had followed him and Anza Istvili was now in danger. He said, "I rode into the city." No explanation, no justification.

The king said, "I have released Lukovian from imprisonment."

Oh, this was dangerous. Nothing to do with Anza at all. Don't give him anything. "Sir."

"He's too good an examiner to waste." With bent forefinger,

he beckoned Esvar closer. Esvar complied. Behind Karolje an open window admitted warm air, but the king wore a thick robe. His pendant looked too heavy for his frail neck.

"Kneel."

Esvar did. His heart sped up. He clasped his hands to hinder any temptation toward violence.

The king leaned forward. His breath was cloying with the scent of medicines. He said, "The arrest was a good move you put your brother up to. But upon reconsideration I find that I am inclined to believe Lukovian after all. He but passed on what his subjects told him." He smiled.

Damnation. Any response would be taken as argument, even not responding. Esvar said, "Lukovian is your servant, sir."

"Meaning?" Karolje said.

"It is your prerogative to take his word over mine." No wonder Goran had been delighted.

"You won't argue?"

He longed to draw his knife. He said, "I aver my innocence. If Your Majesty desires to have this proved as a matter of law, I shall of course present my case." To prove a negative was impossible. If Karolje pushed, did Esvar have any choice but to attack?

The king studied him. Esvar endured it, though a muscle twitched in his jaw. Karolje made few mistakes.

"As touching on your honor, Prince, these stories are yours to dispel. Begin with Nikovili."

That was the twist of the knife. Not a twist, a bloody corkscrew through his heart, his soul, the bits of integrity he had managed to amass. Prove your innocence by torturing your accuser. Who is not even the true accuser.

A good move you put your brother up to. A test. The king knew he was dying. If Esvar followed him in this, he would prove himself worthy of being a successor. Tevin's life would be snuffed out faster than Nikovili's. If Esvar resisted, it was only a matter of time before he was put on trial for treason. If he evaded, Nikovili would simply die, leaving the story of Esvar's betrayal on Lukovian's ready tongue.

"I am sure Nikovili will deny saying any such thing if I simply ask him," Esvar said. "He has no incentive to call me a traitor to my face, especially if I am the one threatening him. It falls back upon Lukovian."

"Smuggling is not so great a crime as treason. If he accuses you, that might buy him his release."

Esvar grabbed the king's thin wrist. The doctor came to his feet. Esvar said, "There's no need for games between us now. If you want to arrest me, do it." He tightened his grip. One quick movement would break Karolje's bones.

The black of Karolje's pupils swallowed the black of his irises. A light glinted in that darkness, cold and distant, merciless. Esvar would have rather stared into the eyes of a demon.

Karolje said, implacable, "Question him. In public."

Had a pardon already been issued? Had Nikovili been prepared with a story that would burn like wildfire? Was the king playing games because it was the only thing he knew how to do?

Esvar wondered if he looked as grey and bloodless as he felt. His fingers loosened. He stood and issued his own challenge. "Will you attend?" Show yourself. Make public your weakness. Your disease.

The silence was a little too long. With an effort, Esvar kept his hands still and open. If he revealed any fear at all, he was doomed. Memory of his mother sitting with an expressionless face at a food-laden table while the king accused her of adultery intruded. She had been terrified, he knew that. He remembered drowning in terror. She forked a piece of meat, the scrape of the metal tines against the ceramic the only indication of emotion.

"Get out!" Karolje snapped. Esvar improperly turned his back and left.

* * *

He went to his rooms first, where he was quietly and privately sick. Better now than later. He wrote a message to his brother, dispatched it and his other orders, and went to the Green Court to wait.

The room was large, a domed ceiling in the center and two rows of green marble pillars marching its length. Gas jets on the walls and pillars were dark with age and carved into sinister shapes of monsters and demons and other fantastical creatures. Shadows crosshatched each other on the tiled floor. At the end opposite the door was a low dais, the chair of judgment in the fore and several seats across the back for witnesses if necessary. There were two side doors, one opening onto an antechamber, one onto a corridor. In front of the dais, iron loops for attaching shackles had been set into the floor.

It was not a court of justice. It never had been. The original throne room of the Citadel, built when might mattered more than pomp, it had for nine centuries been the place where punishments were meted out. The captives who were to be questioned by king or lord or commander were brought here. Blood had seeped into the floor, and fear into the walls. The current throne room, the receiving hall, they were for the bright display of power. Power in the Green Court was as old and dark and savage as wilderness. No one doubted it.

There was no other place in the Citadel where he could more convincingly clear his name.

Nikovili was brought in first, unsurprisingly. He reeked of the dungeons. His clothing concealed most of the marks of torture, but his hands were wrapped in bloody bandages. The guards shackled him to the loops in the floor. One soldier, bowing to Esvar, handed him the weapon he had requested: a triple whip, three metal wires running from the same handle, studded at irregular intervals with small barbs. Most people passed out after only a few strokes. Nikovili, seeing it, turned pale.

Esvar seated himself in the chair of judgment, the flail laid across his lap. The witnesses trickled in as ordered. Marek was one of the first, and Esvar gave him a few whispered instructions. Karolje's chief commander, who would report to the king. The chancellor. A soldier to witness for Tevin. Two lords. Doru. Lukovian the last, clean-shaven, dressed in his most formal uniform. Esvar directed him to stand a few feet away from Nikovili.

He signaled to Marek, who acknowledged it and left the room. Esvar rose.

"You may be seated," he said to the witnesses who had stood with him. When they had settled back into place, he descended the step from the dais to the floor of the room, the flail in his hand. He snapped the whip against the floor, metal on stone ringing through the air. The room went quiet as death. Nikovili was motionless in his chains.

Esvar faced him and said, "You are guilty of smuggling."

Nikovili gulped. "Yes, my lord," he said, voice high and reedy.

"You have defrauded the Crown of its revenues."

"Yes."

"You engaged in unsanctioned dealings with men outside Vetia."

A quick glance at the flail. "Yes, my lord."

Esvar took a step to the side so that the lords and Karolje's commander would be sure to see Nikovili's face. He said, "You claim that I profited from these dealings."

Naked shock and confusion as the merchant went white. He collapsed to his knees. "No—I never—no, my lord—it's not—my lord, no."

It was a convincing denial. Arguably, a man who had not expected to be found out would look much the same. But a man who had already made the claim under torture would not expect not to be found out. He would know the story was out there. No one who had endured what Nikovili had in the past few days would be blindsided by such an accusation unless he was innocent of it.

Esvar said, "You have accused me of collaborating with foreigners."

"No. Please." He was about to break down into sobs.

He looked at Lukovian. "Examiner, you extracted his confession."

"I did, my lord." The man was wary.

"Did he make these accusations against me?"

"Yes, my lord." A pause. "He might not remember."

That was sharp. Esvar's mouth tightened involuntarily. Lukovian had to see the direction this was going and would not set his word against a prisoner's. Much better to evade the problem by setting the prisoner against himself.

"Do you find merit in them?"

"Certainly not, sir."

Whoever had set this up was not prepared to drive it home, then. Lukovian would have produced forged evidence if this accusation was meant to bring Esvar down. It was a taunt, a test of who was willing to go how far for what.

"Then how did such rumors come to be spread?"

"I was not aware of such rumors, my lord. My people are instructed never to speak of what is said during an examination."

"You just spent two days under arrest yourself for repeating this slander."

"A lie," said Lukovian, cool as could be. "As you can see now, the arrest was clearly in error."

Esvar smiled. "But you cannot deny the existence of rumors if you were arrested about them, regardless of the correctness of the arrest."

That bought him a moment of silence. Lukovian was accustomed to dealing with prisoners who were weak and frightened and would never try to trick him. He wasn't prepared to be on the receiving end of an interrogation.

But he was not a fool. He would not have the position he did if he were foolish. He said, a simple and therefore nearly unassailable lie, "I was arrested. I was not charged. I was told nothing."

Esvar struck the floor with the flail again. Even the guards jumped. "Are you sure you want to hold to that story?"

The problem with having backed Lukovian into a corner was that now he could see exactly how things lay. Insolently, he said, "Yes."

"Oh?" said Esvar. He pulled the flail across the stone, the metal rasping loudly. He said to the guards, "Tell Captain Marek to come in now."

Marek was followed by a man robed in black. One of the witnesses audibly breathed in. Nikovili twisted in his chains and, seeing the man, said, "No. No."

The Truth Finder advanced. Any noise his feet made was drowned out by the sound of Marek's boots. Lukovian was the only person in the room besides Doru who did not draw back to some degree, however slight. He looked confident. He had worked with the Truth Finder for years and had to be certain the man would lie on his behalf.

"My lord," said the Truth Finder with a smooth bow. He was tall and thin, with grey hair and pale, long-fingered hands. Esvar had been afraid of him when he was younger.

Am I really going to do this? Esvar thought. If it went well, it was an act Karolje would approve of. If it failed, he was signing his own death warrant. And it might well fail. He knew he was not a traitor, but if Karolje—or Doru—had told the Truth Finder to lie, the Truth Finder would. For an interminable moment he wished he could change his mind.

"My name has been called into question," he said. "Each of these men denies the slander. I have two questions, and two only, for you to put to each of them. Does he have knowledge that I have collaborated with foreigners against the king for my own gain? And has he ever told another person that I have so collaborated?"

The Truth Finder repeated the questions and, on Esvar's affirmation, said formally, "If I report untruthfully, may the gods strike me down." Esvar suspected the Truth Finder did not believe in the gods either, but it was a necessary part of the show.

"Begin," he said, and stepped away. His stomach curled in on itself again.

The Truth Finder placed his hand against Nikovili's forehead. Silver light glowed at the tips of his fingers. At the touch, Nikovili fainted, which was the best thing he could have done for himself.

It was done in a few breaths. Then the Truth Finder turned to Lukovian.

The interrogator stepped backward. Esvar hoped the man

would lose his nerve and run for it. That would be so much easier. Lukovian held firm until the glowing fingers touched his skin. "No!" he shouted. He screamed. Esvar's teeth bit hard on his lip. He was roused, tense; it felt hideously like lust.

The Truth Finder lowered Lukovian to the floor. His limbs jerked violently. His eyes were closed.

"This man," said the Truth Finder, pointing down at Lukovian, "spread the stories. He believes them to be false. The other man knows nothing."

"This is the truth?"

"This is the truth."

"I thank you for your service." He was glad of the ritual words; he would not have known what else to say. The Truth Finder bowed.

Esvar said to the guards, "Take the men back to the cells. Get a doctor for them if they aren't conscious by then. Provide plenty of clean water." He faced the witnesses. "Nikovili remains guilty of smuggling. For him, nothing has changed. Lukovian I judge guilty of calumny against a prince of the realm. The penalty for such false claims is the penalty for the crime alleged, in this instance, death. You are dismissed."

He let his eyes find the chancellor's. Goran looked evenly back. This was not close to over.

His glance slid to Doru, who smiled. The spymaster might regret losing one of his more forceful examiners, but he probably thought it worth it as a blow against the chancellor.

Followed by Marek, Esvar left by the side door and went to his rooms. He dismissed the captain to wait outside. He had forgotten it was summer, sunlit and warm. The chill of the Green Court was all through him.

He was not at all surprised half an hour later to hear the

clank of heavily armed men approaching. He said to Marek, "Get your orders from Tevin. Don't fight," and let the soldiers take him.

They stopped at the second level of the dungeons, whose purpose Esvar knew only too well. He stopped walking and let all his weight go into their arms as they dragged him forward. It relieved him when they went into the third room. He wasn't to be killed then, or blinded, only to be hurt. Pain, he could withstand.

They removed his shirt and chained him kneeling to the whipping post, wrists cuffed to the post-arms. The floor was discolored with years of blood. He was not granted the grace of a hood, and they would report his every expression to the king. There would be no questions, no verbal taunts, just pain. He hoped they would not use the whip he had brought to the Green Court, but he expected it.

After chaining him they went away, leaving him time to think, to imagine, to weaken in body and soul. The chains rubbed painfully against his wrists if he slumped at all, and the stone floor hurt his knees.

Deep in himself was a place of quiet, where he could shelter if he reached it before the pain became too great. He remembered the journey to the mountains five years ago, when Karolje tested him with rebellion. He stood on an outcrop of rock, alone except for the wind, and looked down at the soaring birds and the far, far distant and noiseless river. Mountains filled the space to the horizon. The wind was the sound of the turning earth, and he meant nothing more to the world than the birds did. Whatever he did, whatever was done to him, the wind would always be there.

He was a thing of meat and blood and bone, of skin and hair and nerves, each breath reaching to the ends of his body, and he was in a quiet secret place that expanded beyond the world, both stillness and motion. Sharp incandescent light, balanced with infinite blackness. If he fell, he would float and drift. The wind was the tide of his beating blood, ebb and flow, ebb and flow, every moment a silver spider thread stretched out infinitely across universes.

The whip cut into his back.

It's only pain, he thought. A thing, a sensation of the body. It did not belong to him and could not enter this place without his permission.

A second stroke, thin and fiery. A narrow wire lash, which would cut deeper but heal faster. He was not to be scarred like a slave or a prisoner, back a bark-like mass of thickened skin from whipping upon whipping upon whipping. He pressed his tongue to the roof of his mouth.

Another, and another, and another.

Birds and wind.

A respite. They would come back. This was only a subtler form of torture, leaving him to wonder when the next blow would fall.

Pain was increasingly harder to hold off. It had no edges. He was light-headed. He smelled his own blood, felt the warm moisture on his back. His arms and face were sweating, stinging his wrists and eyes. His breath was ragged and rough. He had bitten his tongue.

I will kill you, Karolje, he thought. He could bring no force to it.

Another lash. His body jerked, and he banged his forehead against the post. For an instant the blossoming pain in his head overtook the pain of his back.

He reached for the silence again. It was gone.

The whip whistled before it struck him. It cut through skin

and into muscle. The world turned grey. He writhed, and the cuffs on his wrists dug into the skin there.

It might be a good idea to pass out now.

On the next stroke, he did for a few seconds. He was brought back by pain in his shoulders and wrists as he slumped, shivering from the cold water they had doused him with. Fresh blood speckled the post in front of him. He imagined the flesh and skin of his back as ribbons. Another lash, and he cried out despite himself.

His knees were miles away, the bloodied floor waving. He could no longer feel his arms or hands. He faced down a tunnel, its dark edges closing in, and his head spun. His scream did not come from his own lungs. He had no breath left. Can't give in, he thought, can't. Kill the king.

Karolje's black eyes stared into him, seeing everything. His mother's blood darkened the white sheet.

* * *

When he came to, he was lying on his stomach on a cot in an interrogation room. His wrists and back were bandaged. It hurt, but not intolerably. His brother sat nearby on a wooden stool.

Esvar closed his eyes again. "How bad is it?" he asked.

"You lost a lot of blood, but the strokes were all clean and narrow. They will heal well enough, though you won't want to put your back against anything for a week or so, I expect. The wrists are just scraped."

"Am I under arrest?"

"No. There's to be no further punishment. What the hell did you think you were doing?" There was both anger and anguish in his voice.

"Tilting the board," Esvar said. He cleared his throat. "I'm sick of playing Karolje's games."

"By using a bloody *Truth Finder*? Any other method, Esvar, but not that one."

It had been hard to justify to himself at the time and was harder to justify to his brother now. He tried anyway. "I needed the king to know I'm willing to use his tools against him." *Even if you aren't,* he did not say.

"That particular tool has a way of slipping in one's hand."

"I knew what he'd say. I knew I was innocent." The words were hollow.

"That's not the problem of a Truth Finder," Tevin said, gone from hot anger to deep cold.

Esvar knew the problem: the invasion of a mind, the damage it caused. There was no good in being found innocent if it wrecked your mind in the process. He had watched men go mad as a Truth Finder probed, seen the sanity drain from the eyes. It was like watching a death, except the light in the eyes changed into a feverish glitter or dull distance. Tevin had ordered him years ago never to use a Truth Finder and he had abided by that, until Lukovian and Nikovili.

"I'm not fifteen anymore, older brother." He didn't have the strength to put all the force he wanted to into it.

"Well, you've made Karolje aware of that too, and now he's going to be scrutinizing you more closely. You didn't tilt the board, you stepped right into the hole he had dug for you."

Esvar opened his eyes and twisted his hand in an obscene gesture. "You play your own cards much too close to your chest," he said. "You started the whole damn thing by complaining to Karolje about Lukovian. Why didn't you just have a quiet word with Lukovian and head all the conflict off at the source? Once the king dared me to clear my name, there was nothing else I could do."

"I told you to be patient and let me act. You didn't question the arrest when you first heard. You should have come to me, since it was my fault."

The mockery hurt more than the whip had. "I sent you a message. What do you think you could have done?"

"Go to Goran, point out that it was a bad precedent for examiners to be telling tales about their betters, and remind him that there were things he wouldn't want rumored about himself. All you've done is give him a reason to slander you further."

"If I knew what you had on him, I could have blackmailed him myself."

"It would have been easier for him to bluff his way past you. You aren't old enough to remember the things that matter."

Esvar glared up at him. We shouldn't keep secrets, he thought. Not now. He was too weak to argue further. "What time is it?"

"Just past dinner. Are you hungry?"

"Thirsty."

"I've water. Can you sit up?"

With an effort, he did. His breath came short. He took the flask his brother offered and drank most of it. Water spilled out of his mouth, and he wiped futilely at his chin. He had never been this weak. He could only remember the whipping in patches now. Had he cried, or begged?

Tevin took the flask. "I'll get it refilled," he said. "The doctor wants you to stay here for the night. You're not fit to walk yet. It's saving you some embarrassment too."

"What's the story being told?"

"Nothing. All the king has said is that the Truth Finder has spoken. Lukovian will be executed at dawn tomorrow."

"I need to be there." He lay down again, carefully. The pain that had been a hum when the conversation started was becoming a roar. "I want to see the doctor."

"I'll send him," Tevin said. "You need rest. Esvar, you went out this morning. What was that about?"

At first he could not remember. "I had to see someone," he said. "It was personal. Not to do with any of this."

No, just with raids and a dead queen and a woman braver than himself, who looked steadfastly into his eyes as he could not with Karolje. Anza, with the dark hair and the dark eyes and the small, strong body. She would always be birdlike, light and quick. Bones made angles on her wrists and shoulders. Not at all fashionable. In a portrait she would be pretty but not beautiful; no painter would be able to capture the diamond-sharp intensity of her gaze. She had no idea what it was to yield, though he was not sure she knew that about herself yet.

He had never met anyone like her. Most of the women of his acquaintance were nobly born, cosseted and indulged, selfish if charming. And afraid. They had been taught by their mothers and sisters and servants to be careful in his presence, to refuse him nothing, to flatter. They had the queen's example before them. Once when he was seventeen, he had looked at the woman lying naked beneath him in the bed, her hair dark and curly with sweat at the sides of her face, her mouth open in pleasure, her eyes like shuttered windows. He thought the pleasure had been real, but the woman had been holding back her soul. Since then he had expected nothing of his lovers but their bodies.

He wasn't going to get that from Captain Havidian's daughter. A soldier's daughter, who should hate him for what had been done to her father. Why had she put herself in his hands again? Mirovian had told him she was not motivated by money, and he believed that now. What did she want?

Revenge. His heart thumped and his mind slid pieces together faster than words. Mirovian had remembered her at the house. He had spent a long time staring at the gable window. She was the missing resister, she had to be. She matched the description. She had somehow acquired a forbidden book. She had the courage, the size, the father who could have taught her the bow and given her arrows. The intelligence to understand politics and the bravery to question him. The resistance would value her.

He could talk to them. His breath hitched. He did not dare waste this opportunity.

It occurred to him that he might be imagining things in a haze of blood loss and hatred for the king. Then he thought of her small, lithe, muscular body, which would have been able to get out the window and onto the roof. The newly healed cut on her hand so like the one Mirovian had got from a slate. It had been bandaged the day he met her, the day after the resister's escape.

Karolje had better not find out about her. If the king got curious, he might subject Esvar to a Truth Finder. Gods, it had been a stupid thing to do, hadn't it, challenging Lukovian. He needed to be at the execution.

His thoughts were spiraling. That was what pain did. He closed his eyes. A door shut.

Hands lifted his head and held a flask to his mouth. He swallowed automatically, tasted the bitterness of opium mixed with wine. He gagged, but it was too late.

Do me the courtesy of assuming I still have a soul, he heard someone say through the fuzziness of descending sleep. Then the darkness.

11

A PARTY AT JANCE'S lordly cousin's house was not how Anza had imagined renewing their friendship. It was a better option than a smoky tavern or a loud coffeehouse, but she hesitated for a long time before accepting the invitation. She had attended such parties with Rumil and was not intimidated by the scene; it was the potential for coming to someone else's attention that gave her pause. Her life had enough secrets in it already. At last she decided that if she kept herself quiet and polite, she was unlikely to be of interest to either suitors or spies.

The carriage Jance had sent for her arrived at his cousin's mansion when the western sky was the fine gold of imminent sunset. It would be dark when she left, but Lord Darvik had been able to get curfew passes. She alighted at the front door. A candle shone on every windowsill, and dozens of paper-covered lights glowed on the drive. Music spilled out the open door and windows. A footman on the right-hand side of the door presented her with wine in a crystal glass, and a footman on the left offered her a choice of eye masks. She gave him the wine to hold while she tied her mask on. It was half-white, half-black, with white and black feathers as trim.

Some of the guests must have known masks were to be part of the entertainment, because they wore masks that covered everything but the mouth and chin. Animal faces, patterns, gems, feathers, anything that could be adornment was. The clothing matched, silk dresses and velvet trousers, short satin cloaks, long gloves and gauzy scarves. Anza expected to see some familiar faces among the commoners, but the masks made it more challenging.

Tables of food and drink were at one end of a great room, and musicians at the other. In between, dozens of people stood in pairs or groups, talking and laughing, while white-clad servants carried wine bottles and collected glasses. Doors opened to a large terrace, steps descending to a lawn and garden. Hanging paper-covered lanterns shone on paths and benches and fountains. Roses climbed profusely on trellises and adorned the flower beds. The Citadel was not far away, but the large trees beside the wall circling the place blocked it from view. Bats flitted at the upper branches.

Anza was not interested in being flirted with by a man old enough to be her father, which described many of the guests. She walked down the steps to the lawn, where more of the younger people were. Jance, in a black and scarlet mask that covered the upper half of his face, was standing with half a dozen other people. He waved her over.

He was already drunk. When he gave her a kiss on the cheek, she smelled the wine on his breath. He put an arm around her shoulders and said cheerfully, "I'm glad you came. There are going to be fireworks later, did you know?"

With a firm hand, she removed his arm. "Introduce me to your friends," she said. "Is there an occasion?"

"It's my cousin's wife's birthday." He made the introductions.

They chatted, mostly about people Anza did not know. Fireflies were green-gold sparks floating on the air. The women had slim necks and elegant jawlines and wore jeweled necklaces, and the men had their hair tied back with colored cords and sported expensive rings. She knew she looked respectable enough in the gown Rumil had bought her for such occasions, but she was aware as always of her so-different upbringing. When these people had been presented at their first formal balls, she had been dancing barefoot on the floor of a barn with loose bits of hay in her hair.

A servant magically appeared and refilled the wineglasses. The sky darkened and the first white stars appeared.

Anza tired of conversation and wandered to the house, where she made herself a plate of spiced mushrooms and peppers. When she finished eating, she put the plate on a small table where other people had done the same. Her mouth and fingers were greasy, and she wiped them on a fine linen napkin. So much wealth.

In the great room, people were dancing. Most of them were fifteen or twenty years older than her, she guessed, old enough to remember life before Karolje was king. Had it made much difference to them? As they danced now, did they have any fear of the king's spies? Surely some were present.

The thought chilled her. She found a servant and took a glass of wine, then went to the side of the terrace to drink it. The cutout patterns on the hanging lanterns seemed letters in another language, suspended in darkness.

"Anza," said a woman behind her, her voice velvety smooth.

Anza knew that voice. She had not expected to ever hear it again. She turned, dreading the encounter. "Thali," she said, trying to be civil. The last time they had spoken she had shut a door in Thali's face. But that had been four years ago. "You're looking well."

Her former lover wore a slim, high-waisted, one-shouldered gown that showed off her excellent figure and her husband's excellent income. Thali's honey-gold hair was piled on her head, artful tendrils hanging beside her face. Her green mask covered the top half of her face and matched the gown. Her sandals revealed narrow, high-arched feet and painted toenails. Beside her, her husband held a wine cup.

"Who's this?" said Doru, eyeing Anza's dress. "Some city girl risen up beyond her station?" His half-mask was gorgeously painted and doubtless expensive.

Anza's immediate impulse was to mock him equally in return. She remembered what Sparrow had told her: *The chief interrogator reports to him.* She dipped her knee, hoping no fear showed on her face.

"An old friend," said Thali. "I was surprised to see her, Doru, it's nothing more. We can move on." Her once-expressive features were sculpture-still. The coldness in her voice might have been intended as insult or as protection.

"But I delight in knowing your old friends," he said. "Hold this." He gave the glass to his wife and stepped closer to Anza. He was a man of middling height with a wiry frame, but he loomed threateningly anyway. She had never seen eyes so cold. Poor Thali, she thought.

With one finger he stroked Anza's chin. She recoiled. His hand locked around her forearm. Dressed as she was, public as they were, kicking was not an option. The only thing to do was to stand motionless. Pretend she was about to shoot.

He caressed her neck, trailed his hand over her chest to the neckline of her gown, and lifted it without touching her breast.

On the other side of the terrace, people were watching. Anza felt as soiled as she had in the Citadel cell.

"You're right, my love," he said, turning. "She's nothing." He reclaimed his glass.

When Thali and Doru had disappeared inside the house, Anza let herself slump. Her heart was pounding. She put her wineglass shakily on the balcony wall. A man across the terrace gave her a sympathetic glance but made no move toward her. She supposed she was marked now as dangerous to associate with. Surely she had been here long enough to politely leave. She would find Jance and ask him to send her home with an escort.

An unfamiliar man's voice said, "Anza Istvili?"

She turned, reluctant, and saw a tall, bearded man. The set of his eyes reminded her of Jance. This must be his cousin.

"My lord," she said with another dip of the knee. "Thank you for your hospitality."

"My cousin has told me quite a bit about you."

"Oh dear." And where are you now, Jance, you ass?

"Not at all. My wife will be delighted to make your acquaintance," he said. "Come inside."

Was she being sheltered from Doru or was it chance? She guessed the former. Reluctantly, hoping not to see Doru, she followed Lord Darvik inside and to a parlor opening off the large foyer. The house reminded her of Nikovili's. She remembered the soldiers' footsteps, the dusty closet, the prison cell.

Several women and men were seated inside. Most were not wearing masks, and Anza removed hers. The room was very blue: the chairs upholstered in a pale blue velvet brocade, the walls papered in patterns of dark blue and silver, the carpet an Eridian weave in four shades of blue, and the vases on the side tables sea-blue glass. The windows were open, heavy velvet draperies pulled aside and light linen curtains hanging straight in the motionless air.

Darvik made the introductions. His wife, Jeriza, was tall and lovely, her auburn hair braided and pinned, her full breasts covered but accentuated by the dark red satin of her fitted gown. Anza felt short and plain.

Jeriza said, "You're Jance's friend? I wish he had invited you previously. Since he joined the Guard he's become so serious."

"Anyone would be, Riza," said Darvik. "But I'm glad something changed enough for him to invite a friend. Have you known him long?"

"Five years, my lord. But we haven't seen each other much since leaving the College."

"Oh!" said Jeriza. "I'm always interested to meet women who have been at the College. I would have liked to go, you know, but my father would not let me. I think he was afraid of what I might do if left on my own."

"I did all sorts of improper things," said Anza. "Once I climbed over the wall around it on a bet. None of the boys thought I could do it. Thank the gods I wasn't caught. I would have been expelled. I did win a lot of money, though."

Darvik laughed. "Please, come sit down," he said.

There was no getting out of it. She sat, folded her hands decorously on her lap, and listened to a conversation that was entirely mundane. Politics, events, ideas, those were all risky to talk about. The wrong words could result in interrogation. Much better to discuss a lady's new necklace or the incompetence of the workmen doing repairs on a house. Comparing horses was about as safe as it could be.

She tried to pay attention, in case anything was mentioned that might be useful to the resistance, but she felt out of place. It had been more comfortable talking to Esvar. Which was odd, as he had so much more power than these people.

He hadn't been afraid. That was the difference. Tense, cautious, demanding, yes, but not stunted with fear. Not that she was much of a threat to him. But if he was in the habit of looking over his shoulder, he had concealed it well.

The talk was interrupted by heavy footsteps, not the tread of guests. The music, which had been a constant background sound, went silent. Anza tensed. Had there been enough time for Doru to have called in soldiers for her arrest? The women in the room looked as though they had been posed, the men had curled hands by their hips. Everyone sensed danger. And these were the people supposedly on Karolje's side.

"Excuse me," said Darvik, rising.

Before the door shut behind him Anza saw four soldiers, whips in their hands. Their swords were sheathed. One of them was holding out a paper with a seal attached. A warrant. They were required in order to arrest nobility. She could not be the target. Which did not mean they would not take her if they wanted to. Who would they be coming to arrest at a party? It would be easier to take any noble present from within the Citadel.

Though not, perhaps, so publicly.

An argument was happening, voices low and indistinct but rapid with anger. Jeriza's hands were locked together over her belly with worry for her husband. Through the door, Anza heard Jance say, "I'm an officer. What's all this?"

A moment later the door opened. Darvik said, much more bluntly than Anza would have expected, "They only want Lady Jeriza. The rest of you are in no trouble." He extended a hand to his wife, who stood, pale and proud. Everyone else relaxed guiltily.

The lord left the door open this time, and Anza had a clear

view of the foyer. Jeriza took the warrant and read it, then thrust it back at them. "This is ridiculous!" she said.

One soldier shifted his whip suggestively from hand to hand. The leader said, "It's our orders, m'lady. We have to carry them out."

Darvik put his hand on his wife's arm. "Let's get this over with, then," he said. "I'm sure it will be resolved quickly. Cousin, if you would be so good as to take over as host, I will be grateful."

"Of course," Jance said.

The men shook hands. Escorting his wife formally, Darvik followed two of the soldiers out. The other two fell into place behind them.

No one said anything until the front doors of the mansion had swung shut. Then everyone spoke at once. Anza got up and went to Jance's side. He placed her hand on his arm as though they were about to dance, but his fingers gripped much too hard. They might leave bruises on the inside of her wrist.

He guided her into another room, smaller and more comfortably furnished, and closed the door most of the way. He said, "That's a way to get sober in a hurry. Hell. Let me know when you're ready to go home, and I'll order the carriage for you."

"What was she arrested for?"

"The warrant didn't say, which means it's likely sedition or treason of some sort. Whatever it is, she's innocent." He wiped his face. "I may be next."

"Have you done anything wrong?"

"I'm Darvik's cousin. That's enough. She was taken to put pressure on him, I expect, though he hasn't done anything wrong either. Except be liked. But he's not about to lead a revolt."

"You don't—never mind." She had been about to ascribe rational behavior to Karolje. "What happens if they aren't released?"

"If the property isn't confiscated by the Crown, it goes to Darvik's younger brother. Nothing comes to me; our mothers were sisters, and the property is from Darvik's father."

"At least that means you're unlikely to be framed," said Anza.

"Unless this is the first step in a purge."

"If it's a purge, they wouldn't bother framing you. What about Prince Esvar?"

"What about him?" said Jance. "It's my job to protect him, not his to protect me. He has problems of his own. When I got back to the Citadel after taking you home, he'd had some sort of quarrel with the king. It was about one of the interrogators. He told me later he had been punished. That was his word. This business with Darvik might be related. I feel pretty damn helpless, Anza."

She had no words to encourage him. She was shivering at the thought of the interrogator. *He misjudged a political situation. In other circumstances, he might have come out on top.* That was about Esvar's reprimand, which had been about her. Was the prince going to pay for having freed her? The thought made her stomach hurt. She didn't want to bear that obligation.

Jance continued, "None of it's your responsibility. But there are games going on I don't understand, and after what happened tonight, I'm afraid you might get sucked in. There are other people who can fight the king. You can't do anything against him if you're in a cell or dead. You got away once. It won't happen twice. You need to go back to your aunt and help her with her farm. This is war, and you're not a soldier."

"You're wrong. I am a soldier, even if I don't have a uniform.

And I'm not talking about weapons. Anyone who doesn't resist Karolje helps him. I won't do that."

His face reddened. She realized she was condemning him and braced herself for a quarrel. But all he said was, "Because of your father?"

"Because the king is evil."

Jance sighed. She wondered how much effort it had taken for him to refrain from saying that her father had not resisted. To refrain from defending himself. She had been unfair; he had warned her at risk to himself, had appeared ready to protect her from the prince, had not turned his back when he learned the truth. He was a good man. Her hands were bloodier than his, and her father's had been even bloodier.

She still didn't know if killing made her evil. The rules all changed in war.

And were the rules the arbiters of morality? Had she nothing at her center that was constant, that was good? Law and justice were distinct—that was obvious to anyone living under Karolje—but were justice and goodness? Was there such a thing as a just war?

"I'm not blaming you," she said, trying to soften things between them. "I'm going to step outside and clear my head, and then I'll be ready to leave."

Standing on the terrace again a few minutes later, she rubbed her arms against a nonexistent chill. Even obscured as it was by the trees, the Citadel threatened. The night felt enormous.

She heard footsteps and knew before she turned that it was Thali again. This time Thali was alone.

"Where's your husband?" Anza asked.

"Don't accuse me," Thali said. "Please." Her hands went to her temples, and she nervously loosened a strand of hair. "I didn't come here to pick a fight with you. Doru is back at the Citadel. He left shortly after we encountered you. When I saw the soldiers, I was afraid you were the one they'd come for."

"He went back without you? Isn't that improper?"

"There are a great many things about our marriage that are improper." The contained anger in her voice was alarming. "It was a mistake. I don't need to have you tell me that, by the way. I know it. But here I am."

If Thali still held a grudge, it was a small one. Apparently she wanted to talk. They would never be friends again—they had been too different in the first place—but at least they were not enemies. Anza pushed back the thought that wanted to come in, that her split with Rumil had been no neater, and said, "Why did you marry him?"

"All the usual reasons. He was charming and handsome and he wanted me. I thought I loved him. I didn't know how coldly cruel he is. Or how much he watches. He watches everything, every step, every word. He married me because I came without a fistful of established Citadel alliances, and he tried to force me into ones that would be useful to him. He's a spidergod, watching from the dark and pulling threads other people don't see. He vanishes at times, and people die."

"I'm sorry," Anza said, meaning it. "Can you divorce him?"

"No magistrate would grant it. They're too afraid of him. His enemies find their lives difficult and short. I would have to ask the king. And you can imagine what that would be like."

Anza could, only too well. The marriage might be sundered with an axe. Esvar might grant a divorce, but only if he dared oppose the king. Thali was unlikely to be worth that much to him.

"I wish I could help."

"I didn't come talk to you expecting you to save me." Thali

slapped at an insect. "But you might try to save yourself. If Doru starts poking about and finds that you were invited here by Jance, he'll get quite suspicious, since Jance has been taken up by Prince Esvar. That's probably half the reason Lady Jeriza was arrested. Any people at the College together will continue to know each other afterward—it's nothing. But Doru won't see it that way."

Four years ago Anza would have flared angrily at Thali's brisk *You might try to save yourself*, sparking one of their frequent quarrels. Thali had been her first lover, and that part had been delicious, but she could see now how they had rubbed against each other in all the wrong ways in every other thing that mattered.

She said, "Thank you. I don't know what Jance was thinking, inviting me to this party. Or what I was thinking in accepting."

"When he gets that sincere pleading look in his eyes, he's hard to say no to."

"He's hardened in the last two years. I suppose we all do after we leave the College."

"It's called giving up your illusions."

Anza glared in the direction of the Citadel. There were half a dozen things she wanted to ask Thali now, and speaking of any of them would be dangerous. Even if Thali never told anyone about them, a Truth Finder could get them from her. The only real way to keep a secret was to forget it.

The musicians were playing again. Lights, music, a pleasant evening. What was happening to Lady Jeriza?

"I'm a clerk for a lawyer," Anza said. "He might know someone who can secure your money for you."

"I have a lawyer. And a bank. It's the marriage contract itself that is the issue. He hates to lose."

Should she say it? "I heard that he is the spymaster."

"He is. I didn't know that when I married him, of course. Anza, I can't stay talking to you. Word will get back to him, and then you will become even more interesting. I just wanted to warn you to be cautious. Especially if you are doing anything illegal. He's got spies everywhere, and there is no shortage of people who would inform. Be careful."

"You too." She wanted to offer help again, inadequate though it would be, but she knew Thali would rebuff it. Underneath her self-possession, her unreadable coldness, Thali was scared. Terrified, even. Anyone who had their arms extended for balance didn't dare reach for assistance.

MIRANTHA

KAROLJE RETURNS IN the late summer a year and a half after he left, the Tazekhs routed for the time being. He brings with him a boy who has gained five inches in height and an uncountable amount of power. He isn't fourteen yet but is being treated as a man. He has his own Guard now, a handful of men sworn to him. They were vetted by Karolje, but Tevin chose them.

He is lost to me, Mirantha thinks as she looks up at Tevin for the first time.

"Hello, Mother," he says, his voice deeper, and hugs her.

"I am very proud of you," she says.

"Can I come tonight to tell you about it?"

"Of course. Please."

But Karolje orders Tevin to stay beside him all evening for celebrations, and by midnight he still has not come.

* * *

They are finally able to see each other alone three days later. He is bursting with stories about battles he watched from a distance, men he met, the winter in Densk, the meetings with generals he spoke in. She listens, attending more to the sound of his voice than to his words, looking at this child she birthed who will one day be a king.

He fades into silence. Then he looks at her, with eyes that are not a child's, and says, "We didn't really win this war."

"What do you mean?"

"Thousands and thousands of Vetian conscripts were slaughtered. There's no one to do their work. Their families are angry with the king. And there are—on the way back—there are Tazekhs living in Vetia, and he killed them." The maturity flees his face. "He did bad things to them, things they didn't deserve."

She goes to the door and opens it. No one is in the antechamber beyond.

"Tevin," she says. "You know to tell these thoughts to no one else, don't you?"

"Yes."

"The safest place to keep them is in your head. Now listen to me, and we will never speak of this again after tonight.

"Your father is cruel and unjust. A king is supposed to protect the powerless. Instead he hates people without power, because he sees in them what he fears most for himself. He will hurt anyone, hurt anything, in order to get what he wants, because he is too cowardly to face adversity. You will inherit a kingdom in tatters.

"You are too young to confront him. Wait. Keep your own counsel and be careful whom you trust. Listen much more than you speak. He will turn on you if he thinks he has to. No matter what happens, don't try to protect me. You have to be strong and brave, and you can't fall into hating anyone, even him. Don't think about vengeance. Think about justice.

"And do everything you can for your brother. I've had time with him, but Karolje won't let that continue, so it's up to you."

He kneels before her. "Mother," he says. "You talk as if you're going to die."

"This might be the only chance we have. Once he learns you've been to see me, he'll keep us apart. Don't fight him about it. It's not worth it. Save yourself for a later battle. Promise me, Tevin."

He stares, now looking much younger, and licks his lips. His face is bloodless. He has had to promise difficult things before, but this is the first time he has to put into words what he already knows, that much of his life will consist of giving up the things he loves.

"Promise me," she says, knowing he is too well-trained to weep, and fearing she is not.

He opens his mouth, shuts it, says in a voice that breaks, "I promise."

His hands are larger than hers. She raises him and kisses his cheek. She says, "Whatever happens, you are my dear son. Now tell me what is next for you. What new duties do you have?"

✦ ✦ ✦

When he learns of the talk, Karolje slams her into a wall so hard she cracks a rib. She stays in her rooms for a week, seeing no one. Twice she turns away Esvar, knowing it will hurt him, knowing she can't risk him coming to his father's eye. She reads and thinks. The Rukovili, over and over, not just the harpy poem but also the others, the love poems and the meditations, the sonnets that are painful with compassion.

Then she goes to the chapel.

Instead of Ashevi, Tahari is there. Lord Goran swooped down to marry her as soon as he heard rumor of her pregnancy, hoping no doubt to use the king's bastard for his own gain. Mirantha did nothing to prevent it, though she knew Tahari might be harmed, as she has done nothing to prevent Goran's other schemes against the king. The boy is a year old now and Tahari is pregnant again with Goran's child. She has much to pray about; Karolje claimed her again his third night back. Mirantha wonders if there are bruises on her body too.

She must pretend that she has come to pray instead of to see her lover. She kneels a proper distance away and looks up at the god on the tree. The god who is not a harpy, the god who twisted suffering into power. Who demands sacrifice and returns nothing. Her cracked rib throbs.

Her hatred of Karolje blazes up from the pit where she has buried it. It is not right, it is not good, of her to hate, but is she supposed to love cruelty and injustice and oppression? He is evil, a demon in human form, a man who should not have power over a worm. And he has a kingdom to tear and rip as he pleases, to beat and torture as he beats her.

Beside her, Tahari sniffs loudly, the sound of someone trying to hold back tears. Mirantha looks at her. The girl's face crumples. Mirantha pushes the libation bowls back and sits on the edge of the dais, one hand extended to Tahari.

"Come here, girl," she says.

"I'm sorry, my lady, I'm sorry," Tahari says through tears. "It's all right, I shouldn't be crying like this. It's just the baby, everything's all right."

"If it was all right, you wouldn't be here," says Mirantha. She asks the question she is not supposed to ask. "Is it Karolje?"

Stricken, Tahari opens and shuts her mouth. Then it all spills out. "He wants to take my son from me. He says I cheated him by marrying Goran, that he will not have his child raised by a whore. Goran tells me to submit. I have submitted, over and over and o-o-over." She turns away, covering her face with her hands.

The hatred narrows and sharpens into a point. It is too much. He has done too much evil. She trembles with rage, and the rage is joy that she drinks in, strength that she breathes in.

Tahari wipes her face and says again, "I'm sorry, my lady." She stands and hurries out.

Mirantha gives her time to get well away, then sends a guard to find Ashevi and waits. He comes to the chapel half an hour later and locks the door. In that time she has committed herself.

She says, "I am done with him forever."

"How done?"

"Done."

It is the first time they have seen each other privately since Karolje's return. They are standing beside the dais. The candles lit for the king's safety have been removed, but the wall behind the altar is smudged with soot.

He says, "How much did he hurt you?"

"It's painful to breathe. Don't touch me."

"Do you want me to help you leave?"

"I want you to help me kill him."

He stares at her. She stares evenly back. "How?"

"I want you to bribe a guard to knife him in his sleep, or a woman to give him poisoned wine. I want it quick and clean."

"If it's quick and clean, it will look like murder," he says. "You'll be the first person they suspect."

"There are many other people who hate him."

"But if he dies, you're the regent for Tevin. You benefit the most."

"I don't care if they kill me," she says, but she does. Not for herself, but for her sons. "Is there no other way? Can it be done so that Goran is accused? He benefits too."

"I'm a priest, not an assassin," he says, tone edged with impatience.

"Then call a succubus to kill him in his bed!" she snaps.

"Don't be a fool."

"So there's nothing. Are you going to tell Karolje I asked for it?"

"He knows about us," Ashevi says, and she goes cold. She has feared it for years, but it is a different thing to hear it said. "He knows you hate him too. There is nothing to tell him."

If he knows about us, why does he let it continue? she thinks. Perhaps Ashevi is lying. She can't remember what truth looks like. She fears what he will do if she challenges him. It would not take much to hurt her, not now when she is already battered by Karolje.

She has been a fool, hoping for love, for kindness, for someone to take her part.

* * *

She considers ways to kill her husband. He is never unguarded, unless they are in bed, and she is not strong enough to fight him. It would have to be a trick, a hidden knife in his neck or heart. She would be hanged for it, or worse. There is no opportunity to feed him a slow poison. Guards stand duty in the kitchen when the king's food is being prepared. None of the servants who support her will give their life. If she knew the tangled intricacies of power among the lords, she might find an ally, but she has been kept apart from them.

The knife is likeliest, but Tevin is young, too young to withstand the pressures that the lords will push against him when he sits on the throne. He is clever and brave, but he is not yet a man. Right now she can still support him, lend him her presence, and advise him, but if Karolje dies soon, it will be her own death warrant too, because Goran will not want to share power. Then who will there be to look out for her sons?

She wants to be free of everyone. Of Ashevi, of Karolje, of her sons, of the lords and servants. She wants to ride north and not stop until she is hundreds of miles away, surrounded by stone and pine. Away from hands that touch her and voices that implore her and eyes that distrust her.

It is a simple want, a pure want, cold as mountain snow.

I have never been Mirantha, she thinks. Father, husband, sons, always there is someone between her and herself. Ashevi holds the door open, but if she tries to step through, he will block her too. He brings her body to life, he knows how to give her ecstasy, but he doesn't love her, not really. He loves the idea of her.

She recognizes that if things go on as they are, at some point she will tip over the line of caution. She writes letters to her sons, then tears them up and burns them. They are too dangerous. Love of any kind is fatal.

12

ESVAR THOUGHT HE had lost the capacity to be surprised or shocked. It had bled out of him during the whipping. When Marek told him Lady Jeriza had been arrested for treason, he felt only a dull curiosity as to why he had not foreseen it. He never should have spoken to Darvik.

"Where is she being held?" he asked.

"They brought her directly to the Green Court. Your brother is on his way. The arrest was on a king's warrant."

Karolje's personal order. That and the Green Court meant there was to be a full indictment. The more usual thing would have been to put her uncharged in a cell, especially because then Karolje would not have needed to appear. If the king was showing himself, it was a trap of some sort, and Esvar had to walk into it with his eyes wide open.

"Am I ordered there?" he asked. He would go, regardless, but he needed to know Karolje's expectations.

"No, sir."

This game involved his honor, then, what he had left of it. He wondered if he should wear his sword. No. If there was to be physical violence, the plan would be for him to be outnumbered.

He was a good swordsman, but the best of the Guard were better.

He dreaded the thought of returning to the Green Court, and when they arrived he let Marek open the door. He was half-afraid Lukovian's ghost would try to steal its way into him. The execution had been quick, the heavy blade slicing through his neck in the space of a single breath.

Within were Tevin, Darvik, Jeriza, and six armed guards. Tevin had taken Jeriza aside. Her red gown looked close to black in the dim light. Two of the guards Esvar knew as loyal to Tevin despite not being his own sworn men, but the other four were ordinary soldiers who would follow Karolje's orders.

Darvik hurried to him. His fine clothing was disheveled. A smear of dirt on his shoulder was probably from a hand restraining him. He said, "She's not a traitor, she hasn't done anything." His voice was rough with suppressed fury.

"I know. Have you been told the specific charges?" Esvar asked.

"No, my lord."

"Did you do anything? Loan money to someone? Contact the resistance?"

Darvik's denial came a few breaths too late.

Esvar didn't have the time to consider the transgression. It might have been petty. He said, "You're not under arrest. I advise you to leave the chamber now, before the king comes. Wait in the antechamber." Karolje meant to use Jeriza against her husband, and half his leverage depended on Darvik's presence. The lord should realize that.

"I can't leave Riza."

"All you can do in staying is make yourself a larger target. And her. They'll hurt or humiliate her more if you are watching. Leave, my lord."

"She's—" Darvik's response was interrupted by the opening of a side door. The king entered, two more soldiers behind him. He walked slowly and looked weak, but he seated himself in the chair without awkwardness. His gaze flashed from one prince to the other as the room silenced.

"Up here," he said. "You will witness this."

Neither of them moved. Tevin's body was set with defiance.

Karolje gestured. Steel whispered from scabbards like wind in a tree. One of Karolje's men stepped forward and leveled his blade at Jeriza's stomach. Everyone except the king froze.

"If you value the lady's life, you'll obey me," said Karolje.

Darvik, who had turned to look at the king, glanced back at Esvar, who could do nothing from where he stood. Tevin was not close enough unless he could surprise the soldier. If she was killed, Darvik would blame them. He might get himself killed too. Karolje was going to have to be obeyed. Again.

Jeriza said, "I'm pregnant."

The soldier's sword wavered. The warm tones of his dark skin flattened. To kill a pregnant woman was a sin. Karolje might be able to get away with it if he killed with his own hand, but his soldiers wouldn't.

Darvik was taut with fear, not surprise. She spoke the truth.

Good, Esvar thought savagely. Karolje was going to have to alter his plan.

"Come here, woman," Karolje said. "And you, Darvik."

Don't do it, Esvar thought. He kept his mouth shut. The lord and lady obeyed and stood before the chair. Esvar followed as quietly as he could. No one seemed to notice; their attention was all fixed upon the king.

The king said, "I void your marriage. A child born in prison to an unmarried woman belongs to the Crown. I will allow you to live long enough to give birth. Be glad, Lady Jeriza. If the child is a boy, I will raise him as my heir."

Darvik was so white Esvar could not see how he was still standing. He said, "You're mad."

"You're superfluous," said Karolje.

Esvar moved before the nearest soldier could, shoving Darvik aside and pulling Jeriza behind him. The tip of a soldier's sword came to rest against his ribs.

"Traitor," Esvar said. He heard Jeriza stumble toward her husband and Marek but did not move his eyes from the soldier's face. "You've drawn on a prince of the blood. You know the penalty."

The soldier, wisely, kept his mouth shut, but his blade did not waver. Esvar put his hand on his knife hilt. The pressure of the sword increased.

This isn't how I die, he thought. He was calm, certain. He had never seen his own death, had no claim to see the future, but this could not be the moment, so ignominious, so empty.

Deliberately, he turned his head to the king. "What do you command, Karolje? Do you countenance this betrayal?"

"Put up your blade, soldier," Karolje said. "You may have his life, Prince, if you will take it now, with your own bare hands. If you are not man enough to do that, he has my pardon."

The cage had slammed around him with no room to breathe. He could be a coward, or he could be a murderer. Either way he was Karolje's tool.

Tevin spoke, his voice dripping with venom. "Are you ordering an execution, or a brawl?"

Karolje's guards each stepped closer to Tevin. The king halted them with a raised hand. "Clear the room," he said. "I will speak with the princes alone. But it is death to anyone who leaves the antechamber. Or who attempts to listen."

Esvar nodded at Marek, then leaned insolently against the nearest of the pillars. He would not stand and be disciplined like a child. Karolje wanted something, or he would not have bothered to send the others out. Tevin folded his arms. It was the most outward and unified expression of defiance from the two of them in Esvar's life. It might be the last.

The door shut. The silence built. Karolje hadn't held power all these years for nothing. Even in his weakened body, his authority dominated the space.

At last the king spoke, not breaking the silence but controlling it. "You're a pair of jackals frothing at the mouth with eagerness. Give it up. You can't kill me, and I refuse to die."

He grinned. His cheeks drew back, and Esvar had the horrible image of Karolje sitting on the throne in two hundred years, thin and frail as a dead leaf, flesh withered down to nothing, skin tight over bones, eyes as black and potent as they were now.

Tevin said contemptuously, "What is the point of this performance? You haven't got an audience."

Esvar knew there would be no explanation. The performance was its own point, and he and Tevin were part of it. Karolje was showing the puppets the strings. Because it amused him to do so, because one of them had tugged too hard, because he wanted them to see their weaknesses. It almost didn't matter why.

He wished he could think the king possessed or mad. But he wasn't. This was Karolje, a man, an ordinary man in a line of men, who had over and over chosen to do evil. The king had shaped himself. Gods and demons had not brought him to this spot. Power had, and cruelty and selfishness and vicious joy, and the unshakable certainty that the world existed to do his bidding. With time and circumstances, any person could become like him.

"I always have an audience. And so do you, both of you. There are no secrets in the Citadel. You're a fool if you think you can hide your actions from me, or the actions of your tools."

Esvar opened his mouth and shut it again at the glance from his brother. Tevin's senses must be finely tuned right now to have heard Esvar's intake of breath.

"I have done hundreds of things you have never seen," Tevin said. "And when you are dead, I will undo your works. I will erase your name from the records, and you will be known only as the traitor king."

"Will you boast of your goodness? That will be a lie greater than any I have ever told. You were conceived in filth. You don't know what manner of whore and adulteress your mother was. I shall tell you. You are not my sons. She lay with her father, and it was no rape. She used to taunt me with it, tell me how he suckled her breasts and rubbed his cock against her belly. I hurt her, and she laughed."

It was a lie, of course. Esvar had only to look in a mirror to see how like he was to Karolje. The same shape of forehead and nose and set of eyes, darkness of hair, line of brow. Tevin's coloring was lighter, but the face was the same.

His revulsion was no less for knowing that. Shame and revulsion. He was unclean. He could not help imagining his mother, naked and golden-haired upon a bed. *It's not true, it's not true,* he thought. *He lies. He always lies.*

"You are impotent, then?" Tevin said, striking back with a sword Esvar would never have thought to lift. "And powerless to hold a woman's affection?"

"You are not my son."

"But you named me your heir. You can't undo that." He took two calculated steps closer to the king. "And you won't live forever."

"The woman is pregnant," Karolje said. "I have raised two children as my sons who are not. I can do it again. Proclaim you bastard and traitor. The priests will not interfere."

"No one will believe the first. As for the second, if you name me traitor, I will prove it on your body."

Careful, Tevin, Esvar thought.

"I did not think you so foolish as to threaten me," Karolje said.

"You don't know me at all," said Tevin, cold and hard as marble.

The king sat unspeaking. His fingers gripped the chair arms. That's something you weren't ready for, Esvar thought in satisfaction. The repudiation struck at the heart of Karolje's self-conceit. It was inarguable. Tevin had found a weak place and pried it open. Esvar wished the court could see his brother now. The lords would hesitate to cross him.

Esvar went to Tevin's side. Neither Karolje nor Tevin broke their stare at each other.

"You tried once before to prove my mother had betrayed you," Tevin said. "It was in this room. You failed. Do you remember that? Or does your memory fail you too? I remember who was here that day. If you try to cut me off as your heir, I will call those men as witnesses to your madness, and they will give the crown to me while you yet live."

Somehow Esvar kept from exclaiming, from staring at his brother, from doing anything that would interrupt Tevin. His heart fluttered in his chest like a butterfly against a pane of glass.

What had happened? Had Karolje killed her after he could not prove betrayal?

"You are a fool unworthy of a crown," said Karolje.

His voice cracked on the last word. He convulsed violently, then slumped, his hand to his heart. His face was deathly pale. It more than ever resembled a skull.

Tevin ran to the door and yelled. Light from the antechamber flooded across the floor, banishing the darkness. Esvar's mouth was dry. Die, old man, die, he thought. It was the only clear thought he had in a swirl of emotions. His heart ached with old grief, stained with fear and anger, but he could not have said what the pain arose from.

Guards came running. Esvar watched impassively as they carefully placed the king on the dais beside the chair. Tevin stood near him, looking for all the world like a worried son. One guard felt for a pulse, then looked up and said something Esvar could not make out. Tevin nodded and took a few steps backward.

Esvar joined him. "You never told me that about our mother," he whispered.

"Later. Go wait in my rooms."

Dismissed, he thought. Protected.

* * *

He pulled a book from Tevin's shelves and paged through it without reading. For the first time he wondered what each of them held to himself that was in fact known by both. He knew things he would never say to his brother because the secrecy of them was etched into his bones; Tevin might know them too. Fear pushed them apart from each other and corroded the trust they should have had.

I'll have it out with him, Esvar thought. Hoarding secrets played into Karolje's power.

And what secret would he give up when Tevin asked? Alcu Havidian's daughter? The book that had been his mother's, which he had sent away forever? His foolish hope that he could leave the Citadel and join the resistance to fight Karolje?

Gods, he hated waiting. He needed something to do with his hands. A table in the corner had wine and glasses on it, and he poured some. It was a dark wine, velvety, not too sweet. Had it been sold to the Citadel by Servos Tashikian? He put his fingers under the cup of the glass, cool and smooth and unyielding. He took a polite, unsensuous sip. Through the open windows he heard the familiar noises of guards changing watch somewhere below.

Finally Tevin came in. He too filled a glass with wine and sat down. His face was tense.

"He's conscious," he said. "I expect he'll live. Everyone present is sworn to secrecy, and the halls were cleared before they brought him to his rooms. The doctor said it was his heart without any prompting from me, so I think we will escape a murder accusation."

Someone would tell. Someone always did. Rumor would run, and poison might get added to the story. Hell, some people would approve of murder and would think that Tevin had failed. You should have let him die, Esvar thought.

"Why did you call the doctor?" he asked grimly. "There weren't any marks on him. No one could think you killed him."

"That doesn't matter. I would still be accused."

"You're afraid to kill him." Esvar regretted the words as they left his mouth.

"No," Tevin said, cold. "But if I do it, it has to be when I am surrounded by those who will support me. Not alone, like a thief in an alley."

"Just tell me you have a plan."

"I have a plan, damn you!"

Esvar knew he had pushed his brother too far. For an instant he remembered Mirantha in the last few months of her life. She had been quick-tempered, even harsh. Her hands had become very thin and the planes of her face angular and sharp. He realized now she must have been waiting for Karolje to kill her.

More subdued, he said, "And Jeriza? What's happened to her?"

"I sent them home and will get them off-island as soon as possible. You'd better not know more than that. I told them they were still married, and right now my word is law," he said bitterly. "Don't blame yourself for this one, Esvar. Darvik sent most of his money to Traband and encouraged others. That looked like preparation for treason."

"I understand arresting Jeriza and Darvik. That's political. But I don't understand the rest of it. The taunts. The claiming of the child. Has he gone mad?"

"If so, it would give me grounds for Articles of Deposition. But I don't think he has. Everything that happened tonight is in keeping with things he's done as long as he's been king."

Esvar took a breath. He wasn't sure he was ready for the answer. "What did he do in the Green Court to our mother?"

"It was after Ashevi was arrested. He made her submit to a Truth Finder about infidelity. The Truth Finder said she was innocent."

The Truth Finder could have torn Mirantha's mind apart. "How do you know?"

"I was there," said Tevin, jaw set.

Gods, Tevin had watched it. No wonder he was so set against the use of a Truth Finder. But—Esvar frowned. "You told me she was unfaithful, though. Were you wrong?" He remembered that clearly, the anger he had felt at his brother when Tevin finally told him.

"No. I saw how they looked at each other. He at her, mostly, as though he owned her. The Truth Finder lied."

Truth Finders lied when they were directed to, but lying to the king himself was a different matter. "What happened to him?"

"Slipped on a staircase a few weeks later and broke his neck. Karolje knew what was going on with Ashevi, but after Marantha was declared innocent, he couldn't prove anything. He'd known for a long time, I think. I don't know what moved him to get rid of Ashevi then."

"I do," Esvar said. "He knew he had lost you. He was afraid he would lose me. He needed to put someone completely loyal to him in charge of me." The man who had replaced Ashevi as his tutor had been stern and humorless. It could not have been a comfortable position, teaching a prince when your predecessor had been executed.

"That was part of it," Tevin agreed. "Karolje usually has more than one reason for what he does. Ashevi might have been conniving with Goran. He was damned ambitious in his own right."

Esvar said, "Tell me what you have on Goran. I might need it."

Tevin hesitated. "I will tell you, but don't use it unless something has happened to me. I don't want it to explode in my face. I need to wait until the next time he falls out of favor, and I prefer to wait until Doru has been eliminated. Do you remember when Goran's son died of winterfever?"

Esvar nodded. The Citadel had been full of illness and death that year, nine years ago, and when the chancellor's son died, no one had been surprised.

"Goran killed him." Tevin picked his wineglass up off the table and drained it. "I watched him do it."

"How?"

"The old servants' passage in that wing runs behind the rooms. Some of them have peepholes. They're all forgotten about now. Nihalik showed me when I was about nine, while Karolje was at the border before Piyr died. He was uncanny, that old man, I have no idea how he knew about them.

"I happened to see Goran go down the corridor to his son's room, and I knew he was going to do something bad. I just knew, the way one does sometimes. There was no one around, so I slipped into the servants' passage and went down to the peephole. I heard him talking to the nurse. I saw her go out. He sat down and talked to the boy, then sat by him and waited. His son fell asleep. Goran put a pillow over his face.

"It was quick. The boy might have died anyway. He hardly struggled. He was five, I think. Goran put the pillow back and went out and told the nurse he was sleeping and not to disturb him. The next time the nurse went in she found the boy dead and thought it was the sickness that had killed him. No reason not to think that."

Appalled and fascinated, Esvar said, "Is that enough to blackmail him with, though? He can call it slander."

"Ah, but there is something I know that only a few others know. The boy was Karolje's son. Goran knows it, and the king does, and maybe a servant or two suspects."

Gods. Poor Tahari. "How do you know?"

"Our mother told me. I asked Tahari once, in confidence, if

the boy was Karolje's, and she confirmed it. I didn't tell her Goran had killed him."

"But—" Esvar could not see how this gave his brother leverage. Not in a court where Karolje could whip his own son and Disappear his own wife. "That will be your word against his, and no one will care enough for it to threaten him. The only person who will be hurt is Tahari."

Tevin refilled his cup and had a generous swallow. "Karolje doesn't know about the murder. He would probably have liked to make this boy his successor, since you and I are so unsuitable. Kill us, kill Goran, put the boy in place as Karolje's heir. Everyone thinks his claim comes through Goran, but Karolje has the satisfaction of knowing it's his own son. What do you think would happen to Goran if I told Karolje this now?"

Goran would go to the block. Why had he even married Tahari? He must have thought raising a king's bastard as his own would give him influence with Karolje. The man was a fool.

Esvar said, "Goran can say you're lying. And if the king finds out you kept this secret, he'll kill you too."

"As to the first, I'll tell Goran that I am willing to submit to a Truth Finder. That should keep him from risking disclosure. As to the second, Karolje understands political expediency. But in any case, Goran won't go running to him to spill the story. I trust you."

"And if Karolje dies before you blackmail Goran? What will you do then?"

"Tell Goran I know, and threaten to try him for murder if he doesn't submit."

"You could have used this years ago," Esvar said.

"I want to control Goran, not give him to the king to dispose of and replace with someone worse. Now." He drank. "Do you see the red book there, on the third shelf from the top?"

"Yes."

"There's a letter in it for you if Karolje and I kill each other and you are somehow still alive. Nothing in it would be useful to anyone else, to use against me or for their own profit, but there are things in it I want you to know if you become the king. No facts or plans or coded messages, only thoughts."

"Is there anything I should know if they take you away tonight?" He tried to sound droll, ironic, but he expected Tevin would see through that. Voices carried in from outside as people went about their ordinary business, unaware or unconcerned that the king had turned on a lord that evening.

"Once when I was seventeen," Tevin said, "a man came to me and offered to help me overthrow the king. He was wealthy and had friends among the courtiers. I wanted to trust him, but I couldn't be sure it wasn't a trap. I ordered him killed. Quietly, without notice or fuss. For years I told myself it was the only decision I could have made. Even if he did truly support me, it seemed a bad idea to hurry to the throne on the shoulders of someone else. That kind of secret gets found out, or collects interest. I had no desire to owe anyone a favor for my crown. And you weren't old enough to take my place if necessary.

"It was a mistake. I could always have said I intended to double-cross him."

Esvar had only a little wine left. He finished it. "You were seventeen, Tev. You didn't have support. There was no one to advise you. What could you have done?"

"Challenged Karolje as I did tonight. He's never been invulnerable. No one is. He has just succeeded at looking so. The weakness was there, if I had had the nerve to strike."

"He might have exacted a bloody revenge on someone else," Esvar said. He was not used to reassuring his brother instead of arguing with him.

"It's no use playing 'might have.' The time is past. But I'm not going to let caution rule any longer. If the king's soldiers fight mine, mine will fight back." He drank again. "There are other secrets. Do you know that Karolje murdered our mother's family? It was her brother first, during the war. He was injured, and Karolje's doctor poisoned the wound. Our grandfather was beset by bandits and our grandmother was thought to have hanged herself in grief. The murders shouldn't surprise you, though it's interesting that he bothered to conceal them." Another drink. "He turned on the doctor later and had him killed. I talked to the doctor while he was waiting for execution, and he told me about the wound. He said it wasn't the only time he'd been ordered to kill instead of to heal, and he told me where he kept the poisons. They're now in a box under a false bottom in the chest that holds my winter cloaks.

"There are a few other things there that were our mother's that I managed to get out of her rooms before Karolje had them thoroughly searched. She had her own hiding places. No papers—she wasn't that foolish."

Esvar was clutching the stem of his glass too hard. He relaxed his fingers and put the glass down at his feet, far enough away that he would not kick it accidentally. Tevin looked feverish. He wasn't revealing information; he was confessing. Slicing away rot.

"She hated him, you see. I think she was working up the nerve to kill Karolje herself, and that's why he had her Disappeared. She had learned how to be cruel too, just as you and I have. Because that's how you survive Karolje. You bathe in acid and everything is dissolved that isn't hard and inflexible and essential. If you think there's anything left of who you are but that, you're deceiving yourself.

"And that, Esvar, is why no matter how much you try to be right and good and just, you will fail. You keep trying because you have to. If you don't try, he wins. But you will never know what it is to love, or to have joy, or to not be shadowed by fear. Every time you look at yourself, you think you see Karolje looking back. You won't let anyone come close because you don't want to hurt them, but you will pretend to love them so they don't know how much you're like him. However you try to turn things, you are yourself a lie."

Then Tevin, Tevin who never lost control, dashed his glass against the floor. It rang one high sweet note and shattered. The wine splashed, red everywhere among the shining fragments of glass. Some of the wine stained his fingers and the back of his hand, lay on his forearm like freckles.

Esvar was mute. This was a brother he had never seen, on the knife-edge of madness. His own fear of Tevin told him not to move, to be invisible, unimportant. He's your brother, help him, said one voice in his head, while another said, If you do anything wrong, he'll take that broken glass and slash your neck.

"It's all right," Tevin said, rising. His voice shook. "I didn't mean to say all that."

"Are you drunk?"

"No. Well, maybe a little. Wait."

They didn't speak again until a servant had come and gone, the glass in a pail and the floor wiped clean. Then Tevin said, "His next move will be to use us against each other. Be watchful for that. It will come in some way neither of us expects."

"You have a hold on Goran if you need it. Do you have one on Doru?"

"No. He's considerably slipperier."

"Discredit him," Esvar said. "Whisper in Karolje's ear that he should have put down the resistance entirely by now. Let the king brood upon Doru's failures. I'll grant you that Karolje's sane, but I think he's breaking."

Tevin considered it for longer than Esvar expected. "You'll bear some risk," he said at last. "Since you're responsible for the raids, Doru can spin your own actions back at him and blame you for the failures. Or aim downward, at your soldiers."

"I'll chance it. He's dying, Tevin, your way needs to be clear. Don't worry about me."

"I won't, if you don't go rogue," Tevin said without heat.

"I won't," Esvar promised. Then he thought of Anza Istvili, who was in the resistance, and knew he might be lying.

13

ATTENDANCE AT THE execution of the arsonists could not be entirely compelled—there was not enough space in Temple Square, large as it was, for all the residents of the city, for one thing—but Anza and Radd worked much too visibly not to go. A little before midday they left his office. On their way to the square, they passed soldiers going in the other direction, ready to search shops and offices for people who had hung back.

On an ordinary day, vendors on the perimeter of the square offered religious charms: amulets with the signs of the gods, special candles and herbs and oils for offerings, prayer stones, and holy scrolls. The public scribes were there too, and untrustworthy apothecaries. All of them had been removed. Soldiers lined the square and stood with bows at the ready on the upper balconies of the nearby buildings. The priests would watch from the Temple steps, ready to receive the spirits of the condemned.

Anza and Radd took a place on the Temple side of the square, next to a row of ancient mulberry trees that provided some shade. The heat of the day was already intense. The pyre must have been prepared the night before. It was one long pyre with separate posts and chains for the victims, raised a few feet above the ground. Fitting for arsonists, but so cruel. Soldiers with unsheathed swords held the crowds back from all sides of the pyre. The Vetian flags, dark blue with the silver wolf's head of the house of Kazdjan on them, were limp and motionless in the heat.

People talked, but in low voices. This sort of public execution had stopped being entertainment a long time ago. One never knew who would be next. The harpies were gathering in the trees and on the rooftops. From the walled Temple garden behind Anza, honeysuckle released its scent. Fallen and trampled mulberries had attracted wasps. The insects' wings moved up and down as they sucked.

If she looked over her shoulder, she would see only the Temple, a large ancient building with its gilded dome shining in the sun and its tall bell tower obscuring the Citadel. It was no protection. Mirantha had not turned to the Temple for sanctuary, not even after her priestly lover was killed.

Esvar was up there in the Citadel, biding his own time. They weren't done with each other, he and she, but Anza had no idea what to do next.

Radd said, startling her, "As soon as people are allowed to leave the city again, I want you to go to my family in Osk. I'll come as soon as I can after that. We can start over there. It's closer to your family, too."

"You've taken care of me more than enough," Anza said. "I can't leave now."

"Why not? Now that you have left Rumil, what other obligations do you have?"

She wanted to tell him everything, starting with her father's death. Tell him about that, and the resistance, and Sparrow, and the prince. Tell him about the queen's journal. She said, "My friends are here. Mid-country isn't home anymore. If it gets dangerous, I'll leave."

He gestured at the pyre, the soldiers. "It's dangerous now."

"I have to stay. I can't tell you why."

That brought his head around sharply. He said, "I'm not going to pry into your secrets, Anza, but are they worth your life?"

Jance would say no. So would Esvar. Would he? He had not tried to talk her into leaving, even when he mentioned war. He left her to assume her own risks. Or perhaps she didn't matter to him and he had forgotten about her entirely by now.

She remembered Irini's face when talking of Velyana. River's firm voice as he corrected her stance. "They aren't my secrets," she said.

"Be careful about that. When someone gives you a secret, it can be a trap, even if it's not meant that way. If you had to climb down a cliff and this person held the other end of the rope, would you go over?"

"Yes," she said at once, thinking of Sparrow. And Esvar too, for that matter. She had gone into her father's house with him, alone, and emerged again. "I already have."

He put a hand on her shoulder. "All right. I know better than to argue with someone your age in a passion. But you have good sense and generally good judgment. I would not have kept you with me if you didn't. For the gods' sakes, don't throw those to the wind. Karolje won't live forever, and we need strong people after he dies."

They were standing close to each other, voices soft and drowned out to observers by the other noises around them: conversation, soldiers' feet, the faint stir of leaves in the breeze. She said, "What kind of a king will Tevin be?"

"That will depend on what he has to do to get and keep power. Now we've talked enough. Save your other questions for my office."

It's not safe, it's not safe. The thought pounded through her, driving in a sharp nail of fear. She wanted Esvar to leap onto the stand and proclaim his brother king. She wanted the crowd to turn on the soldiers. She wanted a bow in her own hands. The world was on the edge of terrible change, and there was nothing she could do.

✦ ✦ ✦

They waited for at least an hour before the prisoners were brought out. Two men, one woman, all blindfolded. The men were both Tazekhs by their dress and untrimmed beards. Anza shuddered. An example. The crowd would be frightened and turn its fear on the Tazekhs in the city, while the act sent a covert message to the resistance: *every act you do I will counter with the death of innocents*. Sparrow had anticipated this. Anza thought bleakly that Karolje could twist anything to his advantage.

Guards chained the prisoners to the posts, their backs toward her. Radd's hand came to her shoulder. A chant arose. *Burn the Tazekhs, burn the Tazekhs*. The soldier nearest to Anza had a frighteningly eager face. *Burn the Tazekhs*. The chant wanted to suck Anza into it. Clapping began, rhythmic and relentless.

A horn blew, echoing around the square. The chant died raggedly out. Scroll in hand, a man dressed as a commander ascended the stand beside the pyre. He unrolled the scroll and read. The words did not carry as far as Anza's ear, but she knew what they were. The charges, the names, the sentences. Lies.

He rerolled the scroll and raised his fist. As soon as he brought it down, other soldiers would approach with the lit torches and toss them on the oil-soaked kindling. The posts and chains would conduct the heat and burn the prisoners' skin before the flames did.

The paper fell from his hand as he staggered. Something long and black protruded from his chest. Another arrow shot into his neck. He fell. Screams and shouts broke out. Her eyes followed the path of the arrows to a balcony where several soldiers were struggling with each other.

"Run," Radd said sharply. "They can't kill everyone. Go east. By the time you reach the street, the soldiers will be in the crowd. Go." He pushed her.

She was pressed between the crowd and the wall. The crowd was moving. She started running. She heard screams. She was shoved hard against the Temple wall. Run. Everything was heat and panic. No smoke yet. An elbow in her side, a foot coming down hard on hers, the scrape of her arm against tree bark. The furious hum of wasps an undertone to the shouts. If she fell, she would be trampled.

Another scream, much closer, and the crowd turned, pushed her backward. More screams. Soldiers nearby.

A column of fire erupted, violet-white at the core, and a wave of heat blasted against her. The crackle of wood. Something sharp struck her on the arm. A thunderous noise took her hearing. She stumbled and fell, the last sight in her eyes a soldier with a raised and bloody sword in a silent and slow world.

• • •

The sun was painfully bright. She turned her head and saw a bandage on her arm. She had enough strength to put her uninjured right arm over her eyes, to block out the light. She lay, hardly thinking. Around her she heard pain and grief and some stronger voices, commanding. She heard the word *water*. Her mouth was dry and her body was a mass of pain. The ground vibrated a little as someone walked by. She smelled clean grass and burned flesh and bitter salves all at the same time.

She slipped in and out of consciousness. Time had no meaning.

✦ ✦ ✦

A voice, calling her name. Familiar.

She lifted her head. She lay in early evening shadow on a folded cloak on the ground. A man squatted beside her. A soldier. He was familiar. She could not remember why. Not Jance. Her mind felt clotted.

"Anza Istvili?" he said.

At the tone, a memory snapped into place. *He wants to see her. Now.* Esvar's captain. She did not know his name. "To the prince," she mumbled. Her tongue was thick and cumbersome.

"Yes," he said. "Good."

"Radd, what about Radd?" She tried to sit, but he pushed her gently down. Full memory of what had happened was coming back.

"Wait. You've been hurt. Lie still. I'll bring you a drink."

She waited, staring at the sky. A flock of starlings swooped blackly against the blue. Her eyes watered from smoke, and dull pain throbbed in her left arm.

Footsteps. The captain put an arm under her shoulders and raised her to a sitting position, offered her a flask. The water was sweet and cool and reviving.

"Why are you here?" she asked.

His dark eyebrows went up. He said, "Orders. I've been here

for hours. It's chance I happened to see you. How much pain are you in?"

"Everything hurts." Each movement made her wince, but none of the pain was the pain of a broken bone. "It's not too bad. What happened to my arm?"

"A cut, the doctor said. He was worried about your head."

She felt. A lump on the back of her skull was tender and sore to the touch but not bloody. "I'll be all right."

"Let's see what happens if you get up." He reclaimed the flask and helped her to her feet. She was briefly faint, then steadied.

She was in the Temple public garden, not far from a wall. A flock of harpies was gathered, waiting. Several soldiers stood alertly. The covered shapes of the dead lay everywhere, too many to count. Two men were walking among the wounded. It looks like a battlefield, she thought.

"I want to see Radd," she said. He would not have left her. "Where is he?"

"The gravely wounded are in the Temple," the captain said.

Oh gods, if he died, if he died . . . Light lay golden on the grass. Their shadows were long. She caught a faint scent of honeysuckle. The sounds of people in pain intruded on the peacefulness.

Ten narrow steps led up to the Temple's garden entrance. Oil lamps burned at the bottom and top steps. Stone figures in demonish shapes, streaked green with moss where rainwater spilled out of their grinning mouths, loomed from the roof. Inside, torches cast parts of the room into shadow and illuminated others. Tiled on the surface of the high dome was an angel with a raised sword, standing with one foot on a demon's stomach. Patches of dirt-encrusted tiles on the walls and ceiling showed gold and blue and red against the dull stone. Carved faces stared down from the walls and pillars, faces with wings behind them. The building was enormous, and old, and patient.

Columns formed an arcade along three walls, sheltering the wounded. Radd was halfway along the western side. He lay unconscious, a blood-soaked bandage where his eye and cheek had been and a swelling black bruise over his stomach. He wouldn't live the night. Anza went to her knees beside him and picked up his wrist. His pulse was faint and unsteady. The movement of his breath was barely visible. She touched the bruise and felt the pressure of the blood pooling underneath the skin.

No, she thought, no. It wasn't fair. Her throat ached.

She sat with him until he died. It might have been an hour.

Two years ago she had knocked on Radd's door with a letter from Master Tinas. He had taken it and read silently in that way he had, then shown her into the next room and to her desk. He had paid her and taught her and respected her, and now he was gone.

She leaned against the wall, her face pressed into her forearm. The gloom of the Temple enveloped her, the old smells of stone and incense, the hundreds upon hundreds of people who had trod the floor and prayed. Grief was a cloak, thick and sheltering, protecting from the ever-watchful eyes of the god. From the wingbeats of the Messenger.

After a few moments, she drew herself up and called over the nearest priest. She hastily made burial arrangements, then went in search of the captain.

He was talking to a priest. She waited until he broke off. "I need to talk to you," she said.

The captain said, "What about? I'll give you an escort home. You're in no danger. From anyone." He put a slight emphasis on the last word.

"And when I'm home, then what? Soldiers outside my door to watch me?"

"Excuse us, please," he said to the priest. He escorted her to a shadowed alcove and said harshly, "Don't waste my time, girl. The prince wanted to meet you once. That doesn't give you any claim on me. Do you want an escort home or do you want to spend the night here?"

"I want to see Esvar."

"Why?"

Why? was better than many other responses. She had no good answer to the question, though. She wanted to rail at the prince for Radd's death, she wanted to know why Lady Jeriza had been arrested, she wanted to shout at him to do something. She wanted him to prove he was not his father.

She realized she was shaking. She breathed out deeply, calming herself, and said, "Please. Just tell him I'm here."

He considered it for a long time. He must have some discretion of his own, which she counted on him to exercise. At last he said, "I'll send. I can't promise an answer."

✦ ✦ ✦

She was not sure how much time passed after that. She dozed, but her dreams were too horrifying to sleep through. The Temple was cold and quiet. Like a tomb, she thought. If this were a play, a ghost would appear and tell her what to do next. She drew her knees up to her chest and leaned into them.

"Anza."

She raised her head. Esvar himself. She was immediately wide awake. She came to her feet, trying not to seem as wary as she felt.

"We'll talk in the priests' garden," he said.

Priests and soldiers accompanied them as far as the door, but no one followed down the steps. An oil lamp burned at the base. The walled enclosure was small, a fountain at the heart and white-skinned birches lining the path to it. Anza resisted looking back as Esvar led her around the fountain to a bench on the other side. No one could see them through the water. No one could hear her if she yelled.

He sat first. She lowered herself carefully to the opposite end of the bench. Her sore muscles had stiffened again, and she felt graceless compared to the feline litheness of his movement. It was too dark to see into his eyes.

"Why did you send to me?" he asked.

"Why did you come, my lord?"

His laughter was sharp and humorless. He said, "What did you see out there in the square?"

"The commander was shot. Twice." She remembered the men struggling, the strangeness of motion when the rest of the square was still. "After that was the explosion. I was knocked out."

"Did you see the man who shot?"

"I was close enough to see that he was a soldier. I think everyone could see that. Is he still alive?"

"Yes. He'll be hanged. He was an experienced soldier. He confessed to supplying weapons to the resistance."

Why had the man exposed himself when the only death he bought was a commander's?

Because it was public. No one could think the Tazekhs were responsible when the shots came from one of the king's own soldiers. The man had sacrificed himself to show that Karolje did not have the loyalty of all his troops. She wished Sparrow had told her the plan so she and Radd could have stood farther away.

"What was his name?" she asked.

"Tarik Ashvili. He wasn't married; he could afford to take the risk." Esvar's soft voice demanded her attention. He had taken the time to learn something about this soldier.

"But he didn't set the explosion off."

"After the commander was shot, someone lit the pyre. There was an explosive laid within it. That would have happened even if there had been no archer. The pyre was rigged to kill as many people as possible. It's like the war. Everyone will think it was Asps."

Burn the Tazekhs. Burn the Tazekhs. She thought of the soldiers standing around the pyre. They had been the targets. "How many soldiers died?"

"Twenty-two so far. Sixty other people. The numbers will rise."

Four score people dead. But the explosion would not have been part of a resistance plan, unless someone had broken with Sparrow. Sparrow would not have ordered anything that killed sixty ordinary people and could be blamed on Tazekhs. Karolje must have done it. Killed his own soldiers, his own people, to turn their hate and fear away from him. She was afraid to make such an accusation to Karolje's son.

Her left shoulder ached. She rubbed it.

"How badly are you hurt?"

"Just a cut, and I was bumped around. I hit my head. I'll be all right."

"Good."

He shifted and sat with head bent, clasped hands dangling between his thighs. He was thinking. She watched the bubbling fountain. It would soothe her into sleep if she let it. Fireflies winked against the water.

Esvar raised his head. Staring at the fountain, he said, "The poems by Rukovili—where did you get them?"

It was a right angle to anything she had expected. "At the College," she said. "I found it in the library. The room was locked, but I had a key."

"Why did you take it?"

"It was an impulse. I had been drinking. Then there was no way to put it back."

"It belonged to my mother," he said.

She swallowed. "I know, my lord. There was an owner's mark."

"Why did you keep it?"

She could not see where he was leading. She decided to give the conversation her own twist. Her heart hammered; if she had misjudged him, she was giving him reason to kill her. "When I asked my father why he remained a soldier, he said that when the king dies, someone needs to be there to set things right."

Esvar's lack of reaction told her that her words had struck home. She waited, thinking of the first time they had met. She had been terrified when she was brought before him. Then he spoke, and his face was no monster's face, and his voice was concerned.

On the bench, he shifted again to look at her. The skin of his hands was light against his dark trousers. "I hadn't intended to broach this with you yet. But since you brought me here, I shall. I want to employ you."

"In what capacity?"

"To be my messenger to the resistance."

"I know noth—"

"Anza," he cut in, "don't lie. Please. We both know better. You killed three men during the raid. It was quite clear once I talked to you. Your father was a very good archer, did you know that?"

"What was clear?" she asked sullenly. A firefly winked in front of her face. On the other side of the fountain, the Temple loomed against a starry sky.

"That you are the woman who got away. You fit the description. You had access to a man who could teach you. You're strong and quick. You have personal reason to hate the king and did not deny having owned an illegal book. You did not collapse under Lukovian's attempt to kill you. You stood up to me. That all adds up. And I did know your father."

"Did Jance—"

"He hasn't said anything. But he cut himself on a slate just as you did."

She had brought herself to this point. By her acts, by her very mention of her father. By asking to speak to the prince. What for if not to reveal herself? She had taken a risk and he had called her on it; there was no backing away. Radd's question about the rope and the cliff had been a good one, and she had not considered it carefully enough.

Avoiding his gaze, she said, "What if I refuse to go to the resistance? Will you arrest me?"

"No." His voice was patient, the tone one might take when calming a recalcitrant child. She could not hurt him personally with her rage. Nor did he owe her anything. Yet he was far from passionless.

She watched the fountain for a while. At last she said, "I can take a message. But they might decide to cut me off instead of sending me back. They won't want to take the risk that you could spy on me or suborn me. They might even get rid of me one way or the other." She did not want to imagine Sparrow ordering her death, but she knew it was a grim possibility. Sparrow wanted to win.

"They won't. Not when Karolje is busy shifting the blame for all their actions to the Tazekhs. That explosion was planned for days, I assure you. Even if the resistance claimed it, they would not be believed. And no one is going to remember the commander getting shot."

So he knew who was behind it too. It should have assured her that he was trustworthy. Instead it made her fear Karolje more.

"Is that what I am to tell them?"

"That will do nicely to begin with," he said. "All I want right now is to know if they will talk to me."

"They're not likely to believe me," she said.

"Oh, I think they will. You're forthright. But if they don't, ask what they will accept as proof, and I will endeavor to provide it."

"I don't understand why the resistance has been allowed to continue," she said.

"'Allowed to' is not the correct phrase. The leaders are good. It's only in the last year or so that it's been evident to people not in it. Before then there were lots of smaller groups squabbling. They competed with each other, which served Karolje. Now Sparrow, and Stepanian before her, have managed to spread resistance like witchgrass."

"Are you still trying to weed it out? Because if you are, they won't have anything to do with you."

"I was. For my brother's sake. But things have changed. I hope to give them something that they want: an end to Karolje's reign."

"You said the king is dying."

"He is. His heart came close to failing a few nights ago."

"Your brother—"

"My brother's position is not secure. If it were, I would have no need of the resistance. I could just wait for Karolje to die."

The resistance is not your tool, she thought. She had no idea what ambitions he had for himself. "How can the resistance secure Tevin's position? Or do you want to use the resistance against him? Do you want to be the king?"

He recoiled. A hand rose, went down. "No. I support my brother. I thought you knew that. If not for him I would stab Karolje in the heart and let myself be killed." He said it so factually that for a moment she did not hear the pain.

Mirantha would not have wanted Karolje's death to come at the cost of her sons' lives. Speaking more softly than she had been, Anza said, "For some people, an end to Karolje will be enough. Others want power of their own. They're going to question why they should put their trust in either you or Tevin instead of toppling the throne altogether."

"I doubt there's anything I can do to convince everyone. All I can do is convince you."

"Why should I trust you?"

"You shouldn't."

For an instant terror stopped her breath. Then reason asserted itself. He was not saying he would betray her. He was holding her at a distance, walling her off. From friendship, from risk, from reliance.

Friendship. What a foolish word that was. This man had no friends, and if he did, she would not be one of them. What did he hold himself accountable to? Not her, that was for certain.

He was still talking. "That's the thing about trust. It's faith. Without it, there's nothing but fear. The king trusts no one and fears everyone. He is convinced every person he meets is against him, and so he makes them enemies. It's impossible to hurt him, because he's hollowed himself out."

"Did you trust my father? Did he trust you?"

"I would like to think so on both counts. It was never put to the test. He was in the king's command, not mine or my brother's, so I did not have much to do with him. I can't fault him for obeying Karolje's orders. I obey them. Your father didn't let his men be cruel, and the men who trained under him are good soldiers. When I was a boy, before he was made a captain, he helped me a few times. You have nothing to be ashamed of in your parentage."

"You told me he served you better than he knew. How?"

"He showed me that a man could be kind." He was quiet. "That's a rarity in the Citadel. I'm not much good at it."

"You let me go."

"That wasn't kindness."

She got up and walked to the edge of the fountain. Spray cooled her face. She dipped her hand in, sliding her fingers under the smoothly resisting surface of the water to the rough stone basin. It was colder than the air. The lamplight reflected in the water and gilded the mist.

The falling water was too loud for her to hear Esvar approach, but her body sensed it before his hands came down on the basin rim. His face was newly shaven, his shirt crisp. He had not come carelessly to her.

"Let's go in," he said. "I'll have Marek take you home so you can rest."

And then? she thought. Radd was dead.

She slapped her hand hard against the surface of the water, splashing them both. She did not have obscenities enough.

Esvar wiped the water from his face. "You're angry."

"You're bloody right I'm angry!" She hit the water again.

"Let me tell you about rage," he said.

The words were an axe of ice, severing her from her anger. She wiped her own face and stared at him.

"Rage burns hot. It stays a coal one can curl around and warm oneself with. It keeps one moving. It's an incendiary, and when it goes off, it destroys everything around it. That feels powerful, oh so powerful. But all the smoke gets in the way of what one needs to see.

"Karolje's not like that. When he gets angry, he gets cunning. His rages are calculated, intentional. Anger makes him crueler and stronger. It's not his weakness. When one goes up against him and he's angry, he wins every time. He enjoys it when people throw themselves furiously at him. They burn themselves out. It's no use for the resistance to try to make him angry, or to manipulate other people into being angry at him.

"The resistance needs to erode the power of the lords who support him. And that needs to happen fast. Or we might have a Tazekh war on our hands."

He was frightening. Every line of his body spoke of contained violence. "Why are you doing this?" she blurted. "Why oppose him?"

"When I was eight years old, Karolje made me watch the execution of my mother's lover." In the speaking of his father's name, she heard something cold and implacable that resonated in her spine. Not hatred, not hot enough for that, not contempt nor scorn, but unyielding opposition. "Three months later he killed her. There is nothing he can do to buy my forgiveness. Or my brother's."

Her stomach lurched. *He was staked, not ganched.* Mirantha

had spoken of Esvar watching, but it was far worse to hear it from him. "Did you look?"

"I closed my eyes. I couldn't keep them closed forever. It was worse for Tevin, who had to stand next to the king. My guards told me not to look, but they didn't dare cover my eyes or let me turn my head. It took a long time for him to die. I had nightmares for weeks.

"The soldiers came to arrest him while he was teaching me. I yelled at them, and one of them looked at me and said, 'It's the king's orders, boy,' as though I belonged in the kitchens. Karolje could have taken him quietly at night, but he thought I should have a show."

It seemed impossible Esvar could have survived such brutality without having learned to be brutal himself. She wondered how much it cost him to try to keep to an honorable path.

"I want a favor," she said. It wasn't really a favor, it was a test, and it was edged.

"For yourself?"

"No. The things I want for myself you can't give me."

"What?"

"I have a friend whose lover was arrested for no reason last year. Find out what happened to her. Her name was Velyana Roshikian."

"She's probably dead."

"I know. But uncertainty is terrible." She left unsaid, *You of all people should know that.* The words hung between them nonetheless. Show me you can have compassion. Show me you won't let Karolje win this point too.

"I will inquire," he said.

"I will take the message, my lord," she said. "It might be a few days. How am I to bring you a response?"

"Take it tomorrow. I will meet you two days later in the Red Hawk Tavern, near the College."

To see Sparrow tomorrow, she would have to ask Radd—Radd was dead. There was nothing she needed to do tomorrow, or the day after, or the day after. She would send the pending business back to his clients. A letter had to be written to his children.

It was too much. Her vision blurred. *Who else can Karolje use to hurt you?* Sparrow had asked, and she had been able to name no one except Radd. She had made herself into a person alone without even knowing it.

"What time?" she asked, hard.

"Six."

"As you wish, my lord."

He shook his head, then walked away and up the steps. He did not look back.

She followed. Marek waited inside the Temple. "Are you ready?" he asked her. Esvar was speaking to a priest several yards away.

"Yes," she said. "Get me the hell out of here."

Marek went to Esvar's side. The prince said something, then looked over his shoulder at Anza.

Their eyes met. She felt exposed. Everything he had said to her, kind or moderate or firm, covered the depths of who he was. She understood Jance's loyalty. This was a man she did not want to fail.

MIRANTHA

An assassin tries to kill Karolje and nearly succeeds. He has been in the king's guard for years, and when he knifes Karolje, the only thing that keeps the wound from being fatal is that the king twists away at the first prick, and the blade slides against a rib. The man kills himself before he can be questioned. Word is given out that he was a Tazekh spy, but Mirantha does not believe it.

Karolje's survival is accounted divine, the protection of the gods upon him and his kingship, and a holiday for prayers and libations is ordered. When Mirantha takes the cup from Ashevi to pour the water into the basin, their fingers touch. Run, her instincts say, run now.

• • •

It is a cloudy winter morning a week later when Esvar brings her the news of Ashevi's arrest. The boy comes pelting into her rooms, his guards behind him, and says, "Mother! They took him. Ashevi."

Mirantha goes still with shock, but recovers herself at once. "Tell me. Slowly," she says.

"It was my mathematics lesson. The king's soldiers came in and said he was under arrest for treason. Will he be killed?"

Treason. She will be next. Karolje has learned, he has heard, he suspects. She has to be completely calm about it.

She says, "Your father will decide. If he finds Ashevi is a traitor, then he will be killed. It is nothing to do with you, Esvar, I want you to remember that."

He thinks it over. He is a few months shy of nine, no longer a little boy. Clever, bookish, but with some of his father's temper. She once saw him strike another boy with a hard, efficient blow that sent the other child to the ground.

"Will I have another priest as tutor?" he asks.

"That is up to the king too."

"I hope not. The other priests don't know as much as they think they do. Will I be allowed to see him?"

"No." She looks up at one of the guards. "Do you know where they took him?"

"To the cells, my lady. In chains."

He will be executed within days, then. She says to Esvar, "You're not to seek him out. No one in the cells is to have visitors. To make an exception would weaken the king's power. Did he say anything to you about your lessons?"

Esvar shakes his head, but the soldier says, "My lady, he says to tell you the plan is in his workroom. He didn't fight them at all."

Thank the gods. "Take Prince Esvar to his archery lesson," she says. She has to search Ashevi's workroom before Karolje's soldiers do.

* * *

She looks quickly for anything she does not want to fall into Karolje's hands. In one drawer she finds a cake of opium and a book of erotic drawings and stories that disgust her and arouse her at the same time. She leaves both. His papers are letters from priests and scholars and notes for tutoring her son. No journal, no letters in Tazekh, no papers of debt. Nothing that shows he has any sort of lover. She is safe.

A soldier raps on the door and opens it without waiting for a response as she is making a pile of the books Esvar had been using and Ashevi's notes. "The king commands your presence, my lady," he says. He is a few years younger than herself, black-haired and handsome, and she can tell he does not want to take her.

She follows him, heaviness growing in her. This is it. She hopes she will be allowed to say goodbye to her sons.

The soldier takes her to one of Karolje's formal rooms, the Green Court. Several people are present, but only one she cares about: Tevin, at his father's right. This is not fair. He should not be made to watch this. His face is studied, impassive, but she knows him. She sees the anger and fear in his eyes.

Karolje says to the soldier, "What did she take?"

"Nothing, my lord." He is wooden.

Karolje says, "What do you have to say for yourself, woman?"

His stare separates her from her body. She watches from a twilit distance as a woman says without insolence, "About what, my lord?"

"Ashevi has committed treason. As soon as you were told of this, you went to his workroom. What did you destroy?"

"Nothing, my lord."

He looks at the guard. "Is that true?"

"Yes, my lord."

"Why did you go?"

"To see where he left off in his teaching," says the woman.

"Those papers and books might be destroyed, and Prince Esvar's next teacher will need to know what they were."

"So you are certain Ashevi will not be freed?"

"My lord, no one who goes to the cells is ever freed."

"You will not try to persuade me of his innocence?"

"Why would I do that, my lord?"

"Look around."

The woman turns her head. Mirantha, watching, follows the gaze. The king's general is there, and a Truth Finder, and Goran, who will be regent with her if Karolje dies. Cold-eyed Doru, who spies and watches. The soldier standing to Karolje's left holds a whip. If the woman needs help, there is no one to turn to. Tevin is too young, and Mirantha cannot help her either.

Karolje says, "You have no allies. Kneel."

The woman obeys. Coward, thinks Mirantha. But there is little choice.

Karolje rises from his chair and walks to the woman until he is almost touching her. He grabs her hair and pulls her head back.

"Ashevi planned to kill me," he says. "Do you tell me you knew nothing of it?"

"Nothing, my lord." Her voice is strained from the position.

"He wanted Lady Tahari to poison me. She reported it at once."

That's interesting, thinks Mirantha. Had he decided to help her after all? But the king might be lying. Perhaps the arrest is nothing to do with assassination, it is some other kind of treachery or Karolje has grown tired of his counselor. Or she has done something offensive and Ashevi's death is to be her punishment.

The woman says, "I know nothing about it, my lord." Goran's foot moves a nervous half step forward before he catches himself.

"Ashevi is your lover."

"Never, my lord."

"Don't think I don't know about the two of you," he says. "I brought him here to do me a service and gave you to him as a reward. There are peepholes in the chapel. I've seen you fuck him there, more than once. It made you feel powerful, didn't it, to think you had a secret from me? There are no secrets, Mirantha. There is no place you can hide from me, ever."

It almost shocks her back into her body.

Karolje is the one lying.

The woman says, "My lord, I will swear on anything you like that I have been faithful."

He gestures to the Truth Finder.

Mirantha knows what will happen next. She feels sorry for the woman. It will hurt. She looks at Tevin and sees his entire body ridged with tension. Karolje has misjudged. His son is going to hate him for this.

The Truth Finder puts his hand on the woman's forehead. The room goes quiet. It will be over quickly. The woman doesn't know anything, after all. The woman's hands go to her ears and her face crinkles with pain.

The Truth Finder brings his hand down and says, "She has been faithful, my lord. Ashevi tried to seduce her and she rejected him."

Clearly Karolje has not expected to hear that. He sits back down. "Is she a traitor?"

"No, my lord. She cares only about her children, and nothing else matters. She is loyal."

"A cow," says Karolje. "A bitch."

The woman's face colors. Mirantha knows the worst is over. When the king descends to insults, he has given up on getting anything.

"Get her out of here," he says.

Outside the room, Mirantha almost collapses. Returned to her body, she can barely see through the pain in her head. The guard stands patiently while she regains strength. He hadn't liked what happened either. How many are there like him, who still believe in honor? Tevin will need such men around him.

✦ ✦ ✦

Karolje comes to her that night. He leaves the light on and undresses her. The room is cold. He has brought the whip.

I can't take much more of this, she thinks.

DO YOU BELIEVE him?" Sparrow asked.

"Yes."

"Why?"

"He gave me my freedom when he gained nothing by it. Then he gave me my father's worth, before he knew I was the same person he had freed. That's two times he helped me when he didn't have to."

"He's using you."

"I know. We can use him." Anza said it with more confidence than she felt. They were at Miloscz's house. She felt the skepticism emanating from the circle around her. She did not blame them—she would find it hard to believe herself—but it was tiring. Irini's face was particularly grim.

"Use him?" Miloscz said now. "To what end? Is he going to kill the king or slay his brother? Of course not. The most likely thing is he gets himself killed. Or worse, goes into hiding and we're saddled with protecting him. Even if he's telling the truth, the risk is all on us and the benefit is to him. We don't need more spies within the Citadel."

"I think we do," Sparrow said. "The ones we have are not

placed highly. If we'd known about Karolje's plans to blow up his own men, we'd not have killed that guard commander yesterday. We could have planned some other destruction of our own to happen during the chaos."

"Did the prince know this was planned?" asked Miloscz.

"From what he told this girl, he didn't. He's no more useful than a Citadel cook. Less, perhaps. A cook could poison the king."

Sparrow said, "Karolje's blaming everything on the Tazekhs, and we're out of sight. A prince can put us into view. We need that."

"What we need," Apple said, "is a strategy. Ever since Ivanje was killed, we've been acting like a drunk in an alley, staggering around and bashing into things. We need to plan further ahead than a week or a month. When we have that in place, we can decide how useful one of Karolje's sons can be. Since he's not offering himself as a hostage, there's no hurry."

Anza said, "He's no use as a hostage. The king would let him die."

"The reason we don't have a strategy," said Jasper, "is that we have failed to agree on our goals. The prince wouldn't be making this offer if we had shown we were stronger."

"He wouldn't be offering at all if he thought we were weaker," Anza said. Her body ached from the violence yesterday, and her heart ached with grief for Radd, and she had no patience for subtle argument.

"Why is he offering?" asked Sparrow. "What turned him?"

"I have a friend in the Guard. He told me the king is dying." Better to put the secret on Jance than on the prince. "He's afraid of what might happen in the Citadel when Karolje dies. I think Esvar is too. We might be headed for a civil war."

Sparrow said nothing at first. The silence was unnerving.

Finally she said, "How sure is your friend that the king is dying?"

"Sure. And he is sure enough there will be trouble that he advised me to leave the city."

Miloscz said, "I mistrust all of this. It's too tempting. We're being trapped. Even if the prince means what he says, he could still be being used by Karolje. Or by his brother. I am not willing to make Tevin a king in his father's mold. We should consider that this invitation might be meant to split us."

Anza said, "There's no way to know what either Esvar or his brother want without listening to them. He wasn't lying when he told me he hates the king. Karolje's been as brutal to him as to the rest of us." She thought of the story of the man he had been forced to kill. Remembering hurt more than hearing it had. Damn it, was he coming to mean something to her? She couldn't let that happen.

Sparrow said, "I have no doubt that he wants an end to Karolje. But the resistance is not to be used as a step stool for anyone. We aren't kingmakers."

"If Karolje is dying, someone will come to power. This way we have some influence in the matter," Anza said.

Jasper said, "A country needs a leader. Is this a resistance or a revolution?"

He was a quiet man, brown and nondescript like a sparrow as Sparrow herself was not. That didn't lessen the impact of his words. He had exposed the turning point.

"Who among us would you trust to rule?" asked Sparrow. "The resistance is not about taking power for ourselves. It's about ending the tyranny."

"That's not enough," said Miloscz. "We need to end the lock the Crown has on us altogether. There can't be an opportunity for another Karolje to arise."

"Tyrants always find a way out of ashes," said Apple.

"We shouldn't make it easy for them," Miloscz said.

The wooden planks beneath Anza's feet were smoothed and polished. Miloscz was a rich man; his goals could not be the same as other people's. Did he care who ruled as long as he had lower taxes? Sparrow wanted Karolje dead. Irini wanted revenge. Apple, Jasper, River, the others, she did not know what they wanted, but she doubted they all wanted the same thing. People were more complicated than that.

Apple said, "I don't want to discuss this in front of Esvar's messenger. If we decide to listen to him, she can't be allowed to tell him what we intend. And he certainly shouldn't know anything if we decide not to listen."

"That's fair," said Sparrow. "Harpy, leave the room. I know you wouldn't willingly reveal secrets, but they can't force out of you anything you don't know. If you're going to be an intermediary, you only get to know what we decide you should tell him."

"I'll be outside," Anza said. She could at least practice shooting.

After collecting her bow and arrows, she walked down the lawn toward the pavilion, stopping when she was close enough to hit the statue within it. Drawing the bow made her shoulders ache more. Her first shot fell short and to the side. The second was wild.

Her mind would not break free of the memory of the arrow piercing the commander's neck, of the sudden terror. The explosion.

Karolje had taken her father, her friends. She would not let him take her ability to shoot away from her too. Her father had said, *To shoot, you must breathe into your entire body. Every muscle you have must be aligned with your eyes, and there is no room for anything else. Breathe. Don't think.*

She centered herself, shot. This time the arrow struck the statue. Not where she had aimed, but a hit was a hit.

Soon she had fallen into the rhythm of it. Afternoon sun was hot on her hair and back, loosening the tight muscles. Set, draw, release, over and over. The only noises were the occasional buzz of insects and the soft coos of a dove somewhere in the trees. It would be easy to forget about everything else.

When her name was called, it startled her. She turned around. Sparrow was walking toward her. Anza pointed at the quiver and the statue, went to gather the arrows. By the time she finished, Sparrow had reached her.

"You shoot well," Sparrow said. "I watched for a while."

"You didn't see me start. If I only have one chance to shoot, I'm afraid I'm going to miss."

"Do you intend to go back to Radd's?"

"No." She had gone earlier. Inside it seemed the same place it had been when they had left to go see the execution, just waiting for their return. Papers untidy on her desk, a glass with the dregs of wine, a stack of closed ledgers. She pulled out the three contracts she knew Radd had been working on and the two letters that needed to be answered and wrote brief responses advising of his death. Then she locked the door and went to meet Sparrow. "That's all done."

"You could stay here."

"Then people won't know how to find me."

"That's the idea," Sparrow said, her mouth hinting at amusement. "And it would give you much more time to practice."

"I'm not your only archer. And if I meet Esvar and someone follows me back, it gives you all away."

"Why do you trust him? What you said inside is good enough, but it's not complete."

She unstrung the bow. The sun was hot, and she walked forward a few paces until she was in the shade of the pavilion. Sparrow followed. The lake was intensely bright. For a moment Anza considered telling Sparrow about the journal, about the faith the queen had had in her sons. But that was not her secret.

She said, "He told me why my father was executed. He led a raid on the resistance. The leader of the resistance was killed instead of being taken prisoner. That was accounted a failure. The prince seems to think it wasn't. And he told me that before we ever talked about me being in the resistance."

Sparrow said, "Skilled manipulators lay their traps well before anyone starts looking for them. As soon as he determined you were in the resistance, he began thinking about how he could use you."

"So you think this is a trap?"

"I think the possibility has to be considered. And Miloscz was right when he said Esvar could be being used by other people. You always have to look below the top layers."

"Do you trust anyone at all?" Anza asked.

"Only a few. It's a hard way to live, but I do live." Sparrow flexed her hands. "You're to tell the prince we will listen, but there are conditions. He needs to send you back with something only he could own, something that is of great value to him. If he will give it into my keeping, I will treat with him through you. Not face-to-face, ever. I want to know what sort of help he expects. We aren't an army. I won't risk any more of my people in the Citadel as spies. I want a promise from his brother not to turn around and jail us when it's over. If he won't do all of that, we won't talk."

“What are you going to ask him for?”

“That depends on what he offers. He has to satisfy my other conditions first.”

“I doubt he carries anything valuable with him. I’ll have to meet him twice.”

“He can take all summer if he needs it,” Sparrow said. “It’s his move. Don’t bring his answer back to anyone but me.”

“What if something happens to you?”

“Jasper is the only one likely to negotiate in good faith. And that you are not to tell anyone else. Anyone.”

“I know how to keep confidence,” Anza said. “Isn’t River trustworthy?”

“He’s too hurt. He would try and fail. I’m going to have to keep other things from you for the moment, too. Meet the prince tomorrow, see what he says to our conditions. Treat the negotiations as you would work for Radd.”

“And then? Will you still be here?”

“I don’t know. I’ll send someone with a message.”

Anza nodded. She and Sparrow stood in an almost companionable silence, looking down the lawn to the water. The smell of smoke had lifted by that morning. Nothing indicated the city was anything but peaceful. A duck flew by and landed on the water with a splash.

“Come back in,” said Sparrow. “You’re needed. We have work to do.”

• • •

The Red Hawk Tavern was familiar to Anza; she had spent many evenings drinking in it while she was at the College. She thought that was why Esvar chose it. He was meeting her on her ground, not his, which should have signified more equal terms but only made her more suspicious that he was trying to get something from her. She had already fortified herself with two glasses of wine in a different tavern. The door was propped open. The inside was dark and smoky, as usual, and crowded and hot. It smelled of beer and grease. She didn't see Esvar. She made her way to the back, excusing herself and sliding by and pushing. Only one man pinched her.

Someone said her name. It was him, perfectly concealed in workman's clothing and cap. Since the people in the tavern had probably never laid eyes on him except from a distance, he didn't need much disguise. His guards needed more.

She slid in on the high-backed bench opposite him. A wall was on her left, and they weren't likely to be heard over the amount of noise other people were making. His chin was stubbled and his hair mussed under the cap. He seemed younger. Part disguise, part a way to put her at ease. She needed to be careful.

"I ordered," he said. She had to lean forward to hear him. He poured beer from a pitcher into a mug for her, then drank from his own. "I hope it's to your taste."

"You're paying," she said, cutting off a *my lord*. She would play along with the disguise. She lifted the mug with both hands. "How did you know about this tavern?"

He took off his cap and spun it on one finger. "When I was younger, I used to come to places like this pretty often. No one ever recognized me. I was damn proud of myself for living wildly outside the Citadel. Later on I realized my little rebellions had been watched and permitted like everything else. The box was bigger than I had thought, that's all."

His contemplative tone was more frightening than rage or resentment would have been. She thought of Mirantha. *I don't remember anything of the trial. A woman went each day and watched, but she was not me.* To make people deaden themselves, that was an especially vicious way to kill.

"Why did he allow it?" she asked.

"It was a form of winnowing. If I was stupid enough to get killed in a brawl, he was well rid of me. If I lived, he could have turned dissipation into need." He put the cap down. "Why didn't you tell me Radd was killed? I would have been gentler that night."

"It doesn't matter. It didn't matter. He's gone."

"What will you do now?"

"I don't know," she said. She had been turning the question over and over with no conclusion. "I thought Radd took me on, that the College admitted me, on my own. Sparrow says my father bribed them."

"They would not have taken you if you weren't fit," he said. "Your father didn't have the money for that sort of a bribe. I know what a captain's rate of pay is. But for you to succeed at the College, you must have had an excellent tutor as a child."

"Karolje became king," she said. "Men of learning found it prudent to hide."

"They did." He paused. "I found out about your friend. Velyana Roshikian. She was killed shortly after she was arrested. Do you want to know more?"

She tried to imagine telling Irini. It would be awful. "Was she tortured to death?"

"No. She resisted a guard and died during the fight."

There was a whole story unspoken, an attempted rape or a desperate suicide, a shattered skull or broken neck. A trumped-up reason for arresting her. Whatever had made her a target in the first place. Esvar could find it all out if he hadn't already, but to what end?

If it was not invention. "That's enough, but give me your word it's the truth."

"I so swear."

There was no point in asking for his word if she wasn't going to believe it. "Thank you."

"Karolje's recordkeeping is meticulous," he replied, hard and bitter.

Anza had no response. She was no good at giving comfort, and Esvar was probably no good at receiving it. If she tried anything to ease him, they would just crash into each other. More, if he was going to oppose the king, he would need his edge.

He drank, lowered his glass, wiped his mouth with the side of his hand. Much more calmly, he said, "Did you talk to Sparrow?"

"She wants proof. She'll believe you are serious if you give me something to give into her keeping that only you could own. It has to be of great value to you. If you do that, she's willing to talk, but only through me, not face-to-face."

"That will do to start. It can't hold forever. Anything else?"

"She wants to know what kind of help you think she can give. She said to tell you that the resistance is not an army."

"No," he agreed. "It's not. As to what I want, it is little more than for the resistance to do what it intends to do. I will provide some targets. And names of people to leave alone. There will also be letters to deliver. There are more people than you know who can help, but I can't go to them directly."

"Does your brother know about this plan?"

"My brother," he said. He circled his finger on the table a few times. "No. And I don't intend to tell him."

"I thought you trusted him."

"*Trust* isn't the word. We promised years ago that we each

would try to keep the other from becoming like Karolje." A statement, delivered neutrally, yet freighted with intimacy. More than she needed to know, more than she wanted to know. A history that went back a lifetime, lit with suffering.

"I see," she said.

"Do you?" His face had gone still, no friendliness flickering in the eyes or curving the mouth now.

"I know about promises. Why haven't you told him, then?"

"He has to be able to prove himself innocent if he's questioned by a Truth Finder. This is all outside his compass."

It had not occurred to her that Karolje would use a Truth Finder on his own son, even if he had done it to his wife. Sons were different.

"Sparrow wants a guarantee that your brother won't turn around and jail her or her people when it's over. She told me that was one of the conditions you had to meet before she would negotiate substance. But if he doesn't know, you can't speak for him."

"Yes. That's the rather large flaw in my plan. I can't offer amnesty. I don't have that power and I won't be forsworn. Tell her that. If it puts a halt to talking further, I will have to find some other way to fight the king. I can't let Tevin risk knowing how much I am a traitor." His lip curled. "For all I know, he is saying the same thing about me, but we don't dare question each other. There may be thousands of people in Karegg who would rise against Karolje if they had a leader, but no one will be the first. That's what I need the resistance for."

"You don't expect them to storm the Citadel," she said. The Citadel had been taken only twice in all its history, and those had both been by treachery from within.

"No."

The server appeared with the food, seasoned chicken and fresh brown bread. They each ate a few bites in silence. The bird was strong-tasting and oily. Anza broke off a piece of bread to soak up some of the grease. When she was younger, she hadn't noticed the poor quality of the food in the tavern. Esvar must find it ghastly.

She said, "This is a colossal risk to you in return for little. I don't understand."

"I can't strike at Tevin's enemies myself. But they need to be weakened or eliminated for him to succeed without a war." He took a bite and said through the food, "Right now Karolje thinks I am obedient, if unreliable. I need him to stay confirmed in that belief. To look weak, I must to some extent be weak."

That can't be true, she thought. Esvar exuded strength. She told herself she did not know what face he turned to the king, what ways he had found to protect himself. Perhaps he lurked like a deepwater fish.

She attacked the chicken with her knife and chewed. *I have your mother's journal,* she wanted to say. It would be disastrous. He could never escape the ruins of his parents' marriage.

She said, "Some members of the resistance want to do away with the Crown altogether."

He held his hand out, palm up, fingers spread. "If it were up to me, I'd listen. It's not."

"You would? Can I tell them that?"

"No. It would only make Tevin a more favored target. He isn't going to give up power. He may not be averse to sharing. I don't think he has considered it, but there are some things we don't talk about. He certainly knows it's possible. He's read the same histories I have. If I don't miss my guess, you have read some of them too. Even—or perhaps especially—the illegal ones."

The ones Nihalik had refused to let her take out of his cottage. Books that described the follies and weaknesses of Vetian kings, that compared the state unfavorably to other nations, that spoke of a prince's duty to his people, that argued for governance by all citizens. If Esvar knew she had read such books, he must know she was evaluating everything he said in light of them. "Is that why you want me to be your messenger?"

"No. You happen to have crossed my path at a convenient time. The captured members of the resistance who are still alive are not fit to be released. Even if they were, I'd be brought up as a traitor if I did it."

She said, "If we go on with this, you aren't going to be able to hold back from being a traitor. You're going to have to turn sometime, or Sparrow will wash her hands of you."

"I know. I have as slender reason to trust Sparrow as she does to trust me. I'm sorry you're caught between the two of us. If we start shooting, get out of the way."

His words sat uncomfortably on Anza. She remembered Sparrow's face that night in the Anchor, hard and ruthless. Had Anza given her allegiance to someone who could be as merciless as Karolje?

"Who is she?" she asked.

"She first turned up about five years ago. She seems to have no family but all the money she wants. I suspect she began as a thief."

"A prosperous thief."

"Oh yes."

"Why didn't you arrest her?"

"You don't get rid of a wasp's burrow by killing a single wasp. You poison or plug the whole thing."

"You can kill the queen," she said.

"The queens don't come out." He said it as though he were presenting an ordinary fact, but the hand that had been reaching for the mug stilled momentarily. Anza thought of Mirantha, locked away. The analogy did not hold. The words had power nonetheless.

"If your brother was made king tomorrow, what would he do?"

"You mean with no obstacles or wars?"

"Yes."

His eyes flicked back and forth. He had said living in the Citadel was like treading constantly around broken glass. She thought she was starting to understand what that meant.

He said, "Repeal those of Karolje's decrees that don't involve money. The decrees about property and taxes have to be done more carefully. What Tevin needs to do is get married. The best thing would be for him to marry one of the chancellor's daughters, but they're much too young—the oldest is ten—and he can't wait so long."

"Why the chancellor's daughter?"

"Because the chancellor is Karolje's cousin and next in the succession after me. He would like to be king himself, which is why Tevin and I are not safe from him. But if he could make his daughter queen, that would satisfy him for now. He might even join Tevin in unseating Karolje if he thought he had that chance. It's moot, though, since they're still children. Tevin will need an heir of his own body sooner than seven or eight years from now."

His fears of civil war were much more grounded than she had thought. "The resistance wants to target Goran. And the spymaster."

"As they should. They're both dangerous."

"I know Doru Kanakili's wife from the College. Jance knows her too."

"You do? How well?"

"We were lovers for a few months. I've only seen her once since, but we talked. She's scared."

"Of what?"

"The king. Her husband."

Esvar said, "Is there any chance she might poke around and find out things about you better left hidden?" *Including me,* his tone implied. "She could buy herself safety, even power, if she did."

"I don't think so. She has no reason to think I'm involved in anything. She more or less warned me not to be."

"This could be a problem. If she finds out that you and I have been meeting, tell the truth about your father. Who else do you know who might know me?"

"Possibly some of Rumil's friends. But I've hardly seen most of them for months. And I didn't tell anyone about my father."

"Rumil was your lover?"

"Yes. The last time I saw him was before you gave me back the book."

"All right. Be careful, though. Old lovers can be malicious." Esvar picked up his glass and drank. She wondered if he spoke from experience. "And talking of malice, I'm going to give you an escort home from here. I don't want you to be easy prey for anyone."

"I know the area," she said. "As long as I leave before sunset, I won't be in any danger. It's not as if this is Beggar Island."

"I'm giving you an escort anyway," he said.

She wanted to tell him it would only make her more noticeable, but something in his voice stopped her. He was trying to protect her because he had not been able to protect his mother. He might not know that was the reason, but she had to honor it this time.

"Thank you," she said. She reached across the table and touched his hand.

He gripped her fingers tightly. It was not a lover's clasp; it was the grip of a man who is falling. The noise of the tavern faded out as they stared at each other. Her heart turned over and resettled itself.

He raised her hand to his lips and let it go. Sound filled in around her again. She knew this was a moment that sharply divided her life into a before and an after.

"We will win," he said. "We must."

MIRANTHA

A FEW WEEKS AFTER Ashevi's execution, she sends for the soldier who took her to the Green Court. He is a lieutenant named Alcu Havidian. "I need you to do something for me," she says. "It might be dangerous. The only reason it is not forbidden is because it has not occurred to the king to forbid it. You will have to do it quietly and tell no one."

She waits. This is the moment when she knows whether she can trust her instincts at all or if the soldier's fear of Karolje is too great. Havidian can obtain advancement and favor if he goes to his captain upon leaving this room. She will deny her orders to him if asked, but the king won't believe her.

"I serve you, my lady," he says, passionate, convinced of her rightness. Her heart nearly breaks.

Her journal and her books are in two bags. She hopes that one day the journal will come to her sons, though it will hurt them to read it. Of the books, most have no special meaning to her, but they are illegal outside the Citadel. She wants to preserve their knowledge. Their sense of history and beauty and of a world greater than the one Karolje is making.

One is the Rukovili. It is a wrench to let go of this book, because Nihalik gifted it to her and because the poems have been her refuge. But Karolje will destroy it.

"Take these bags to Master Tinas at the College," she says. Nihalik had trusted Tinas. "Don't look in them. Give them only to him. There is no other message."

"Yes, my lady," he says. He picks up the bags, one in each hand. He is shorter than her but his hands are larger, and the bags aren't as eye-catchingly huge when he is holding them. The muscles on his arms barely stand out with the weight. He is strong, capable. She wishes she could have him guard Esvar. To request it would bring him to Karolje's notice.

"Do you have children?" she asks.

It startles him, but he answers readily enough. "A daughter, my lady. But I haven't seen her in two years, not since I was sent north."

"You could bring her and her mother here."

"They are happier in their village." He does not need to say *safer*. "Her mother and I are not married."

"How old is she?"

He smiles, amused by some memory, no doubt. "Eight. Clever enough for older."

"Make sure she is taught, then," Mirantha says. "There will be a time when Vetia has need of learning, and a time when learning is the coin that buys a woman power."

He stills, an almost intimate response she had not expected. She wonders if she has made a mistake, if he believes that women should be men's servants and playthings. His eyes have darkened with thought.

"Do I alarm you?" she asks, testing.

"No, my lady."

"What, then?" She realizes. Money. He is probably still in

debt for the cost of his commission. She can't offer to pay; it would shame him. Worse, it would draw attention to the girl. Perhaps there is someone she can have help the girl discreetly. "Where does she live?"

He tells her. The world falls into a different pattern.

She says, "I know a man near there who will teach her for nothing, as a service to me. If she does well, he can see that she is admitted to the College on the same terms."

His face colors. "Thank you, my lady. But I have done nothing to deserve such a boon."

She has noticed this before, that the common people want far fewer favors than the nobles. They want to prove their own sufficiency. She says, "This is not a boon for you. I do it for Vetia. For my sons."

With care, he lowers the bags to the floor. He kneels, which soldiers do not do. She gives him her hand to kiss and in the same motion raises him. It is the first touch she has had from anyone besides her sons and her maids since Ashevi was killed. There is nothing sensual about it. It is almost unbearably painful, ripping the scar she has built over her loneliness.

But pain is something she knows. She says, "Do this errand when you safely can. If it fails, do not report to me. You were here because I needed to know the truth of a rumor about one of Prince Esvar's guards, a rumor that you have assured me is false."

"My lady," he says, and salutes and takes the bags.

When he is gone, she weeps a little, for herself, for her children. Then she dries her eyes and writes the letter to Nihalik. She sews her rings into the hem of a shirt.

✦ ✦ ✦

One night she wakes to the sound of a scream cut off, and she hears boots in the maids' room. She slams the bolt to her door shut and turns the key in the lock. They pound on the door.

Part of her has always known this night was going to come, and she is ready. In seconds she is dressed in riding trousers and the jewelry-hemmed shirt. She opens the window. It is a twenty-foot drop to the ground. She had meant to have a rope. She would rather die falling than be killed.

The door hinges screech as they are forced out of the frame. She extends one leg over the sill, then the other, but before she can prepare herself for the drop, the soldiers' hands are on her, pulling her back into the room. They strike her on the head, and she blacks out.

* * *

When she regains consciousness, she is in a small arched room. Four men wait. She recognizes one of them. He has guarded her door many times. She stares at him, and he looks aside. The walls are stacked with bottles; this is someone's wine cellar. She thinks rapidly about which lords Karolje might want to frame for treachery.

Out the cellar door, and up steps, and into a kitchen. Mice scuttle away. Her mind wants to slip its moorings as it did at Ashevi's trial.

The men take her outside. The moon shines. Blossoms froth on the trees in the yard, two long rows of them against the surrounding wall. The house is one of the large ones near the Citadel on a silent street. If she screams, no one will come.

She stops walking. The soldiers draw their swords. Sorrow for her sons almost overwhelms her. She says, "What are you going to do?"

"Cut off your head and take it back to the king," one says with malicious glee.

"You know what he'll do next, don't you? He won't leave you alive to speak of this. You're signing your own death warrants as well. Does he know you have me?"

"Of course," says the man she recognized. She hears a note of false bravery in his voice.

She pushes. "He has some other story ready. Traitors or Tazekhs. He will have you executed for failure to keep me safe. If you go back to him, you are fools."

"Shut your bloody mouth," says one of the other men. He is afraid too. He is very young.

She almost has them. They know what Karolje is like. "Listen," she says.

The man she knows brings his sword point to her neck. "On your knees."

"He probably let you loot my room. He'll say you're thieves."

"Kill her," says the first man.

"Flee," she says.

The man who hasn't spoken yet says, "If we desert, that's our heads too, and for certain."

"Not as certain as if you return to the Citadel. He had you kill my guards. Do you think he wants you back in the Citadel with that story on your tongues?"

They stare at her. She pushes the sword away from her neck. The soldier does not resist.

"What the hell are you doing?" says the first man to the other.

The man she knows says, "She's right. He won't want any witnesses to this."

"She's a whore and you're a fucking traitor," the first man says, and she hears pleasure in his voice. He has been looking forward to killing her. He lunges at the other guard.

The blades ring, the moonlight cold on them. The remaining two guards are watching, dumbfounded. They are paying no attention to her. Their hands are lowered, fingers slack on their sword hilts. Bad discipline, she thinks. The moon is on their faces, shadows behind them. She should run. But she wants to finally fight.

With one quick grab, she snatches the sword from the nearest of them. He jerks and spins, but she already has the point of the blade against his knee. She thrusts, severing a tendon, and he crumples as she pulls the sword out. Blood darkens his trousers.

His companion, the young one, swings around, sword raised. She brings her blade up in time to parry the blow.

He is not well-trained. It takes only a few exchanges before she has seen his weaknesses. She learned how to use a sword before he was born, and though she has not practiced regularly in years, her body has not forgotten. It is not for nothing that she watched her sons learn. A slash at the knee, a feint to the groin, and he responds, leaving his upper body unguarded. Her sword slides through his neck. He staggers, almost pulling the sword from her hand before she manages to pull it free, and falls heavily.

She takes a step back, her breath still even, and observes the other fight. Both men have been wounded slightly; blood slicks their arms and runs from a cut in one man's cheek. The smell of blood is stronger than the fragrance of the blossoms. The blades clash and slide against each other, the silver light following the motion. Distant and unconcerned, an owl hoots, low and throaty.

Then the man she knows stumbles on uneven ground, and his sword flails wildly. His opponent is much too good to miss the opportunity. He thrusts his sword through the other man's heart. Blood gouts, a black fan of liquid that reminds her obscenely of the fountains in the Citadel garden, and before the dead man has struck the ground, she is under attack herself.

She parries, and knows immediately that she has met her match. He is stronger, faster, more skilled. He is impelled by some deep hatred of her that she does not understand.

So she does the only thing she can. Still facing him, using her sword only for defense, she retreats. He advances on her. Her sword pulls him along as if he were tethered to it. If he were to lunge at her, she might not be able to hold him off, but he seems intent on toying with her. She smiles grimly. He has no idea what else she has endured. This is nothing.

He follows her under the trees.

Then it is only a matter of putting a few trees between them and circling back. The tangled moonlight and shadow are confusing, like a spell. It is a twilight she belongs to. He is loud and large and breathing heavily. She slides among the shadows. The soldier knocks against a branch, and petals fall softly down, obscuring his vision. He halts, looks around. He has lost her.

She has no compunction about stabbing him through the back. The harpy, rending. He staggers, and she drives the blade in farther. He cries out in pain, a liquid gurgling cry, and she knows she has punctured a lung. He sinks slowly to his knees as she withdraws the blade. The iron scent of blood is stronger than ever. The owl hoots again.

She runs.

ANZA RECOGNIZED JANCE'S tread on the balcony and realized she had been waiting for it. Two days had passed since the meeting with Esvar, and dusk was settling over the city. Jance himself looked haggard. He carried a package in one hand.

"What's wrong?"

"Nothing. It's hell in the Citadel, is all. My cousin and his wife are gone—Prince Esvar tells me it was his brother who arranged it and not to worry. As if I couldn't. And I had to lead a raid at dawn this morning. I didn't want to do it, and then when we got there, the place was abandoned, leaving me at fault. Despite the fact that it was abandoned before I got my orders."

She got the raki out and splashed some into a glass for him. After a moment's consideration, she poured some for herself. "Did Esvar send you here? He told me he would."

"You've seen him since that day at your father's house?"

"Twice. Once immediately after the executions and again two days ago. Don't say it, Jance, it's business, not a love affair."

"What sort of business?"

"If he hasn't told you, I shouldn't," she said. "Did he send you tonight or not?"

"He sent this." Jance nudged the package across the table toward her. "I thought it was something of your father's. I take it this is connected to whatever you're up to with him."

"I'll find out when I open it." She put the package out of easy reach. "Can you stay a while?"

"I shouldn't." He drank his glass down and refilled it. "I will. Anza, I realize you aren't going to tell me what's going on between you and the prince, but you don't owe him anything. If the king finds out, you'll get used against Esvar and then killed. You need to cut him off."

"I can't."

"Why not?"

If it hadn't been for the raki, she might not have spoken. But the secret she had been carrying was too heavy. "Do you remember the night we snuck into the library?"

"Yes. What's that got to do with Prince Esvar?"

"That key you gave me—it let me into a room where there were some books. They were the queen's books. She must have sent them there to keep Karolje from destroying them. One of them was her journal. And now no one remembers about her. I need to be her witness. Her voice."

"She's dead. You don't owe her anything either. It's stupid to risk your life for the sake of a ghost. A ghost that isn't one of your dead."

"Her life was controlled by men. Her death was used to start a war. She deserves better."

"And so does your father! Do you think he wanted you to get killed?"

"He wanted me to fight. Not to run away. That's what I'm doing."

"Anza . . ." Jance closed his eyes in seeming exasperation. "All right. I won't argue. But at least think about it. Please."

"I will," she said. He would know she was lying and hope she wasn't, and that was enough to silence him for now. "Do you think there's a chance of civil war?"

"Not from the resistance. It's not strong enough," he said. "But you would know better than I if they intend to try."

He had probably not intended to hurt her, but it stung as much as if he had called her a weakling directly. She said, "I'm not talking about the resistance! I'm talking about the infighting in the Citadel. Don't tell me it doesn't exist."

"Then, yes, there is conflict between the princes and the other lords. I think that is behind what happened with my cousin. I don't know if it would lead to actual war." He pushed his chair back. "I've stayed long enough. I've got other duties."

Anza walked with him to the door. She said, "Don't tell Esvar any of this about his mother. Please. It will only hurt him."

"Caring for his feelings, are we now?" he said. It was not malicious.

"How am I supposed to contact you again?"

"I'm sure that if the prince wants to speak to you, the prince will find a way." He kissed her cheek. "Stay safe. I mean that."

"You too," she said.

She watched him ride away before she opened the package. It contained a wooden globe about the size of a peach, a child's toy. The continents were carved on it in relief, and mountain ranges stood out as bumpy ridges. Karegg was marked with a single diamond chip, almost too small to be seen. The equator was a seam, and Anza tried to turn the top half. It unscrewed easily, opening to reveal two hollow sections, constellations painted on the inner surfaces. It was a place to put in beans for a rattle. Or to hide things. At the moment it was occupied by a tightly folded paper.

It was meant for Sparrow. Anza unfolded it. Esvar's handwriting was neat and small. *This was given to me by the queen when I turned five. Keep it safe, and return it from your own hand.*

Soberly, she put the paper back and screwed the globe together. There was pain in this gift. She hoped Sparrow would appreciate it.

✦ ✦ ✦

Two days later, walking through Temple Square on the way to meet with Sparrow, Anza looked grimly at the masons working on the wall around the Temple. The square itself was strewn with mourning flowers. The amulet sellers and scribes were back. Soldiers with hellhounds guarded the entrances to the square and kept the beggars away. She passed a man talking loudly to a group of about a dozen people. She stopped to listen, then hurried on as she realized he was complaining about the Tazekhs.

Her meeting was in a garden behind a shrine. Dangerous for the priest who kept the place, she thought. A walkway paved with white stone led to a statue of the god, a pitcher at his feet for libations from the nearby pool. A plum tree was to one side, a pair of benches and flower bushes on the other.

Sparrow was waiting on a bench. She said, "What delayed you?"

Anza sat down. Sun was warm on her back. "There's a man in Temple Square stirring up trouble."

"What kind of trouble?"

"Against Tazekhs."

"Damn." Sparrow shook her head. "We should be quick then. I want to hear what he's saying. How did things go at the tavern?"

"He agrees to some of the conditions. He can't promise amnesty. He says he can provide a list of targets. He sent this." She produced the globe.

Sparrow took it almost gently. She ran one finger along the coast of a continent, across a sea, and brought it to rest on Karegg. "This is well made," she said. "What does he want from us, and what does he intend to give in return?"

"I think—he was not specific, this is my inference—that he wants the resistance to serve as his assassins, which benefits us too. He said he only wanted us to do what we would do anyway."

"But under his guidance."

"He said no one would rise against Karolje unless someone else went first. He wants us to be first."

"So we take the risk and he gets the reward? Or his brother does? He's not the general of our army."

"You said yourself we aren't an army."

"So I did." She turned the globe, round and round. "You have a great deal of faith in a man raised by Karolje. He can't escape that even if he tries. Children are bound by their childhood."

Anza thought of Esvar's face when he said that neither he nor his brother would ever forgive the king. That was too private to share. She remembered a line in the journal: *He made Esvar come too. I am afraid that alone will be enough to ruin him.*

She said, "He was raised by the queen also."

"Of course," said Sparrow mockingly.

"He told me my father showed him a man could be kind. That's not the sort of thing one makes up. There are other reasons I believe him, but that's the one that counts the most."

In a flowering shrub nearby, bees hummed loudly. She listened for the noises of the city—dogs, carts, voices—but the silence of the shrine extended over the garden. Her own words echoed back in her mind, a rough note of dissent.

Sparrow said, "I knew your father."

"What!"

"Not well. It would be more accurate to say I met him. I was there the night he led the raid on us. He could have killed me. Instead he let me go."

"That's why he was executed," Anza said, low and furious.

"If that was why, Karolje would have had him hanged in public as a traitor. No. I think he let me go because he already knew he would be killed for failing. But I owe him something."

Sparrow's attention to her took on a different aspect. The ease with which she had been recruited, the private meetings with Sparrow, they were not about her.

"You lied to me," Anza said. "You knew who I was."

"I did. But he didn't ask me to take you in; that was my decision, based on your ability. He probably would have liked some better return for his gift than to have his daughter put in danger." She looked at the globe as if surprised to see that she was still holding it and put it in her bag. "I am willing to extend credit to the prince's honor, for your sake and your father's. I understand why he thinks he can't promise amnesty, but he's going to have to give on that eventually if he wants negotiations to mean anything. He doesn't get to pick and choose his powers. I will talk to him without a promise, but I won't *do* anything for him. When you see him next, tell him that we will accept his list provided that we are promised a voice in the next government. We don't demand the throne. But we are not going to risk ourselves killing men he targets without a promise of power. If he can't make that promise, he doesn't have anything we want."

"All right."

"And in the meantime, I'm sending you out with River tomorrow. Meet him by the Port Island bridge an hour before sunset. Wear dark clothing." She drew a finger across her throat.

At last. This was better than being a messenger, which had happened by sheer coincidence. An attack used her skills. "I will," she said.

Sparrow rose. "I'm going to go listen to this man you say is speaking out against the Tazekhs. If he and others like him attract a following, we might have to put an end to them before we move against the king. It's a distraction that plays into his hands, not ours. Wait ten minutes or so before you leave, and don't go through the square."

"You think there might be violence?"

"I think it's possible. Karolje might push things in that direction. This man might even have been planted by him. Then his soldiers ride in to restore peace on the one hand while on the other the fever for a Tazekh war grows."

That kind of cunning was beyond Anza's imagination. She felt naive. She remembered something and rose. "I asked Esvar to find out what happened to Moth's lover. Velyana. He told me she died before she could be tortured. Can you tell her that?" It felt strange not to say Irini's name.

"Of course. Did you ask him that as a favor or as a condition?"

"As a condition for me to be his messenger. I know he might

be lying. But Moth deserves my effort. And he knows what it feels like to have someone go missing."

Sparrow's gaze shifted to the pool. She said, "Be careful, Anza. Don't sympathize with him. You and he have very little in common."

There was no explaining her trust in Esvar without revealing the queen's journal, which was a secret that did not belong to anyone in the resistance. She said, "I know. I loved my father."

Sparrow edged her chin up and down, the slightest affirmation. "Do what River tells you to tomorrow," she said, dismissing the prince. "He'll keep you safe."

Once alone, Anza went to the statue and poured a libation without a prayer. The stream of water was calming. She knelt and washed her hands, expiation of the deaths that had not occurred yet.

✦ ✦ ✦

She was early to the bridge. The area was crowded even late in the day—laborers and workers crossing from one island to the other, fishmongers closing up their stalls, servants performing the day's final errands. She found a bakery that had not shut its doors and bought a costly sweetbread, which she ate standing on the quayside. Greedy birds gathered, and she shooed them away.

River joined her. He was not carrying any weapons. He said, "We have to walk about two miles. Some of the streets are rather nasty. Try to act normal."

"I've walked streets on Beggar Island."

"Good. This won't be that bad. Come on."

He set a steady but not too rapid pace and led them inland to the southeast. At first the roads were lined with well-kept shops and houses, but as they progressed, more and more of the buildings stood abandoned. The streets became narrow, full of doglegs and closes, twisting, old. A thousand years ago they must have been sheep trails.

They crossed a wider road, and the character of the place changed again. Now smoky rushlights burned outside large, once elegant stone houses that might have been built four hundred years ago. The windowsills were chipped and the porticoes were crumbling. The streets were laid out neatly. This was the part of the city that had been summer homes for the wealthy, fields and gardens around, before Karegg had spilled outside its walls and spread across the island.

Some of the windows showed light, and people walked outside despite the curfew. Drums and pipes, the sweet smell of kenna weed. Women leaned against walls and stood on corners. They had bright painted lips and bare shoulders, thin necks, cheap jewelry. Anza was glad that in her drab trousers and dark shirt she was clearly not one of them. River stayed close to her. She watched a man approach one of the women, heard the clink of coins.

River turned on a cross street and then into an alley. It was dark. The buildings' roofs almost touched overhead, and there were no windows. About halfway along to the next street he stopped. Anza bumped into him, and his hand came up to cover her mouth in warning.

He opened a narrow door and stood aside for her to enter. The dark house smelled vacant, as her father's house had: no cooking odors, a hint of dust, staleness in the hot air.

"No one lives here," he said. "The owner died a month ago. His children are fighting about possession of it. I'm not sure how Sparrow found out about it."

"It's not a brothel like the others?"

"They aren't all brothels. Not on this block. This is much smaller. The house next door is rented by a draper. The other side is someone respectable too. It's a safe street, which is why Lord Ruslan rides along it on his weekly visit. Lord Ruslan is a close friend of the spymaster."

She knew nothing about Lord Ruslan otherwise, but if he was Doru's friend, he was corrupt. He could doubtless take ordinary pleasure in much finer places; whatever brought him here must be something nasty and illegal, which Karolje allowed for devious reasons of his own. When word of Ruslan's death got out, he would have few mourners.

"I see," she said. "Are we going to kill him in a way that makes it clear he didn't run afoul of a thief? There must be a fair number of murders down here that aren't connected to the resistance."

"You are going to do nothing but watch. Sparrow's not going to trust you with a killing until she knows you have the nerve. You'll wait upstairs while I deal with the lord."

I've already killed three people, she thought. But they had been soldiers and she had been scared. This was assassination, not defense. "How long to wait?"

"Two or three hours," he said. "It's early now. You can have a nap if you want. They haven't taken all the furnishings away yet. There's still a bed."

"I don't need a nap."

"Patience," he said. She could hear that he was grinning. What he was doing tonight was as ordinary to him as sweeping the floor or saddling a horse. The hatred or anger that had led him to join the resistance didn't color his actions.

She thought of Esvar, murdering on command when he was a boy. Of Sparrow, who wore cold anger like a second skin. Of her father, who had delivered prisoners to Karolje's interrogators and kept her illegal book for her. Of Radd, who had been kind and thoughtful and had nothing to do with killing and now lay dead as a result of Karolje's trickery. How much better all of them could have been if not for Karolje. How much better she could be.

"Are you all right?" River asked.

"Yes. I was just thinking how much I hate the king."

"My mother was a lutist. She taught girls, rich girls and the daughters of lords, how to play. Ten years ago she criticized the king to someone she shouldn't have, and Karolje sent a soldier to break her fingers. They healed, but the pain was unbearable in the winters, and she couldn't play anymore. She killed herself five years ago."

The darkness hid his face, but she knew it had to still hurt, in the way old pain did. "Oh gods, River, I'm sorry."

"The problem is that all of us would like to kill him, and he can only die once. What you said about the prince that day—I believe you. Anyone so afraid of losing power as to do what Karolje did to my mother, who was no one, and evil enough to kill his own wife, I hate to think what he would do to his children."

"Miloscz doesn't agree with you."

"Miloscz spends too much time reading. He's very certain of what the world should look like. I suppose I shouldn't have said that."

"Why not?" Anza said. "Aren't we supposed to be equals in this? And I don't think Sparrow likes him."

"No one likes him," said River. "I have concluded that he doesn't want to be liked. He wants to be attended to. Not the way I want to live, myself."

"And Sparrow? What does she want?"

"I don't know what drives her. But she's the strongest person I've ever met. She likes you, by the way."

It startled her and pleased her. She had been afraid that she was seen as an annoyance. "Does she? How do you know?"

When he spoke, she could hear the grin again. "If she didn't, you'd be doing whatever it was you did before you first came to Miloscz's. But don't fail her. Which doesn't mean you have to have the stomach for assassination. Not everyone does. If you have bad dreams and the shakes after tonight, she'll find some other way to use you."

"There's nothing else I could do. Where's your bow?"

"It will be close work tonight, no shooting. Get up to the top floor and open a window so you don't die of the heat. I'll be attacking from the street, so there's no reason anyone will think to look here. If you have to run, go out the back and turn left. They don't enforce the curfew in this part of the city, so you'll be fine. If all goes well, I'll collect you."

Anza went dutifully upstairs and opened the windows in all the rooms. Most of the houses on the street were dark—lamplight showed here and there—and the streetlamps were on the corners. River would have no trouble being obscured in the darkness. It would be hard for her to see much of anything, even if the assault was right under her nose. This was a test of her ability to stay calm and follow orders.

One of the rooms on the third floor had a footstep-softening carpet in the center and a set of armless wooden chairs. She moved one close to the window and seated herself in it. For a while people passed on the street, most on foot but a few on horse. Music played distantly. Then the lights went out in the other houses and the traffic lessened to almost nothing.

Her mind drifted. She got up and paced to keep herself alert, stretched, practiced her stance. The house was still besides herself; River must have gone out to wherever he intended to hide.

Hoofbeats, the dull thud of shoe on dirt. The horse was walking. She saw the man on horseback, the flicker of the streetlamp bright enough in this darkness to cast his shadow ahead of him. His face and hands were pale against a dark shirt.

He was almost directly across the street from her when River emerged from a niche and walked briskly toward the horse. "Lord Ruslan!" he called. Anza's hands tightened on air. The dull pain of tensed muscles settled below her rib cage. Her eyes were well adjusted to the dark, and although she could not see details, the men and the horse were more than shapes. The horse had white socks. Ruslan's posture was relaxed.

"Not so loud," said Ruslan. His own voice carried. "What's all this?"

"An urgent message, sir." River stopped beside the stirrups.

Ruslan bent over and extended a hand expectantly. River took it, jerked him from the horse, and flung him to the street in one smooth motion. He knelt over him.

She was about to watch a murder. It shouldn't disturb her—she had seen hangings enough to know what violent death looked like—but this was different. It flowed from her, not to her. She was full of the sick feeling of failure. She shuddered and put her hand over her mouth. She could not look away. He killed my father, she thought. He killed my father. He killed my father.

Ruslan struggled. He squirmed, struck out at River. River evaded him easily and moved his hands. Ruslan's cry was cut off, and his feet beat against the dirt. His arms flailed. Then he stilled. River fussed briefly with the body, then stood. He whacked the horse on the rump and walked away.

Still feeling sick, Anza barely heard the back door open, River's feet light on the steps. "Come on," he whispered. She stood, catching the chair before it crashed to the uncarpeted part of the floor, and followed him out.

In the alley she stumbled on rutted ground. Regaining her balance, she was overwhelmed with the heat, the alley stench of garbage and waste, the darkness. She could feel the rapid beats of her heart. Her hands were large and heavy. A cat dashed away from them, and she swallowed a scream. She was certain they would be caught. Ruslan's horse must have attracted attention by now. The lord's body would be found, a bell would ring, soldiers would storm through the streets, whips ready.

Gods. She couldn't go on like this. River walked with the steadiness and assurance of a man coming home from market. She told herself that returning from the raid had been more dangerous. Tonight no one knew to look for her. Soldiers were nowhere near. They might not even care that the lord was dead. *He'll keep you safe.* Sparrow's risks were calculated.

Slowly fear faded into caution. Whenever her mind gave her the memory of River pulling the lord from his horse, she wrenched her thoughts in another direction.

After walking a mile or so, they stopped at an ordinary house. River knocked lightly twice. A woman opened the door and stood aside for them to slip in.

The woman said, "There's a room in the back where you can wait. You'll have to leave at first light. And this is twice in six weeks—the next time had better not be so soon. The neighbors got suspicious after the last one."

"I hear you," said River.

The woman showed them to a pantry, narrow and crowded, rich with the scents of onions and garlic. Dried peppers hung in strands from the rafters. It had no windows, and as soon as the woman shut the door, it became completely dark.

"I have a light," River said. "Wait a moment."

Seconds later he had a stub of a candle lit. It cast shadows upward, enlarging the bags and jars, deforming the ropes of peppers. Anza said, "What did you do?"

"Garroted him. Was it too much for you?"

"No." She reached for a burlap sack and folded it to make a rough pillow.

"Good girl. I didn't think it would be."

"Did he—was he like Karolje, that evil?"

"He owned most of the berths on Port Island. Merchants and traders paid a ransom to him in docking fees. If they didn't pay, unfortunate things happened to their cargo, their boats, or their families. He worked hand in hand with Doru—there are nasty stories about the things that went on in Ruslan's house in private. The world is well rid of him. Lie down, now." He blew out the candle.

She could not sleep. Over and over she saw Ruslan's feet drumming on the ground, and all the wretchedness she had managed to hold off while they walked descended on her. Had she made a mistake?

KAROŁJE RETALIATED FOR Lord Ruslan's death by ordering twelve people hanged, one an hour in different sections of the city. Three of them were Tazekhs highly respected by their own people. This despite the notes the resistance had left pinned to Ruslan's body and nailed to shop doors claiming responsibility.

Esvar waited until the day after the executions to order Jance Mirovian to take him to meet Anza in her own house. The lieutenant did not make a show of protest. Dressed plainly, they rode out in the midafternoon of a humid day, the sky hazed with heat. Flies buzzed insistently around the horses' eyes and the men's faces. The shade of the arched entrance to the courtyard was a relief. Esvar was struck with a sudden sharp memory of playing in the royal forest preserve when he was a child, the coolness of trees overhanging the lake. He must have been very young.

Mirovian pointed out the door to him. He left the soldier with the horses and took the steps three at a time, knocked forcefully on the door. A bit of flaking paint fell off.

Some of his anger abated when he saw Anza. There were

dark circles under her eyes, and her face had none of its usual energy. He shut the door quietly.

"This has to stop," he said.

"You wanted us to keep fighting! You have targets."

"I was wrong. Everything that happens now is giving Karolje another wedge to start a war with Tazekhor. Do you know how many people will die if we have another war? It's madness for him to do it, but that's what he wants, and you're making it easy for him."

"Do you think I don't know?" she shouted, and broke into tears.

Two sobs and she had recovered, but it was enough. Esvar put his arms around her and held her lightly to him. Her shoulder blades made him think of a bird. What was it that she had been called by the resistance? Finch, that was it. His own heart was beating rapidly.

"I'm sorry," he said.

She pushed against him and he released her. "What do you want?" she asked.

He wanted to kiss her. It was an impossibility. He said, "I want to talk to Sparrow directly." Ever since he had heard of Ruslan's death, he had been playing this conversation in his mind. "The stakes are too high now to take the time for you to go between us."

"She won't do it."

"She must."

"*Must?* You're the one who wanted this negotiation. The resistance doesn't owe you anything. You aren't going to be the king—that's your brother." She stumbled over some of the words, anger propelling them faster than her tongue.

"Anza," he said, slowly, trying to calm both of them. The windows were open. They had to keep this quiet.

"Stop it." She turned away. The flat was one long room, and she had nowhere to retreat to. He took a careful step backward. Sweat ran down his face and he blinked it out of his eyes, keeping his hands at his sides.

This isn't how a prince acts, he thought. He imagined Karolje mocking him, his brother rebuking him. Would his mother have been disappointed in him too?

She said, "You didn't speak against the hangings. As long as you stay silent, you are giving everything he does your countenance."

"Why in the gods' names—" He was too loud. He tried again. "That's why I want to talk to Sparrow myself. We could be allies. I'm sick of guesses and intrigues."

Finally she looked at him again. "Sit down," she said. "Let's discuss this like civilized people. Do you want something to drink? I have good wine."

"You choose," he said. The table had only two chairs. He pulled one out and sat. She poured wine into ceramic cups for each of them. The wine was much better than he had expected.

She sat and said, "I watched Ruslan get killed. I've hardly slept since."

Her words shocked him. They should not have, not after she had killed his men during the raid. "Did you help?"

"No. I didn't know what was going to happen until too late. No, that's not true. I knew someone was going to be killed. But it wasn't how I expected. They want me to be an assassin, and I don't think I can do it."

He was unsure whether she was troubled more by the guilt

or by the fact that she felt guilt. "Ruslan had deaths on his own soul. He wasn't innocent."

"It doesn't matter. I thought I could kill in cold blood, and I can't, so I'm of no use."

"If you could, you'd be like me. You don't want that. The world doesn't need it."

Her hand trembled as she lifted her cup. When she brought it down, a smear of red stained the upper edge of her lips where wine had spilled over the cup's brim. "How can I fight if I can't fight?"

"Perhaps you can't. Not everyone's a warrior. Those of us who can kill like breathing need to be countered by the people who hate it. When this is all over, it's going to be the ones who know something of mercy and gentleness who set us on the right path."

"Who told you that?"

"My mother," he said. "My grandfather, perhaps. Men like your father. I have to believe that Karolje is the exception, not the exemplar. If the world were only men like him, it would have been destroyed a long time ago. We keep living. We make beautiful things."

She put her face in her hands. He waited. He could not mark the moment his anger had evaporated, but it had. Was that what happened when you paid attention to someone else's pain instead of your own? Did evil have its root in the fear of being hurt? Karolje was afraid—afraid of loss, of defeat, of dying. Of powerlessness. He was terrified of his own vulnerability, and so he tried to control everything.

And what do I fear? Esvar asked himself. The answer was cruel: being left behind, overlooked, forgotten. Obscurity. He drew his breath in.

Anza dropped her hands at the sound. "What's the matter?"

"Nothing. I've just had a reckoning with my own pride."

"It's the afternoon for it. Esvar, what do you think you and Sparrow can *do*? It seems like it's your brother who's the weak point. Why doesn't he have the power to hold back the others?"

He wasn't sure why she used his name. It could have been reckless presumption or casual absentmindedness or a challenge to his claims of cooperation. It didn't matter which. When he put his arms around her he had given her the right to treat him as a person.

He said, "Because Karolje would throw both of us out of the succession if he could, and everyone knows it. He hates Tevin. But he had Tevin sworn as the heir when he was crowned, and he can't set that aside without angering the priests. He won't go that far."

"Surely he could arrange an accident."

"I think—" Esvar began. He stopped and tried to find the words to frame a situation he did not understand. "I think in some dark corner of his heart he needs us. It's not enough for him to have power, to see all the lords stabbing each other while trying to keep his favor. He requires Tevin to be his audience."

"And a player?"

"He's a cat, and my brother is his favorite toy." The thought was a revelation.

"There are some people in the resistance who would like Tevin to fail. Getting rid of Karolje is not enough. Sparrow said I was to tell you that we would not strike against your targets unless we had a voice in rule. She wants a promise of power."

"Ruslan would have been one of my targets. But I don't know what to do about my brother. He's trying so hard to be upright and incorruptible, everything Karolje isn't, that he's boxed himself in."

Anza smiled. It was the first real smile of the afternoon. "Is he trying to look out for you at the same time?"

"Yes. He thinks I'm still about eight."

"Perhaps you should disappear for a while."

"It's tempting," said Esvar. "That would force a confrontation between him and the king. It would not solve the problem of the other lords. The better possibility is to sell the kingdom to Milaya." Bitterness leaked out despite his control.

"How?"

"I go to Milaya and marry one of Nasad's daughters. That ensures my brother's safety. If Tevin is killed or dethroned, I come back with fifty thousand Milayan soldiers. Our child marries one of Nasad's other grandchildren, and within a generation or two Vetia has a Milayan overlord. It would keep the Tazekhs from attacking again, too."

"Don't do that," she said.

"It's the only reasonably believable threat I can make."

She pushed her cup aside. "If it's Tevin or the Milayans, the resistance will accept Tevin."

"But it won't be that choice. It will be Tevin or the Milayans or someone in the resistance." He laced his fingers together and tugged. "It's a knot, and pulling any of the strings we can see makes it tighter."

She frowned again, got up, and paced to the window. The brightness outside silhouetted her slim figure. Esvar shook his head at himself. Even a hint of affection would ruin their capacity to plan. If he wanted to satisfy his body's lust, there was no shortage of other women he could go to.

"Poor Jance," she said, returning to the table. "He's standing out there trying not to look like a soldier on duty and failing miserably. The neighbors are all going to be convinced someone has been arrested. Or worse, informed on them. I think you're right, you do need to talk to Sparrow. But she probably won't agree."

"Twelve bodies on a gallows should be somewhat persuasive," he said.

"We should have expected something like that. I'm surprised Sparrow didn't. Perhaps she did and was overruled."

"She's not the leader?"

"She's the leader. But as far as I've gathered, she doesn't make her decisions alone. If she agrees to listen to you, she's going to want to know why she can trust your brother." She stopped. He could tell there was more.

He decided to come at it differently. "She took the wooden globe."

"Yes. She didn't dismiss it."

It was the only thing he possessed that he thought would convince Sparrow of his sincerity. Nothing else was so individual to him. "Did she figure out how to unscrew it?"

"Not in front of me. I'm sure she did."

"You did."

"I read the note too. I thought you would expect it of me."

"I did," he said. He drank more of the wine. "Where did you get this?"

"It was a bottle Rumil gave me to give to Radd. I reclaimed it after Radd died. I suppose I thought I should have something fit to serve a prince."

She was mocking herself. "Thank you," he said.

He had never had a moment like this, quiet in a sparely furnished hot room with a woman he would ask nothing of. Outside the window was a noise that he identified after some puzzlement as a rug being shaken for cleaning. The light sweat on the backs of Anza's hands glistened. He realized sharply how much it would hurt him if she died.

"Anza."

"Yes?"

"If something happens, and you have to run, where will you go?"

"Jance wants me to leave the city."

"Before that. You would need a place to hide until you could get off-island."

She was silent. He knew trusting him was a risk to her. He knew that whatever she told him might be a lie. If she refused to answer, he did not dare push her.

At last she said, "Would the king use a Truth Finder on you?"

"He might."

"Then I can't tell you, Esvar. I'm sorry."

"I understand," he said, disappointed but unsurprised. He would have done the same.

"What of you?" she asked. "If you can't get off-island and there are spies crawling everywhere looking for you, do *you* have a place to hide?"

At the bottom of everything, he didn't. The people he knew who lived outside the Citadel were known to the king. No ordinary person would risk sheltering him. He should have taken the time to cultivate allies in the city, but he had not.

He said, "I don't know. The traditional place for sanctuary is the Temple, but I doubt even the Hierarch would resist the king for long. There might be some negotiating involved." He drained his glass and set it firmly on the table.

Anza took the hint. Standing, she said, "I'll try to convince Sparrow. I'm sorry I lost my temper."

"It's understandable." He rose. "I'll send Mirovian or Marek to you in two days to find out what she said."

She walked down to the horses with him and exchanged a few words with Mirovian. Esvar mounted. The horse was taller than she was. He leaned over and said, "Soon."

She dipped her head slightly and said, "My lord." A courtesy, a formality, a distance. For Mirovian's benefit, perhaps also for her own.

He opened his mouth, closed it. He had nothing else to say. He put his hand on the reins and looked a thousand miles across the space between them and kicked the horse. Exiting to the street, he glanced over his shoulder. She was still there, watching him. Then the horse trotted forward, taking him out of sight.

✦ ✦ ✦

He was talking to Tevin that evening when they were interrupted by a soldier. The man, only a lieutenant, was red faced and breathing hard. Esvar's first thought was that the king had died.

"Sir," the soldier gasped, looking at Tevin, "there's a mob down in the city. They started at Temple Square and are headed toward the Tazekh quarter. There's hundreds of them."

"What's the watch doing?"

"Nothing. They can't. There are too many."

"All right. Listen." He issued a series of orders with such calmness and certainty that Esvar guessed Tevin had foreseen such an event. So many soldiers here, so many there. The Citadel would be left with essential men but not more.

Then, the lieutenant gone, Tevin stripped off his fine shirt and said, "Go put on armor and something splendid over it. We're going out."

"We shouldn't both go."

"This is the sort of thing that could go very badly wrong. Mobs don't start like this by accident, and until we know who is behind it, I want us together. We might have to run."

"The Citadel is the safest place in Karegg." He caught the unintended irony of it at once and was embarrassed. He was a fool.

"Put your armor on, Esvar. Now."

Under other circumstances he would have argued. Not now, when delay could mean death. They could have it out later. He went to his rooms, armed and armored himself, and rode out of the Citadel gates with his brother and two dozen soldiers.

It was too hot for the armor. Esvar was glad his hair was short under the helmet. He had on a cool silk singlet under the short-sleeved mail shirt and a silk vest over it, the wolf's face of the house of Kazdjan embroidered in gaudy silver thread. Tevin was in similar dress and wore a silver circlet that appeared much more valuable than it was. The horses' trappings were bright and showy. Royal might descending, a clear target for any person who wanted to do away with two princes at once.

They went at a quick trot. It was full dark, and the streets were empty. In the Old City the lamplighter had been by, but on the other side of the walls, streets that should have been lit were not.

A hellhound barked. The horses were trained not to respond to those barks, but the men did. Esvar's legs tightened around his horse.

The indistinct sound of many shouts grew louder. Tevin came to a stop at the top of a steep hill. Farther down the lamps were on. Near the bottom of the hill, soldiers made a band across the street. Some held raised swords. Beyond them a crowd, extending into the darkness of the next block, jeered and hooted. A body dangled from a second-floor window, a rope around its neck.

Tevin ordered two men to question the soldiers. Watching them, he said to Esvar, "That's not a mob. It's been contained."

"Can you make out what they're shouting?"

"No. But I want to know how that hanging occurred."

"It's probably a Tazekh."

Tevin nodded. He wiped the side of his face with his hand and said, "If this happens again, I'm afraid it might start a war."

"Tevin," Esvar said. "The resistance—"

"Do you think they're behind this?"

"No."

"Then wait till this is over." One of his soldiers was returning and would be in earshot soon. Tevin was right—it was not the place for secrets.

The man reached them and said, "The crowd's controlled now, sir. They're being sent off from the back. But there's a dozen dead, and the Tazekh there, and another Tazekh a block away. Captain Estaru says it all happened before he got here. The men who were here when he came told him the same."

"Was the other Tazekh hanged too?"

"Yes, sir."

"I'm going to talk to the crowd. Come with me, Esvar."

The horses walked down the hill. The street was clean and weedless. As Tevin came into the light, the noise of the crowd lessened. Jeers were cut off mid-word as recognition spread. Esvar recognized the quality of the silence; he had seen it when courtiers waited for the king. Fear mingled with a nervous desire to be noticed. There would be women pushing themselves forward, hoping to catch a prince's eye.

Tevin said, "Bring that man's body down." He spoke to the

soldiers, but his voice carried over the crowd. Ripples of movement began. The cleverer people were retreating.

A soldier, signaled, blew a horn. Tevin stood in the stirrups and swept his arm from right to left, muting the last murmurs. He said, "This is an unlawful gathering. And that man's death"—he pointed at the body—"was murder. No one takes the Crown's justice into his own hands."

"He was Tazekh scum!" came a yell from the back.

"I decide who lives and dies in Karegg. When you call another man's life forfeit, you strike against me." Tevin paused long enough for any hecklers to call back. None did, and he dropped back down to the saddle. "The Tazekhs are not your prey. The guilty will be punished by the Crown. Beware lest you become the guilty."

Then, to the soldiers, "Break it up. Peacefully."

Esvar looked at the lamplit swath of faces, some fair, some dark, most of them sobering with the realization that they had misstepped. "'I'?" he said as soon as the soldiers were gone. "When that gets back to Karolje, he'll have you whipped at best."

"Who's going to tell him?"

"You don't know who's in that crowd. You're taking a lot of risks tonight."

"I told you. I mean to be the king. Caution isn't going to gain me a crown, as you well know."

Esvar was glad it was too dark for Tevin to see him flush. "You're no coward," he said. "But which side are you playing, white or black?"

"White, of course. And—"

The interruption was an arrow. It struck Esvar's left arm, just below the mail.

The pain was immense, but training took over. He yelled a

warning and swung down sideways from his horse at the same time. He crashed onto the hard cobbles and felt his breath go out of him. The horse screamed and reared as it was shot. Esvar rolled out of the way of descending hooves, which drove the arrow deeper into his muscle. He blacked out.

When he could see again, soldiers had control of his horse. He heard a great deal of shouting and guessed he had lost consciousness for only a short while. Blood ran freely down his arm, and the pain spread from shoulder to elbow.

"Lie still," Tevin said from a squat beside him. "The shooting has stopped."

"Will they catch him?"

"Maybe. If they get the door down in time."

That was the other noise, the pounding. Esvar turned his head from side to side, decided he would not faint, and sat up. He swore. He put his free hand around the arrow shaft.

"Don't pull it out here," Tevin said. "I'm sending you back to the Citadel. Let the surgeon do it."

"It's not that bad."

"You don't need to take chances. We're lucky neither of us got killed. If I hadn't had the mail on, I'd have been down too—I took an arrow to the chest. It's a good thing it's dark."

"What about my horse?"

"It's hurt much less than you are. Can you stand?"

He saw no reason to remind Tevin of how long he had endured at the whipping post. "Yes," he said, demonstrating. Soldiers were still dispersing the crowd. He turned his head in time to see men force their way into a house. It had probably taken too long.

One of the soldiers was ready to help him onto a horse, and he gave in. The stirrups were short and he had to wait for a soldier to adjust them. He refused to yield the reins. He could ride one-handed, even with an arrow shaft sticking out of his flesh. He kicked the horse forward.

He was not feeling as strong by the time they passed through the Citadel gates. The blood had stopped flowing, but the pain had spread, and his head was thick. He dismounted carefully, stumbled, righted himself.

He walked to the surgery without assistance. The surgeon took one look, directed him to a cot, and started barking orders to his assistants. Esvar lay down, eyes closed, and let the world recede.

"Here, my lord," said the surgeon, holding a spoon of something bitter-smelling to his lips.

"I don't need it."

"It will make it easier for me, sir." The surgeon tipped the spoon.

Esvar swallowed, coughed madly, and passed out.

✦ ✦ ✦

The first thing he noticed upon waking was the bitter taste in his mouth. His arm hurt. The bandage was neat and white against his tanned skin. His bloodied overshirt and armor had been removed. A full glass of water was on a table next to him.

He sat up and drank the water down. The surgeon entered as he was finishing and said, "It's been about two hours that you slept. Your captain wants to see you."

He stood. A flutter of faintness as his body adjusted to the loss of blood, then he steadied.

Marek waited in the antechamber. There were guards too, so Esvar walked out without saying anything and drew Marek aside in the hallway. "What's wrong?" His mind was a trifle sluggish yet from the drug.

"Your brother hasn't come back, sir."

Had he fled? Been captured? "What happened?"

"It took a while to disperse the crowd. He left with his men while that was going on. Everyone thought he'd come back here, of course, but he didn't. There aren't any signs of an attack."

He hoped that meant Tevin had gone into hiding. A plan long laid, not confided, waiting for the right moment of chaos in the city. That was why he had wanted Esvar with him. Why he had worn the damn silver circlet. The arrow shot had ruined the plan, at least as far as it concerned Esvar. Too much risk that he would hinder or delay the escape, but other events had already been set in motion.

That was all wishing. Karolje might have arranged the whole thing. "Does the king know?"

"He's been told. He hasn't issued any orders."

"Call off the search by soldiers. If someone had killed him, he would have been found by now. Make Karolje rely on his spies." He hoped he could get away with shutting things down instead of continuing to search as a loyal and dutiful son would. The decision might land him in a cell.

Marek said, "Is there any chance it was an action by the resistance?"

"There's a chance of anything. I think it unlikely." He could not so easily shake off the likelihood that someone in the Citadel had ordered Tevin's death. He resumed walking. "He didn't say anything to me about this. Do you think Karolje will believe that?"

"What will you do?"

"There's nothing *to* do."

"If he doesn't come back—"

"You don't need to tell me, Captain! If I want your advice,

I'll ask." He did not often lose his temper with Marek, and he regretted it at once. "What do we know about the mob? Who started it?"

"There are several men who have been speaking against the Tazekhs since the executions in the square, sir. It was one of them. He's being interrogated now."

The interrogation would yield whatever Karolje wanted it to. The interrogators didn't do their work for the truth.

"Arrest the others, quietly. They need to be held until things have calmed down. Lock them in a watchhouse, not here. I'll talk to them myself when I get a chance. And increase the patrols around the Tazekh quarter to keep fools from causing any violence there. Make sure the soldiers know it's not the Tazekhs I'm worried about."

"They're not going to want to protect Tazekhs."

"If Vetians kill more Tazekhs as they did tonight, Korikos will start his war. That's what I'm trying to hold off." He moderated his voice. "Have all the shops within a mile of everywhere the mob marched closed for two days. Shop owners can enter their properties but not sell. Say it's for their safety, that we fear what another mob might do. If anything was broken or stolen, let them invite their insurers in." Redirecting the cost and putting the blame where it belonged would give merchants incentive to shut down Tazekh-haters instead of joining in.

"Do you think you're safe now?" Marek asked. An innocent enough question, since Tevin had disappeared, but a dangerous one too, because the captain was asking about the king.

Esvar shrugged. If Tevin had been gotten out of the way, he would be next, and there wasn't much he could do to prevent it. There was more to be said, but not within the confines of the Citadel. "That's all."

* * *

Alone, Esvar walked to his brother's workroom. A servant had removed the wineglasses they had been drinking from when word of the mob came and turned down the lamp, but otherwise it was as he had last seen it. The clock said after midnight. Its ticks were loud.

The red book Tevin had said held a letter for him was shelved among volumes of history and political philosophy. He had no idea what Tevin thought was the source of kingly authority. The gods, as was signified with the priests' bestowing the crown? Force? Precedence? Karolje claimed divine right, as had his predecessors, but his actions suggested he believed in force more than anything else.

Cautiously, as though he were doing something forbidden, Esvar eased the book off the shelf and opened it. He found the letter about a quarter of the way in, a thin piece of paper folded in thirds. He slipped it out, held it, realized he could not bear to read it. Not now. That would be acknowledging that his brother was dead. Which was impossible.

He returned the letter to the book, the book to the shelf. He turned off the lamp and pulled the door of the darkened room closed. He walked the short distance to his own rooms undisturbed.

There he found Lady Thali Kanakili, most improperly waiting.

It was much too late for her to visit him, even if he were not wounded and drugged, and she should have come to his workroom, not his private rooms. "You shouldn't be here," he said.

"I know, my lord."

Simply said, without cajolery or servility. It caught his attention, and he opened the door and waited for her to precede him.

The samovar was cold, and he did not want wine, but there was a pitcher of fresh water. He poured for both of them and sat opposite her.

"What's this about?"

"I want a divorce, my lord," she said.

Very softly he let his breath out. "On what grounds?" He was not the person she should be asking, but she knew that.

"Cruelty to me and treachery to the state."

Oh, he had to be careful. "This is not the best time to ask me," he said, gesturing at his arm. "My thinking is not as clear as it might be. Do we need to do this now?"

"Between the mob and your brother's disappearance, there is no better time for me to leave the Citadel. I don't want to be in Doru's reach when he finds out."

"He'll expect you in your rooms tonight, surely."

"He won't come to bed, not with what's happened in the city. He'll want to take part in any interrogations and direct the search for Prince Tevin. I ask that you not tell him until as late as possible tomorrow. If you grant it, that is."

The precision of her words reminded him that she had been educated at the College. Like Mirovian, like Anza. Anza, who had been her lover.

He said, "I've shut down the search for my brother."

"That won't stop Doru. Not when he's on the hunt."

"Have you got a secure place to go?"

"Yes," she said. "And I've already sent most of my money to a bank in Traband. I just need enough hours to get out of Karegg before he knows."

The hours Mirantha had not had. He said, "I think you've already answered this, but I must ask. If your only grounds were those of cruelty, would Doru oppose it?"

"Yes. Out of spite and habit and possessiveness. I have proof aplenty."

"Need we reach the other grounds?"

"That rather depends on what you want for yourself, my lord. If you want the opportunity to get rid of him, I can provide the evidence."

"That's more likely to end in a beheading than a divorce. Which would mean all his property is confiscated by the Crown and you are left with nothing. Do you want to risk that? I can't have you change your mind partway through." He would dearly love to prove Doru a traitor, but the evidence had to be unassailable. If Esvar misstepped, he would find himself in Lukovian's position.

"If you grant me a divorce, he has to make a settlement on me before the Crown confiscates the rest."

"He can invoke a husband's right to keep you quiet about what happened in the marriage, even if it's over. Is there evidence other than your word?"

"Yes. But can't you use a Truth Finder?"

He had learned his lesson from his brother. He said, "I can't. Doru would be tried by Karolje. If the king doesn't want Doru to be found guilty, he won't be. The Truth Finders can be bribed, you know. They're just men. And some of them might lie for Doru on their own accord." His arm ached.

"He's a traitor," she said.

He drank his water slowly, making her wait. If she was going to crack at all, better do it now than later. She matched him sip for sip, which almost amused him. He and Thali had never liked each other much, but neither had they underestimated each other.

"Cruelty first," he said.

She told him. He made a written list. Any single incident was inconsequential alone; taken together, they gave good reason for her to be afraid.

"You'll get your divorce," he said when she had finished. "I have two questions before we advance to the other matter. If he goes on trial for treason, you can't leave Karegg until the trial is over. Are you prepared to take that risk?"

"I'm prepared, my lord. My life is already at risk in being married to him."

"And why accuse him of betrayal at all? I did not, to be frank, think you had any special loyalty to the Crown. I would have imagined that you sought your own advancement."

"You're right. I have no loyalty to Karolje. That's why I'm here, asking *you*. Lord Prince."

"That's very thin ice you're stepping on now, my lady."

She looked steadily at him over the rim of her cup. "I know. Who doesn't? But the king is too ill for me to trouble him about so minor a matter as a divorce, is he not?"

"A divorce from the spymaster isn't minor," he said. "Doru will demand a hearing from the king."

"Who would be glad to try him on grounds of treachery. I don't think he'll chance it. Even if we say nothing, he'll know what could happen. I made a mistake when I married him, my lord, but I've never had reason to think he's stupid. That was one of the attractions."

Esvar turned a chess piece on its rim against the desk. Round and round. He wished his head was clearer. Was it the moment to bring Doru down, with his brother unaccounted for? If the lord's followers aligned themselves with Goran, Esvar would be alone.

"What is the betrayal?" he asked, not bothering to correct her assumption that Karolje would want treason squashed.

"There are a great many. The most urgent one is this: when Karolje dies, Doru planned to accuse Tevin of poisoning Karolje. Now they probably will turn it on you. They intend to wait until you've gone to see Karolje's body, and Karolje's guards will take you on the way out."

"Has he acted at all against the king?"

By Thali's account, Doru had been loyal to Karolje, albeit corrupt; it was in his acts against Tevin that charges of treason could lie. He had ordered spies and soldiers killed, stolen and forged letters, and threatened people who would have been Tevin's allies. The arrest of Lady Jeriza had been the most blatant of such actions, not the first.

But the evidence itself was scant: two letters that Thali had managed to steal before they were destroyed, money in the wrong place, and what she had been told or overheard.

"This won't work," Esvar said reluctantly, refolding the letters. "It's too easy for him to explain everything away. I can't accomplish anything with it except angering him. I believe you, but Karolje won't execute him on it. He's not providing aid and comfort to any enemy of the state, and he hasn't willfully disobeyed any direct orders. It's all against my brother, and may have Karolje's countenance."

"If things were reversed, Doru wouldn't hesitate."

"My lady. You gave me this information to do with as I chose. Don't question my actions."

"If someone had questioned Doru's actions, we would not be here," she said, and for the first time he saw how frightened she was. Her posture reminded him of a nervous cat. He realized that his disappointment in the weakness of the evidence was nothing compared to hers.

"You're quite right," he said. "But you're asking now why I

don't murder him. An execution isn't going to happen while Karolje is king."

"Doru's murdered hundreds of people."

"You didn't come to me about them. You came to me about yourself."

She put the empty cup down. She said, "And if someone else were to murder him?"

"Don't do it, Thali. I can't look the other way when a man is murdered by his wife."

"Even if she was defending herself?"

If he had not been wounded and drugged, the question might not have been the blow that it was. It caught him cold. He thought he might faint. The world hazy before him, he bent his head and felt the rush of returning blood. His hand went to the injury, an excuse to Thali and to himself.

When he was steady, he said, "Doru won't want to settle anything on you. Will you contest that?"

"My lawyer will. Amil Vasanian."

"I'll do the divorce as a separate decree then, and the two of you can argue out the money before a magistrate." He inhaled deeply, trying to recover some of his vigor. "I'll send Vasanian the decree. Good luck, my lady."

"Thank you, my lord." She stood. "I know there are political considerations that restrain you. I wish a woman's life could weigh the same."

"So do I," he said. It was the best he could do.

He showed her out and waited until he could not distinguish her footsteps to shut the door. He bolted and locked it, which made him feel even more of a coward. But one prince missing and the other injured might prove too great a temptation. Where are you, Tevin? he thought.

MIRANTHA

SIX YEARS AFTER leaving, she returns to Karegg. It is where her sons are. She has no fear of being recognized, even by the few people who might know her: her hair is short and heavily threaded with silver, her body has lost its wealthy softness, and she has a limp from a broken ankle that took months to heal. She has been living in a village in the mountains, isolated, where she has learned to kill, butcher, and preserve a deer, to make bread, to tell direction by the stars and hours by the sun. She has honed her skill with the bow and the blade, can haggle ruthlessly, and runs fast despite the limp. When she first fled, she imagined going south, going home, but that would put her remaining family at risk. It was too chancy.

Tevin is twenty, and there are stories of him. He is said to be more moderate than Karolje, sometimes fair. He is much adored by young women, and his patronage is sought after by young men. Like Karolje, he rarely appears in the city. All she learns of Esvar is that he is training as a soldier and is healthy. She wonders what her sons have done to survive this long.

Her hatred of Karolje has not abated, but it has become a cold thing, nestled in her soul where she scarcely notices it. She sees the city through the eyes of its people. In the narrow, crooked streets, the dingy public houses, the stinking wharf district, the broken courtyards, she hears the voices she never heard in the Citadel. The note that sounds in all of them is fear.

Karolje's soldiers are everywhere. In the market, walking the streets, watching as barges are loaded and unloaded. She is afraid too. Not for herself but for her sons. She hears whispers of a resistance but does not pursue them. If the king is overthrown, the princes will die with him. Nothing will bring her to raise a hand against them.

Then one of Karolje's soldiers rides down a boy who did not get out of the way in time. The boy's parents are hanged for not teaching their son obedience. It is not the worst thing Karolje has done, but every time she thinks of the boy, she imagines her own sons at that age.

Days later, she wakes weeping from a hideous dream, and she realizes she cannot go on as she is. If she is to stay in Karegg, she must fight. Her sons are no longer children. Moreover, they are princes, born with a duty to their people. If they died in battle against the Tazekhs, that would be a grievous thing, but she would accept it. The same is true of a battle against a tyrant king. For the first time she understands how her parents must have felt when they married her to Karolje. She had been sacrificed not for the power and prestige the marriage brought her father but as an attempt to give Piyr another way to control his son. It is no one's fault the attempt failed.

She still remembers the names Nihalik gave her, and one afternoon in late summer she opens the door of a lawyer named Radd Orescu. She has to begin by trusting someone. He looks up, polite, no sign of recognition on his face. She has a scarf tied around her head to keep the dust off her hair.

She sits in the chair he indicates and says, "I won't tell you my name, sir. It will be better for both of us if I don't. All you need to know is that I am a friend of Nihalik Vetrescu."

His glance goes to the window, which is open to let in air. There is enough street noise that no one can hear them without being visible. "Lock the door," he says.

She does. Her plan seems impossible. She licks her lips and says, "Nihalik told me there were people in Karegg who stood against the king."

His eyes are a striking green in a brown face, under a shock of thick, slightly curly black hair. She wonders what has happened in his life to make him willing to take the risks he does.

"There's another man you need to talk to," he says. "Not me. I can get a message to him to expect you. His name is Ivanje Stepanian. He is a steward for Yenovi Galik. You will need to appear richer to be admitted to see him, though."

It is a kind way of telling her what she knows, that she looks poor and exhausted. "I have money," she says.

He writes the address down on a scrap of paper and gives it to her. It all seems so easy. Is Nihalik's name that powerful? Or is she being trapped?

Outside, people walk past in their light summer clothing, their heads bent even if the sun is at their backs. Their pace is perfectly steady, neither rushed nor dawdling. It is the pose of daily submission.

"Can I buy you dinner?" she asks.

✦ ✦ ✦

For the occasion she finds a seamstress, who makes her a simple dress of pale green linen and silk. She touches the silk almost as a child would. It is six years since she has worn anything pretty, anything soft, anything new. In the mirror her face is thin and sharp and belongs to someone wearing a sword, not a dress.

Her other attempts to appear more feminine only make things worse, so she goes as she is. They eat at an inn on a veranda framed by vine-covered trellises. The grapes hang in full bunches, rich with color. In the center of the veranda, water pours ceaselessly from a stone pitcher held by a stone woman. Her sculpted legs are bare from mid-thigh down. It is an old statue, pocked and cracked and lichened, but the noise is even and pleasant.

They are served a different wine with each course, beginning with pale gold and moving through pink and deep red. The last is blue-black, sweet and heady. It tastes good with the sharp, crumbly cheese served at the end of the meal. They have greens, onion soup, seasoned lamb, melon, something creamy and icy and sweet. It is the best food she has had since she left the Citadel, and she worries that it will be too rich for her stomach.

They carefully avoid speaking of anything dangerous. Radd tells her about his work, his children being raised by their grandparents, his time as a boy spent fishing on the river. She tells him about her neighbors, about hunting, about her favorite flowers. He is a good listener.

He won't let her pay. When they have finished eating and the fireflies are out, a musician starts playing in a corner. Sunset is a violent, glorious reddish-purple. Without discussion, they leave the table and go up to the room he has taken for the night. The windows face north, toward the Citadel, and Radd closes the wooden shutters. A single oil lamp spreads warm light over the room.

They kiss. He is careful. She thinks that he senses how long it has been since other lips touched hers. With the windows closed, the air is hot, and their bodies are soon slicked with sweat. Clothes go to the floor. She expects she will be nervous, quick to jerk away, but the wine has made her skin less sensitive and her body more relaxed. When the time comes, she is ready.

Afterward, shutters reopened, they lie together in the dark. The night cool moves in. She realizes she has never slept with another person in the bed; Karolje always left. It is odd to have this sense of another body beside her, to stretch out her hand and make contact with flesh.

✦ ✦ ✦

In the middle of the night she wakes, disturbed by some dream or the unfamiliarity of the place. She gets up and walks to the window, looks out. The city is dark, a few roads dotted with lamps. The Citadel is a sleek blackness. Tevin is in it somewhere. It is hard not to think of him as a child.

When he was a child, she did not resist Karolje, did not confront Goran, in part because she wanted to be sure the throne remained for her son. She stares painfully at nothing. Guarding the throne for Tevin was a mistake. He is a man now, and if he is not fit to be a king, she will have to stand in his way too.

Radd is ready for her when she comes back to bed.

✦ ✦ ✦

They make love one more time, in the morning, knowing it is the last. She washes and dresses. She is about to leave when Radd says, "I can get a message to your sons if you want."

Tears well in her eyes. There is no point in denial. She dashes the tears away and says, "Thank you. It's not worth the risk. Don't try. I won't come see you again either. Forget all this, Radd. Go back to Osk and your children, and be safe."

His hands come to her shoulders. He lowers his head and kisses her lips. For an instant she clings to him, wishing she could have this comfort.

Then she steps back. "Goodbye," she says.

✦ ✦ ✦

She goes to Ivanje Stepanian. When he asks her name, she lies. The questioning is long and sometimes painful. Her story is simple: her father was a loyal officer who was captured in the Tazekh war. Karolje refused to ransom any of the captives, and he executed their commander when the man argued for them. The events are real.

Do you have children? she is asked, and she lies. *They were born and died.* It happens to too many women to be remarkable. She thinks of her lost sons and struggles with pain she thought she had put aside. *What about their father?* She says, *He left me a long time ago. I haven't seen him for years.*

Ivanje Stepanian is a good leader. He is prudent without being overly cautious, patient, and knowledgeable about how power works. She discovers in herself a genius for organizing. All those years of listening to her father talk about military strategy have paid off.

Karegg has an undercity. She supposes all cities have many selves. There is the public self, the shops and markets and craft halls, where money and goods pass from hand to hand and voices mingle in dozens of different accents. There is the domestic self, which encompasses both the quiet tree-lined streets where the wealthy merchants and guildsmen live and the crowded houses of the laborers and clerks and gutter sweepers. There is the ruling self. There is the revelrous self, the taverns and theaters and rings for games, performances, and races. There is the self of thieves and murderers. These are all known, all seen by anyone who walks through the city, all closely watched by Karolje's soldiers and spies.

But there is also the city that he cannot see, because it has no buildings and has no patterns. It is a city of color and movement and language, which shifts constantly and is not observed because it is too big and too close. It is a city of secrets and transgressions and obscure defiances, of shifting and bubbling ideas of what could be and pokes at what is, of both betrayals and confidences, of hidden things.

Slowly they build a thin tissue of resistance, connections wound and woven across each other like fishing nets. They find the people who remember Karegg as it was decades ago and have no strength or will for arms but can provide a place to meet, the booksellers who now lay bricks and will carry messages, the stable hands who will hide a few weapons in the straw, the occasional merchant or wealthy man who can go unquestioned to the docks and observe the changes of watch. The merchant knows the wagon driver who knows the baker whose sister works in the Citadel. The old herbwoman knows the candlemaker who knows the perfumer who sells things to the lords' wives. The carpenter has a cousin whose wife's brother is a locksmith for the soldiers in the barracks. Because she knows which kinds of people in the Citadel are never noticed, who learns things under the lords' gazes without being seen, she knows what kinds of tendrils to extend within Karolje's inner domain.

They have their codes and signals, the yellow cloth and the spiral symbol and the innocuous-seeming words. They begin to choose their targets, to chisel at the weak places in the king's authority, to plan more daring and more violent acts. They wait for whispers to become a roar.

She takes a new name. She considers and rejects calling herself Harpy; this is about more than her own hurt. She settles instead on Sparrow. The plain brown bird that is seen everywhere and thus never noticed. She must be not a person but a symbol.

17

SPARROW AGREED TO meet with Esvar more readily than Anza had expected, insisting only on a mask. Anza thought the hangings had shaken her too. It took four days and several visits from Jance for Anza to arrange. The third time he came to her flat he brought flowers, saying that otherwise the neighbors would be suspicious. Sparrow and Esvar settled finally on the College as a meeting place. It was between terms, and there would be few people on the grounds.

Anza was to record any agreement made. She had intended to walk, but she heard hoofbeats and looked outside in time to see Jance and Esvar pull up outside the building. Damn it, this was hardly inconspicuous, even if the other guards were up the block. Reluctantly, she went to the door and opened it to wait.

Esvar came up, his step lighter than she would have thought. They greeted each other, and she shut the door. The room was already getting hot. At one end of the table, the flowers drooped in a vase, petals darkening at the edges. Anza had not given them the care she would have if they had actually been brought by a lover. Duplicity exposed by death.

"Why did you come?" she asked. The journal burned

through the chest as it had when he had visited before. She did not know how much longer she could keep it from him. "Did you think I might not show?"

"No. I wanted to see you. I'll leave if you ask it."

"You can stay. But it's too early for wine, and I don't have water heating. It's well water or nothing."

"Well water is fine," he said.

Suddenly she was glad he was there. She filled two cups with water and sat across from him. His clothing was good but plain with nothing to mark any rank.

"What happened?" she asked, looking at his bandaged arm.

"Did you hear about the mob?"

"The one that killed two Tazekhs? Were you there?"

"Yes. I was shot. It isn't bad, as arrow wounds go. And it's not my sword arm. The archer got away without being questioned. I've been hoping it wasn't one of your friends."

"Sparrow wouldn't have you shot now that you've entered negotiations," Anza said. She was not so sure about some of the other members of the resistance.

"You shot me once, you know."

"I did? You were at the raid?"

"Yes. You got me right in the back. I had mail on underneath, fortunately. It was my own fault. I should have stayed where I belonged, out of range."

"I was scared," she said. "The explosive wasn't part of the plan. Everyone panicked."

"It was a hell of a thing you accomplished, getting out and over the roofs in that storm. Where did you learn to climb like that?"

"I grew up in the country. I was wild as a girl. I climbed everything. We had a donkey, an old slow one, and I used to stand on its back as it walked. I was a great trial to my aunt."

He grinned. It made him look about fourteen. "I'm sure you were. Do you ever want to go back?"

The question was an unexpected intimacy. It reminded her that they barely knew each other. Their conversations had all been negotiations, exercises in seeing how much they could withhold. I can't keep the journal from him, she thought. It wasn't fair. Mirantha could have destroyed it, but instead she had sent it away. Who could it have been meant for but her sons?

"I like the city," she said. "If I went back, there would be nothing to do except farm. Farming is—it's exhausting, and it's all-encompassing. My aunt could never see beyond the edge of her fields. Sometimes I think she didn't even know there had been a war."

"Why did you live with your aunt?"

"My mother died when I was eight. My father was here." It threw a shadow between them.

He slid his glass from side to side. When his eyes met hers again, they had darkened. He said, "I granted Lady Thali Kanakili a divorce from Doru. Has she come to see you at all?"

"No. There's no reason she would. We aren't friends any longer."

"He was furious when I told him. She told me she was prepared and that she had a way out. But I'm worried."

"If Thali told you she had a way out, she did. She knows how to make plans. She wouldn't have asked you if she wasn't certain she could get away. You aren't the only person who makes choices in things."

"I feel like I should just kill him. I'm not afraid for my own life, but he won't hurt me directly, he'll find someone else to hurt me through. It might be you."

"It's been several days, hasn't it?"

He nodded, drank. His upper lip was compressed and angry on the edge of the cup. She wished she knew a way to take that anger from him.

"Doru knows how to wait," Esvar said, putting the cup down. He tilted it on its base and spun it with the palm of his hand. "Several days mean nothing to him. The blow might not come for weeks. He will enjoy watching me worry."

"Esvar," she said. Then she did not know what to add. The quick embrace he had given her the last time he had been here, when she had raged at him, was not enough for her to feel sure she could touch him.

He said, "You know how to be careful. I know that. I want you to be more than careful. I'll tell Sparrow today that she needs to find another intermediary. We shouldn't see each other anymore, Anza. It's my fault. I dragged you in."

This wasn't a conversation either. It was a confession, an expurgation. She left the table. His head shot up, wary.

"Don't find another intermediary," she said over her shoulder as she bent to open the chest. "Did I tell you that my father spared Sparrow's life? She said he could have killed her, and he let her go. He told her he already knew he would be executed for having failed in the raid. That dragged me in as much as anything you've done. More."

Silence. She took her bag out of the chest and slipped paper, pens, and ink into it. She tightened the strap and turned around. He was looking at his hands. They were well-formed and beautiful.

"My lord," she said, which got his attention. His lips moved in a soundless *No*. "What do you want from this meeting?"

"An alliance."

"An alliance to do what? Think about it. You don't want to push for the wrong thing." The statement could be an insult, implying as it did that he was not prepared, but she needed to get him out of his own head. "Radd told me the contracts his clients were most dissatisfied with were the ones where they failed to ask for what they really wanted. If they asked and didn't get it, they moved on. If they never asked, it ate at them long after the contract was signed." And underneath that, the thought she would never dare speak aloud: *You're a prince, and your life has been hell, but you can ask for help. You're only twenty-one.*

He stood and poured what was left of his water into the vase. "Those poor flowers," he said. "Come here, please."

Anza did, placed her hands in his extended ones. As sudden as flame she wanted him, and she reached up and touched his chin. His throat moved as he swallowed. His free hand slipped through her hair to the base of her skull and cupped it. His mouth came down on hers, hard, and her lips opened to invite him in.

Her arms circled his waist, his fingers stroked her hair. The kiss went on for a hundred years.

At last, reluctant, she turned her mouth away. "We haven't time." She had to force her hands to stay planted on his lower back instead of caressing him.

"I know," he said.

He didn't move either. She was aware of his scent, leather, the bite of fine wool, a hint of metal. It further aroused her, and she stood on her tiptoes and kissed him again. His hand found its way under the hem of her shirt.

"Your guards," she said, one last protest in the hope that he had more strength to resist the pull of their bodies than she did.

"They all think this is what we're doing anyway." The tip of his tongue circled on the roof of her mouth.

The leather of his belt was soft and smooth against her palm. She pulled him, navigating around the chest, to the pallet. Their legs tangled as they lowered themselves, and he reached out to catch her. They laughed. Then her shirt was off, and his mouth was on her breast and her hands were unbuttoning his waistband.

✦ ✦ ✦

They were quick despite themselves. As they dressed afterward, Anza saw the lines of new skin on his back. They crossed each other repeatedly, as though his torso had been shattered and glued back together. She stilled. So much pain.

After a long pause, Esvar put his shirt on and said, not looking at her, "That was done at Karolje's orders. It doesn't hurt anymore."

"When did he do it?" She thought she knew. Her voice was pitched higher than normal with emotion.

"It doesn't matter," he said. "We need to go. Will you ride with me or with Mirovian?"

"With Jance." Then she would not be tempted. And while she did not think Jance wanted to sleep with her, there was no point in making him jealous if he did.

She washed her face and carried the bag down the steps. The horses were very large. Jance helped her up and, when she had settled herself, swung up in front of her. They had ridden this way before, when he took her to her father's house to meet Esvar. It felt familiar, safe.

At the College, they left the horses and all the guards but Jance outside and went into the classroom building. Master Tinas showed them into a classroom on the second floor. Anza's feet fit comfortably into the depressions on the stairs made by years of passage. The smell of wood and scholarship had not changed in two years, and she tried to imagine she was a student again, with nothing more to concern her than a question of rhetoric or a mathematical proof.

Jance stood guard outside the room. He looked preoccupied, and Anza almost delayed entering to ask him what was on his mind, but she decided he would not answer honestly in Esvar's presence.

Inside the classroom, door shut, Anza brought out her writing materials and set them on the table, not too close to Esvar. He looked preoccupied too. She was reminded of their first meeting, when she sat trying to keep all her fear hidden while he read a report and they waited for Marek to return. She had known by then he wasn't going to hurt her, but he had still been dangerous. When had she learned to overlook that danger?

The windows faced east, and she saw the sun falling brightly on the tiles of the library roof. Red and blue and orange and green and brown, they were laid in geometric patterns, predictable and even, far older than the reign of Karolje. Two harpies perched on the ridgepole. The building's shadow was still substantial on the square, but it would begin shrinking rapidly within the next hour. Half the table lay in golden light.

She heard footsteps in the hallway and looked at Esvar. He was watching her. "I won't ask for another intermediary," he said.

"Thank you, my lord," she said as the door opened.

The arrival was Sparrow, alone, dressed in black trousers and a dark green men's tunic. Her face was half-masked and her silvered hair newly cropped, barely an inch in length. The downturned edges of her mouth were pronounced. She took a seat at one end of the table and said nothing.

Anza felt she had been forgotten as the other two looked at each other. In profile they were curiously alike, jaws set with determination. Neither intended to yield anything.

"Shall we begin?" Esvar asked.

"I have someone else coming."

"This was to be just us."

"I need a witness. If I am to bring orders from you back to my people, they need to know I'm not lying. Some of them won't be convinced on my word alone."

"Very well," Esvar said. It turned Sparrow's assertion into a request for a boon. He was claiming the room for himself. He was the default. Sparrow would not accept that.

She didn't respond. The three sat in a stiff silence for several minutes until more footsteps sounded in the corridor. They were too heavy to be a woman's.

Again the door opened and shut. Miloscz. Anza looked at her fingernails. She wished it had been anyone else. He would be arrogant and contentious. Why had Sparrow picked him, of all people?

Because people in the resistance who would not believe her would believe him.

He seated himself on the same side of the table as Sparrow, with an empty seat between them. His gaze slid across Anza to rest contemptuously on the prince.

Esvar spoke to Sparrow. "Now that Miloscz is here, are you ready?" Even said politely, his words were an attack. *I know who your companion is. You don't have secrets from me.* Or, *Your own people don't trust you, and you shouldn't trust them.* They would strike whichever part of her was soft.

Sparrow grinned. Anza realized she was looking forward to this. Perhaps there were no parts of her that were soft. She said, "Why are we here? Your initial message was that all you wanted was for us to keep doing as we were doing. That's all we've done. Was Ruslan to be spared?"

"Things changed. If I were giving you names of people to kill, Lord Ruslan would have been on the list. But that strategy is no longer viable. It's too easy to blame murder on the Tazekhs, even when explosives aren't involved. Even when you leave notes. You have to stop. Korikos could decide to start a war. He's no less bloodthirsty than Karolje."

Once Anza had seen a practice sword fight, the combatants circling each other with blades extended, not touching. Watching feet, hands, deftness of movement. They knew what would come next and were strategizing. Sparrow and Esvar were evaluating each other the same way.

Sparrow said, "We're already in a war. The king against the rest of us."

"I know that's how you see it. But you're struggling. Do you want people to join your resistance, or do you want them to march in mobs and break windows and hang Tazekhs?"

"You have the power to call out those lies. You can make speeches and tell the watch. We won't be believed."

Karolje would kill him, Anza thought. He carried the proof of that on his back.

Esvar said, "To do that, I have to name the king as responsible for what he's done. I'm willing. But I'll only get one opportunity. He'll have me killed."

"Horse shit," said Miloscz.

"I thought he was here as a witness, Sparrow. I didn't invite him to participate."

"I don't tyrannize my people. He speaks for them as much as I do. If you don't listen to him as well, there's nothing to negotiate."

"Oh, I'll listen," said Esvar. A first lunge. He looked at Miloscz. "To argument, not to insult. And I tell you now that if you think for one moment that I am protected by virtue of my birth, you are naive. For all I know, Karolje's already disposed of my brother."

Sparrow interrupted. "He's really missing? Not locked away or killed?"

"He's really missing. I have ideas about what he's doing, but that's all they are, ideas. His body may be in the lake. I've sent a message to the Temple, and he's not taking refuge there."

"The king would tell you if he'd killed him," said Miloscz.

Esvar shook his head. "No. That's not how he thinks. He likes having secrets. If he killed Tevin and I succeed, I spend the rest of my life wondering if I am really the king."

"If your brother went into hiding, that's different," said Sparrow.

"If he went into hiding, he'll reappear. But he didn't tell me he was going into hiding. He sent me back to the Citadel because I was injured, and I haven't seen him since. We can't count on him to still be in the picture." The tip of his left index finger pressed the table.

Hell, Anza thought. He really didn't know. She had heard of

Tevin's disappearance before Jance told her—the whole city had—but she had assumed it was part of a plan made by the brothers. Jance had seemed unconcerned. It had never occurred to her that Karolje might have Disappeared him.

"You wanted to meet with us before he vanished."

"Yes. My aim remains unchanged. Karolje has to be overthrown."

"You could kill him yourself."

"I don't have the backing," said Esvar. His skin reddened slightly. Anza thought the admission had been harder for him than he had expected it to be. "Killing him now sends me to the gallows as a regicide and, with Tevin missing, puts the chancellor on the throne. You don't want him to be the king either."

"Why not?"

"He's ruthless. He murdered his wife's son. My brother watched it."

"Your brother, your brother," said Miloscz.

Sparrow said, "His *wife's* son? That would be his own son."

"She was pregnant when they married. He smothered the boy during an illness."

"You're certain?" Sparrow's jaw was clenched. Anza was sure the anger was not directed at Esvar. Sparrow could almost be a superior officer receiving a report. Something in the balance had changed.

"Yes," said Esvar. "I told you, Tevin watched it. Through a spyhole. The Citadel is full of them. Goran put a pillow over the boy's face until he died."

Sparrow's eyes were deadly behind the mask. This mattered someplace deep, beyond words, beyond explanation. She said, "Does his wife know?"

Esvar said, "Not unless Goran told her himself. Tevin kept it from me until very recently. It's a secret he did not intend to use until the best moment. I'm afraid now that he might have held it too long."

"Tell her."

Esvar's eyebrows went up. "Even if she believed me, and even if she didn't report the accusation to her husband, it would serve no purpose but to pain her."

"You don't protect a woman from pain where her children are concerned. She deserves to know everything." Another twist. Anger shifting to anguish.

"Do you have children?" Esvar asked, challenging.

You fool, Anza thought. She wanted to shove something into his mouth to silence him. The question was indecent. Almost obscene. She had never thought Sparrow would show pain. Her past was being exposed, an old wound torn open.

"They died."

The utter lack of feeling with which she said it was worse than sobs would have been. Esvar shifted. That had got through to him, then, echoing off the walls he had built up to foreclose loss.

He said, "I hear you. I can't risk telling her now."

"She could be your ally," Sparrow said.

"Keeping silent wouldn't be the first mistake I've made. But we're only discussing the chancellor by way of my other limitations, namely my lack of power."

"Don't tell me you're powerless!" said Miloscz. He had been waiting for the chance. "That's a self-indulgent fantasy. If you have no power, why should we stay here at the table?"

"Miloscz," Sparrow said.

"It's absurd for him to say he has no power when one word from him could get our heads cut off. This is a farce."

Esvar said, "But I haven't ordered that, and I won't. I don't give a damn whether you attribute that to my own self-interest or to cowardice or to some other better reason. Regardless, I'm circumscribed. I could arrange to kill my enemies and become the king, and how would that profit me if you keep burning buildings and killing lords?"

"The Crown would profit you exactly as it profits your father!"

"That's the rub, isn't it?" said Esvar. "You burn and kill and it's had no effect on Karolje's power. Perhaps you're going about this in the wrong way."

Sparrow said, half rising, "We haven't hurt anyone who didn't deserve it."

"Tell that to the people Karolje hanged."

"I can't take responsibility for what he does, only for myself."

"Have you no conscience at all?"

Anza thought Esvar spoke out of anger and not deliberate cruelty, but the words struck Sparrow as she had never seen. The woman dropped back into her seat, her face white. Even Miloscz noticed and stayed quiet.

Her voice softened, Sparrow said, "Vetia has suffered too much under Karolje. I will do whatever I must, even if it is a terrible thing, to end it. He has to pay."

"I agree. So what do we do?"

She locked her fingers together, thinking. It was not an argument anymore. "You want backing," she said. "I think you're right that you need it. I don't see how we can help."

"You have supporters in the Citadel."

"Not ones with the power to make you the king. Servants see things and hear things because they're overlooked. As soon as they come to anyone's attention, they lose their advantage. And they're worn to the bone with fear of discovery."

Esvar half smiled. "Rumor can be potent. The chancellor's power is built on rich merchants who expect him to favor them in matters of trade and taxation. They have no personal faith in him, most of them—sow doubts, and it won't take much for them to begin to crumble. You can sweeten things by spreading vague promises about what a different chancellor under a different king would do."

"And the spymaster?"

"Oh, that's easy. Competence. If the Tazekhs are such a threat, why hasn't he been watching? How come he could not prevent the explosion in the square? How did he allow Ruslan to be murdered? Why hasn't he found my brother?"

"Most people in Karegg have no idea who Doru Kanakili is."

"Everyone knows that someone like him exists. You don't have to name him to cast aspersions on him. He hates being thought wrong."

"Rot," said Miloscz. "Rumor won't bring down a throne."

Esvar tipped his head back. Anza realized he knew how to deal with Miloscz. Angry, blustering men must have been part of his life since he could walk. It was the people like herself and Sparrow who were unfamiliar.

He said, "You're not going to bring down a throne. Not this way. You can shove everyone of Karolje's lineage off it, can try to rule without a king for a while, and you'll crown someone a dozen years later. The people who lead bloody revolutions want power for themselves. And the people who follow, the artisans and traders and booksellers, they aren't fighting about principles of rule. They're fighting about their taxes and their comforts and their safety. They'll accede to any ruler who treats them well."

"You're talking about ruling," said Miloscz. "I'm talking about governance."

"The king is dead," said Esvar, snapping his fingers. "The lords are dead, all of them. You're in charge. What do you do now?"

"Oh no. I know this game, and I'm not playing it."

"You'll concede that I have more than a scholarly interest in the outcome."

"Gentlemen," said Sparrow. "We're straying."

"Are we?" said Esvar. "When Karolje dies, however he dies, there's going to be a reckoning for all of us. If my brother is dead, I'm the heir, and I have no intention of handing the Citadel over to the two of you."

Miloscz shoved his chair back. "Enough. There's nothing we both want. And nothing you can give us."

Sparrow said, "If you leave, Miloscz, you're leaving me too. Prince, we can spread rumors. It would be helpful if you have truths to include with them, especially in regard to Kanakili. In return, we want your word not to punish us or anyone we vouch for after Karolje dies. Even if Tevin succeeds him, not you. We want our jailed members freed and blood price paid for the ones who have been executed. We want laws and taxes restored to what they were when Karolje was crowned. We want him publicly denounced instead of being buried with honor."

"I can't promise all of that. Not now."

Miloscz said, "Everything we demand is within your power. There's no balance. What we ask for will even things some."

"Those are things a king can give you. I'm not a king."

That won't convince him, Esvar, Anza thought. She could see the chance of an agreement slipping away.

"You're asking us to do your work for you without any promises."

"I'm committing treason with you," he said, staring at Miloscz until the man looked away. "If you want to continue as you are without me, you can. Get up and leave. But I swear to you that I will do everything I can to prevent the king from using you to start another Tazekh war. Anything you do, I will have to expose to the entire city. If a war starts, I'll have to bring the Milayans in. Is that what you want?"

"Don't threaten us."

Sparrow said, "It's not a threat, Miloscz. It's a possible consequence. We might still choose to decide we'd rather have the Milayans than Karolje. He's right about the Tazekhs. You've been silent, Harpy. What do you think?"

Anza's mind went blank with surprise. She recovered herself. It was not so long since she had been in this room being asked sudden questions by the masters.

"The king killed his own soldiers and blamed the Tazekhs. I think he will twist anything we do to his own purposes. I think Esvar is who we have, and we take what we can get, even if it's not everything we would want. And I think he knows Karolje much better than we do. The king is evil. Evil. We can't lose sight of that."

Miloscz said, "You're rather conciliatory for someone trained by a lawyer."

"It's sound strategy not to let your enemy divide you," she snapped.

Sparrow said, "Rumor has it that the king is dying. We could just wait."

Esvar said, "He's been ill for months. But he's still on his feet. He might last until winter." He leaned forward. "The longer he lives, the more time I have to consolidate my own power. The more time there is to weaken Goran and the spymaster. I have to balance that against the damage that will be done while he still gives commands. If you help me, he can be got rid of sooner."

Anza found him convincing. Judging by the expression on his face, Miloscz did not. He opened his mouth.

Her temper was high. Miloscz was being stubborn for the sake of listening to his own voice, not to anyone else. She said, "Why are you here, Miloscz? You're rich. Why do you want to overthrow the king?"

Sparrow said nothing. Esvar said, "Answer her."

Miloscz glared at all of them. "No man should have that much power, especially when he only acquired it through birth."

"That's a principle," said Esvar. "A fair one. But not one people risk their lives for unless something else is driving them. What is in your heart?"

"You have no right to ask that, or to get an answer."

Something had hurt him, still hurt him. A father killed, a lover killed, a loyalty broken. Even if it had been a dozen years ago, it still stabbed.

I don't want to be like that, Anza thought. That path lay ahead for her if she was not careful, quiescent rage that smoldered and destroyed. She could hold on to her father's death forever. Sparrow held that rage too, but Sparrow had managed not to be consumed by it. She wanted Karolje dead, wanted her revenge or justice or whatever she hoped to gain, but if she gave up her anger, something of her self would be left. Rage was powerful, but all power needed to be reckoned with.

"Very well," said Esvar. "Just tell me this. Are you with me or against me?"

"I will never in a hundred lifetimes trust you," Miloscz said.

"Will you betray me to the king?"

In the fraught silence Anza clasped her hands together under the table. She wondered how much of this Jance was able to hear. If Sparrow and Esvar could not agree, who was she to go with? She hoped she would not be forced to choose. It would have to be Sparrow, if Sparrow would still have her. The resistance mattered more. Gods.

Miloscz said, "No. No, I won't betray you." He rose. "But I can't side with you either."

Esvar rose too, pushing his chair away from the table with controlled force. He was closer to the door. He said, "If the resistance splinters, none of us win. You have the power right now. If you walk out, it's over for all of us. What will it take to keep you here?"

"I want an insurrection."

"Bloody hell," said Esvar. "You don't demand much, do you."

"This is a war, and the other side holds all the ground. Half measures are useless, and you can't convince me you don't know that. *Your father* won't hold back."

The room was too small for all of them, the anger between the two men almost visible. Please, Anza thought, please. Esvar's face twitched. He had one hand around a bar on the back of his chair, and the tops of his fingers and his knuckles were white.

Then Miloscz broke his gaze and strode past Esvar to the open doorway. As he went through, he paused. His back moved as he breathed in. He spun and looked at Sparrow.

"Don't come back to my house," he said. "Not you, not any of your people." He grabbed the door and slammed it shut behind himself.

Slowly, Esvar sat back down. He kept his hands flat on the table in front of him, braced. He looked at Sparrow. "Will he change his mind?"

"No."

"How deeply will the schism go?"

"He'll bleed off people. The fanatics. Not enough to revolt on his own, but enough to cause mischief."

"Will the loss be enough to damage the resistance?"

"No. He doesn't know how to find the threads that matter. But he's right about one thing: this isn't going to be settled without bloodshed, Prince."

Anza heard the door to the building slam. The sun had shifted, and no light slanted onto the table now. The negotiations were going to fail. Esvar's goals and Sparrow's goals were too different. A common enemy was not enough to plan a future.

Esvar said, "An insurrection must meet two conditions to be successful. There have to be enough people for it to be a true threat, and there have to be leaders who can keep it from becoming a mob. Do you have the people? Do you have the leaders?"

"Yes to both," Sparrow said. "We aren't an army, and if we go directly up against the Citadel, we'll face too many experienced soldiers. But we have enough people to take the docks, the watch posts, the banks. The lords' fine houses. Not all at once, of course, but once the resistance begins to act, other people will follow. What we don't have are the arms."

"How do you intend to get them?"

She shook her head. "I can't divulge those plans to you."

"I might be able to help," Esvar said. "I don't want to do it this way. I would far rather have a few successful assassinations than see the city run with blood. If there's an insurrection, many people will die. But if an insurrection is the only way to get rid of Karolje, I will support it. Provided that I am at the head. Or my brother, if he is still alive."

Things were suddenly going much too quickly for Anza.

How had Esvar leaped from wanting the resistance to stop killing to planning a revolt? She had not thought he desired the throne. If he was willing to support insurrection, why had he waited until Miloscz left to make the offer?

Because he did not trust Miloscz, and because he knew Miloscz would not agree to his terms. Sparrow might reject them too, but she would do so in good faith.

Sparrow said, "How do we know you will be better than Karolje?"

"You don't. If you consider the things I've done, you don't have much reason to think I will be better. I can't make you believe me."

Sparrow tipped her head upward, staring at the ceiling to think. Her hands were in her lap, out of sight. It was a vulnerable posture. A harpy croaked in the distance. Anza wished she could touch Esvar. To do so now would be to align herself with him against Sparrow. She was glad he seemed to have forgotten she was in the room. If he made any movement toward her, she would break.

At last Sparrow looked back at Esvar and said, "What do you want for yourself?"

He laughed, a short bitter sound. "Not to be king, I assure you. It is a poor substitute for what I want, which is impossible. I want to have clean hands again."

No, Anza thought. He was better than that. She ached for him.

Sparrow said, "Sovereignty belongs to the people. We don't need a king."

"I almost agree. But if people like you and Miloscz take power by force, that is no different from how Kazdjan did it nine hundred years ago. And I have a duty."

"A duty to what?"

"A duty to justice."

The silence was much longer than any yet. Finally Sparrow said, "For now, I accept that. If we win, we will have this conversation again."

"I accept that." He removed his ring and placed it on the table. "If there is something you need authority for to overthrow Karolje, I will place my seal on it."

Anza shivered. There was a desperate bravery in the act that seemed almost suicidal. He was his mother's son. The time had come to give him the journal.

IT WAS MIDAFTERNOON when they left the College. In the shade of the arching gateway to the grounds, Esvar touched Anza's shoulder. She stopped walking. He was sending Mirovian with her. They might not see each other again, and he was too wrung and exhausted not to give in to the desire for one more moment of closeness. She looked as he felt. He had thrown himself into the resistance's hands entirely. He had passed everything he knew about the defense of Karegg and the Citadel to Sparrow, and he was a traitor.

"I have something for you," Anza said. "It's at home. You have to promise not to look at it until you are alone and safe and have time."

"What is it?"

"It's better if I don't tell you," she said. "Please. You'll see."

"Give it to Mirovian, and he can bring it to me," he said. Coyness was unlike her, which meant whatever she wanted him to see might go off like an Asp's explosive.

"All right," she said. Her hand came up as if against her will and touched his arm. He wanted to gather her up and bring her to his bed with no one to disturb them for days. If circumstances were different, he could love her. He could not stop himself from lightly touching her shoulder, so that he could feel the softness of her hair against his skin.

"Stay safe," he said. It was a nonsensical admonishment after what they had done this day, but it was all he had.

"Esvar." His name in her mouth was a summons, an intimacy, an affirmation. No one had ever said it quite like that.

He kissed her forehead, then wheeled and walked to his waiting horse. He mounted, lifted the reins. Looking back at her was too hard. She would understand.

◆ ◆ ◆

He wanted to see the city, the city he now pushed to rise against the king. The people who might die for his ambition. The places where his brother might lie in wait.

Through the streets around the College then, past stately houses that had once been homes for masters. Now they were owned by rich men and were let by the room to shopkeepers' assistants and clerks and young people just beginning in their trade. Each room was taxed, which benefitted the Crown.

He led his guards to the street where Ruslan had been murdered. The horses trotted past shops: milliners, jewelers, chandlers, drapers. Apothecaries, bakers, tailors. No booksellers. The streets bent around squares, widened and narrowed, went up and down. He kept to the paved roads when he could, and the horses' hooves clopped loudly. There were shrines, some tucked between other buildings and some almost large enough to merit the name of temple, market stalls and market buildings, green squares or circles with empty fountains in the center.

Everywhere he was watched. Carters edged their donkeys or horses to the side of the road; older children scattered; men and women stood warily on the edge of the street. He was not sure if he was recognized or if it was the presence of the soldiers alone that made people draw back. When he chanced to make eye contact with someone, they ducked their head. Taverns had their doors open because of the heat, and music came out, strangely jolly against the stillness of the watchers.

He wanted to rouse them, to scream out that they should follow him to the Citadel and bring it down with kitchen knives and rocks and chair legs. They would be slaughtered. He wanted to tell them he was not Karolje. He wanted one of them to throw something at him that would knock him from his horse, so they could see that they had power.

The impulse toward chaos was one he knew. It ran hand in hand with the desire for violence to be done to him, to destroy him because he was not worth saving.

Nothing marked where Ruslan had died. The streets were dirt, and dust puffed around the horses' feet. The tenants were at their work, the children somewhere more crowded. Begging, or stealing, or selling their bodies. The only sign of life was a black cat watching from the sill of an open window.

Onward then, west to the strait between Citadel Island and Port Island, where boats bobbed at dock. The lake glittered beyond. On Port Island the visible buildings were all warehouses, vigorously patrolled now since the earlier arson. On this side were the business offices: insurers, banks, shippers, traders, buyers, sellers. People moved with more confidence, secure in the knowledge that they were law abiding and the soldiers could not be here to arrest them.

Esvar looked at his guards. He had handpicked all five of them as loyal to him and not Karolje. But if he ordered them to go grab a man walking blithely along the street and beat him to death, they would. And none of the other people would run to the man's defense. Nor would they start a riot. What would it take to rouse them?

If he wanted them to follow him, how would he prove he was unlike the king?

He understood Miloscz's point. He had understood it in the negotiation. He could even agree with it in principle. When princes leaped for power that was not theirs, they did it with poisons or with battles. When the people rose to overthrow a tyrant, they chose one of their own to take power instead. A prince leading a revolution of the people was an absurdity.

He wasn't a prince. That was his brother. He was a weapon. He had put himself into Sparrow's hands to be hurtled at Karolje because her aim was a thousand times sharper than his own. If, when it was all over, he took the throne, it would be for her, not for himself.

He had to get back to the Citadel before his absence aroused any more curiosity than it already had. He kicked his horse.

* * *

Upon returning, he threw himself into routine tasks with a passion. He read reports of fruitless interrogations and dictated polite, noncommittal letters to merchants agitating for the Crown to put down the resistance, the Tazekhs, filthy thieves, and interfering priests all at once. Each time the clerk gave him something to sign—*By my own hand and seal*, over and over—he thought of how he was complicit in Karolje's tyranny. The historians of the future would elide his name with the king's. His mother was gone and his brother had fled. He was left to bear the guilt.

The light was balanced between twilight and full night when Mirovian came to his room with the parcel from Anza. Outside the leaves were dark, dark green, not quite black, and fireflies sparked. The cicadas had started buzzing. He thought he could see mist rising from the lake water.

The parcel was book-shaped, dirty burlap tied with coarse twine. Esvar took it and laid it on the desk.

Mirovian said, "She said to tell you it was with the Rukovili, sir. That's all she said."

With the Rukovili. Stolen from the College library? Another one of his mother's books? Had she been holding on to this for years too? Mirovian seemed twitchy.

"Does anyone besides you know where it came from?"

"I don't think so, sir. I brought back a bottle of wine, and put them in the same sack. No one followed either way as far as I could tell."

"Good. Thank you. Go enjoy your wine."

"Sir, I—" He broke off. His eyes shifted back and forth. Esvar had seen men's eyes do that too often not to know what it meant. Bad news coming.

"Has something happened to her?" he asked, holding his voice steady. Thinking of her skin, her eyes.

"No, sir, nothing! It's just—" He swallowed. "I know it's irregular. I want to resign my commission."

Esvar hadn't expected that. "Why? Sit down. How much did you overhear of what was said at the College today?"

Still standing, Mirovian said, "Only a little, sir. It's not that. It was being back at the College. I remembered what it was like to be learning. I could see the library. There are thousands of books in there that might never be read again because the king forbids it. I can't help kill the people who want it to be otherwise."

Saying that was an immense act of courage and faith. Esvar

was surrounded by people who were braver than he was, braver and more honorable. He didn't deserve the trust they were putting in him.

"What will you do instead?"

"Work with my father."

"The despised bills of lading," Esvar said, which was unkind. He gathered himself. "I need you. I swear I won't order you to kill anyone in the resistance."

"Someone else will."

Which was true. Mirovian was technically under the command of a captain under the command of Karolje. If Esvar interfered with that chain of command, it would raise questions.

"Can you be loyal to me? Or am I too tainted? I need your honesty, Jance, not your appeasement. If you think you can't trust me, I'll discharge you."

"I trust you, sir. It's the rest I can't bear." He gestured broadly.

"It's not going to go on much longer," Esvar said. "Sit, damn it. I don't want to shout up at you. What do you know about what happened today?"

"I'm pretty sure you were meeting with the resistance, sir."

"I was. There's going to be an uprising."

The liminal dusk was gone. Full darkness pressed against the walls, hot and thick.

"When?" asked Mirovian.

"It's not set yet. We need to try to find Tevin first. He may have his own plans. But soon. A matter of days, two weeks at the outside. When it happens, I'll need men I can rely on. And until it happens, I need someone to take my messages to Anza. If you leave, I'll need to find another person or go myself."

He could almost read the thought on Mirovian's face: *And*

I'm the one who brought her to your attention. Honor was very close to guilt.

"If I stay . . ."

"If you stay, obeying me from here out is treason. If we fail, you'll be executed or a fugitive. You can take your discharge and go home, or you can stay and risk your life. The only other choice is to turn me in to the king, but if I thought you would do that after hearing me now, I wouldn't let you leave this room."

The silence went on a little longer than Esvar hoped it would, but when Mirovian looked directly at him again, his face was set. "I will stay, sir," he said. Esvar waited for a *But*. It didn't come.

"Go on, then."

Mirovian rose, walked slowly to the door. There's something else, Esvar thought. Last time Mirovian tried to hide something, it had been Anza.

He almost let the man go. Then he considered the cost of being wrong. "Mirovian!"

"Sir?"

"What are you not telling me this time?"

He looked more relieved than affronted to be called on it. "It's only a feeling, sir."

"About what?"

Mirovian returned and leaned over the desk. Voice lowered, he said, "It's Lord Doru. I saw him a few hours ago. It was chance, I was coming back from the training yard and he was coming toward me in a cross-corridor. I stopped to let him go past. He looked at me. I swear I have never seen a man holding in so much anger. I would have rather faced a rabid dog. It was only a glance, but I will admit it scared the hell out of me. He's going to do something hideous." He swallowed. "I think that is when I realized I couldn't do this anymore. I don't want to end up like him."

"You won't," Esvar said. "But I understand the fear. Stay out of his way. And the next time I send you to see Anza, make arrangements to meet her somewhere else after that. A tavern, a square, a shrine. Continue the pretense that you're courting her." He should never have gone to see her that morning.

"Yes, sir." He left, lighter in step.

When he was gone, Esvar sent for Marek and gave orders for Doru to be constantly watched. Esvar had been more frustrated than serious when he told Anza that perhaps he should just kill the spymaster, but it might be time to act. Tevin would have wanted him to wait, but Tevin wasn't here.

There was still the matter of Goran. He remembered Sparrow speaking of Tahari: *She could be your ally*. Did he dare bring Tahari into this? More, would she dare to come? He couldn't ask her to murder her husband. And what had she felt about that first son who was killed? Karolje might not have raped her with violence, but she could not have refused him if he wanted to bed her. Had she gone to him out of desire or as submission? Could she have loved a child born from a forced union? Perhaps the boy's death had been a kind of terrible release.

He closed his eyes. Everything he knew was slipping away. He wrestled a monster that changed its shape every time he thought he had a grip on it.

A deep breath. Another.

He gathered himself, poured a cup of wine, and cut the twine on the parcel Jance had brought. He unwrapped it to reveal a book, green leather. If he had been holding the wine, he would have dropped it. For an instant he was five again, sitting at a table in a chair too tall for him to touch the ground, swinging his feet while he copied letters onto a piece of paper with a shaky hand. The pen nib tore at the paper, ink spattered. He remembered the smell of the ink. And Nihalik, a presence, comforting but not one he could disobey.

Tevin had used books like this. When Esvar was small, he had aspired to one. Then Nihalik was gone, and Ashevi in his place, and Tevin went south with the king.

It was with the Rukovili. His mother's? He opened it, carefully, and saw Tevin's childish hand. He turned the pages.

And then writing he did not recognize, an adult's, the Eridian characters graceful and firm. *I know it is dangerous to write this, even in this foreign script.*

His arm swept across the desk, knocking the book, his wine, a few loose papers to the floor. The breaking glass tinkled dully on a cushion of paper. Across the room the wall receded into darkness. His mouth was stopped with rage that had no target, no core. Over the thunder of the blood in his ears he heard pounding, steady and hard, coming from a distance.

His body saved him, or betrayed him, and he fell. The pounding stopped. Language returned, obscenities and profanities. He beat against the floor with both hands. Pain shot down his arm from the arrow wound, shocking him to stillness.

He lay, breathing hard. Slowly the edge wore off, and he heaved himself to his feet, righted the chair. The green book had been spared the wine, but the loose papers were ruined. He glanced at them, decided they did not matter, and balled them up and put them in the fireplace. He swept the broken glass into a pile and covered it with a rag.

Now he was ashamed. Who was he angry at? Anza, for keeping the book from him? For taking it from the library in the first place? His mother, for writing it? For dying?

At that thought, the anger swelled again. He put the book back on the desk and sat. He had more self-discipline than this. He had to. He had to.

He breathed.

Finally he thought he had reclaimed his core. He opened the book.

The new chancellor cornered me last night after a formal meal. He said nothing of import, but I did not like the way he looked at me. I don't think he knows my own secrets—he did not act as though he was preparing to blackmail me. Or if he knows, he doesn't care. It was more as though he were holding back some weapon he intends to surprise me with, for the sake of hurting me. He would be happy if Karolje died, of course, because then he would gain the regency and be one step closer to the throne, but I didn't think he wanted to be rid of me too.

I hate this, all this secrecy and slyness and fear. It's not necessary. It's inherent in power, some would say, and the gods know I have read enough accounts of kings and their intrigues. But this goes beyond politics. It's a kind of rot. They serve us spoiled meat and we pretend to enjoy it, and we're going to die of it.

When Piyr was alive, he and his chancellor used to summon the merchants to hear their complaints. They told him what roads needed to be repaired or how other merchants were underselling them or what Milayan tariffs were too high. Goran has not held any such meetings, and a few merchants who have come to see him have not left the Citadel. Their homes and goods have been confiscated. It's as though any complaint is seen as blame, any request as accusation.

So they aren't coming anymore. They aren't fools. But they aren't buying, which means they aren't selling. The Hierarch sent a message saying that more people are asking for alms. The chancellor ignored it. I sent a little of my own money, but it won't be enough.

Gods. There had been so much more to her than he ever saw, ever heard. Had Tevin known this aspect of their mother? He must have. Those early years Karolje was at war, she had had the chance to shape him. That was where Tevin's rigid determination not to follow the king had come from.

A new order has come from the king. He has required all Citadel servants and guards with Tazekh blood, no matter how distant, to be dismissed. They are to go to the Tazekh part of the city to live, and the king's soldiers are sent there to build a wall around it. Tazekhs, even wealthy ones, who live in other parts of Karegg are ordered to the Tazekh section too. They are to be penned like animals, not allowed to work, not allowed to leave. They will starve. Most of the lords and ladies in the Citadel approve of this order. Korikos and his Asps are evil, I have no doubt of that, but I remember the Tazekhs and half-Tazekhs in Timor, who were no more warlike or hateful than ordinary Vetians.

Goran wants to marry Tahari, and I have encouraged it, though I fear she will be hurt. He is terrible. He takes bribes and steals from the treasury and uses the money to buy property and power from weakened lords and merchants, who sell at great losses to keep their families safe. There are fines for the most minor infractions, and fees and taxes for every act of commerce. My heart aches for the ordinary people he has impoverished and frightened, for the poor who must give up the few things they have to pay his taxes, for the women who sell their bodies to keep their families out of jail.

But I let him do it without any protest. Every bit of power that Goran gains hurts Karolje. This is weak of me, and cowardly, but I have come to a point where I will let others suffer because that is a tool to break his hold.

People are starving in the city. There was a bread riot, which Karolje's soldiers put down bloodily. I do not know the details, but at least a hundred people died. Vetians, all of them. The bodies were sent off-island to be burned, and soldiers left the Citadel with hellhounds to patrol the streets.

Somehow, and what a fool he was, he had not thought of his mother as political. She had only been his mother, with golden hair and a soft voice and the scent of lavender. But of course she had been political. She had been a queen. Her infidelity itself had been political, a renunciation of the marriage she had been forced into for state reasons. Had she hated her own father for giving her to Karolje?

A letter has come from Tevin. It is in his hand and his voice, and I think it may not have been seen by the king. He writes very little of the war, which is to be expected; he has to be wary of Tazekh spies. Instead he tells of things he has seen, southern things such as olive groves and the peddlers with the bright blue carts. He sounds well and satisfied. He says that he is a participant in the strategy meetings, and that Karolje has praised him. I think this is true. He has studied war since he was small. I fear that when he comes back there will not be much boy left to him.

I go to the chapel daily to pray. Usually I am alone, but sometimes he comes. He is getting careless. I am afraid we are going to be discovered. I am afraid he wants to be discovered. There is no reason he would, but I cannot shake the thought.

He has not touched me in weeks. We quarreled. Soon the king returns.

He was intruding into a place no one should be allowed to go. If Tevin read it, it would rip him apart.

Tahari and Goran's child, a son, was stillborn. I am sorry for her. She has become much admired, but sometimes when she is not careful, her face betrays a bleakness. She is unhappy, and there is nothing I can do to ease her unhappiness. If both my sons died, she would be queen.

Today Tevin turned fourteen. I was given time alone with him. We watched the snow falling, the year's first, and drank tea and ate sweet cakes. He will make a good king if he gets the chance.

Last night I dreamed. The details are not worth recording, and by now I remember hardly anything anyway, except that I was being chased in moonlight, and I woke frightened and sick to my stomach. The feeling has not lifted all day.

I used to think I knew what love was. Then I thought I knew what it was not. Now I think I have no idea of either. What the body wants, the body will find a way to have. That isn't love, that is need.

He put the journal down and clenched his fists, unable to contain, unable to name, his emotions. He wanted to weep for his mother and hurt Anza for having read the journal and put a knife in Karolje's heart and drown himself in the lake all at once. His clothing felt like sandpaper. He was afraid that if he touched anything, he would destroy it.

> *I have walked in terrible places and done terrible things. Karolje would have driven me mad if I had not had my sons to protect. But he will kill me soon. I can see it in his eyes. He has had his Truth Finders trying to pry secrets from my mind. But what they want to know is not held in words or thoughts, and they cannot understand that.*
>
> *When I am gone, Karolje will pay.*

When she vanished, he had not been allowed to weep and had held it inside, a tight ball compressing more and more on itself each day until it took up almost no space and was immovably dense. He learned to keep himself away from that grief, to veer off course anytime he approached before it could draw him in. Now it threatened to pummel him.

Every time he had talked to Anza, she must have had the journal in her thoughts. Weighing him, wondering if he was more like Karolje or Mirantha. Knowing the pain that had been the air he breathed since he was small. Seeing him through the veil of his mother's love. So many times Anza could have turned away, and instead she had put herself in his path. Put her body in his arms. When she touched him, the air had rung like a bell against his skin. She deserved far better.

He closed the journal. It could not stay in the Citadel. He would give it to Mirovian to return to Anza.

He took out ink and pen and paper. He intended to write a

long letter, telling her what she already knew, all the reasons he could not let himself love her. But the words would not come right. He scratched things out over and over. Tevin's voice echoed in his mind: *You will pretend to love them so they don't know how much you're like him.* He tried to write that—*if I seem to love you, it is a lie, because lying is all I know*—and blotted it out because it too was a lie. She compelled him to honesty. That was one of the things for which he loved her.

What he finally finished with was only a few short sentences, inadequate but true. He signed his name, sanded and sealed it, and placed it between pages of the journal, which he rewrapped.

He had an awareness, distant, like a storm on the horizon or a sleeper wave offshore, of waiting force. It was coming, the wreckage of the past, ready to crash over him. He couldn't stop it. History was inexorable.

Despair overwhelmed him. He went into his bedroom, bolted and locked the door, and flung himself on the bed fully clothed. His knife pressed uncomfortably against his hip, and he took off the belt. Without conscious thought he drew the blade. The edge was sharp. He put his hand on the hilt and pressed the tip against his heart, not with enough force to go through his shirt.

Not now, not when he owed his brother so much. To kill himself now was to waste everything Tevin had done.

Not now, while he remembered the feel of Anza's hair in his hands.

He sheathed the knife and tossed the belt onto a chair. He undressed and got into bed, but he left the lamp on. The low, golden light at the end of the wick burned through his dreams.

MIRANTHA

IN THE CITADEL, she never carried anything deadlier than her small scissors made for snipping threads or flower stems. The knife she wears now—at six inches the longest that is legal for a citizen of Karegg—has become a familiar weight on her hip. She has a pair of longer knives, the edges so sharp they cut your eyes to look at them, that she brings with her on the nights she is involved in resistance activities. They have plain hilts and plain sheaths, the weight perfect in her hands. She knows how to use them together and singly.

One evening in the dreary period where winter and spring bleed together, a day of sleety rain followed by a day warm enough for shirtsleeves, she puts the knives on and slips out of her lodgings. It is cold enough for a concealing cloak. The moon shines fitfully through clouds, but she smells rain on the wind. Twelve years have passed since Ashevi died, twelve years since Mirantha vanished. Esvar will be twenty-one soon. It seems hardly any time at all since she held him, a red-skinned newborn with still-blue eyes and fat wrinkled fists. She has seen him a few times since she returned to Karegg; unlike his brother, he comes from the Citadel on occasion, without pomp and clamor. She has never been close enough to clearly see his face. She wonders what atrocities her sons have committed to keep themselves alive.

Tonight the resistance is meeting in a small, filthy house jammed onto a hillside with others like it. The nearest well is three blocks away. The streets are unpaved alleys not wide enough for a cart. In places it is so steep the dirt has been carved away and planks laid down to make crude steps. Getting out will be a mess if there is rain.

She is the last one to arrive. Herself, Ivanje Stepanian, six others, sitting in too-close quarters in a room that reeks of poverty. They have a single candle in a holder on the floor. One man is the householder, a grey-haired shrunken person whose right hand was chopped off a few years ago as punishment for copying seditious writings. His livelihood lost, he retreated to the slums to brood upon revenge. Sparrow feels a strange, terrible kinship with him that she does not with other resisters; his mutilated body seems the physical form of her own loss. The shiny scar tissue of his stump catches the candlelight.

The wind rattles the door fiercely, and thunder rumbles low and deep. She goes out to check the weather, shutting the door behind her. The clouds are thick and dark, obscuring the moon. Her eyes sting from the woodsmoke, which can no longer rise in the heavy air. In the west, lightning streaks across the sky. The wind gusts, and her nostrils flare like an animal's. She hears a distant bay that is not thunder.

She dashes back into the house. "It's going to storm," she says. "And there are hellhounds coming. I heard them."

"Where? Which way?"

"I'm not sure," she says. Ivanje grabs her arm.

Her years in the Citadel come crushingly down on her, memories so vivid she thinks she is there again. Her mouth tastes like she has swallowed something poisonous. She bends over, retching and retching, tears running from her eyes with the force of it. She cannot think. Karolje grabs her by the hair and forces her onto the bed. He opens her wardrobe and with a knife slices through the new gown her mother has sent. He knocks her wineglass to the floor and stands over her with a belt while she picks up every sliver. In the throne room he presents to her a handsome necklace she had seen another lady wearing a few hours ago, and the lady stares viciously at her while Karolje's fingers fasten the clasp. She huddles in the corner of her bed, weeping with shock and shame, after the first time he strikes her hard. She is so afraid.

"Sparrow!" Ivanje says, hurrying her to the door. "Run!"

She is shaking and trembling, and to her shame lets him push her away. Then her body takes over, run run run, feet thumping against dirt it is too dark to see. She skids, falls, picks herself up, keeps running. She feels the breath of the hellhound on her neck, its teeth on her skin, and looks back, gasping. She imagined it. She falls again and twists her left wrist when landing. The pain is sharp and immediate. Run run run. Lightning flashes, and the thunder comes close upon it.

She finds herself on the lakeshore, where she smells fish and tar and hemp. Her senses are all too vivid tonight. There is a rip in one knee of her trousers, and the cloth is sticking to her leg. She must be bleeding. A scrape, like a child. The wooden jetty she is standing on is slick. The water slapping against it is threatening. A cat in heat yowls behind her.

It's over, she tells herself, over, over, over. She still has both her knives. They will never take her. She will kill herself first, even if it means smashing her own head into a wall.

She is shivering now from chill rather than fear, her teeth

clicking together, and she turns around. She sees a shrine half a block away, a single lamp burning at its door. Unthinking, almost unaware, she hurries to it. The door is dark, blue or black or green, it is hard to tell, and it opens when she pushes. She stumbles in, kicks the door shut, and collapses on the tiled floor.

✦ ✦ ✦

The priest, a thin, dark-skinned man a few years older than her, gives her hot tea and cleans her scrapes and binds her wrist. At first she has no words, only animal-like moans. The warmth from the hot liquid—it is more than just tea—spreads through her, and she stammers her way to a thank-you. There is nothing left of her but exhaustion.

He shows her to a long, windowless room where there are several cots, and she lies down on one, still dressed. He spreads a blanket over her, says a few things that she does not have the attention to hear, and leaves the room. The door stays ajar. Sparrow stares at the yellow rectangle on the wall where the light from the corridor falls, and for a long time there is nothing in her awareness.

Something moves in the light. A spider, crawling down the wall. It moves so confidently. She watches until it has crept back into shadow. She does not feel so raw, so exposed, anymore. Thunder cracks nearby, rousing her back to full alertness.

There is a soft thud. The main door to the shrine closing. A dog's bark.

They have tracked her, followed her scent. The priest will not refuse them. No one would.

She is on her feet, a knife in each hand, but already she hears the priest's voice and the sound of men approaching. She has nowhere to go. Her breath is coming short and fast, and she is sweating.

The door opens. A soldier enters, light shining on the blade of his sword.

Suddenly she is calm. If she is to die now, it is an honorable death.

He will try to disarm her first; resisters are to be taken alive. She drives the knives forward, one aimed at his gut and the other at his throat. His sword comes up expertly to block the knife at his stomach, and when the blades clash, it sends a stab of pain through her sprained wrist and forearm. With his other hand he grips her right wrist and immobilizes her arm with the knife inches from his neck. She kicks hard at his shins.

He evades her. His grip on her arm shifts, and then before she knows it both knives are on the floor and he has pushed her up against the wall, his arm pressing on her throat. He can cut off her breath just enough to keep her alive. She has no way out.

"Hands on top of your head," he says.

Viciously, she lowers her head and bites his arm. He slams her against the stone as Karolje once did, and pain freezes her. The world is a chaos of lights. One hard punch to her stomach, and she cannot help doubling over, and he chops at her neck with the edge of his hand. Her arms turn weak as water.

"Now," he says, "you can come quietly and have this over with, or I can drag you out of here hamstrung in both legs. Which will it be?"

The pain and the threat and the utter futility of it all come together, and the fight goes out of her body. Out of her heart. She stands limply while he shackles her hands behind her back. Her sprained wrist throbs against the metal shackle.

He puts one hand on her shoulder and steers her forward. She feels a pang of loss for her knives.

In the front of the shrine, the priest says, "Don't hurt her. There shouldn't be blood spilled in a shrine." He has lit incense somewhere, and the scent propels her back to the Citadel chapel, to Ashevi. The helplessness of years long gone crashes back down on her.

The soldier laughs. "Don't hurt her? What do you think is going to happen at the Citadel? Stay out of it, priest."

Outside, rain falls lightly. There are three more soldiers, one holding the chain of a hellhound. Another has a captain's insignia on his tunic. Sparrow looks around for horses, a donkey cart, anything. Are they going to be walking back to the Citadel? She wonders if she should reveal herself and ask to be taken before Karolje. They wouldn't believe it.

A hellhound's bite seems a better death than torture. She kicks at the dog. It is not close enough for her to make contact, but it growls, low in its throat, and its back bristles. The soldier yanks on the chain, restraining it. She kicks again. The man who chained her grips the shackles and pulls, jerking her arms toward him. Her body follows.

"Back off," the captain snaps to the man holding the dog.

The soldier obeys. Sparrow keeps her eyes on the hellhound. She knows how well-trained they are. One lone woman can't make it go wild. The weakness is in the soldier. And he, unfortunately, looks experienced and well-trained himself. The dog is no way out. Moisture on her eyelashes makes it difficult to see.

Lightning whitens the world, the thunder deafening and immediate. Everyone jumps, and the dog howls.

She breaks free of the soldier's hands and runs at the dog. It turns, snarls. It lunges at her. The soldiers are yelling, and the rain is falling harder. Another flash. She sees the sharp white fangs.

The dog's handler pulls the chain. The thunder booms, and he jerks in surprise.

That is all it takes for the hound to pull forward and turn, sink its teeth into the soldier's hand. The man screams in pain and horror, and the hound breaks free, runs, trailing its chain.

"Go after it!" the captain shouts. "Both of you!"

They obey. The man who was bitten writhes in agony as the venom courses through him. His mouth is open, his face twisted, while the rain beads his skin. His hand has already started to swell. There is no cure for a hellhound's poison.

The captain squats by the bitten soldier. His arm moves. Blood sprays outward. The flailing body jerks once. She could run now, but she doesn't. Nothing matters.

Sheathing his knife, the captain rises. He and Sparrow look at each other in the rain and lamplight. The world stills, teeters on its axis.

"I know you," he says.

His face is familiar to her too. She cannot name a time and place. But he is a captain in the Citadel; she probably saw him often. He would have been younger then.

"I know you," she says. They step closer to each other. The hellhound barks frantically in the distance. "Tell me your name."

"Alcu Havidian." He swallows. "My lady?"

"No longer," she says. Her memory of what they did for each other is clear now. *I do it for Vetia*, she had said.

They stare at each other, the dead man a silent witness. The barking breaks off, and a man screams.

Havidian unlocks the shackles. "I'm sorry," he says. "Go. Hide. Keep fighting."

"You'll be killed for this," she says in a flash of lightning.

"I think I am soon going to be the only witness," he says, jerking his head over his shoulder to renewed barking. The dog sounds frantic now, trapped. "I may be killed for what happened to the dog."

"Don't go back. We could use you."

Thunder drowns him out. He shakes his head. "I can't. Go. We depend on you."

"The others—my friends—"

"The leader was killed. The others are captive. I will try to help them die quickly." He pauses, smiles suddenly. "My daughter is here. She graduated from the College two years ago. Thank you for that. And I can tell you in return that your sons are men worth serving. Now run, my lady, please."

She does, back to the lake and along the deserted wharfs. Boats rock beside her on the high water, and she hears the slosh of waves against the pilings. Even when she is gasping for breath and her side aches she keeps going, stumbling over coils of rope, sliding on boards covered with fish scales. The shifts between a lightning-bleached world and utter darkness confound her eyes. The rain picks up its pace, the drops striking against the water and fountaining between her feet. The cats and the rats have all taken cover.

The cats and the rats. The phrase repeats itself continuously, forms the rhythm of her movement. The cats and the rats. The cats and the rats.

She is pushing herself too hard. She turns onto the next street and finds a gap between two buildings where she is at least out of the wind. The overhang of the roofs keep most of the water off her. She sits and huddles against the wall. Her skin is numbed from cold. The cats and the rats.

She is so cold and wet and exhausted that it takes time for her to realize she is crying. Her heart is broken. Her sons, her sons.

19

ANZA COULD NOT see across the courtyard when she opened the door. The thick mist smelled of the lake: wet, muddy, green. Rivulets ran down the stone, and the iron railing was covered with beads of water. She watched one enlarge and drop. She had a cup of hot tea in her hands, a comfort against the greyness. The air was chilly for summer, nothing like yesterday's heat. The fog had moved in beginning at midday, several hours ago, and seemed unlikely to lift anytime soon.

The hoofbeats that had brought her to the door clattered to a halt in the courtyard entrance, out of sight. She heard the rider dismount, the tread of boots on stone. One man, alone. It wouldn't be Esvar, then. I'm not in love with him, she said to herself. I'm not.

A figure emerged at the top of the stairs. Jance. He wore a short black cloak over his uniform. His hair was beaded with moisture. They greeted each other and went into her flat. She had lamps on, and his belt buckle caught the gleam.

"I've brought this back," he said, handing her the wrapped journal. "He wanted me to tell you that it's not a rejection. He thinks it's safer with you. There's a letter in it."

She nodded. She was not surprised. His other choice was to burn it. She would read the letter after Jance was gone, though she thought she knew what it said. He would sunder their connection. It was the only thing he knew how to do.

"Was he angry at all? Do you want tea?"

"He didn't seem to be. Although it's hard to be sure. He did look like he hadn't slept much."

The kettle was on the hearth, keeping hot, and she poured a mug of tea for Jance. "It's nasty out there. Stay a bit."

Jance looked at her windows. The fog obscured the building across the street. "We aren't supposed to continue to meet here. Esvar is afraid that either you or I or both of us are being spied on. Is there a tavern nearby that would not be too suspicious for us to go to the next time?"

She planned like that with Sparrow. "There's one a couple of blocks away that would work," she said. "Go up to the top of the hill, turn left, and it's on the next corner. Every time I've walked by it's been crowded."

"Is the food edible?"

"It's not splendid, but it won't kill you either. The beer is adequate."

"Can you meet me there in two days, an hour before curfew?"

"I can. I might not have any messages, though." She was still waiting for Sparrow to tell her where they were going to go next, since Miloscz's house was no longer an option. She hoped Sparrow had retrieved her bow.

"That's all right." He sighed. "Anza, I tried to resign my commission last night. The prince told me a few things."

"You tried to leave? How could you do that? He needs you." It was a mad thing to say after the self-righteousness she had inflicted on Jance at other times, and it brought home to her how much faith she had come to place in Esvar.

"I know. It's just—there's not a lot of honor in this job right now. I feel dirty. And worse, I have to lead the raids, and the person who tells me where to raid is Doru Kanakili, and he is evil. And cunning. Anything he orders me to do could be a trap. I'm not worried for myself, but for Esvar and for you and for other people. It would be very easy to manipulate me into a situation where Doru gets secrets from me. I tried to explain this to the prince, but he didn't want to listen."

"I think he knows it," Anza said. "He's warned me about Doru. If it didn't seem like he was listening, it's probably because yesterday was hard. I shouldn't say anything if he hasn't, but did he tell you what it was about?"

"Yes, although I would have had to be an idiot not to have guessed most of it." The word *treason* hung unspoken between them. "That's what convinced me to stay, the chance that things might change. Otherwise I was ready to go home and work for my father. I don't know how your father did it."

"He thought he needed to stay to help pick up the pieces. But he turned too. He—he had a chance to kill Sparrow, and he let her go." Saying it was a relief. At the end he had been on the right side.

Spinning his mug, Jance said, "Are you in love with Esvar? I'm not jealous, I just want to know."

"I'm not. I could be. I don't need you to tell me that would be stupid. I won't see him again, so it doesn't matter."

She knew she was probably lying. She had been trying hard not to think about sleeping with Esvar. Lips on her mouth, her skin, the hard muscles of his arms, the mixed scents of horse and leather and soap. She wanted to do it again, slowly, properly. The shadow in his eyes when they parted yesterday had been enough to tell her there would be no *again*. He had cut her off, which was the best thing for both of them. They had no future together, even if they survived the uprising.

That was who they were. Survivors, both of them. Like Sparrow. Love would interfere, so it could not exist.

Why would it interfere? she asked herself. Why was it a loss and not a gain? Was this another thing to lay at Karolje's feet, the fear of loving?

She had no idea whether her parents had loved each other; they had parted when she was small, and she had not been told why. They had not fought with each other, she remembered that much. It was one of the many things she had never asked her father. The past was a country whose boundary they had never crossed.

"It might matter to him," Jance said, to which there was no possible response. Anza refilled her own mug. The tea steamed in the chill air of the flat. She would light a fire tonight.

Jance went on. "He—what was that?"

"What was what?"

"I heard something."

"It was just one of the neighbors, Jance. No one could have followed you in this fog."

He was closer to the door. He got up and shut the bolt. Anza heard the feet: several men, heavy, determined. Fear seized her briefly as it had in Nikovili's house, then was gone. She rose and looked around for anything that could be used as a weapon.

"The table," said Jance. He knocked it over, shattering the teacups and sending the journal flying, and pushed it against the door. "Go, get out the window, you're small enough." His sword was in his hand. A dark pool of tea spread across the floor.

"Don't be ridiculous." She grabbed the sharpest of the kitchen knives. "I'm not a coward."

"Fuck it, Anza, run. You're more important than I am right now. And if you die, I don't know what will happen to Esvar."

The words cut into her. But the roof of the building was an overhang, and she would not be able to pull herself onto it. Someone would be watching on the ground fifteen feet below. She didn't see how even the fog would protect her from being caught after the drop.

Weight thudded against the door. Her mouth went dry. *Thud. Thud.* The frame wasn't built to withstand such force, and the wood splintered below the bolt.

"Go!" Jance shouted.

Another blow, and the frame gave entirely. The door edged open. The table was too light to hold for long. They would push it aside as easily as Jance had pushed it against the door. She slid the knife through her belt and grabbed the kitchen kettle. The table scraped against the floor.

Jance stared furiously at her. He was going to die, trying to save her. Was she going to waste his life?

The door opened far enough for a man to shove through and kick the table farther out of the way. Without thinking Anza heaved the kettle at him. The lid and then the kettle itself clanked to the floor as hot tea sloshed out and over the intruder's face. He screamed. Jance stabbed him in the stomach.

Blood blossomed from the wound, a crimson flower unfolding and unfolding. It shone on Jance's sword. For a moment the fragrance of the tea filled the air. Then there was a sudden stench as the man's bowels released. He fell, still screaming. His body blocked the door more effectively than the table had.

The next man through had his sword ready, and he brought

it down against Jance's blade as he took a long step over the body of his comrade. The clang of metal made Anza's teeth hurt. Jance parried, thrust, was blocked. Another man entered. He saw Anza and grinned, took one step toward her.

She ran for the window. There was nothing else to do. She sat on the sill, feet out, and twisted onto her stomach. She looked up in time to see a fourth man enter and the three of them engage Jance. No, Jance, no, she thought. This couldn't be happening.

A low swing from one man caught him in the thigh while he stabbed at another. He stumbled. The third man brought a sword down forcefully on Jance's shoulder. Blood fountained everywhere as he screamed. The scream was cut off as another blade sliced through his neck. She dropped.

The impact resonated through her whole body, but she kept her footing and ran. Up the hill, into another courtyard and across it to the wynd, through the next courtyard and down that street, a left turn onto another street. The fog was so thick she couldn't see the places to turn until she was almost atop them. An alley, a courtyard, a narrow path that turned into a flight of steps descending a steep hill. She had never seen them before. She hurried down, almost slipping twice, and came out onto a street she did not know, which vanished into the fog in each direction.

She bent over to get her breath. She was panting now, loud and rough. Pain in her side jabbed as sharply as a knife. Her heart beat far too fast. She listened for pursuers but heard nothing over the sounds of her own body.

As soon as she could, she started walking again, then jogging. Down streets, along alleys, through more tunnels. The streets got wider and she began to see people about, dim shapes that loomed up suddenly. Gold light shone from windows through the mist.

They killed him, they killed him. She saw again the blood as his arm was parted from his body, the white knob of bone swallowed up by the spray of blood, brighter than anything else. She bent over and vomited, retching long after her stomach was empty. Bile burned her raw throat.

⁂

She let her feet lead her and realized after a while that she had stopped being lost and was headed toward Sparrow's house on Beggar Island. She stopped, considered as best she could if that was where she should go, and went on. She could have gone to Irini or Rumil or some other friends, but those choices would cut her. They were too close to her memories of Jance. And the only one who could help her anyway was Sparrow.

Crossing the bridge, she paused in the middle to look back at Citadel Island. The fog obscured it entirely. She could just see the edge of Beggar Island, the soft grey lines of buildings that shifted in and out of focus as the fog moved. The water below the bridge was iron grey. She stood, suspended in a featureless world where the only sound was the light lap of water against the pilings. Her hair was damp, her skin pale and chilled.

Time was imaginary in the unchanging fog, but she supposed it had been about an hour when she came to Sparrow's house. She recognized it by the peeling blue paint on the door. She knocked three times. If Sparrow wasn't here, she would sit against the door and wait. The killers would have left her flat by now, but she was never going back to it. The letter from Esvar would never be read.

The door opened, and Sparrow stepped aside for Anza to enter. "What's happened?"

"Jance is dead," Anza said. The words were heavy as ingots. She felt desolate, yet at the same time, none of it seemed real. "I didn't know where else to go."

"My poor girl. I'll bring you something to sit on."

Sparrow went up the narrow staircase and returned a moment later with a large stained red pillow. The fabric was coarse. She threw it on the floor next to the wall and said, "You'll be more comfortable on that. Do you want tea? Raki?"

"Tea," Anza said. Her throat ached from grief. Wearily, she sat. Her feet and shoulders hurt. Her palms and forearms were scraped from the scramble out the window. Gods. Jance was dead. She shivered and jerked.

Sparrow brought her a chipped mug full of tea and sat down facing her. "Tell me," she said, as softly as Anza had ever heard her. The room was dim and grey. Moisture trickled down the glass of the two small windows, the fog colorless against them.

"He came to see me. Then men broke in. He actually killed one of them first. I was a coward. I ran. I couldn't think of anything. So I came here."

She could not help sounding desperate. She felt desperate. The sword, the blur as it moved through the air, the explosion of red from Jance's neck. Her shoulders drew in and her body tightened.

This was worse than when her father had died. There had been grief and anger and fear then, but not this terrible sense of urgency. She had been alone, very carefully alone, and now she was wound round with threads tied to too many other people. She couldn't move without tugging at things that perhaps should not be tugged at. There was no untying of the knots, no return to the past.

When Jance didn't return, Esvar would know that something

had happened and would send men to look. He would know who had done it. What would he do?

"Shh," said Sparrow, leaning forward to touch Anza on the arm. "Who were they?"

"I don't know. They weren't in uniform, but they knew what they were doing. Jance couldn't possibly win. He was trying to fight three of them."

"Were they after him or you?"

Anza had not considered the question. She did now, sluggishly. "I think him. They didn't try to stop me from escaping. But it was very fast. I'm not sure."

"Why would he be killed?"

"Does it matter?"

Sparrow said, "Yes. You have to be strong, Anza. Harpy. You can mourn, but you can't give up. Think. I don't know Jance at all. Who are his enemies?"

Anza sipped the tea. She could not imagine Jance having any enemies. That caution required by a hot drink, the slowness, the smallness of the gulp, the careful movement of the lips to avoid being scalded, struck her as important. It slowed time, cushioned awareness of things that would be an onslaught otherwise.

"They did it to hurt Esvar," she said, the knowledge clear and certain. To make him feel vulnerable, to shame him, to immobilize him with fear of what his actions might bring down. Tears of loss and injustice swarmed her eyes, and she furiously blinked them back.

"That probably means it wasn't Karolje. He has other ways to do that. He doesn't need to bother with indirect threats."

"Esvar told me yesterday he had granted a divorce to Lord Doru's wife. So it could be Doru. And also . . ." She hesitated. "Would Miloscz do something like that?"

"No. If he wanted to strike at the prince, he would fight directly. Doru is much more likely. This kind of murder is personal."

Jance. Radd. Her father. Her dead were accumulating. Was this what it meant to keep living? Did more and more people die around you as you went on? Or was that unique to Karegg?

"I want my bow," she said.

"And then what?"

Kill them all, she thought. Hide on the old walls and ambush lords when they rode out from the Old City. Climb on rooftops and shoot the watch when they walked by.

"I want to kill him. Doru."

"He rarely leaves the Citadel."

"I'll offer to turn myself in to him, tell him I know where Thali is."

"That won't draw him out. He has people everywhere who could abduct you. You might have to leave this vengeance to the prince."

"No."

"You're angry," said Sparrow. "As you should be. But anger will only carry you so far. A resistance that is only about revenge fails when it has achieved that revenge. When your anger fades, what will you have left?"

She remembered watching River kill Lord Ruslan, the pit at the center of her being when she imagined doing murder herself. Esvar had said, *Those of us who can kill like breathing need to be countered by the people who hate it.* He had softened as he spoke, almost as though it was a revelation to him too. That was the moment she had entirely stopped seeing him as the enemy. The moment she had begun to see him as someone she might love.

We are marked by what we do, she thought. And by what we don't do.

She could not bring Jance back to life. Jance, who had once told her it was stupid to risk her life for a ghost. What had she said to him? *I need to be her witness. Her voice.* He needed a voice now too.

Slowly, stumbling over the words as she thought it through, she said, "Terror of Karolje keeps people silent. Not just about him and his laws. About everything. Vengeance is only another kind of silencing. But justice is about speech. About hearing and being heard. That's what I want."

"To be heard?"

"To make a space for everyone to be heard."

Sparrow's face was very hard to read, as usual. She said, "Can you give up Doru?"

"It appears I have to." She took a breath. "I can't kill someone like River does, Sparrow. Not in darkness and cold blood. But I can still fight. I will still fight. And help build afterward."

"You don't need to fight. You've done so much already. We owe you."

"Because of Esvar?"

"Yes. I don't for a moment think it was easy for you to be a go-between. It took courage. Regardless of how much you trust him or think he's unlike the king. We have the keys we've needed, and that wouldn't have happened without you."

"I can fight," Anza repeated. "I'm not done."

Sparrow looked at her for a long moment. Anza looked steadily back.

"All right," said Sparrow. "Tomorrow we spread the signal. The next day, or the day after, we will rouse. But we have to be ready. River's armory raid is tonight."

In the negotiations, Sparrow had finally admitted the resistance had stolen uniforms. Once he heard that, Esvar had provided a complicated sequence of passwords that would get a few men posing as Citadel soldiers with orders from the king admitted to an armory. He had put the royal seal on blank paper for Sparrow.

"I'm glad River didn't go with Miloscz." It was a justice of sorts. The world still had some balance.

"Most of them didn't. Moth didn't. You don't need to worry over what Miloscz might do. He won't betray us, and he won't sabotage us, and that's what matters. I have your bow and a few other things that were at his house."

"Does that mean this is the only place you have to live now?"

Sparrow grinned. "You're thinking how dreadful it is that the leader of the resistance lives in a rat-infested hovel on Beggar Island with no furniture. It *is* good not to be dependent on things, but I have a flat on Citadel Island. You're lucky you found me here. I'll be going back there tonight. It's important not to stay in any one place too long."

"Where do I go?"

"I'll take you to River. He'll take you somewhere safe before they raid."

"With Jance dead, I don't have a way to reach the prince. He can't find me if I'm hiding."

Sparrow said, "There are ways to get him a message. They are extremely risky, which is why I haven't done it, but it's getting on time to take those risks." She stood. "Now, you need to rest and I have things to prepare. When we go out, you'll have to be alert. With luck the fog won't lift until tomorrow."

Anza drank down the last half of the tea and got up. Her

legs were shaky. She said, "If you send him a message, tell him Jance died bravely."

"And for yourself?"

Everything was much too intimate to pass through another person. "Nothing," she said.

Sparrow looked at her thoughtfully. "Have you slept with him?"

That's not your affair! Anza thought, but of course it was. Sparrow needed to know where there were weaknesses.

"Once," she said. "We both know it won't happen again. That was why we did it. It won't get in the way."

"Are you sure?"

"Yes. Killing Karolje matters more."

"Very well," said Sparrow. "Go rest."

Anza went tiredly up the steps. Her legs had stiffened. At the top she turned around and glanced back at Sparrow. The woman was staring forward, her thoughts clearly elsewhere. On her face was an expression of loss. Anza remembered her first impression that Sparrow would do anything to win. She had been wrong. Even for Sparrow, some things cost too much.

20

THE FOG STILL hung heavily over the Citadel and the city at nightfall. Esvar was hollow and exhausted. He snapped at the servants and slammed doors. Ever since the men he had sent to find Jance Mirovian had returned with news of his murder, he had felt himself unraveling. His soldiers had recognized the other body in the flat, a man who had been exiled from the Citadel Guard to the city watch some months ago for brawling on duty. Doru did this, he thought. He was afraid that if he summoned the spymaster, he would kill him.

There had been no sign of Anza, which distressed him more than he could say. He was tempted to go riding off in a blind rush to look for her. Only the knowledge that he would himself be followed kept him in the Citadel. If she had managed to escape, he needed to leave her that freedom. He wondered if she had had time to read his letter.

He sent for Marek and fought with the captain in the practice yard. Mist swirled around them in the lamplight. It was like fighting underwater. They used blunted blades, but the clang of metal against metal, the force of impact when he was hit, assumed the weight of a genuine fight as he went on. He looked at

Marek's familiar face and saw an enemy. He could trust no one. This is how I become like the king, he thought. It didn't matter. He kept raising and swinging his blade. His arm ached with strain.

Marek stepped back and dropped his sword, yielding. At first Esvar didn't understand, and only the muscle discipline of years of practice kept him from striking an unarmed man. Then his mind caught up to his body, and he lowered the sword. He turned his head and saw the visitor whose arrival had halted the fight. An ordinary soldier, his hand extended, palm up.

"What is it?" Esvar asked raggedly, sides heaving. He expected some new calamity.

"The king wants to see you, sir. He sent a while ago. No one knew where to find you."

Not quite a calamity, but he would have preferred nearly anything else. He retreated to his rooms to wash and change, splashing cold water in his eyes to waken. The physical tiredness from the exercise was creeping up on him. He put on formal clothing, not out of respect for Karolje but as an assertion of his own power. There was a chance, as always, that he would be killed or locked away.

The king's doctor waited outside Karolje's bedroom, obviously unhappy at having been dismissed. Crossing the threshold, Esvar staggered with the corruption in the room. The fruitwood and herbal medicines could not cover the stench of a long sickness. Karolje sat in his chair, papery skin drawn tightly over sharp bones, eyes black and sunken and still vital. The lesions on his face had increased in size. But his voice had lost none of its command.

"You took your time."

"I was in the practice yard." That could not be disapproved of.

Karolje looked him over. "Sit down, my son."

You're dying, Esvar thought. He had never felt more naked. He sat, not wanting to, unable to disobey. His legs and feet yielded as little to his will as chunks of marble.

"I'm your son again, am I?" he said.

Karolje laughed spitefully. It sent him into a spasm of coughs, his body jerking. His face reddened, then blanched. He reached for something beside him in the chair and tossed it at Esvar's feet. A letter, battered with transit.

"Your brother is a traitor. Read it."

Esvar obeyed, feeling sick. He saw almost immediately what it was, but he read the entire thing, slowly, hoping to irk the king. It was Tevin's letter to Nasad, shah of Milaya, proposing marriage to one of the shah's daughters.

He raised his head. "A forgery. I learned recently that Doru is falsifying documents. He intends to take me and Tevin down. He killed one of my men today."

"Don't be so innocent, boy. You know that letter's treason. You're my heir now." He spoke almost invitingly. Esvar reminded himself that the king had attained much of what he wanted by presence rather than by force. Had he not been so evil, he could have been great. "I will abdicate in your favor. Do you want the crown?"

Esvar's breath caught. His left hand clenched and his heart sped up. Everything he had said to Sparrow yesterday about fighting for his brother vanished in a surge of desire. Gods, he wanted it. He didn't want it for the people of Karegg, of Vetia, he wanted it for himself. All his life he had been second, the ally, the support, the listening ear. He wanted to be the one to order himself. He wanted the control. Needed it. Power was safety. Power was life.

It's a trick, he told himself. That did nothing to convince the hungry part of him.

"Why?" he managed to get out.

"I'm not answering questions. There's an offer. Do you want it or no?"

His mouth opened. He was going to say yes despite his better sense. He wasn't strong enough to refuse.

He remembered his words to Anza: *He finds a lie that will make the hideous more palatable.* Karolje never gave, always took.

On Esvar's ninth birthday, in the time between his mother's death and Karolje's return south to fight another Tazekh war, the king had summoned him to his chambers for dinner. There had been all his favorite foods, musicians playing during the meal, and a juggler afterward. *Well, lad,* Karolje said, *it is time we get to know each other a little better.* He was kindly, deep-voiced, and charming. After the entertainers left, they played chess. The king promised him the beautiful new horse he desired, and ruffled his hair affectionately and kissed him on the forehead when it was time to go to bed.

And then, a week later, when Esvar dared to ask about the horse, Karolje said, *I never promised you a horse, boy. Why would I give you a new horse? You won't grow out of the one you have now for a few years. And I've already sold that one to Lord Imru. A king gives horses as rewards, and you've done nothing to earn one.* Esvar said, *But Father—my lord*—and Karolje struck a blow that sent him reeling against the wall and said, *Don't snivel, you brat. Sometimes I wonder if you're even my son.* That was the last time Esvar had called the king "Father."

He's lying, he's lying, he's lying.

“There must be conditions.” He forced the words out like mud through a strainer.

“Three, in fact,” said Karolje. He smiled, an obscene death’s-head mask, his gums an unhealthy white. “First and most obviously, you don’t get to turn around and hand the throne to your brother if he reappears. If you do that, I’ll kill both of you. Second, you may recall that I gave you the opportunity once to kill a guard with your own hands, no weapons. You declined. Now you have to do it to your cousin Goran. And third, you marry one of his daughters and consummate the marriage. Which daughter, I leave up to you and Tahari to negotiate.”

Revulsion, far stronger than his desire to be king, shocked through him like ice. It was not in him to do that to a girl of ten. Part of his mind gibbered in relief.

In the Temple garden, Anza had been injured and afraid, and she had challenged him. She would lie or thieve or trick if she had to, but not betray. Her god was justice. She held on to her truths and became immovable. If he gave in to Karolje now, he dishonored everything she had done. Some things were worth dying for, and the shreds of goodness in himself were among them.

“My brother is the heir. Why do you want Goran dead?”

“You surprise me. I thought you had ambition to match your station.”

“If you thought I had such ambition, you would have made this offer when I came of age. Or eliminated me.” And three years ago he might have been fool enough to accept it. His breath was steadying. “What happens now?”

“That depends upon your brother.”

Did that mean Tevin was alive after all? “Am I your hostage for his return?”

"That would be useless. His regard for you is not so high as yours for him. Come here." He beckoned with one skeletal finger. Esvar couldn't disobey. Karolje's hand shot out and caught him by the wrist. "You think I'm bluffing."

He pulled free. "I do not. I have never known you not to carry out your threats. You taught me that, at least."

"Why do you fight me so? What have I ever done to earn your enmity?"

"You killed my mother," Esvar said, sudden viciousness escaping him. All that kept him from attacking the king were fatigue and grief. Violence required more strength than he had.

"No. That's your brother's lie. It was Asps. Don't you remember? They killed her maids and the guards and took her. An Asp's knife was left in one of the maid's hearts."

Tazekhs would have either sent back Mirantha's head or held her for ransom. Her disappearance did not serve them at all. It was hard not to say it. Not to let the king stir him up any further. Karolje could be so convincing.

The king was staring at him, waiting for opposition. Esvar smiled thinly and said nothing. So must his mother have been silent for years. Even in his illness Karolje seemed invulnerable.

Yet Mirantha had not lost herself in silence. She had never submitted. She had if anything grown stronger. That was why the queen had had to be Disappeared; subtly killed and buried royally, she would have been an endless rebuke to Karolje. Gone, her body vanished, she faded from memory. She had seen that coming and had sent her journal away to protect what she could of her voice. For her sons, yes, and also for the other people the king had silenced. She could not know what manner of men Esvar and Tevin became; it was the people like Anza she had to rely on to preserve the memory of her. To say, *The king is unjust.*

"A weapon proves nothing," Esvar said.

"If I killed her, I could kill you."

"I've known that since I was eight years old."

"Where is your brother?"

"I have no idea." He touched his bandaged arm. "He said nothing to me. I was drugged in the surgery when he disappeared."

"I find it hard to believe, that he would not tell you."

"Why? You've made sure each of us are good at keeping secrets. That's how you keep your power. You don't like having it turned on you." He felt almost drunk with recklessness. "He's still trying to shelter me. All these years, and it's our mother he's loyal to. Not you. It will never be to you."

"Let me tell you something about your mother. I let Ashevi have your mother. A few times I even watched. Shall I tell you what they looked like together, how scared she always was that they would be found out? That was what he liked the most, to see her frightened. He—"

"You killed her because she was stronger than you. You're weak, old man, and you always have been."

Karolje laughed. "We're more alike than you think, you and I. Tevin takes after his mother, but you, you've learned to survive. What do you say to my offer if I don't make you marry one of the girls? Kill your cousin and you can have the crown. Then you can execute Doru too. Why wait?"

Tevin was the heir. Esvar said, "If you want to abdicate, abdicate." Arguing would only give him strings for Karolje to pull. Offer nothing. Take nothing. As soon as he started bargaining, he would have to give up ground.

"You know it's what you desire. Don't punish yourself for wanting." The king's voice smoothed. "Want is how you know you're alive. Those who want nothing become nothing. Their hearts are straw, their skin is a husk. This court is full of such people. You're better than that. They will follow you. They—"

Esvar interrupted. "Save your breath. You need it."

Karolje's clawlike hand curled, released. "I didn't think you were so weak. Should I reverse this offer and have Goran kill you?"

That threat was so futile he almost laughed. "Goran's a coward," he said. It occurred to him that he had an opportunity to strike back. "And before you decide to choose him over me as your successor, there's something you should know. Tahari was pregnant when he married her. With your child. My brother." How strange those words were. His brother had always and only been Tevin.

"Who told you that?"

"It doesn't matter. What does matter is this. The boy took ill one year with winterfever and died. The death wasn't natural. Goran smothered him. Tevin saw him do it, through a peephole."

Karolje hissed. "You lie."

"No. Imagine it, the boy just lying there, ill, a pillow over his face. It wouldn't have taken long. You wanted him as your heir. Tevin and I wouldn't have survived past his majority, and neither would Goran. He must have been very pleased when the fever struck."

It was the first time Esvar had ever by himself brought the king to silence. He wished it had come as a result of his own strength, not his brother's secrets.

"I'll test the truth of this," Karolje said. "Your brother is a liar."

"As you wish," Esvar said, letting a bit of insolence color his voice. "Here, or in the Green Court?"

"Here, of course. You have a lot to learn." He rang a bell.

Sickeningly, Esvar realized that he had just become the king's collaborator. It might be only for this moment, but it was real. He was supposed to have threatened Goran with divulging the information, not to actually do it. Karolje had baited him, and he had swallowed it completely. He turned.

"You're not leaving," said Karolje.

The door opened and a guard entered on those words. The man looked at Esvar warily, as though expecting to be commanded to arrest him. His hand was close to his sword hilt. Esvar imagined kicking him, wrestling for the sword.

"The chancellor," said Karolje. "And a Truth Finder. Now."

The guard twitched. "Yes, my lord," he said. He retreated.

Esvar went to a window and stood with his back to the king. His reflection, deformed with shadow, framed with mist, looked back at him. The lake was invisible. Had Mirantha ever looked at it and wanted to throw herself in? *I have walked in terrible places and done terrible things*. Such as he was doing now?

The words echoed in his mind with some other familiarity. Terrible things. *I will do whatever I must, even if it is a terrible thing, to end it. He has to pay*. Sparrow's words yesterday.

He saw it then, her face, the shape of her jaw like Tevin's, the grief when she spoke of her children. The concern for Tahari.

It couldn't be. The words were a coincidence, the resemblance his own desire. His mother was dead. What his heart wanted deceived him. Sparrow led the resistance that might kill him or his brother. What mother could do that?

When they acquiesced to Karolje, how could she know it was out of fear and not agreement?

Sparrow had refused to see him. Had demanded he show his honesty with something only he would value. A test, that was, of what in the past still mattered to him. And he, all unknowing, had given her the thing that might most resonate with her. A toy, still treasured, or he would not have kept it.

Sparrow could not be Mirantha, but she was, she was.

The knowledge was more than he could countenance right now. He had to. He could not let Karolje even guess at any of this. He tried to find inside himself that silent place where he had gone during the whipping.

"What do you look at?" Karolje asked. "Your kingdom?"

"Darkness," Esvar said, turning. "Even you can't avoid it. Have you thought what happens next, when Goran is dead? You have to leave the throne to me, unless you want it to go to a child—a girl—and be taken from her through marriage by a man not even of our family. Your legacy will be the end of the lineage."

"Well argued, but incomplete. You are not thinking through all the facts."

"You're dying. What other facts are there?"

Again Karolje's lips moved in that parody of a smile. "When Goran dies, Tahari will be a widow. I had one son with her. I can have another."

"No one in this court is going to kneel to an infant," Esvar said. "Not even yours. If you kill me and marry Tahari, Doru will kill her and make his move. He'll sit on the throne while the worms feast and make merry with your body. The Messenger is waiting for you. Your words stink of decay, and they neither frighten me nor tempt me. You've missed your chance."

"You are a fool, boy."

There was a rap on the door, startling both of them, and Goran entered. He bowed to the king and looked smugly at Esvar.

"Sit," said Karolje, as though he were inviting Goran to take tea. Esvar remained by the window, arms folded.

Goran took the chair Esvar had vacated, edging it back. He acted confident. A sudden summons to Karolje was not unusual, even this late. Esvar supposed the chancellor expected he was here to testify against the prince, instead of the other way around.

Karolje said, "Your loyalty has never been doubted," a sentence that would have made any reasonable person prepare for the worst. Goran inclined his head. The king went on. "Except for a lapse of a few minutes, nine years ago."

"My lord?"

"Your wife was pregnant with a son when you married her. You killed the boy."

"Who tells you such lies? Him?" He jerked his head back at Esvar. "He is jealous. And ambitious."

"In this matter I find him credible."

"The boy had a fever, my lord. He died. I grieved at his death. These accusations are baseless."

"The boy was my son, as you well knew. That was why you married her. To raise a royal child as your own, not a cuckoo but a hostage."

"Why would I kill him then? What did I gain? All that came of his death was grief. And how could Prince Esvar know? He was a child himself. Winterfever takes the old and the young and the weak, and that year was a bad year for it."

Esvar clamped his mouth shut, holding back words that would only ally him more firmly with Karolje. Goran's surprise and affront were genuine; he could not have expected that death to be laid at his feet so many years later. But he had not yet said the words that mattered: *I didn't do it.* A guilty man might say them, but an innocent man would never omit them. Goran ought to know that.

"My lord chancellor. My dear cousin," said Karolje. "The motive is clear. The boy would have been next in the succession. My son, not yours. As my son Prince Esvar has convincingly noted, you would have been in the way. I have never wanted you dead, but this crime arises from your imagination, not mine."

"It arises from his imagination, if any. For the argument to work, he would have to claim that you wanted him dead as well."

"He's made that claim."

"He's mad."

Perhaps I am, thought Esvar. If so, he was not fit to rule. He remembered more of his mother's words, her fear of the chancellor, her pity for Tahari. She had not been mad and neither was he. Poor Tahari. He wished he had not exposed her.

Goran had stood to face him. "Did you fabricate this? Or are you deluded?"

"You can't expect me to answer that, can you? Be quiet." It felt good, that little snap of anger, a jab he had long wanted to make.

Another knock. This time the guard admitted a Truth Finder. Not, Esvar was relieved to see, the man he had used in the Green Court. Goran paled. Esvar clasped his hands together behind his back, making it more difficult for him to use them on either chancellor or king. He would have liked to be invisible. If Karolje set the Truth Finder on him, far too many secrets would be exposed.

Karolje said, "Would either of you care to retract anything you've said?"

Esvar shook his head. Goran hesitated, then followed suit. He was going to try to bluff his way through it, the fool.

The king pointed at the chancellor. "Begin with him. There is one question. Has he smothered an ill child, nine years ago?"

"My lord," said the Truth Finder, stepping forward.

He stood between Goran and the door. The chancellor turned, shoved the Truth Finder out of the way, and fled before the startled guards could stop him. Their pursuing footsteps slapped loudly in the corridor. He would not make it far.

"It seems you are vindicated," said Karolje. "It's the spymaster you'll want to dislodge next, I suppose. I advise you to wait."

Esvar wanted to be gone, away from this evil place. Karolje's malevolence coated his skin and filled his lungs. Anything he did or said—even silence—ceded authority to the king. There was no way out. He would be safer himself in a dungeon, where the games were over and he had nothing to confront but actual darkness.

"Silence?" the king asked, mocking. "There won't be a trial. But I might not execute him right away. He still has uses. I could even pardon him."

"Why?" Esvar could not keep it in. It was a larger question, encompassing years of actions, interrogating Karolje's core.

"You can't expect me to answer that, can you? Be quiet."

If Esvar had been armed, he would have attacked then. The rage rushing through his head was dizzying. He spoke, and his voice was not his at all, it was someone else's coming from the hollow box that was his chest.

"I don't want your crown. Ever. I wish you joy of it. But you don't know what joy is, do you? That's where you will always fail."

He stalked out, expecting every moment for Karolje's voice to freeze him, for the guards to take him. Nothing happened.

In his rooms, he prepared to do the only thing he could think to do. He gave the orders, and half an hour later, just as the bells were tolling midnight, he rode out with Marek and two men he considered loyal, his saddlebags packed. He did not intend to return.

21

RIVER STOWED ANZA in a small house not too far from the Temple. The fog burned off with the rising sun, and when Anza left the house, the bright morning was as if the day before had never happened. But Jance's death was still sharp in her waking memory. At least she had not had nightmares.

She had money. River had appeared earlier with a few coins and a change of clothing, along with a promise to retrieve her possessions from her flat. She feared Esvar might have set a guard, and she made River swear he would not kill anyone for the sake of getting her belongings. They could no longer know for sure that every soldier was an enemy.

She found a coffeehouse a block away from the Temple and settled down with a cup of coffee, a sweet bread, and a wedge of cheese. The sugared frosting on the bread formed a spiral. Sparrow had begun getting the word out. *Be ready.* The raid on the armory must have succeeded.

The shop was crowded, a few day workers and crafters and a much larger number of shopkeepers and clerks. Anza sipped her coffee, thinking. Slowly the conversations of other people edged into her awareness. Esvar's name caught her attention. It was a common name, but she heard *both princes missing* and then *chancellor*, and she went alert. Esvar too? she thought. But had he left, or was he in the dungeons or dead? If he had left, where was she to find him? She was already on edge, and she felt herself approaching panic.

She heard *executed*, and her heart skipped. The man who had said it, a large grey-haired man with brown skin, was well-dressed, and she took him for a merchant of some sort. He continued to his companion, his voice not especially low, "With Goran dead and Karolje's sons missing, that puts the succession in doubt. Anyone could be king next."

Goran dead? That changed things. Slowly she reclaimed her calm.

"If Karolje ever dies. But the princes will show now, I expect."

"If they are living. One has to wonder why the king hasn't found Tevin yet. He's losing his touch."

"Or his subordinates are. There will be more of them going to the block."

Another man said loudly, "If you're going to talk treason, do it somewhere else."

"It's not treason to state facts."

"It's not you as decides what treason is. And I don't want to be tainted by your talk. I'm a loyal man. Shut your mouth or get out."

In a different place or among different men, it would have turned into a brawl. The grey-haired man swigged his coffee and left. His companion, who was ten or fifteen years younger, left less than a minute later. The man who had yelled at them settled smugly back into his seat.

Were those genuine rumors? Or was the grey-haired man a

resister trying to spark something? Hell, the loud man could be in the resistance too, drawing attention to the first two men.

Who in this shop would obey the call to rise?

It's about more than killing soldiers, she thought. More than violence. Violence was the surface of it, the cover, the igniter. The resistance was about how one lived in an unlivable world. She had known she had to fight Karolje's injustice, but the people who had no weapons, who had families to protect, who were maimed in body and spirit by his rule, fought too.

No other talk of Karolje was loud enough for her to hear. After she finished her coffee, she got up and went outside.

Facing east, she was almost blinded by the brightness of the sun on the Temple dome. If Esvar had fled from Karegg or gone into hiding, there was no use in her looking for him. But the Temple was a refuge of sorts. He had looked there for his brother. He had mentioned it when she asked him where he would go. Karolje had not flat-out killed Esvar when he had the chance, so he might not violate sanctuary this time. It all depended on what the king wanted from his son.

She walked to the Temple and stood a while on the square, looking at the ancient cobbles. The sun played in the leaves of the mulberry trees. She could not tell where the execution pyre had been situated; the stones had been scrubbed clean of char and blood. There was the balcony the soldier had shot from. She imagined holding her bow, the weight comfortable in her hands, an arrow on the string. She was ready to fight, to be a soldier.

A horse clattered, several horses, and she turned around. She recognized Esvar with Marek and two other men. Relief, wordless, all-encompassing, spread through her. She took two steps toward him. Three. He swung down and strode toward her. Neither ran, but she could see an urgency in his pace that was matched by her own.

They met. Their arms went around each other. For the first time since Jance locked the door of her flat yesterday, she felt safe. She pressed her head against his chest, listened to his heart. It was suddenly very hard to keep from weeping.

"Anza," he said. "I feared you were dead." His embrace tightened.

"I got out and found a place to hide."

"So why are you standing in Temple Square in broad daylight?"

"Why are you?" she asked, pulling back from the embrace to look up at him. He was so damned tall. "I heard a rumor you were missing. The only place I could think to look was here. Is the rumor true?"

"Not missing. Gone. I left the Citadel openly. I spent the night in a rather nasty inn." His arms dropped. "Will you come with me into the Temple? I want to talk to one of the priests. I intend to ask if I can stay here."

"Karolje will send troops in to take you if he wants."

"I know. I don't want to be sheltered. I want to be seen. No more fighting from the shadows. Come inside."

She was reluctant to go into the building. Radd's death was too close. "I'll wait here," she said. "Have your talk with them first."

"All right." He reached for her, drew his hand back before he could touch her. Words spilled out of him with the same jerkiness. "I've renounced it all. Karolje offered me the crown last night. The terms were unconscionable. Worse than that, evil. I should have left right away. But I didn't, I stayed talking to him, and I made several mistakes. I was—manipulating things so that he would offer terms that were acceptable, gods help me. I wanted to be king. So I had to leave."

You are brave, she thought. Tears pricked her eyes. Sparrow had warned her against sympathy for him, but Sparrow was wrong. If he had to face despair alone, he might well throw up a shield of evil to protect himself.

Her hand went out toward him. He grabbed it. The roughness of his calloused palm rubbed against her skin, and her bones ached from the force of his grip. Carefully she raised his hand to her mouth and kissed it. A lover's kiss, not a vassal's. Then she released it.

"Go," she said. "I'll wait on the steps."

He nodded, turned, walked to the steps. Marek dismounted and joined him. Their shadows fell blue and long.

She waited until they were in the Temple to follow them and sit on the warm stone. The wall and the row of trees lining it cut off some of her view of the square. A man muttering to himself was hunched over a piece of bread on another step, closer to the wall. Despite the heat, he had on a ragged cloak, its hood brought up over his head. His beard was matted. If she looked as much a beggar as he did, the priests might try to drive her off. And what would she say then, that she was waiting for the prince? They would laugh in her face.

The sun felt good, as though yesterday's fog had leached all the warmth out of her. The soldiers waiting at the bottom of the steps, holding the horses, were alert. She hoped Esvar was right to put his trust in them.

The bells rang the hour while she waited, the toll loud enough that she put her hands over her ears. The sound echoed off the buildings. Several harpies swooped over the square and came to rest in the trees, invisible in the dappled leaves.

In the quiet that followed, she became aware that something had shifted in the world. The light, the warmth, should have calmed her, left her relaxed as a lazy cat. Instead she felt edged by danger. She was reminded of the night she had found the journal, but this tension was larger, greater than one locked room. Her fingers drummed nervously on the stone. Something was building. Did it extend all over Karegg?

She stood, paced. The soldiers watched her for a moment, then turned back to the square. Across the square a vendor unfurled his banner. The design on the banner was the spiral. She stilled.

The beggar got up and shuffled off, head lowered, toward the other side of the square. Three sparrows were picking at the crumbs of bread he had left, and she walked over to them. They flew away. On the stone where the man had been sitting, a rough spiral was drawn in chalk.

Esvar came out not much later and said, "You and I need to discuss things. We can go through to the priests' garden again if you don't want to be inside."

"All right," she said, and followed him up.

The garden was all green and golden, the water in the fountain sparkling in the sun. There were small rainbows in its mist. He said, sitting on the bench, "There are fountains in the Citadel garden. And pools. My mother loved them."

Anza bit her lip and sat beside him. "I couldn't keep it from you any longer. I needed you to know she had strength. Were you very angry with me?"

"No. A little, at the beginning, but you didn't do anything wrong and I knew it." He stared at the fountain. He was about to say something difficult. "Tell me how you found it."

"Jance and I snuck into the library. He had a key to one of

the rooms in it. I went in. There were books on the shelves. The Rukovili, and others that had belonged to your mother. They're all illegal now. The journal was with them. I looked at it, and I read it, and I knew whose it was. I didn't want her to be hidden any longer."

His throat moved. He twisted to look at her. He laid his hand against her cheek, and she pressed her own hand over it. Her body was quivering like an animal's. He kissed her, slowly. She wanted to respond with passion, with hunger, but she held herself back. She could tell he was in pain.

He said, "Last night the king—*my father*, I have to say it, that's what he is—he got the truth out of me about Goran killing the boy. My other brother. He killed the chancellor for it. I don't care about that, but he was proud of me, before he mocked me. I can bear anything but his approval.

"And while this was happening, while I was trying to figure out what to do next, I thought about the journal. I thought about my mother. I understand why she had to write things down; you can't be sure anything you remember is real when you're dealing with Karolje. I remembered a few things she wrote. A few things I had heard someone else say. I knew—and this is the real reason I left, I suppose, not because the Citadel was poisoning me—I knew then a truth." He gripped her hand. "Sparrow is my mother."

She required no convincing. It all fit. Sparrow's hardness when she talked about Karolje or the princes, the way she had held Esvar's wooden globe, the initial refusal to see Esvar at all. Her skills at strategy and knowledge of the Citadel, her leadership. The Mirantha of the journal had been sad and frightened and desperate, but she had also had the nerve and certainty that Sparrow did. The core of justice.

She said tentatively, "Will you tell her you know?"

"No. It's her secret. If she wants me to know, she will tell me." He paused. "Once I saw it, I was afraid Karolje would use a Truth Finder on me. If he did, I might have revealed everything. I've become my own liability."

"She sent the journal away with the books. She didn't need to do that. She could have burned it. It was meant to be read someday, probably by you and Tevin."

Esvar said, "I doubt that when she sent it away she imagined she would be leading a resistance twelve years later. She didn't know she would be concealing herself."

What did Sparrow—Mirantha—want for her sons? The first time Anza talked to her, she had said, *The gate to power is locked by accident of birth or by force or both, and it must be unlocked.* That had sounded genuine. Her motives for fighting Karolje were clear, but would she fight Tevin too? If she thought he had become like his father, she would.

"I thought my mother's body had been sunk in the lake," he said after a silence. "I used to look out at all that water and consider how well it kept secrets. Karolje made me look at her bed with the blood on it. I believed him at first, that it was Asps. Tevin convinced me otherwise when I was older. I threw that at Karolje, and he said it was Tevin's lies. He's lying, I know that, but I'm not going to rest now, wondering what happened instead, how she escaped. What if Karolje knows she's still alive?"

"That was a dozen years ago. What would he have done then?"

"Kill anyone who might shelter her, any of her friends from my grandfather's day. I was too young, but Tevin would have known if he killed those people. So Karolje must think she's dead."

"That gives you an advantage," she said. "I'm not sure how, but it's something you know that Karolje doesn't. That's power of sorts."

"I've had enough of power!" he burst out.

She slid closer to him and put her arm around his waist. His face twisted briefly. It might be a long time before he learned again how to weep.

"What next?" she asked.

"I don't want to see her again, at least not until this is over. You should remain the go-between. If you can, knowing this."

"I can." A bird chirped in a tree. She looked up at the light splashed upon the branches. It wouldn't last much longer; soon the sun would be high enough to lose its golden quality.

Esvar said, "What happened yesterday?"

"They broke in on us." A flash of sword, a bloom of red. "I got out the window. I don't want to talk about it."

"Did they hurt you at all?"

"No. I hurt myself a little."

His arm went around her shoulders. Don't say it, don't say it, she thought. She could not bear to know he loved her, not yet. Not when the world was so fragile. She needed the armor of silence between them still.

"I didn't have time to read your letter," she said quickly.

"It doesn't matter anymore. Everything is different, now that I know who she is. The man who wrote that letter is already gone."

"Do you hate her for leading the resistance?"

"How could I?" His free hand was resting on his leg, and he turned it palm upward, exposing his wrist. His veins were a cold blue beneath his tan skin. "Karolje must be overthrown. She couldn't know from the outside who Tevin and I had grown to become. There are times I have thought myself deserving of death."

"No," Anza whispered.

"Not now, don't worry. I won't give Karolje that gift. But neither am I fit to be a king."

Discovering his mother still lived was not supposed to be so painful. She reached across him and placed her palm over his. His skin was sun-warmed. Her thoughts were tangled, but it didn't matter; they had to look to Karolje's end before anything else could be decided.

The door opened. The fountain obscured their view, but the descending footsteps were martial, not priestly. They both stood up. Marek came around the fountain.

"Sir," he said, "your brother's here."

Esvar ran. Anza was several steps behind, but she went into the Temple in time to see the princes greet each other with a hard, long embrace. This is it, she thought with a kind of vicious certainty. The beginning of Karolje's end.

The men separated. "You have good spies," Esvar said to Tevin. He looked back and beckoned to her. She frowned, thinking their reunion should be private, but he gestured more vigorously. She walked to him.

Tevin looked down at her. He wore plain brown and grey tradesman's clothes and sandals and held a cap in one hand. His chin was heavily stubbled. He was not as tall as Esvar and had fairer skin and lighter hair, but the resemblance was obvious. Their faces had the same shape, the line of bone and curve of eye and even the scrutinizing expression. Now, knowing the truth about Sparrow, Anza could see the similarity to their mother. And to the portraits of Karolje as well. But while her first impression of Esvar had been one of restrained danger, Tevin quelled her with authority. He was not going to erupt, but he would have little patience with mistakes.

"Who's this?" he asked. Judgment was held in abeyance but ready to fall like an executioner's blade.

"I withhold her name," said Esvar, "though she may choose to give it. She is my messenger to the resistance. If you're going to act, you need them to move in concert with you."

"You have been busy," said Tevin.

"I've made some promises on your behalf. An amnesty and a voice in government."

"You *have* been busy," Tevin repeated in a different tone. Anza felt the judgment swing from her to Esvar. "What did you get in exchange?"

"Let's not talk here in the hall," Esvar said. "The priests gave me a room."

It contained a single narrow bed, a chair, and a table. They stood. Anza would have preferred to be outside with Tevin's guards and Marek, but Esvar wouldn't let her edge away.

"How did you find me, Tev?" he asked.

"I heard you were gone, and I set people to looking. This seemed one of the likelier places. The chancellor was executed this morning—does that have anything to do with why you left?"

"Yes. I told Karolje that Goran had killed the boy. That was after the king produced your letter to Nasad and offered me the crown. I tried to shift the letter to Doru, but he didn't believe me. So I left. I didn't make a secret of it."

"Why didn't you accept his offer?"

The expression Esvar turned on his brother was faintly dumbfounded. "You're the heir, he wanted me to rape one of Goran's daughters, and he didn't mean it anyway."

"That's why you should have taken it."

"I told you, I'm not playing his games anymore."

They glared at each other. Anza wondered if this was how they had expected their reunion to go.

Tevin said, "Do you want to have this argument in front of her? What's your name, girl?"

"Harpy," Anza said. She decided not to tell him who her father had been. She might need that information later to convince him of something else.

Esvar said, "She can hear everything."

"She'll take it back to the resistance."

"I'm part of the resistance now."

"Do they agree that you are?" Tevin asked, his voice cutting. "Why would they trust you?"

Anza said, "He was convincing in negotiations, my lord. He can't betray them—us—now without betraying himself to Karolje. It's gone too far for him to retreat."

The prince stared at her. She stared back. Esvar moved to her side and laid his arm across her shoulders. His voice soft, he said, "They can hold her hostage against me if they want, and they know it. I might fail them, but there will be no betrayal."

Oh gods, Anza thought, is this true? Did she mean so much? His arm tightened. Gently, she leaned her head against him, accepting his care.

After a long silence, Tevin said, "What have they promised?"

"To support you now in an uprising against him. If you and I die, the resistance will survive us. I've given them the means to arm themselves. They'll start with the watchhouses."

"Some of the men in the watch are mine. I've been sliding them in over the last few years."

"Then you'd better get them to desert their posts and join you openly."

Tevin looked darkly at his brother. "How soon can your people move?"

"We've been negotiating it. Soon."

Anza said, "There was to be a raid on an armory last night. If that succeeded, they're close to ready. There are signals out now."

"A mob isn't going to be any more successful at taking down the Citadel than armies have been." Tevin ran his fingers through his hair, which made him look younger and more worried. "If Goran's gone, all we need to do is get rid of Kanakili and then the king. We don't need a mass of people for that."

"A month ago I would have agreed with you," said Esvar. "And you're right that if they try to break down the Citadel gates, they'll be massacred. But they're sick of kings. If you and I go in and assassinate Doru and Karolje, you'll get the crown, but the resistance won't stop. You don't want to start your reign using Karolje's methods."

That struck home. A muscle in Tevin's face jumped. He pulled the chair closer and sat down.

"Stop being a general for a moment, Tev," Esvar said. He left Anza's side, squatted, and looked up at his brother. "The king trained you how to win a war. But you have to be a king. You don't fight your own people. The resistance isn't like the mob that hanged the Tazekhs. It's the life of the city. To govern you need the people's consent, and you need to be worthy of that consent."

It was Mirantha speaking, Anza thought. And Sparrow. When she gave the journal to Esvar to read, she had been thinking about his missing mother, the woman he had loved. But he had learned something about power from it too.

Tevin said nothing. He had clasped his hands together and was staring at them. His eyelashes were dark crescents against his skin. The room's sole window overlooked the garden, and Anza heard the distant, gentle splash of the fountain. On the other side of the door, the narrow corridor extended along the building and opened into the central hall of the Temple. Priests walked back and forth, people knelt on prayer mats, incense-scented air moved in dim light.

"All right," Tevin said. "I agree. How do we do this? And when?"

Esvar rose. "We're both gone and Goran's dead. Karolje will do something public to reestablish his power. That's when we should move."

"He won't do it in the city. Or perhaps he will, send out as many soldiers as he can. If he does that, that's the time to take the Citadel. But I think he'll be wary of an attack from one or both of us."

"Do you have loyal men in the Citadel?"

"Some. Enough to get us in without a battle. After that, it will turn bloody," Tevin said.

"The resistance has people in the Citadel too."

"Enough to hold off the Guard? I don't think so. It would be slaughter."

"I could go back," Esvar said. "Give myself up. He would want to make a show of that."

"No! I need you with me. This has to be about both of us."

There he was, that was the brother Esvar loved, the son Mirantha had raised. Anza relaxed. It was going to work.

She must have made a sound, because both men looked at her. She thought they had forgotten about her for a while. Esvar said, "Can you go back to Sparrow and tell her Tevin has emerged?"

"She probably has a spy among the priests who will tell her. But I will. I won't see her until tonight, though."

"By tonight we might know what the king intends to do. Her plans and ours need to not clash."

"I think you can trust Sparrow to know how to take advantage of any show the king puts on." She hoped Esvar heard the second meaning to that, the reminder of what knowledge Arantha had. She knew Karolje better than any of them.

"So be it," said Esvar. He plopped onto the bed. "It's time for specifics."

✦ ✦ ✦

Anza left in midafternoon, her head full of plans and possibilities. The room had become very close with three of them in it for so long, and she was glad to be in more open space. There was hammering somewhere. It got louder as she approached the Temple entrance.

Shielding her eyes from the day's brightness, she left the building and walked down the steps. Esvar's guards and the horses were gone. She hoped they were somewhere safe on the Temple grounds with Marek.

She stopped. In the square, several dozen soldiers were building something. Piles of planks and beams were laid to one side. The soldiers hammered boards into place. A platform. A gallows.

WE CAN'T BURN it," Sparrow said. "He's got far too many soldiers on guard, and it's fresh wood. It won't catch without oil. Even if you shot a few flaming arrows at it, the guards could stomp those fires out before they spread. The solution is going to be to do something at the executions themselves." The announcement had been made that they would take place at noon the next day. When Anza walked back from the Temple, she had seen the uniformed men distributing the notices. The victims were not named.

"Something that won't be blamed on the Tazekhs," Anza said.

"Yes. Although we're getting to the point where that won't matter much. Karolje will be dead or we will. But you are right that we need to be seen and credited. This will be the first strike."

It was night. They sat in the front room of the house Anza was staying in. The furniture was old and worn but of good quality, and the rugs must have been expensive when they were purchased, probably years ago. A single window opened to a narrow street and an elm tree, its limbs sturdy. As a child Anza would have scrambled up it in an instant. She found it comforting now, protective, softening the darkness.

After hearing that Esvar was in the Temple—Tevin had gone to wherever he was hiding—Sparrow had said she would stay with Anza. It was a risk, as everything was, but they needed to be near each other. Anza was to meet Esvar in an hour in another small house not far away.

She picked up her bow from the floor beside her chair and plucked the string. "Can we shoot the guards? There's no chance of getting onto a balcony, not after last time, but maybe a rooftop?" She tried to remember if there were any flat-topped buildings on the square.

"You'd get caught. They'll surround and enter the building in no time. And they can hang everyone anyway. All they have to do is shield themselves with the prisoners. What is needed is a way to rescue the prisoners. But we don't have enough skilled fighters to get through that many guards." Her fingers tapped on the arm of her chair.

"Tevin might."

"He'll need them in the Citadel."

A moth fluttered in the open window and circled above the lamp. A distant cat yowled. Sparrow's face, half in shadow, was thoughtful. What had it been like for her to sit at the same table as her son and oppose him? To test him for trustworthiness? To keep her secret? Anza wished Esvar had not told her, although she understood why he had. It was too great a revelation to bear by himself.

"That night I met you in the Anchor," Anza said, "you said that Karolje's sons would be resistance targets unless they actively defied him. If we win, will you support Tevin as king? Esvar promised things without knowing his brother was alive."

"If we win, Tevin can hold the crown provided he accepts

appropriate restraints. If he doesn't, then we will push him out too. We have to."

You could do that to him? Anza thought. But Sparrow must have considered the question over and over. Karolje's replacement had to be different from Karolje. Not just in policies and tactics, but in how he—or she—saw the people. Tevin could lead, but he had to yield sovereignty.

She forced her mind back to the problem at hand. After Ruslan was killed, Karolje had hanged people, but not all at once, like this. There had been one each hour in a different part of the city until all twelve were dead. The horror and fear of it drove home his message. But this, these hangings were not aimed at the resistance. They were like the pyre, intended as a spectacle for the entire city.

"The resistance hasn't done anything to bring down executions as a warning," Anza said. "Not like the last times. What is he doing?"

"He won't have told the truth about why he executed the chancellor. He'll say it was for treason, and he'll accuse other people he wants to be rid of, people whose deaths matter to the princes. He's setting up a trap that benefits him even if it's not sprung."

"Esvar hasn't let himself get close to anyone in the Citadel."

"Nonetheless, there are people he won't want to see hurt. Some of the younger lords. The servants. Children. The blameless, whom Karolje will blame."

You speak of your sons, Anza thought. It must be agonizing to fear for them in silence. To hope in silence. She wished she could find a way to let Sparrow know that Mirantha was loved, missed, honored.

"If he has filled the square with soldiers, who will defend the Citadel against Tevin?"

"That," Sparrow said, "is a very good question. Don't think he hasn't thought of it. So it must be considered that the executions themselves are a feint, a distraction for us. The princes won't take the bait, but if they move on the Citadel, they'll get pincered by something else. The best thing to do would be to attack now, tonight. But we aren't ready. Not quite. We only get one chance. We can't waste it." She sighed. "He knows how to win a war. And he trained his sons. They will think like him, and so he can predict what they will do. We need something that will distract him in turn. Surprise him."

"A lightning bolt," said Anza, frustrated. She got up and went to the window, leaned out into the night, exposing herself to any spy. She heard the cat again. In other parts of the city parents eased their children to sleep, lovers caressed each other, beggars foraged in garbage piles. Near an empty house on the street where Ruslan had died, a girl extended her palm to receive a coin. In the dark water of the lake, the fish swam, regardless of the starlight that dusted the surface. The world spread outward from this place, out and out and out, life innumerable, ignorant of what happened between the two women.

"I have been thinking of surrendering myself," said Sparrow.

"You can't," Anza said, whirling. "That would—"

"Would what?"

Kill Esvar, she had been going to say, but she had to keep the secret. "Be a waste. My father didn't spare your life for you to throw it back at Karolje a few months later."

"Would it? He would gloat. Summon everyone to see his prize. And in the meantime Tevin could invade. I might even get close enough to Karolje to try to kill him. If I was lucky, Tevin would break in in time to save my life. If I wasn't, I would still be sufficient distraction."

"No," said Anza. "We need you."

"If the resistance fails in this, it will be shattered. It will need new leaders. If it succeeds, it will dissolve. Did Tevin tell you how many soldiers he had?"

"A dozen with him, I think, and another thirty or so in the city. Some in the Citadel itself. He's counting on the men in the Citadel to get him through the gates and into the building."

"If I came in with them, if Tevin claimed to be delivering me . . ."

"The king would see through it," Anza said firmly. "We need to keep thinking about the city. The gallows."

Sparrow's fingers drummed again. "If we incite a mob, innocent people will die. It's no use freeing the prisoners if fifty other people die instead." She thought a moment, then said soberly, "We might have to stay with the original plan and let the executions go ahead. Our aims are to get control of the docks, the banks, and the watchhouses. If we do that, we're in a position of strength even if the princes fail. Freeing the prisoners is a distraction."

"That's not acceptable," said Anza.

"None of this is acceptable!" Sparrow snapped. It was the first time Anza had seen the strain break through Sparrow's composure.

Neither spoke for a moment. Then, in a much calmer voice, Sparrow said, "He'll have to bring the prisoners in. We'll set an ambush close to the square. The ambush will draw off soldiers from the square, and as soon as people see that the soldiers are distracted, they can leave. There's still a risk Karolje's men will start grabbing them to hang instead, but I think the ambush will be enough of a commotion to prevent that. In the meantime the princes enter the Citadel. Perhaps Tevin proclaims himself earlier.

That will be up to him. He can make his own plans for how to do his part."

Anza remembered the soldiers in the square after the commander was shot, the way they had immediately turned on the people around them. That could happen again. Perhaps Sparrow was right. If ordinary people died in the square instead of Karolje's selected victims, the resistance would be blamed. Hell. Did Karolje have them trapped? What would her father have done?

He would have freed the prisoners. Karolje's violence was everywhere and could not be defended against entirely, but the king had set the gallows up to drive fear into the heart of everyone in the city. If the resistance prevented the hangings, Karolje's plan failed. The king's power would crack a little, even if his soldiers killed some of the people in the square.

She said, "What happens to the prisoners?"

"I think most will scatter at once, but we can direct any who stay to somewhere relatively safe. I presume you want to be part of the ambush."

"Yes."

"All right. Let's work out the details of this, and then you can go tell Esvar what the plan is. I'll wait here for his reply."

✦ ✦ ✦

She expected that Esvar would not be at the house yet, but he was. He wore a red priest's robe that exposed his ankles. A single candle was lit on a table. They sat across from each other, the candle to the side, not touching.

After he heard the plan, he said, "It will do. I would like to tear apart that gallows with my bare hands, but that's not possible. The prisoners will not be able to help much, I expect.

They'll be chained in the wagons and bound with fire-twine." He tapped his fingers as Sparrow had. "The executions are at noon. They'll bring the prisoners an hour or so before. Make sure you let one soldier get away, to draw off more men from the Citadel."

"Sparrow thinks he'll hang people you care about."

"He probably will. I hope he doesn't choose Tahari and her children."

The horror on his face was insupportable. Anza swallowed. "Esvar," she whispered.

"What?"

"Do you truly think you can win?"

"No," he said. "I think we'll be taken and later executed. But I think this is the best opportunity we have."

"You could wait for him to die."

"Someone else would take power and hunt us down. Even if that weren't the case, lurking would be seen as cowardly, and Tevin would lose his authority. The confrontation has to be public and forceful. There's a time when events propel things forward. A moment history has been building toward. If you want a change, you can't let that moment slip by."

Time spread backward, the past darkened by the layers piled upon it, and in the past itself was darkness, the darkness of night, the darkness of thick forest, the darkness of a mountain cave, and at the center a flicker of red firelight, holding back the unknown. Courage was stepping into the darkness. Men like Karolje worked to make their fires bigger until they blazed too hot to stand by, and they called that victory.

He said, "Are you going to fight?"

"Yes. I'll be part of the ambush." It felt incomplete. Sparrow's presence was a ghost in the room, an authority they deferred to. The candle flame's reflection fell gold on the varnished table. The world was precariously balanced, and Anza was afraid to stir.

"No more hesitation?"

"Not after Jance. I told him once—I told him I too was a soldier. I can fight in a war."

Esvar reached across and laid his hand on hers. She got up and walked around the table to stand behind him. She leaned forward and pressed the side of her face against his, her arms dangling over his chest. His stubble scratched at her cheek.

"Either one of us, or both of us, could die tomorrow." She stopped before she said anything else. He knew how to accept or reject an invitation.

He caught her hands together and turned his head. Lips on lips, on eyelids, on cheek. He stood and slid his hands down her back, fingers beneath her waistband. Anza read in his eyes what she hoped he read in hers: this was about gathering strength for battle. About armoring themselves.

When it was over, she walked back with his scent on her hands and a sharp, certain courage in her heart.

✦ ✦ ✦

Like most streets that ran into Temple Square, this one had been designed to be narrow. Wagons could get through, but in only one direction at a time, and there was no passing slow-moving oxen or balking mules, so it was usually free of all but foot traffic. Karolje's soldiers used it whenever they needed to approach the square; it was the quickest route from the Citadel.

A little after dawn, when the sun had just cleared the eastern hills and was still red, Anza took up her place on the second floor of an abandoned house. Another archer was in the next room, and two more were on the floor above. The house reminded her more of the house she had watched Ruslan's death from than her father's, although it shared with both those buildings the dust and silence. Once it had been grand. Its ceilings were high and painted, its doors carved, its floors made of narrow boards, finely planed and polished. But light fixtures were empty, discolored patches on the wallpaper revealed where furniture and pictures had been, and black lines of rat droppings crisscrossed each other in every room. The rats had drawn cats, and one room on the ground floor was almost unbearably acrid.

The house across the street, from which River and three others were to shoot, had not been abandoned. Sparrow refused to tell her whose house it was, or what had been done with the inhabitants. When Anza thought too much about it, she squirmed with uneasy guilt.

Occasional hammering sounded from the square. The wait would be hours, but no one had dared bring bows along the city streets in daylight. More resisters would come later to hold the street. Still others would gather in the square to secure the opposite end when people came to watch the executions. The ambush needed to be contained. Anza and the other archers were to shoot as many of the soldiers bringing the prisoners as quickly as possible, then bolt when it turned to hand-to-hand combat. If all went well, the resisters would gather again at a house a few blocks away.

Anza waited. The ceiling above her creaked as another archer walked back and forth. She traced lines in the dust and thought about her father, the hours he must have spent standing guard with nothing to do but watch. She tried not to think about Esvar. The sun moved along the street, growing whiter and hotter. The angled shadows lost their crispness and shrank. Her mouth was dry, and she drank from her flask frequently. A rat gnawed in the wall. Her energy was too high to drowse.

The hammering was replaced by the sound of people talking, a low roar that was funneled down the street and amplified. It reminded her of the crash of a waterfall on a river. She looked toward the square, and through the narrow gap between buildings at the end of the street she saw the crowd. The gallows themselves were blocked from view.

Then, finally, the clatter of approaching wagons and horses. She laid an arrow on her bow and resisted the impulse to put her head out the window and watch. Sparrow had anticipated two wagons, each drawn by two horses, and eight or ten soldiers. The soldiers would be in mail, which meant the shots had to be precise. Neck, eye, mouth.

Now she could see the procession without revealing herself. Damn. Hellhounds, four of them. They would have to be killed first so they didn't cause carnage in the square. Vile beasts. The men leading the hellhounds walked in front. Two soldiers on horseback were between the two wagons, and two more at the rear. With the drivers, that made ten. On each wagon there were six prisoners, hooded and bound.

A sharp whistle pierced the silence. That was the signal. The soldiers stopped almost instantly. Their heads went up, and the fur on the dogs' backs ridged.

Energy coursed through Anza at the sound, and she aimed at a hellhound, drew, fired. Other arrows darkened the air. Her dog went down, and she grinned in pleasure. One other hellhound and a soldier had also fallen. She turned and shot again, aiming this time at a soldier behind the wagons. The arrow went wide, but her next struck him in the forearm he raised to protect himself. Another shot, and this one penetrated the base of his throat.

He tumbled from his horse. A hellhound was howling in pain, and she had to pause, gather her breath to shut out the noise.

Several of the prisoners were screaming too. The driver of the first wagon was slumped and bloody on his seat. Ahead of him, two soldiers spurred their horses toward the square. They would be back with reinforcements immediately. She fired, saw her arrow bounce off one man's back even as another archer's struck him in the neck. She aimed at the second rider, that narrow patch of flesh between head and back. Her arrow hit, and he fell. The horses came to a stop, nervous, the whites of their eyes showing and sweat darkening their glossy coats.

At the end of the street, one of the mounted men who had been at the rear was galloping in the direction of the Citadel. He had a sword out, ready to slash down at anyone who approached. She remembered Esvar's words to let one get through and stopped watching him.

She shot, and shot, and shot, her pace rapid but steady. So did her companions. Shortly all the hellhounds and two of the remaining four soldiers were dead. The survivors were taking cover between the wagons. The horses whose riders had died were clumped together, tails swishing, on the verge of panic. One of the prisoners had managed to work his hood off in the commotion, and he stared wildly around. His head was shaved, the traitor's mark.

The door to the house across the street opened, and Sparrow came out. A drawn sword in her hand caught the sun. Footsteps thumped through Anza's building as the other archers went running for the back door. Irini and a man who had come out behind Sparrow hurried to the horses that were pulling the first wagon to unbridle them.

One of the two soldiers by the wagons came forward and

engaged Sparrow while the other ran toward Irini and her companion. It was time to run, but Anza could not break away from watching Sparrow. The swords struck against each other in quick strokes, beats on a cymbal, flashing and sparking in the bright light. The clash of metal echoed off the building walls. The soldier brought his blade down, and Sparrow deflected it upward, twisted, and slashed at his shoulder. He lurched backward against the wagon. A knife glittered in Sparrow's other hand.

Before Sparrow could lunge, the soldier recovered and increased his speed. The street went so quiet that Anza could hear Sparrow and the soldier panting. She glanced toward Irini and saw that the resister with her was holding off their opponent too.

At the Temple end of the street, a woman shrieked. The scream was cut off. Anza tensed. The only thing that should be happening at the gallows was soldiers heading toward the ambush. Irini released the horses and hit one of them on its hindquarters. It neighed indignantly and cantered toward the square. The three near it followed. Anza hoped they didn't trample anyone in the crowd.

Sparrow slashed at her opponent's arm with the knife, then slipped past his guard and stabbed him in the throat. Blood jetted past her to the wall. Shouts and screams still rose from the square. What the hell had happened? A pool of blood was bright beside the body of the soldier the other resister had been fighting. Irini was rummaging among the soldiers' bodies, searching for the keys to the prisoners' shackles.

Anza had a dozen arrows left. She gathered them and looked out the window. Metal rattled, a heavy sound, as the prisoners were unchained. At the end of the street, soldiers broke through from the square, their swords raised and bloody. Anza fired at the lead man as soon as he was close enough. Her arrow flew straight and sure and into the soldier's face. He fell so quickly that she must have hit his eye.

She shot again at the approaching soldiers. So did another archer who had disobeyed orders and stayed behind. One fell. Another. The men behind him halted out of range.

From the distant crowd, surpassing the noises of fear, came a tremendous cheer, repeated. The soldiers froze as Anza tensed. This was not part of the plan. *Pray that you never have to improvise.* The cheer came a third time. The soldiers pelted back toward the square. Anza fired at them, but her arrow skipped on the ground.

"Run!" Sparrow yelled at the freed prisoners.

Anza ran too. Descending the steep stairs, she almost slipped. The building's rear door was open, and she ran out to the alley, turned east, and ran for the street.

A blood-spattered Sparrow and the other resisters waited, holding several horses. Irini exchanged a triumphant glance with Anza. In the distance the crowd chanted, the words indistinguishable, the rhythm potent. One prisoner, gaunt and pale, had collapsed against the wall. The others had fled.

Sparrow said, "We need to know what's happening in the square. I'm going to look. The rest of you go to the meeting place."

"We're all going to the square," said River. Dust smeared his face. His red hair was tangled and sweaty.

Another cheer.

Sparrow sighed. "All right. One moment."

She gave her reins to Anza and walked to the freed prisoner at the wall. They spoke. Sparrow gave her something, and the woman nodded. Her hand went up to her forehead, perhaps to shade her eyes from the bright sun, perhaps to hide tears. This is victory, Anza thought. One prisoner freed, allowed to reclaim a life she had thought vanished. It mattered as much as the deaths of a hundred soldiers. Against Karolje, every victory counted.

Sparrow returned to her horse. "Harpy, mount up behind me. We'll go around, not through here." She helped Anza up and mounted herself. The horse, large and well-trained, stood placidly, ears pricked forward. River, who had Irini behind him, walked his horse forward to join them.

They trotted south, then west, then north back to the square. The chant swelled and grew clearer as they approached. *Kill the king! Kill the king!* The sound resonated off the stone buildings, a roar that wanted to suck Anza in. The vitality, the energy of it, sent chills down her spine. Things were happening. She wanted to leap from the horse and join in, roar with all her might. *Kill the king!*

Sparrow's back went rigid. Bending, Anza looked around Sparrow over the crowd.

At one end of the gallows stood Miloscz, fist raised in triumph. He had a bloody knife in his other hand. A semicircle of soldiers surrounded him. Two had swords pointed at him, not touching, waiting.

Sparrow said, "He must have rushed the gallows when some of the soldiers on it headed toward the ambush. He's roused the crowd."

"Why haven't the soldiers killed him?"

"They don't want to start a riot. But if they lose control of the crowd, they'll kill him at once. We should go."

"Instead of being part of it?"

Sparrow looked over her shoulder at Anza. "I'm going to the Citadel."

Kill the king!

"You're needed here," Anza said. "Someone has to lead the crowd. If Miloscz doesn't get killed, he'll be the hero afterward. They'll follow him and get crushed."

"If he survives that, he deserves to be a hero," said Sparrow. "By then whatever is going to happen in the Citadel will be over."

In the crowd, at the other end of the gallows, there was movement. A quick eddy and spin, then another man was climbing onto the gallows. The man raised his fist like Miloscz and shook it in triumph. Two of the soldiers grabbed Miloscz and hauled him backward, pushed him to all fours.

The crowd went silent in a wave from front to back as people realized what was happening. The silence was eerie, the air hot and still. One of the soldiers with his sword drawn advanced on Miloscz, and the men holding him stepped aside. The man who had climbed the gallows stood motionless, statue-like.

The soldier raised his sword. It was not a headman's sword and might take several strokes to sever Miloscz's head from his neck. This is going to frenzy the crowd, Anza thought. He was making a mistake.

A second soldier pushed him aside, grabbed the sword, and jabbed the blade into the wood of the gallows. He held his hand out to Miloscz. Another soldier joined them. The man at the other end of the platform ran forward, his footsteps distinct in the quiet.

The soldiers scuffled. "Kill the king!" someone shouted, and the crowd took it up again. Miloscz and the other resister raised joined hands. The two soldiers did too. Then several of the other soldiers charged. Miloscz vanished in a confusion of bodies and blades. The crowd roared and swelled toward the gallows.

"Get down," Sparrow said. "I need to get to the Citadel before the crowd does."

"And do what?" Anza said. She wanted to be there too, but if there was to be any taking of the Citadel, it would be done by the princes.

"Face Karolje."

There's no reason, Anza thought. Not for the leader of the resistance. She should stay here and make sure she was not eclipsed by Miloscz. If Tevin or Esvar had not won control of the Citadel, going there would be suicide.

But for Mirantha it was necessary.

"I'm coming with you," Anza said.

"No."

Anza said, "You need a witness." She knew Sparrow would take it as witness to the event, but she meant it more deeply, as witness to the life of the queen, in its past and its future. Sometime in the struggle, Mirantha would need to be acknowledged.

The noise of the crowd crashed into the silence Sparrow had wrapped around herself when Anza spoke. Anza waited.

Sparrow shifted position, so Anza could no longer see her face, and looked at River. "When they will listen to you, when the violence is over, lead them to the Citadel," she said. She looked at Anza once more. "Hold tight."

23

ESVAR'S HORSE WANTED to race, and he held it back with effort. Everything was sharp and clear, the movement of the horse against his legs, the movement of his legs against the horse. The vibrations of the cobblestones. The children shouting in play. The walls of the Old City rising against a bright sky. Twenty mounted men in armor looked like a military force, and no one was going to interfere.

Near the Citadel, they slowed to a walk and rode onto a curving side street, out of sight of the main road. One man stayed behind, watching the gates to see what happened when news of the ambush reached the king. It was nearly noon, and the tunic Esvar wore under his mail was soaked with sweat. Tevin's face displayed the same eagerness Esvar felt. If they died, it would be on their own terms. If they won, they won everything.

His brother said his name. "Yes?"

"I need to know one thing from you before we go in."

It made him nervous. Which of his secrets had Tevin glimpsed? He had said nothing about the journal, about their mother. "Go ahead."

"Who can he use to hurt you?"

No one, he wanted to say. But the question was not a challenge. It was Tevin needing to know his limits. So he gave it honest thought.

Anza and Sparrow would not be there. Marek was a good companion, but he was also a soldier. If he died, it was a loss but not an injustice. "You, of course," he said. "And I couldn't kill a child, or let him do it. There's a point where victory isn't worth the cost."

"You have to be willing to let me die."

"Not for nothing."

"Even for nothing. Otherwise he has a hold on you. Don't let him get the leverage." Tevin wiped his face. "I intend to win, but you're right, there are limits to what I will do, which gives him the advantage. If it's die or follow him in evil, I die. Let me go."

"I will," Esvar said, though death at Karolje's hand was not the death he feared for Tevin. It was the spear through the heart before they even reached the king, the slow torture with no goal but pain, the hellhound's bite to demonstrate power. Death without any chance of victory.

"If we win," Tevin said, "if he dies, what will you do?"

The question was too large, too vague, too unthinkable, for him to answer. He ran his fingers through the short bristling crop of his horse's mane. Last night's lovemaking with Anza had been a surprise, fragile and lovely; he did not expect it again. Today would change too much, even if they both lived. But that was what he wanted. If he could have anything, it would be her beside him.

"Live," he said, which encompassed all possibility.

A starling curved out of a tree and landed, tapped at the street. Esvar considered, not for the first time, if he should tell his brother about Sparrow, and decided again not to. Part of him wished he had not realized it himself. The knowledge was a distraction, like an aching tooth or a sprained ankle, a pain that could swell to immobilize everything.

Out of sight on the main road, horses thundered past, not more than fifteen or twenty by the sound. Esvar had hoped for his own sake that the Citadel would be nearly emptied of guards, but at the same time he was glad it was so few. If the king had sent a hundred soldiers, there would be no chance for anyone in the square to escape. Tevin whistled, gathering the men, and heard the lookout's report. Sixteen, the man said, which still left a formidable force at the Citadel.

"They can't all be guarding the king," Esvar said.

"No. But as soon as he heard that we weren't involved in the ambush at the square, he'll have concluded we are coming to the Citadel. He'll want to make a show of it, to remind people he still is king. He'll collect the courtiers and servants. We aren't going to find him on his sickbed."

"The Green Court," Esvar said, certain. Karolje thrived on fear.

"Yes. Possibly the throne room, but we'll try the court first." Tevin lifted the reins, then looked at Esvar. He said wryly, "I never thought I would have help from the resistance. I should have. When Nihalik was exiled, he left me a letter telling me I could not defeat Karolje by myself. He reminded me of my duty to my people. You have known or remembered those two things better than I have. Thank you."

Esvar reached across the space between the horses. They gripped hands briefly. It was an affirmation. He hoped it was not also a farewell.

They trotted the horses the last quarter mile. At the gates, the two Citadel guards stepped aside as they would for any contingent of returning soldiers. Then one of them exclaimed. He darted into the gatehouse to pull the alarm bell. One of Tevin's men dismounted and pursued him. The bell rang once, short and broken off. Metal clashed inside the gatehouse.

Tevin's soldier reappeared, blood running down his sword. The other guard dropped his sword.

"Wise man," Tevin said. He dismounted and strode to the guard. "You can surrender, or you can join me. Which will it be?"

Esvar imagined the calculations running through the man's head. If he surrendered and Tevin lost, Karolje might allow him to live. If he joined and lost, he would be killed. If Tevin won, surrender would leave him ashamed and disfavored; joining would make him one of the early heroes.

"I surrender," said the man. Esvar pressed his lips together with disappointment. Whether it was out of cowardice, loyalty to Karolje, or a practical assessment of the situation made no difference. The man was putting his money on the king. If all of them did that, the prediction would fulfill itself.

"The rest of you, dismount," Tevin said. "We go on foot from here. Take him to the stables with the horses, Vanescz, and tie him up, then find me. You, Mirvik, go with him. If a fight starts and you're outnumbered, forget about stabling the horses."

By now the guards at the entrances should have deduced that something was wrong and would be readying for battle. A message would be going to the king.

Esvar swung down and gave the reins to one of the soldiers. He said in a low voice to Tevin, "Are you going to make that offer to every soldier we meet?"

"If I can. If they all choose surrender, I'll have to just disarm them and leave them. We can't waste men guarding them. My hope is that they'll see which way the wind is blowing. Come on." He raised his voice and gave a few brisk commands.

The ordinary Citadel entrance was thirty yards from the gates across a flat expanse of cobbled ground. The doors were closed, a pair of guards standing in front with drawn swords. Esvar drew his own.

Tevin's hand came down on Esvar's shoulder. "Those two guards are mine, but there will be fighting after that. Say whatever prayers you need to say."

They walked to the entrance. The soldiers fanned out around them in two rows. Two of the men had short bows out and arrows at the ready. Tevin led them up the steps to the large wooden doors. One guard saluted. The other pushed the right-hand door open and went inside to hold it. Passing through, Esvar looked at the guard: an older man, experienced, his face lit with satisfaction. He had probably served under Piyr.

The windowless entrance hall, high-ceilinged, was eighteen feet wide and forty feet long. Three doors, each with a guard in front, opened off each side; at the far end, white marble steps swept upward in twinned curving flights to a landing with a rail. The hall was lined with statues and urns. The gaslights reflected on the marble floor and walls and cast dim shadows of the statuary. Usually there were people crossing the hall, their bodies livening the space. Now it was quiet and cold, funereal.

One of Karolje's men in the hall shouted, then drew his sword. Four of the other soldiers joined him and approached the intruders in formation, their feet striking uniformly on the floor. The sixth broke for the steps. He was much too far away to chase. One of Tevin's archers fired. Over the yelling and the footsteps Esvar could not hear the shot, but he saw the arrow strike the guard's thigh. The man dropped.

The odds were better than four to one in Tevin's favor, and as soon as Karolje's men engaged with Tevin's, the fight broke into clumps. The crash of so many blades against each other echoed deafeningly around the room. Surrender, you fools, Esvar thought. It did Karolje's men no good to fight when they were substantially outnumbered.

Marek and one of Tevin's men engaged a soldier who was huge, six inches taller than Esvar and broad. He had a long reach and surprising quickness. He was on the defensive, parrying and blocking effectively without getting any blows in of his own. Esvar watched long enough to get the rhythm of the movements, then lunged in from the side and struck the man's calf. Not a fatal blow, not even a crippling one, but a distraction.

Or so it should have been. The soldier's only reaction was to turn his head for an instant and make eye contact. Esvar fell back, stunned at the contempt in the man's eye.

He had been thinking of the Citadel guards as Karolje's pawns, obedient, willing to turn on the princes at the king's orders, too afraid of the king to disobey even with the odds overwhelmingly against them. But this was personal. The man hated him. For lack of cruelty, for pride, for weakness, who knew. The guard had thrived on Karolje's poisonous words and would never in a hundred years give his loyalty to Tevin. He was the sort of man who had killed Mirantha's maids.

He also had a habit of raising his left shoulder when he swung his blade from right to left. The next time he did it, Esvar drove forward with his dagger and stabbed at the exposed armpit. His blade was too wide to penetrate far into the rings, but the sheer unexpectedness of it threw the man off balance, and he missed a parry. Marek slid his sword through the opening and up to the guard's throat.

Marek looked as Esvar, who nodded once. A deft movement, and blood sprayed outward, bright and red. More blood spilled out of the man's mouth. He fell, his legs jerking.

Of the remaining king's men, two were down, one was on his knees with his hands held open in surrender, and one was under attack by four men. Blood was splashed across the floor and the base of one statue.

The last man went down. Tevin walked to the kneeling man and looked down at him. "Do we tie you up or will you support me?"

"I'll fight for you, m'lord."

"On your oath?"

"Before the gods."

"Get up, then." He made a hand sign to one of the other soldiers. *Watch him.*

The wounded soldier on the steps had pulled himself up and out of sight. Two men went after him. Tevin waited until one of those men appeared at the railing and waved to lead the rest of them to the steps. Without discussion, Esvar separated from him. They should not be too close to each other now.

Then Tevin's man on the landing fell, and arrows started flying at them.

Esvar flung his free arm up to protect his face and dashed to the side, where he sheltered behind a large statue of Kazdjan wrestling with a wolf. Tevin's two bowmen fired back, but the archers on the landing had the advantages of height and cover. Arrows whined in the air, and the arrowheads that missed clinked against the marble.

One of Tevin's remaining soldiers went down, an arrow through the throat. Esvar looked at the landing, and as soon as he saw the next arrows launch, he raced forward. An arrow bounced off a statue as he crouched behind it. Another one of Tevin's men fell, his mail ringing on the floor. Esvar vividly remembered the night of the raid, Anza's arrows striking his back. The fire casting shadows on the street. He wished she were with him. He was caught for a moment, held by memory and loss.

The nearest gaslight was five feet away. He timed his run again and shut the valve, dived behind a large black urn patterned with cherry blossoms. Across the hall, someone followed his example. The room became much darker. Other men did the same, and in a very short time the arrows were falling blindly and soldiers were clustered near the bottom of each staircase. Tevin's archers had forsaken their bows and rejoined the others. Only two of the lights by the side doors still shone.

Charging up the steps would be the most dangerous thing they had done so far. They had no idea how many bowmen were at the top—at least three. At such short range an arrow might have force to break the rings in the chain mail. They had no choice.

The two groups positioned themselves and, at a nod from Tevin, ran upward. Esvar was packed in the middle. One of the men in front of him fell, and he stumbled over the body. It saved his life; an arrow whirred where his head had been. As he righted himself, he heard the first clang of metal.

The fight on the landing was short and fierce. In the tight space, Karolje's soldiers, four of them, were surrounded. With no room to swing a blade, it was knife work, and the numbers told. Esvar did not even bloody his dagger.

Breathing hard, they paused to take stock. Tevin had lost four men in all, two fatally and two with wounds too serious to continue. All of the king's guards who had opposed them were dead.

Tevin said, "They'll have heard us by now. We need to go straight to the court. If he's not there, it's mine."

Esvar said, "I'll bring up the rear." It was the more vulnerable position; anyone running to the commotion would come from that direction.

"All right. But don't fall behind. I need you." Tevin's face was exultant. He had been waiting for this. For years.

They had another level to go up, and several turns to make before they reached the Green Court. It required passing through three more guard posts, and there would be more guards at the entrance to the court if Karolje was there. The riskiest part would be the crossing of a large atrium where several passages converged.

Esvar said, "Can we expect any more of your men to help?"

"There are others on duty, but gods know where. There might be skirmishes all over the Citadel that we never even see. We can't rely on them. But you and I are both worth more captured than dead, and there will be some more men who change sides. It's by no means hopeless."

The guards at the base of the steps to the next level surrendered immediately. Tevin left two men to gag and tie them, and they went on. They were only a few feet along the passage at the top when a bell rang. The sound was muffled, but Esvar knew what it was: the bell atop the Citadel itself, tolling the alarm. It would bring every soldier on the grounds.

Tevin started running.

They came to the atrium. Esvar slowed just in time to avoid crashing into the men in front of him. Two dozen of Karolje's soldiers waited for them, led by the king's senior captain. Next to him was Doru. Dust showed in the sunlight streaming through the windows.

In the silence while the two groups stared at each other, the bell rang again. When its sound faded, Doru said, "Welcome back, my lords. You don't think this plan went undetected, do you? The king is waiting. Will you come peacefully?" Though he had no weapon drawn, the menace of him was unmistakable. The captain edged away.

You're unprotected, Esvar thought viciously. It took all the discipline he had not to break ranks and rush at the spymaster. He wanted to cut the man to pieces for Jance's murder.

"If you knew, you could have saved the lives of the men we've killed on our way here," said Tevin. His gaze swept the assembled soldiers. "You men are sworn to protect the king, but he will throw away your lives for his own fun. You're worth more than that."

"Save the lives of your own men and surrender," said the spymaster.

Esvar estimated the distance and concluded he could not reach Doru without the captain or other soldiers engaging him first. He raised his sword anyway.

"Not yet," Tevin said to him.

Doru said, "We have your lover, Esvar."

"You don't," Esvar said. He felt speared from groin to throat.

"She's been my spy for months. She came to me at dawn and told me everything you plan."

That was a wrong step. Esvar laughed. He said, "The problem with lying all the time, Doru, is that you lose all measure of the truth. I still know what it looks like. You will never convince me of anything."

"Keep your words for the lord of death," said Doru. He signaled to the captain.

The groups met in the center of the room, stone under their feet. There was no chance for thinking, for observing, for watching the movements of the opponents. It was a straight battle, blades crashing without respite. Esvar's body reacted as it had been trained to.

He fought two men. Arms and armor and skill were more or less equal among the three, and Esvar was in the position of the man he had killed earlier, able to defend without much else. He had a slightly longer reach. He kept his feet moving, slid his sword against one blade and curved it back to fend off the other. Jabbing at knees and slashing at wrists, he drew blood, and the floor around them was soon flecked with red.

The edge of a blade stung him on the forearm. They were at close quarters, no room for backing away without running into another fight. His eyes burned from sweat. He could see the pores on the face of one of the men he fought. Somewhere a man screamed in pain, but Esvar barely heard it. He realized, more slowly than he should have, that his opponents were not trying to kill him. He was to be captured, brought to Karolje and thrown onto the floor. He pressed harder.

His sword arm was grabbed brutally from behind. He drew his knife with his other hand and stabbed backward, to no avail. He kicked, making contact with the shin of the man behind him. It was not enough to break the man's grip. He was losing feeling in his arm while pain shot down his back from his shoulder. And now something sharp pricked his neck.

He stopped moving. His sword and knife were taken from him, and then the grip on his arm loosened. His arm and hand tingled painfully as blood returned to them.

The fight was over. He had been taken, and Tevin had been taken, and so had three of the men who came with him. The others were dead or injured. Marek lay nearby, eyes open and empty. The older man who had been on duty at the entrance had a knife stroke through his throat that nearly severed his spine. That had been punishment, not an ordinary battle death.

Their armor was stripped from them. The captain grinned as he bound Esvar's hands behind his back with fire-twine, then spat on him. You shouldn't have done that, Esvar thought. He kept his mouth shut.

Surrounded by soldiers, he and Tevin were separated from Tevin's men and taken through the corridors. Soon Esvar knew they were going to the Green Court. He could not prevent dread growing in him as they approached the doors. The courtiers would not have the strength or the will to oppose Karolje. His death waited for him inside. They had tried, but it had not been enough.

The doors opened, giving a clear view down the aisle of the king seated on the dais chair. Doru stood beside him, leaning slightly on the chair arm, and there were two soldiers on either side. The room was crowded, all courtiers and officials in their finest clothing. It needed only musicians to be a dance floor. Karolje's eyes locked on them. He lifted in the chair, then dropped back. His right hand waved someone away. The people nearest the door turned to look, their faces blank with fear. A woman brought her hand to her mouth to cover a gasp.

Tevin walked forward as though he saw no one but Karolje. Perhaps he didn't. Esvar followed, a guard on either side of him and one behind. The guards jerked Tevin to a halt in front of the dais, not close enough to touch it. They stopped Esvar a few feet behind him. To one side of the dais was an upright iron frame large enough for a person, shackles attached. That was where you put a man if you wanted to restrain him and still give his body room to shake and jerk with every pain inflicted.

"Ah," said Karolje. "Have you anything to say for yourselves before I have you killed? Either of you?"

Tevin stared directly at him. The bonds and the guards seemed unimportant under the force of his presence. He was bleeding from a shallow cut on his left arm.

"I've come to claim the throne, old man," he said.

MIRANTHA

THE CITADEL GATES are open. That is probably a good thing, but it might be disaster. Not long ago they heard a bell ringing repeatedly, an alarm, which means Tevin and Esvar are within and that more soldiers are on their way. Sparrow reins in outside the gates and says roughly to Anza, "Get down," then dismounts herself. She swats the horse and it goes trotting off to its stable.

She looks at Anza, who is small and fierce and brave. A soldier's daughter, like herself. "You shouldn't come," she says, because she cannot bear the thought of watching another woman die. "Wait here for River."

"I have to come," Anza says. She takes a deep breath. "When my father let you go, did he know who you were?"

The question she has dreaded for years. "A leader in the resistance?" she says. "Yes."

"Not Sparrow. Mirantha."

"You're mad, girl."

"Esvar recognized you," Anza says. "He told me yesterday."

Time stops. The earth no longer moves. The Citadel is a painted stage set and the air is glass. She has had few greater fears than that her sons would know her as they watched her die.

"How?" Sparrow asks, her voice brittle as ice.

"When I was a student, I found your journal in the College library. He's read it. Something you said at the College used the same words you had written. Then he could see you in your face."

She should have burned the journal. It was vanity to preserve it. "When did this happen?"

"Two nights ago. He had no idea when he met with you, I swear. He didn't know about the journal then."

"Why did you decide to give it to him?"

"Because he needed to know he had been loved. Needed to know that there was more to his life than Karolje."

It shakes her. Sparrow wipes her forehead. "You shouldn't have done it. All that can happen to him now is more pain."

"At the time, I didn't know there was any secret to keep besides the journal," Anza says. She raises her head and stares up into Sparrow's face. "I had no right to deny him that. It hurt him like hell, but it gave him courage. He told me after he fled the Citadel that Karolje offered him the crown, and he was tempted. The journal gave him a touchstone. Without it he might have failed when he was set against the king."

Every word is a spike driven into her. She wishes Esvar had never learned this, and she is full of gratitude that it gave him strength. When she saw him for the first time in the College, she feared she would break with pride and love and grief. His eyes had the same alert intensity they did as a child, and his face was a mask. He had learned how to hide. How to be safe.

"Why did you tell me this?" she asks. "To try to stop me here at the gate? I'm going in."

Anza says, "No one has a better right or greater need to face Karolje than you. It just seems—some secrets throw shadows much longer than we can bear. You and Esvar"—she stops, swallows, tries again—"if you see each other, you need to know each other. He still loves you. You aren't alone anymore."

Once she had wanted to be free, tied to no one, encumbered by nothing. She did not understand then that it also meant she would be unsupported. Year upon year, day upon day, of solitary resistance have worn upon her. Anza's words are a gift. Sparrow's grief is like water in a lock, deep, held back. In all these years she has never grieved for herself.

She has to turn away. She stares down the broad avenue, which will soon know the feet of thousands of marching angry people, and wonders if she has doomed her sons. She should have killed Karolje when she had the chance, even if it meant her own life. If a mob she has raised kills Tevin and Esvar in the name of justice, she will be crushed by the weight of her failure. The unfamiliar feeling inside her is terror.

And yet, and yet . . . She knew this could happen when she sent the journal away, when she returned to Karegg, when she went to Ivanje Stepanian. It is her own steps that have led her here, her own choices. And she would make them again. She could not sit by and let others fight the king. She could not let him reign unchallenged.

It doesn't matter. The past is unchangeable now, and she has a task. She can weep over her mistakes later.

She looks back at Anza, who must love Esvar to have given him the journal. That had been courageous on her part. She had to have known it would hurt.

It is time for other secrets to be bared.

Sparrow says, "Your father did a service to me once, when I lived in the Citadel. It was he who brought my books and journal to the College. He told me he had a daughter, just Esvar's age, who was clever and quick. He was proud of her. I found a tutor for her, arranged that she could go to the College if she merited it."

"Why?" Anza whispers.

"For Vetia," Sparrow says. "It is people like you who will help restore the nation when this is over. And for my sons. I am gladder than you can possibly know that Esvar found you. I think I must have known, or wished, that Havidian's daughter would be the one to read my words."

Anza's hands clench and her shoulders tighten. "I took the poetry too," she says. "The Rukovili. It was in my father's house when he was killed. Esvar found it. That's what led us together. It made him curious."

Just a few days ago the world was a formless confusion of violence and desire and unsettled anger. As it had been for years. Now it is taking a shape. She says, "Connections matter. Did you ever wonder how your friend Irini found the resistance? Her lover's brother knows one of us from a time they worked together. Karolje's weakness is that he has no connections. He has chosen to be alone. Today he will need help, and he will have no one to turn to. A tyrant's cruelty lies in his contempt for others, but that's also his undoing."

They face each other. Their shadows are stubby, blue on the mottled cobbles.

"We're going in?" Anza asks.

"We're going in. But I think we should close the gates."

They walk through the open gateway. Sparrow's shoulders tighten reflexively as she steps back into this dangerous place. She goes to the gatehouse and looks in. One soldier, stabbed through the heart, lies sprawled half on his side. Blood darkens the floor around him. His face is waxy. He has been dead a while. If no one has come to his aid yet, Tevin and Esvar have likely got the upper hand.

The gates are designed to slide along the walls. They are polished steel, strong enough and high enough to keep out even determined groups. But they might not hold against a mob. There is a wheel on the side of the gatehouse, and she turns it. Above her she hears the creak of metal forced from rest. The portcullis, which has not been lowered for protection since the end of the Tazekh war, is well-maintained and descends almost too rapidly. It takes all her strength to keep the wheel from spinning out of control.

When she comes out, Anza is staring at the portcullis. "It's so big," she says. "Won't River be angry?"

"No. If the people of the city get in, far too many innocent people will die. And soldiers can't get out to attack them easily either. They can be heard, which will be enough. If we all fail, they can run." If there is a panic, some people might be trampled. But the wide street is safer than the narrow roads in the main parts of the city. "Come."

They slide the other gates shut and bar them as an additional precaution, then advance across the courtyard. Sparrow feels as though she is seventeen again, a new wife, crossing this expanse of cobble to a building that will swallow her. When she came then, the formal entrance doors were opened and fifty guards stood on either side in dress uniform, and King Piyr waited on the steps to greet her and Karolje. She was full of eagerness and hope, her hand on the arm of her handsome husband with the pleasing smile.

"This way," she says, walking briskly toward the ordinary entrance. It is impressive too, but nothing on the scale of the ceremonial doors, which stand twenty feet high.

The guards who should be there are missing. No signs of violence. She pushes on one door, expecting to find it barred, and it gives. It is heavy enough that she and Anza both need to use their weight at first but it swings easily on its hinges once it has started moving.

Bodies lie on the floor of the large room ahead of them. Two gaslights burn, not enough to displace shadows. Sparrow shuts the door again and pulls at the huge bar that slides across the crack between the doors. Anza helps. The bar is heavy but well oiled, and they get it into place, swing down the clamps at each end. Between the bodies, arrows make dark lines on the white marble.

"What happened?" Anza asks.

"The princes had a battle here," Sparrow answers. "I think they were let in, though. Tevin's men must have gotten themselves assigned the duty. It won't be this easy the rest of the way. Get your bow ready." She draws her sword.

The blood on the floor is getting sticky. At the top of the stairs they find more bodies. The air stinks. One man is still alive, unconscious, an arrow in the muscle of his neck and his elbow laid open by a sword stroke. Anza looks away. Sparrow kneels beside the soldier—he is in Tevin's uniform—and looks at the wounds. He isn't going to make it. His pulse is uneven. When she raises an eyelid, nothing happens.

She stands. He will die without regaining consciousness. She doesn't have to apply a mercy stroke. Anza's face is pale.

"If you're going to faint or be sick, do it now," Sparrow says. "Sometimes it helps. We might see worse."

"I'll be all right."

"Are you sure?"

"Yes. If I'm going to vomit, I'll do it on the king."

Sparrow is amused despite herself. Such is the quality of youth. She looks upward a moment, wondering where to go next.

Once she has put the question, the answer is obvious. If Karolje has captured his sons, he will have taken them to the Green Court. If they have triumphed, she will run across their men first and can ask.

So they walk. They have not gone far from the landing when they encounter two guards, bound and gagged, some yards away from the foot of another set of steps. The men's eyes widen when they see the women. Sparrow bends over and loosens one man's gag.

"Who did this?" she asks.

"Prince Tevin. He came back. Who the hell are you?"

Sparrow grins. "His ally," she says, and pulls the gag up.

They ascend the stairs. At the top Sparrow turns right and edges along the wall of a corridor. The gas has been turned off. They walk through dim halls, turning a few times, until they reach a place where daylight falls softly on the floor of a room ahead of them. She knows where they are. It is strange how even after a dozen years her feet fall into old patterns. She is a ghost, a figure from the past who has been summoned to old haunts. The thought disturbs her. She is alive now. It is Mirantha the queen, young and timid, who used to tread these halls lightly, fearing to disturb anything.

She looks at Anza and lifts a hand, halting the other woman. She goes forward and looks around the corner into an atrium. There are at least twenty men dead. Many of them have slit throats, and the floor is covered with blood. The uniforms are a mix.

There should be more activity here, soldiers cleaning up or

servants in the hallways, lords' and ladies' voices a murmur in a nearby room. She goes to the window. The courtyard below is empty of people.

Returning to Anza, she says, "There was combat. Quite a number of men died. I can't tell who won."

"Is Esvar—"

"No. Neither of them. But the blood's fresh. It wasn't long ago. Probably when we heard the bell."

"Do you know where they are?"

"No. But I have a guess. We should have seen more people, so I think Karolje's gathered everyone. And I know where he would do that." It is a relief after all not to have to pretend she has never been here.

They enter the atrium. Anza looks at the bodies, stiffens. "Wait," she says, and goes to look at one of them. She stands for a few long silent seconds, then squats down and closes the dead man's eyes.

"You know him?" Sparrow asks.

"He was Esvar's captain. I think that means they lost."

Sparrow's diaphragm tightens. She says, "Let's go."

They walk. Corridors are wide and ceilings high, windows and paintings on the walls, floors tiled in marble. The doorframes are carved and painted. Marble busts and enameled vases occupy niches in the walls. Anza slows, gawks. Sparrow lets her.

Then they pass through a doorway with a curved arch and enter the older part of the Citadel. Ceilings are lower. The stones are unplastered and dark, stained with centuries of soot. Gas pipes along the walls are mounted on iron brackets, some of them spotted with rust. The air is chilly. The masonry is smooth, the lines clean; these are no underground passages, cramped and rough-hewn. But clearly this part of the Citadel was built as a fortress, not a palace.

Two more turns. When they come to a third, Sparrow stops and looks around a corner. Four armored men stand outside the door to the Green Court. Two are armed with pikes and two with drawn swords.

She pulls her head back and whispers into Anza's ear, "The entrance is down that hall. There are four guards, which I assume means Tevin didn't win his way through. It's within your range. Can you take them?"

"Let me look."

"Careful."

Anza peeks. "I can hit them," she whispers back, "but I can't kill all four before they raise the alarm."

Sparrow thinks. Her goal is to be taken before Karolje. She would like to do this in triumph, as a threat, but a fight might get them killed or hauled away to the dungeon. The soldiers are highly trained and have reinforcements.

"I will surrender," she says. "You can still escape. Go back out and wait for River. If I fail, let them in."

"No," says Anza. "I do this with you."

Sparrow is not going to try harder to convince Anza to save herself. The woman has earned the right to make her own choices, to own her own voice. She says, "Thank you."

They round the corner. The guards see them and tense.

Sparrow removes her sword and lays it on the floor. "Put down the bow," she says. Anza's lips tighten, but she obeys. They walk forward and stop a few feet away from the guards. The carvings on the closed doors shift and bend like living things, and though the lights have not dimmed, the corridor seems to close in and darken.

"I've come to see the king," Sparrow says.

Two of them laugh. A third man looks nervously at the door. The fourth says, "Who are you?"

"Thousands of people are marching to the Citadel right now. The prisoners who were to be executed have been freed, and soldiers are deserting to join the people. Karolje's reign is over."

"And do you intend to be the queen?" asks one of the men who laughed. He steps forward.

"No," says the fourth guard. "Stand aside. We will let them in."

"What?"

In a smooth, skilled blow the fourth man hits the other in the jaw. The man falls, his pike clattering loudly when it strikes the floor. The other two soldiers stare.

"This has gone on long enough," says the fourth guard.

"Filthy traitor," says the other swordsman.

The fourth swings his sword around and levels the tip at the man's throat. "The king doesn't deserve our service." The second pikeman places his weapon against the wall.

The swordsman says contemptuously, "You too?"

The pikeman doesn't bother to answer, just hits the man in the mouth. His head jerks back, away from the sword point, and with a second punch the pikeman drops him. He bends over and picks up the man's sword. "Get your weapons," he says to the women. When they have them, he opens the door.

The two soldiers wait for Sparrow and Anza to enter, then follow, swords drawn. Sparrow cannot avoid the thought that she should not trust these men, that she will be run through with a sword from behind, but she dismisses it and walks into the Green Court. A dozen years are swept away like cobwebs, the room exactly as she remembers it.

Her sons, their wrists bound, surrounded by guards, stand

before the dais, blocking her view of Karolje. She pauses a moment, heartsick. Even wounded and bloody, they are beautiful. She is proud, so proud of them standing together against their father, and terrified that she will watch them die. That would be the worst thing of all.

Somehow she lifts her foot. She and Anza walk forward, the courtiers watching, whispering. Sparrow recognizes people. There is Tahari, dressed in brown, her hair tightly coiled on her head. She is thinner, her face drawn and angry. She does not recognize Sparrow. None of them do. Sparrow's sword is out, blood dulling it in places, and Anza holds her bow.

They approach the king. She counts. Ten soldiers, against the four of them and the two unarmed, bound princes. Winning by force seems unlikely. She never really thought it possible.

"Should I shoot?" Anza whispers. She holds an arrow loosely against the string.

"No," says Sparrow. Her throat hurts. She would not trust even River and his near-perfect aim to kill or wound all the guards before someone slashed a blade across Tevin's or Esvar's throat. If they are going to die, they should die fighting, not captive. She thought she could sacrifice them, but not like this, not in a victory for Karolje.

Esvar looks at her, grim and unsurprised, then sees Anza and goes white. He has given his heart whether he knows it or not. Tevin has no recognition in his eyes. Esvar has not told him. He is bleeding from a swollen lip and a slash on his arm. Traces of the boy she knew remain in his coloring, the set of his eyes, the graceful shape of his hands. Even injured, he has authority.

At a word and gesture from the king, the guards haul Esvar to the right and Tevin to the left, hold swords to their necks. Anza keeps her bow lowered.

Karolje is as alert as ever, and though he is gaunt and weak-looking, he resonates with power. The wolf's-head pendant of office shines malevolently against his robe. He speaks. Sparrow flinches from his voice as she used to. The long-gone ache where he broke her rib comes back to life. The past is thick around her.

"It is a very festival of traitors," he says. "Did you come like a harpy to pick on the remains of the princes, or do you too think to challenge me for my crown? I tell you, you will have to go through them first. Take one step closer, and they die."

"Don't listen to him, Sparrow," Esvar says.

Sparrow says nothing. Silence is her shield and her sword. She remembers the Truth Finder putting his hand to her forehead in this room, remembers floating apart from her body. Such an escape will not serve her now.

Anza says, "A prince who breaks his contract with his people forfeits his power."

"Take her," Karolje says.

A soldier steps away from Esvar and comes to Anza, who does not resist. He grabs her by the elbow and jerks her arm back and up. The bow falls. Esvar stirs, and a bit of red beads on his skin at the sword point. Anza shouldn't have come, Sparrow thinks. Esvar won't be able to bear to see her hurt, and so Karolje will win even if every other soldier in the room turns against him too. Bringing her this far was a fatal miscalculation. Sparrow had forgotten to reckon with love.

Still looking at Karolje, Anza says, "If you kill me, I will haunt you even when you are dead." She has the arrow in her left hand, fingers locked around the shaft.

He shrugs. "I fear no ghosts. Certainly not the ghosts of insolent children like you."

The guard pushes Anza's arm up higher. She closes her eyes and sucks her cheeks in. She says thickly, "Not just my ghost. My father's ghost. If you hadn't killed him, he would be standing here now with a sword at your neck and a hundred soldiers with him."

He laughs.

She goes on. "You don't know how to see what's before your eyes. All anyone gives back to you is your own reflection, and you can't see through it. You're blind. You're alone. No one wants you."

Karolje will not hear those words. The audience might. Sparrow wishes she had had the courage to say such things twenty-five years ago. To speak them aloud, not just to the pages of her journal.

The king makes a sign. The guard jerks his hand higher, and Anza screams, cuts herself off. It is an act of physical bravery such as Sparrow has not seen for a long time. Her face is white and sweating with agony. Esvar has recovered his color but is still taut as a string wound too tight, ready to snap.

From beside Karolje, Doru steps forward and looks at the torture rack. "Is it time, my lord?" he asks.

Some of the courtiers are retreating, hoping not to be noticed. Even the ones who would like Karolje to win are nervous. Violence is ready to fall like a landslide on everyone. The man holding Anza releases her elbow and locks his arm around her neck. Her arm dangles, limp, while her fingers move reflexively, like a dying animal.

"Begin with the girl," Karolje says. He turns his head and looks sharply at Esvar. "That will break this mewling coward of a man."

"Karolje," says Tevin. His voice rings over the room. Heads turn to him. "I challenge you. I demand trial by combat."

Karolje grins. He has always been unable to resist a game, even when simple ruthlessness would suffice. He is very good at games. "I accept." He pauses, and Sparrow knows an agonizing second before he speaks what he will say. "I name as my champion Prince Esvar."

"No," says Esvar.

"Then your brother can kill you, if he wants the crown so much."

"I will give my life to make him king. I always would."

"Not this way," says Tevin.

One of the men behind Sparrow, forgotten, unnoticed, steps around her. He lays his sword on the floor and pushes it, hilt forward, in Tevin's direction. The man kneels and says, looking at Tevin, "You have my sword, my king."

It is a symbolic gesture, futile, perhaps even worse than useless because the man is now unarmed. But in this room, symbols have power. The silence that follows the words has weight. Sparrow's heart aches with pride and love and fear.

"Kill him," says Karolje.

No one moves. Tevin steps back from the blade at his neck without resistance. After a moment, Esvar does the same. The four soldiers on the dais are looking uneasily at each other and at the men around the princes.

Sparrow knows what they are calculating. Probably everyone in the room does. If Karolje wants to win, he has to order his sons' deaths now. Any hesitation, and even the most mercenary of the soldiers will flee from him to a stronger leader.

"Doru," the king says. "Kill them. Start with the younger brat. He won't resist."

"As you wish." The spymaster draws a knife, long and bright-edged. Sparrow fantasizes that he will sheathe it in Karolje's heart, but of course he does no such thing. He steps off the dais.

Anza scrapes the arrow she has been holding sharply against the arm of the man restraining her, and he, startled, loses his grip. In a second she has picked up her bow and put the arrow to the string. Pain contorts her face. She draws and releases. She falls sideways, agonized, and the arrow goes through Doru's neck all the way to the feathers. One of the courtiers screams.

Blood pouring from his mouth, Doru crumples. He grabs at the feathers and tugs. Horribly, he tries to speak. His chest heaves. He convulses, and his eyes roll upward. He is still.

Esvar steps away from his guards, who make no effort to restrain him, and runs the few feet to Anza's side. He kneels beside her, his head bent, vulnerable. The man who had been holding her backs nervously away, his hands held out from his waist, palms up. Of the four soldiers on the dais, three have retreated. The fourth stares at the princes with loathing. He is Karolje's man still.

Tevin hasn't budged. He looks at the king. "Let us make this simple," he says. "Yield to me and I won't kill you."

Oh, Tevin, she thinks. He is being so brave.

"My son," Karolje says, "you are the one who is bound."

One of the men beside Tevin draws his knife. Before Sparrow can even fear that Tevin will be killed, the guard slices through the fire-twine around the prince's wrists. Tevin bends over and picks up the sword on the floor. Burns show on his skin. The guards circle him protectively. Esvar makes a small noise.

"Yield," Tevin says again.

With a flick of his wrist, Karolje sends the soldier remaining on the dais into action. The man leaps off and approaches Tevin, sword raised.

Everything happens fast. The soldier brings his sword down, and it is deflected by two other blades as the circling guards respond. The ring is painful to Sparrow's ears. The soldier jerks back. A guard's sword flashes, and the soldier collapses heavily to the floor. Half his neck has been sliced through. In the crowd someone vomits.

Tevin picks up the sword and takes one step toward the dais. He raises the sword and points it in front of him at Karolje. "Yield."

"Kill him, Tevin!" someone shouts.

She will not have her son be a parricide.

"No," she says loudly. The single word stills him, stills the room. Everyone looks at her. She walks forward, out of the twilight she has been in for years. She glances at Esvar. She is glad after all that he knows, and she smiles at him. At Anza, who brought her here.

The king says, "You are a wretch, woman, and your resistance will die with you."

Tevin says sharply, "Move, Sparrow. His death is mine."

She smiles at him too. Esvar calls, "Let her!" and Tevin turns to stare at his brother in confusion.

Sparrow takes another step. "Karolje," she says, echoing her son. "You failed a long time ago."

He looks at her, still without recognition. Doru's blood has pooled on the green marble. The dead soldier stares upward into infinite darkness.

She says, "It is a mistake not to fear ghosts. You can't escape the past."

Then the king sees it. He cannot hide his shock and surprise. His mouth opens and shuts. "You're dead," he says.

"They lied to you. Everything about you is a lie, and it's torn now like rotted silk."

"They might have lied, but I killed them."

There is a sharp clink as the tip of Tevin's sword touches the floor. His face is a boy's, panic-stricken. She wishes there had been some way to warn him. A whisper is passing through the audience.

She turns her head and says to the courtiers, "He has killed his soldiers. He has killed his chancellor. He intends to kill his sons. Will you stand there and let him do it? Do you think he will want witnesses? The air itself is bloody."

"They're cowards," says Karolje contemptuously.

"I'm not."

"You always have been."

Her breath almost fails her with rage. The only thing that keeps her silent is the knowledge that her voice will be shrill and trembling. She is not weak, but she cannot look weak either.

"No words?" he mocks.

Silent, she continues to stare at him. He cannot be moved by shame or pity or regret. But he has no power over her anymore, and that he is unaccustomed to. The few defiances he has ever seen have always been shadowed by fear.

And indeed, the silence disturbs him. He gropes again for something to hurt her with.

"Your lover, Ashevi—he gained me my throne. He killed Piyr for me, and I paid him with you."

Years ago, Ashevi snapped at her, *I'm a priest, not an assassin.* They had been quarreling. He wasn't brave enough to have killed Piyr. Even if he had been, even if it is true that she had been his reward, it will not stop her now. She has hewn and shaved and polished herself down to the core. Old passion is a castoff. She takes another step forward.

"Have you forgotten how your fear of me aroused him?"

Once it would have hurt. Perhaps it will hurt later. But not at this moment. She decides it is time to speak.

"You used to want to keep me quiet," she says. "It worked for a time. I was your wife. But it taught me something too. I have learned how to wait. How to endure. And how to hunt. I know what a wounded animal looks like when I see it. You're out of time, Karolje."

His expression changes. "Mirantha," he says, his voice a lover's voice, caressing. "You are so lovely."

It sickens her so much she can't think. She recoils. Both her sons are paralyzed with horror.

Anza says, her voice thin and distant, "Sparrow. Mirantha. You have the strength. Use it."

She advances on the king.

"Bitch," he says.

She grabs the pendant and twists the chain viciously around his neck. He gropes at it with sticklike fingers. She clutches harder. His face turns red and his feet kick at the base of the chair. His breath whistles.

She feels his death in the slackening of his flesh. It is done. Karolje is dead on his chair, and she is still alive.

24

TEVIN LEAPED ONTO the dais beside the chair. Crouched beside Anza, Esvar was faint and unsteady. He looked down at her face and saw tears on her cheeks. His wrists burned where his skin rubbed against the fire-twine.

"Karolje is dead," Tevin said, not loudly but loud enough in the shocked silence of the room.

Sparrow—Mirantha—stepped away from the body and looked at Tevin, at the chair between them. Esvar bit his lip and hoped neither of them lost composure. Behind him he heard movement, and he looked to see the courtiers going to their knees. The guards had all taken refuge in expressionless formality, weapons lowered. They were not going to challenge.

"Mother," said Tevin, very gently.

She reached across the dead king for Tevin's hand. His face twisted. He got it under control, and then she said, "You have my love. Always. And my loyalty."

Esvar looked down at Anza. "Go," she whispered. She put her weight on her uninjured arm and tried to push herself up.

A soldier approached and cut Esvar's bonds. Esvar stood awkwardly. His own shoulders ached from having had his hands behind his back so long. He and the soldier both helped Anza to her feet. He wiped one tear from her face, then walked to his brother's side. Tevin was pale. The burns on his wrist were more severe than Esvar's; he must have struggled. Esvar knelt formally on the dais. He had imagined this for years. It felt familiar, right, and also unutterably strange. The king was dead. His brother was the king.

Tevin gripped his hand hard and raised him. They embraced.

"King Tevin!" someone shouted, and the others took it up. Tevin tried to wave them to silence, but it took a while. They stood, cheering. How easily they are led, Esvar thought. How ephemeral this moment.

He faced his mother.

When Mirantha had been masked at the College, he had not seen how the years had marked her face. She was only a few inches shorter than him, straight and slim, firm-jawed. Her eyes were the dark blue he remembered. How hard had it been for her, these weeks?

"Esvar," she said.

He could not frame a question. He felt desolate. He was furious with Karolje for having cheated him of the last twelve years. "I'm sorry," he said. It made no sense but contained everything.

"Before we came in, Anza told me you knew."

"I guessed. You said you would do terrible things. I didn't expect what happened."

She looked at both of them. "None of the things I said as Sparrow were false. The people of Karegg—of Vetia—need a voice. I didn't fight Karolje for revenge."

Tevin's throat moved as he swallowed. He said, voice low, "He hurt you more than anyone. I will listen to you."

"I want you to listen to your people, not to me."

"I will. I will need your help." He looked at Esvar. "And yours, and Anza's."

Mirantha said, "Tevin, the people of Karegg are marching on the Citadel. They have to see he's dead. It's not enough to Disappear him. We have to meet them with his body."

Tevin nodded. "You and Anza," he said to her. "Go out first. Esvar and I will bring him."

Anza. Esvar turned. Beyond the dais, she looked bereft. He jumped down, only vaguely aware of the soldiers around him, and went to her side. She moved tentatively into his arms and pressed her cheek against his chest.

"Anza, Anya, my love, you were so brave."

Tears spilled over her lashes. "I'm glad they're dead, so glad, they deserved it. Both of them. But I hope I never hate anyone like that again."

He kissed her and tightened his hold. She jerked with pain and swore. He stepped back and felt gently. Her shoulder was swollen and bruised.

"Can you move it at all?" he asked.

"Not now. When I used the bow, something tore."

"We'd better wait for the surgeon to put it back in place. Are you in much pain?"

"I can manage for a while. Oh gods, Esvar. Is it really over?"

"This part is," he said. They both looked at the dais, at the body in the chair. Karolje seemed years older. The pendant still hung around his neck.

The courtiers were drifting out of the room. Mirantha stood to the side, alone. Tevin was giving orders. Doru's body had been covered.

Her voice shaking, she said, "Esvar, I'm sorry about Marek."

It muted him unexpectedly, a grief he had forgotten for the

moment. He ran his hand through her hair. She caught it and held it with trembling fingers against her cheek. He was reminded of a bird or a mouse, frightened heart beating in soft body. He loved her. He could, now, without the presence of his father falling between them.

Mirantha approached them. "Anza, we need to go to the gate."

"Go," said Esvar, releasing her. "Tevin's right. You aren't royal, they will believe you."

Guards followed the women out. Did the servants know yet that Karolje was dead? Had word spread to everyone in the Citadel? Were there men still loyal to the king who might attack? It would be a while before he felt safe in this building.

Tevin joined him. His color was high. Soldiers had entered with a bier, a kingly one, nothing like the kind of battlefield stretcher most bodies would get. Esvar would have liked to drag Karolje out by his feet. He and Tevin watched in silence as the body was put onto the expensive leather mat and secured. The sides were black wood, each end capped in engraved silver. The soldiers knelt to lift it.

"Not on your shoulders," Tevin said. That brought a few surprised glances, but they obeyed, carrying it at waist height instead.

Tevin led them. In the atrium and the entrance hall, the bodies had been covered and the floor patchily cleaned. The doors were open, sunlight visible outside. It seemed a dreamworld. They went through the entranceway and down the steps to the courtyard, where not so long ago they had come in. As the sun struck him, Esvar was aware of how cold he had been. Mirantha and Anza stood by the gate, which was open.

The people coming were not visible, but Esvar could hear a chant, the words unclear. Tevin directed the guards to lay Karolje's body a few yards inside the gate.

"Stay back," he said to Esvar, putting a hand on his arm. "Let him lie between us and the crowd."

That was Tevin, who would always know how to stage things. It was comforting.

The bell gonged again, the steady deep strokes that tolled a death. Esvar imagined quiet falling over the city as people knew someone with power had died. They would not assume it was the king.

When the crowd drew near, the leader—a red-haired man who was on a soldier's horse—stopped at the sight of the open gate. He quieted the chant to the ordinary buzz of conversation and walked the horse forward. Mirantha waved at him. He waved back and dismounted. A woman in the front of the crowd sprinted forward, and Anza ran to meet her. They gripped hands, then walked forward to join Mirantha and the man. They stopped a foot or so away from the bier and looked down at the body.

"This is him?" said the man.

Most of the people in the city had never seen him in life, and his aged face looked nothing like the profile on coins. They would have to take it on trust, as they had had to take so much.

"This is him," said Mirantha.

The woman with Anza knelt to look at Karolje's face. Then she rose and stared across the body at Tevin. "You're the king now," she said, hostile.

"Yes," he said.

"Are you going to do what he did?"

"No." He pointed at the pendant. "I will never wear that. A king does not prey upon his people. Tell me what you think I should do."

She took a deep breath. Esvar expected invective or angry

commands. Her face crumpled, and she started crying. Wordlessly, Anza gave the woman a one-armed hug.

The man spat on Karolje's body. The guards stirred, but Tevin waved them back. He said to the man, "He never should have been a king. Come. Tell me what you want."

"I won't go in there."

"You don't have to. I'll come out."

"Sparrow," the man said, almost plaintively. "What happened?"

Mirantha said, "We won."

✦ ✦ ✦

Hours later, Esvar closed the door of his bedroom and put his arms around Anza. Her hair, fresh-washed, smelled faintly of rosemary. She wore one of his robes, which dragged on the floor. He was clean too, soft cloth wrapped around his burned wrists.

This was an interlude. He knew that. A balance had to be found. Even when the principle of something was agreed on, the details were overwhelming and arguable. Tevin had agreed to a ruling council, but who was to be on it? How many? How would they be chosen? There had already been contention about what to do with Karolje's body. Esvar knew his brother would have gladly seen it thrown to the hellhounds, but that would antagonize the loyalists and priests whose support Tevin needed. A compromise had finally been reached, and the body was to be buried whole, without a public funeral or mourning, on the Citadel grounds instead of in the royal tombs. In the city, the work of dismantling the gallows had begun, but people still thronged the square, chanting. Twenty had died, including Miloscz and four soldiers, and that would need to be put right, or as right as it could be.

But now was his own time. He slipped his hand under the edge of Anza's robe.

They lay naked on the bed in candlelight while the evening air moved through the room. He tried not to think about either the past or the future. Her body was lithe and muscular, her skin flawed with the scrapes and scratches of living, her dark hair thick and soft. Her shoulder was stiff and painful, so they did what they could and no more. She had a drug to take to sleep if she needed it.

She blew out the candle. The darkness folded around them, comfortable, safe. His breath evened.

He had thought she was asleep when she said softly, "What happens to us now?"

He would have liked not to consider such things yet, but he was not surprised she asked. It was like her to avoid uncertainty. He repeated to her something his brother had said to him: "In a thousand years we could not have imagined it would end like this."

"With your mother killing him?"

He had spent much of his life with the constant thought that his father had killed his mother. Now it was reversed. My mother killed my father. It had been her right as no one else's to achieve that justice, to throttle Karolje with his own kingship, but it transformed his world.

"Yes," he said. "He always seemed immortal to me. I never really thought we'd win. And I never thought I would have a mother. Things are all askew."

"With me as well?"

He knew it had taken courage to ask that. She might not have been able to in the light. He leaned over and kissed her forehead.

"You hold the world in place. You are an anchor."

He felt the tremor in her body. "Vasha," she whispered, which no one had called him in years.

Taking great care, he laid his arm over her and cupped his hand around one soft breast. He inhaled. "Anza, I want you with me always. I don't know what that looks like."

After a silence, she said thickly, "You're a prince." He knew she was not speaking of freedom and power but of obligation and responsibility. She would not be happy living in the Citadel even if the obstacle of a state marriage could be removed. And she had risked so much to bring down a king.

He said, "What do *you* want? Should we go on as we are, occasional lovers, and let the future bring what it brings?"

She did not answer. An unfamiliar sensation of loss caught him. She might leave.

Finally she said, "I want you. But I don't want to share you with a crown. I don't know what that looks like either." Her voice was strained. She was holding back some deeper sadness.

With his thumb he stroked her cheek. There was only one way out that he could see.

"I told you that I renounced it all. I meant that. I can make it formal, give up my place in the succession."

"I can't—" She stopped and drew herself up to a sit. He looked at her shape, the hair falling over her shoulders, the firmness of her arms. Small and strong. He was not romantic enough to think that if she broke his heart he would never have another lover, but he could never take another woman who looked like her into his bed. She had claimed that much of him already.

She said, "Would you do it without me?"

He remembered the sound of the metal flail striking the floor in the Green Court, Nikovili's terror. The faces turned aside when he rode through the city. The desire when Karolje offered him the crown.

"Yes," he said. "I shouldn't have power I haven't earned."

"Your brother won't want to let you go."

"I don't intend to abandon him, Anza, not as long as he needs me. It will be a while yet. There is a council to establish and ministers to appoint and laws to revoke. It will take weeks to purge the Guard of the soldiers who are unfit and longer than that to have a full accounting of the treasury. But I don't have to be a prince to support him."

He sat up too and placed his hand on her smooth, strong thigh. Wordlessly, she leaned into him. He gathered her hair up and let it fall, again and again. A distant owl hooted.

"Yes," she said.

"Yes what?"

"If you do that, I will stay with you. But I want you to do it for your sake, not mine. I don't want to share you with a crown, and I don't want to share you with regret, either. Love is hard enough on its own."

Softly, he exhaled. Then he put his arm around her, gently, and kissed her hair.

She clasped his hand. "May I ask you one more thing?"

"Go ahead."

"Did you love him at all?"

The question hurt. She had known it would. He said, "I may have once, when I was small. At times after that, until I was nine or so." *I never promised you a horse, boy.* "Children will love where they can. But not for years. Not today, not when he died."

"You must have been so afraid," she said.

Something inside him cracked. His eyes stung. It went no further, not yet. It would. From her he could receive love.

MIRANTHA

At dawn she goes to the garden, having slept only a few hours. The thick dew on the grass moistens her boots. Her footprints lie behind her, dark against the silvery moisture. She walks to the pools and kneels beside one. Mist rises off the water. Here is where she refused to hear Ashevi suggest Karolje's death. Yards distant is where she spoke with Nihalik for the last time. Damp roses, still closed, hang over the trellises. Their scent is faint, waiting for sun to be released.

Her sons are strangers to her in many ways; they have spent so many years apart. None of them want to step into the quicksand of memory yet. Love, there is. But it will be a while before they work out if they like each other.

She trusts Tevin to keep his promises. With Karolje dead and the soldiers and most of the courtiers behind him, he does not need to; but he is anxious to be nothing like his father. She remembers the boy who came back from the war, appalled at what he had seen, what the king had done, and she thinks most of that boy is still there. When he realizes he no longer has to fight for every breath, he will be generous.

Once, it was the sum of her aspirations to see her son safely to his throne. And now? Now she will stay in Karegg long enough to know her boys. To watch Esvar learn to love, to see Tevin and the resistance at peace with each other, to no longer be needed as either a mediator or a leader. Word has not spread yet beyond the Green Court of her identity. She is not sure it will. When she sat with her sons and the resisters, she was only Sparrow.

When peace has come, however long it takes, she will go back to Timor, to the home of her childhood. She will watch oranges and lemons ripen on the trees, and she will walk in the lavender fields while light pours from the bluest of skies. She will sleep and eat and read without fear.

✦ ✦ ✦

In the afternoon, she rides with Anza to the College. Master Tinas leads them across the square to the library and unlocks the door. Their shadows fall across the threadbare carpet in a bright patch of sun.

"Upstairs," she says. They climb the beautiful old steps, the wood creaking comfortably. On the third floor they stand silently in front of the wall. The pointed tips of the arched entryways show above the bricks.

"Are you ready?" Anza asks.

"Yes," says Mirantha. She turns to Tinas, and he hands her the chisel and the hammer.

She holds the chisel against the mortar, level with her chest. She strikes with the hammer. Once, twice, thrice. The noise makes her ears ring in the narrow space. Again. A crack spreads above a line of brick. Again. Bits of mortar and stone dust fall to the floor.

She hammers, coughing a few times from the dust, until she

has freed a single brick. She steps aside and lets Anza pull it out. The air that comes with it is dry and stale. The room on the other side is dark. Workers will come to finish the job.

Tinas takes the tools from her, and Anza presents her with the brick. She holds it. She says, "Let the College keep this, in a place of honor, so no one forgets."

They go downstairs and leave the library. A few harpies are sitting on the roof.

I was a queen, she thinks. Now she is a widow, and nothing binds her to the man she was married to. Not love, not grief, not vengeance. She has no need to replay his death in memory. She has severed herself from him completely. It is time she begins to learn who she is.

THE VETIAN SUCCESSION

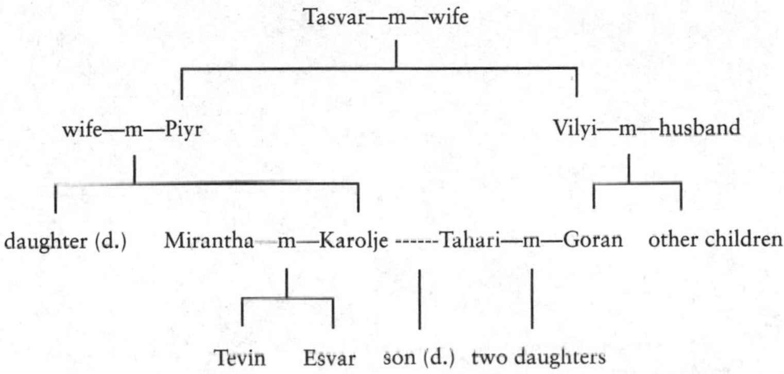

CHRONOLOGY

MONTHS ARE EQUIVALENTS TO THE GREGORIAN CALENDAR

1: Vetian Calendar begins with the reign of Kazdjan
856: Karolje born
872: Mirantha born
889: Karolje and Mirantha marry [September]
890: Tevin born [November]
896: Esvar born [May]
896: Anza born [August]
900: Ashevi comes to the Citadel [December]
901: Tazekh war starts [March]
901: Mirantha and Ashevi become lovers [July]
902: Karolje crowned [June]
903: Karolje returns to war, bringing Tevin [March]
904: War ends, Karolje and Tevin return to Karegg [September]
905: Mirantha is Disappeared [April]
905–908: Second Tazekh war
912: Anza begins at the College [September]
914: Anza finds the journal [October]

Acknowledgments

This novel would not let go of me no matter how often I trunked it. I am so grateful to the many people who have helped it to see the light of day.

Judith Tarr edited an early draft, simultaneously encouraging me and forcing me to face the truth about the work that was needed. My amazing agent, Bridget Smith, saw what the manuscript could be and found it a good home when it was ready. Navah Wolfe fiercely believed in this book and relentlessly asked questions that made me tear my hair out but made the novel so much better. Thanks also to Rebecca Strobel, Lauren Jackson, Valerie Shea, Davina Mock-Maniscalco, Alan Dingman, and all the other folks at Saga/Gallery who worked on the book.

J. M. McDermott's poem (Sonnet #212 on his blog Dogslandia) serendipitously crossed my Twitter feed just when I was looking for a poem to attribute to "Mikos Rukovili." Great thanks to him for allowing me to use it with slight modifications.

My early readers and critiquers were Jamie Lackey, Jenna McKenna, Laura Pearlman, Daniel Roy, K. B. Rylander, Luther Siler, and the late Chris Kelworth. I also thank my many writer friends and colleagues who sustained my energy, cheered me on, and listened to me babble.

I could not have done this without the support and love of my husband, Adam Hill, who has been steadfast with me for all the years this took. He has my love and gratitude.